TRYING TO LIVE WITH THE DEAD

B.L. BRUNNEMER

DEDICATION

To Dad, thank you for always believing in me.
And Robert, who taught me how to laugh.

I owe a huge thank you to several people who have
helped me get this book out of my head.
Ovie, thank you for all the late-night plot texts and
advice whenever I got stuck.
Melissa, the first person to read my writing besides Ovie.
The first chapter would have been torture to read without you!
And to all my beta readers who gave me the push to actually publish,
thank you!

CHAPTER 1

I pulled my Dad's old '89 Chevy Blazer to a stop outside my Uncle Rory's house. I sighed and turned off the truck. New town, new house, new school and new people. It's not like being the new girl in school is anything new. I'd been forced to go to twelve different schools in the last five years since Dad died. I found it amazing I passed anything at all.

I looked back to the house. It was an old two-story craftsmen with its multiple pane windows and a new coat of sage green paint. Thanks to Uncle Rory, this year was going to be normal. No more moving, no more changing schools, no more having to work a part-time job to make sure we had enough food in the pantry. I rested my head against my seat and closed my eyes. This year was going to be normal. As if I would know what normal is.

A chill ran down the back of my neck, I groaned. Come on, I just got here.

I sighed and opened my eyes. Standing at the side of the wooded road not ten feet away stood a man who looked to be in his early thirties. His eyes fixed on the lake, moving over the surface like he was searching for something. My throat ached as I watched him. I knew before he turned to walk down the road; his throat was slashed wide open, and white bone glistened out of the gaping wound.

I gritted my teeth while I fumbled for my phone in my pocket and pretended to check my messages. He came closer. Shit. My throat closed, pain radiating up to my jaw and down to my chest. I took deep breaths and pretended I couldn't see the dead man. As he came closer, the pain increased. My head throbbed as he walked past me. Come on, buddy, move faster.

I was struggling to get air into my lungs. The pain in my head increased as his memories poured into my mind. No, nope, don't want to know. I closed my eyes and focused on pushing them away. I knew what he wanted; I felt it. He needed to tell someone his story. And I really didn't want to deal with this right now.

It felt like hours later when the pain finally faded and I was able to take a deep breath again. When I couldn't feel the dead man anymore, I opened my eyes and adjusted my side mirror, my hands shaking. He was about fifteen feet down the road -- it didn't look like he noticed me. I've been in town not even ten minutes, and the dead were already walking by. It was a new record even for me.

I don't want to see the dead, but I didn't get much of a choice. The Sight has been passed down through my family since the beginning; though it only affects the women. Lucky me.

I closed my eyes, suddenly tired. Please just let the dead stay away tomorrow.

I don't know who I was asking, or if I'd ever get an answer. All the other answers to my request have been no. This one will probably be the same.

Tucking my cell phone back into the inside pocket of my leather jacket, I slid out of the Blazer. I pulled out my duffel bag and the small box of art supplies that I had managed to collect over the years.

Shutting the door with my hip, I headed for the house, ignoring the paved pathway. I was grateful to Rory for letting me stay here, but I knew he had his hands full already with my cousin Tara.

I rang the bell, promising myself that I wouldn't be a pain in the ass for him. The door opened, and I looked up. Tall and fit, even I could admit my uncle was good looking. His brown eyes had always been filled with mischief. Even though he was a police officer for the Spring Mountain Police Department, he never lost his childish streak when it came to practical jokes.

Rory ran a hand over his short copper hair. He was blinking against the daylight. His blue jeans were rumpled, as was his white t-shirt.

"Lexie?" Rory seemed to be waking up. "Sorry, I must have passed out."

He reached out and took the box from my hands. He gave me a small smile that didn't quite reach his eyes. These weren't the best circumstance for a reunion, but it is what it is.

I gave him a small smile back as I stepped into the house.

The house looked like one big room. The family room area was to my right, with a blue couch and matching armchairs. A big entertainment center filled the wall a few feet from the door. The kitchen was further in the back, to the right, in its own alcove. It was clean and full of stainless steel, and had a big window above the sink. The dining area was to the left with a dark wood dining room table that could easily seat eight.

It looked homey. I liked it.

"Come on, honey, let's go get your things from the car," Rory said.

"This is everything,"

I started checking out the photos on the wall to my left. They continued all the way up the stairs to the second floor. I could see Tara in most of them.

It took a minute before I realized that Rory wasn't moving. I looked back to him; he was frowning.

"This is everything?" he asked with an edge of disbelief. "A duffel bag of clothes and a box of stuff? That's everything you own?"

I took a deep breath, refusing to be embarrassed. I had busted my ass for that box of stuff, not to mention my clothes. I didn't have much, but I'd earned everything I had.

"Yeah, Rory. That's everything," I said honestly, trying to keep the challenge from my voice.

I don't think I managed it. Rory gave me a small grin.

"Well, we'll have to fix that," he said before turning and heading up the stairs before I could ask him what he meant. "Come on, I'll show you your room, and then we can figure out what you need."

I followed him up the light pine staircase. It had a railing so you could look down into the living room and at the front door. There were three doors in the hallway; one on the left, one directly ahead, and an open door that looked like the bathroom.

Without turning around, he pointed out the left door with his thumb.

"That's Tara's room." He then pointed to the door at the other end of the hall. "That's the bathroom for you and Tara." He turned to me, his face serious. "That bathroom is for both of you. She'll probably give you a hard time in the morning, don't let her"

He reached the door straight across from the stairs and opened it. "And here is your room, sorry it's so small."

I stepped into the bedroom and smiled. The room looked huge to me. The white walls were plain but bright, the dark wood floor was clean. Across the room and against the wall sat a twin-sized mattress on a wooden platform frame with three drawers underneath. To the left of that was a metal and wooden desk with different colored drawers. I stepped further into the room and looked at the light wooden shelves on the left wall.

"It's the biggest room I've had in a long time," I told him, not bothering to keep my surprise from my voice as I went to examine the closet. There was an actual closet! Not a cabinet! I opened the door and was amazed by the room I was getting.

"I was sleeping on that pullout bed from the dinette set," I said absently. I left the closet and put my bag on the bed. When I turned around, Rory's face was frowning again, his lips in a tight line.

"Damn it, Alexis." He cursed, running his hand over his face before catching my eyes with his. "What your mother kept putting you through...."

I swallowed hard as I looked around, trying to find any way to avoid this conversation.

He stepped into the room and dropped the box onto the desk, then pulled out the chair and sat down. "Sit down, kid."

I sighed deeply. I didn't want this conversation. I sat on the twin bed, absently noticing how soft it was.

"How are the bruises?"

My head jerked up, his eyes stared into mine demanding an answer.

"Big red marks, big bruises, and soreness," I answered lightly as I felt my collar to make sure my jacket still covered any bruises near my neck. "You know how redheads bruise, it looks worse than it is."

I didn't want to talk about this. I just wanted to forget it ever happened and move on. By the look on Rory's face, that wasn't going to happen.

"I talked to your mom's doctor today," he began.

I put my hands on the bed behind me and leaned back. I instantly regretted it as pain shot through my shoulders. I sat back up, hands dangling between my thighs.

Rory waited until I stopped moving before continuing. I paid attention even though I was sure I knew what Rory was going to say.

"She was way over the legal limit on alcohol. They also found cocaine in her system."

I nodded; yeah, that's what I thought he'd say. I didn't care. My mother had come after me. She beat the shit out of me. I was done with her.

"They're charging her," he continued. "They'll send her to rehab for a couple months, then she'll either be released until trial, or she'll be held until trial. If she tries to come get you, she can go to hell." His voice was hard as he looked into my eyes.

My heart slammed in my chest. I dropped my gaze, fighting to keep control of myself. Rory actually cared. No one had cared in a really long time.

"I've already got a lawyer working to get me permanent custody of you. Even if she's acquitted, which I highly doubt will happen, my lawyer said he could tie her up in red tape long enough for you to turn eighteen."

Rory reached out and lifted my chin till I was looking him in the eye again. "You're never going back with her, Lexie."

I didn't say a word, I couldn't. No more moving, no more new schools.

I was going to be able to have a normal life--well, as normal as it can be with the Sight.

I didn't know what the hell to say.

"Thank you," I managed to say, my voice choking off as my eyes filled. I bit down on the tip of my tongue to push them back; it worked.

"You're home now, Lexie," Rory said, smiling a small smile. "You're stuck with us."

I snorted. It was more the other way around, but I'll take it.

Rory clapped, startling me. He stood up, rubbing his hands together. "Now, show me what you have for clothes and we'll go shopping to fill in the gaps."

I got up, opened my bag, and began pulling out the few clothes I had.

"You don't need to buy me clothes, I'll get a part-time job and..." I began laying out my clothes for him to see.

"If you want a job, that's fine." His voice grew firm. "But I want you to focus on researching the Sight, finding anything you can."

I met his eyes again; he was serious.

"I'm sick of the women in our family dying from this," he continued. "I want you to have control. Understand?"

I nodded, my heart warming. Having someone who actually cared about how I was doing was new, but good.

"I've already got some feelers out working on that," I answered, fighting a smile.

I picked up one of my shirts and went to put it on a hanger.

Don't bother with that now, we need to head over to the school and get you registered. Hopefully, they got your records by now." Rory was already heading back downstairs, clearly expecting me to follow.

I tossed the shirt down on the bed and went to my box. I dug through it until I finally found the flash drive I kept my school records on. I tucked it into the pocket of my black leather jacket and followed.

Rory was already opening the door and heading out. I hurried downstairs to walk out the door then stopped cold. Rory was standing in front of the Blazer with a strange look on his face.

"Is this your dad's old Blazer?" he asked, his voice thick as if he was holding something back. I walked over to stand next to him, looking over the old SUV.

"Yeah, I've been trying to keep her running." I hoped he didn't mind, it was the only thing of Dad's that I managed to keep Mom from selling.

He nodded, seeming to make up his mind about something.

"Needs a new coat of paint," Rory mumbled before opening the door and looking inside. "New interior, new seats."

Was he making a list?

"Rory?"

My voice seemed to snap his attention back to me.

He gave me a sheepish grin. "Your Dad loved this thing, did you know that?"

I shook my head, my heart heavy. I remembered riding around in it as a kid. The weekend camping trips he'd decide to take at the drop of a hat.

"How's it running?" he asked as he shut the door and headed back toward the driveway.

"Not bad, but it shakes when you go to seventy."

We were climbing into Rory's newer Toyota when I added, "You're not fixing my Blazer."

He snorted. "How about just getting the engine checked? The Blazer shaking worries me." He pulled the truck out of the driveway and headed down the road back to town. "It could be dangerous."

He acted as if he didn't want to mention it. But I highly doubted it. Rory had always been a charmer. Dad used to say he had a silver tongue and the charm of a devil.

I sighed, giving in a little.

"Fine, just the engine, Rory. But I'm paying you back for it."

Rory snickered. He actually snickered.

Spring Mountain High School was unlike any other high school I had ever seen. The single-story brick buildings were spread out. The students were traveling from building to building. The roofs had enough overhang that it created covered hallways between the buildings.

I watched several other teenagers hurrying from the front of the gymnasium towards the other buildings as Rory parked the truck in a small parking lot.

"Come on let's get your schedule set up."

AN HOUR LATER, we were back at the truck. I was looking over my new schedule. AP World Civilization, English, Algebra 2, AP Chemistry, lunch period, then gym and Art. I hated being stuck with a gym class, but the woman in the office said the class was actually a good one. Apparently, they did yoga or something.

I was too busy going over my schedule and finding the rooms on my map to notice where Rory was driving. When I finally looked up, I realized we were out of town and on the highway.

"Where are we going?"

"Shopping," Rory told me smugly.

I looked over at Rory and glared at him. Rory just smiled, pleased with himself.

"Lexie, this isn't California, you need winter clothes; it's going to snow next month," he explained, gesturing towards the surrounding mountains. "You don't have to go crazy, but you need at least enough to get through the week without doing laundry." He took a deep breath then mumbled. "And then some."

I pretended to not hear that last part. I sighed deeply. I hated to admit it, but he was right. It would be nice not to have to do laundry every few days.

"Fine, you win," I said.

Rory snickered again. I rolled my eyes; he was such a kid sometimes.

We drove into a larger town than Spring Mountain; Northridge, the sign said. It wasn't long until he parked in the mall parking lot. I got out of the truck, resigned. Rory came around the front of the truck beaming.

"Come on, we'll hit a department store or something," he said as I followed him into one of the larger stores. I resigned myself to the inevitable as we walked past make-up and perfume counters. Between the fact that I hadn't bought new clothes in the last year and his demand for my need of winter wear, I wasn't really that unwilling. I just hated having to spend the money.

We walked into the women's section of the store. Rory turned around twice and scratched his head. He gestured at the clothes. "Have at it."

I bit the corner of my bottom lip, suddenly uncomfortable. I hated feeling uncomfortable. I pushed it aside and began looking around at the racks of clothes. In no time at all, I had almost more than I could carry. I looked around for Rory, but I couldn't find him. An older girl, around her twenties, came over.

"Hi, I'm Karen, are you Lexie?"

I nodded.

"Your Uncle Rory asked me to help you get everything you needed, including bras and underwear."

I bit my tongue to keep from cursing at Rory. The guy just had to keep pushing.

"He said he's going to walk around the mall and come back after a while," Karen said.

Sighing, I gave in and handed over a bunch of hangers.

"Let's get a room started for you and put this stuff inside. Then we'll get some bras and try on everything at once. Oh, and your uncle wanted me to tell you to pick up some sheets and a comforter," she said with a big friendly smile.

In the end, Karen was a godsend. Karen helped me get the bras in the right bra size, which was way off what I had been wearing--no one ever told me bras could be comfortable. I now had more than enough clothes for school and at home. We were just bringing out the clothes when Rory showed up outside the fitting rooms.

"How'd we do?" he asked, looking at the large pile of clothes on the counter.

"We did very well She should have everything she needs through till winter. Several pairs of shoes, and a couple hoodies. But she will probably need a heavier coat when it gets colder," Karen explained as she finished ringing up the clothes.

My mouth dropped at the price.

Rory gave me a huge smile.

"I like the way you shop, Lexie." He handed Karen his credit card. "Fast and frugal."

"T-That is not frugal," I stammered.

Rory laughed. "You should see the pile Tara tries when she goes shopping. I give her a limit and make her stick to it." He signed the receipt before continuing. "You're under even her cheapest shopping trip."

I couldn't believe it. How could someone need so many clothes?

We carried it all out to the truck and piled everything into the small space at the back of the cab. It was completely full of bags. I got into the truck and still couldn't believe it. I kept looking back at the pile in disbelief. Shopping for myself had always been at second-hand stores. Even then, it was only when something was beyond repair. I had actually liked shopping today, and I was starting to look forward to school tomorrow.

WHEN RORY PULLED into the driveway, a red Ford Focus was parked in one spot of the driveway.

Rory sighed. "Tara's home," he announced as he shut off the car. "Tara might have a fit since I took you shopping. Don't let it bother you or make you feel bad. Alright?"

I nodded before climbing out of the truck.

We loaded up our arms with bags and headed for the front door. When we stepped inside, Tara was closing the fridge. My cousin was pretty. Long blonde hair, blue eyes, and a sweet face. Too bad the effect was ruined when she opened her mouth.

"You took her shopping? You've got to be kidding me!" Tara yelled shrilly, making my ears hurt. I stuck a finger in my ear and wiggled it around. Damn, how did she make her voice that high?

"Damn, Tara, nice to see you too." I never could keep my mouth shut.

Tara's face was pink, her arms crossed over her chest. If looks could kill, Rory would be a puddle of bloody pulp on the floor.

"I asked to go shopping last week, and you said no!" Tara shouted again.

"Stop screaming, Tara." Rory's voice was hard and quiet.

Tara's mouth snapped shut.

"I'm going to help Lexie take her stuff upstairs. When I come back, we can have a discussion."

Tara huffed before flopping down onto the couch. I took the opportunity to head up the stairs and into my bedroom while Rory followed closely. I put everything on the bed, Rory followed suit. He dug into a bag and pulled out a large flat box. He turned and handed it to me.

"You are going to need this for homework."

I looked down to find a laptop box in my hands. My mouth dropped, I was stunned. First the clothes. Now a computer? Why the hell was he buying all this stuff? I looked up at him probably still looking like a stranded fish.

"W-Why?" I stuttered.

Rory shrugged. "You need to know how to use computers these days. You can't use mine, and I doubt Tara's going to share," he told me matter-of-factly before heading for the door.

"Thank you, Rory." I blurted out, my voice full of repressed emotion.

Rory waved his hand as he headed down the hall

"Anytime, Lexie."

I smiled down at the computer box. I was still trying to control my emotions when Tara's shouting began downstairs. I put the box on the desk and closed my bedroom door. MY bedroom door. I had a bedroom! It's weird the things you get excited about when you've lived in a travel trailer for four years.

Tara really had a set of lungs on her; I could hear her through the door as I pulled off my leather jacket and hung it on the back of the chair. I pushed it out of my mind and began unpacking and putting clothes away. When I was finally done, I stuffed all the plastic bags into one and hung it on the doorknob. I quickly made the bed with my new sheets and comforter--a dark gray comforter with a white geometric pattern with the teal sheets giving it a pop of color. I liked the way it looked. I tore into the computer box next and focused on setting it up. It was an hour later when I heard my name called.

"Lexie! Dinner!"

Before heading downstairs, I shut my new laptop and closed my door behind me--is it sad how happy I was about a door? Heading downstairs, I decided I didn't care if it was.

Tara was frowning as she put paper plates on the table next to a pizza box. Rory grabbed a plate and served himself. I followed, taking three pieces of pizza. I didn't notice it before, but I was starving. I was halfway through my first piece when I felt eyes on me. I looked up to find Tara watching me as she cut her pizza with a knife and fork.

"So, Alexis, are you planning on joining any school clubs?" Tara didn't sound like she really cared about the answer.

I shrugged and swallowed the food in my mouth.

"What clubs are there?" I asked, before taking another bite.

Tara smiled. "Well, I imagine for you, chess club, yearbook, and 4H, of course." She seemed very pleased with herself. Was Tara trying to insult me or something? I decided to ignore it.

"Are there any art clubs? Painting?" I tried to make nice with my cousin.

Tara raised a perfectly plucked eyebrow.

"I don't think so." She took another perfect bite.

"I didn't know you painted," Rory said. finishing off his first piece of pizza.

"I want to try. I've been mostly drawing and using soft pastels." I shrugged. "Student level pastels are cheap."

I looked over at Tara, watching her chew slowly. Was she still on her first piece of pizza? I got curious.

"What school activities do you do?"

"I'm a cheerleader; I'm also a member of the fashion club and the student council." Her eyes ran over me before she leaned forward and whispered across the table. "I can help you dress better for tomorrow."

I raised an eyebrow at that. Wow, Tara was rude. I smiled sweetly at her, not wanting her to realize she'd just irritated me.

"No thanks, I know what colors look good on me and I stick to them. Besides, I'm really not that into fashion," I explained, picking up my third piece of pizza. "I like my clothes to be comfy and still be able to climb onto the Blazer to check the oil."

Out of the corner of my eye, I saw Rory smile. Tara seemed horrified. I reminded myself I needed to get along with her.

"But if there's a formal dance or something you'll be the first person I call, Tara."

Tara smiled again then continued eating.

Rory was giving out chores for the week when I felt a familiar chill run down my neck. I froze, my heart slammed in my chest as my throat closed. I lifted my head slowly. Standing between Tara and Rory was the dead man from earlier today. His clothes looked like they were from the forties. His eyes were on me, he knew I saw him. Damn it. Pain ran up my jaw and down my chest.

"Alexis?"

I barely registered Tara's voice as the man started coming towards me. I held up a hand, palm out, and motioned for him to back up. He stopped and stepped back; the relief on his face made my heart ache. When he was far enough back, the pain eased, throat loosening. I finally took several deep breaths.

"Tara, go upstairs," Rory stated calmly, his eyes never leaving my face.

I shook my head as I was getting to my feet. "I'll take him outside," I mumbled as I hurried upstairs to get my sketchbook and pastels. I came back downstairs and hurried across the living room. I needed to get outside before the ghost decided he wasn't waiting anymore.

"What is going on?" Tara asked loudly.

I ignored her and headed for the back door.

"Are you sure you got this?" Rory asked.

I kept my focus on getting to the door without the man getting too close. I nodded, opening the door and flipping on the back-porch light.

"You have five minutes, Lexie, then I'm coming out," Rory said.

I waved that I understood and shut the door behind me. The dead man stepped out through the wall of the house.

"I'll listen, but you can't get too close, it really fucking hurts," I told him firmly.

He nodded emphatically.

I led the way away from the house down the small paving stones to the patio furniture that was about 10 feet away from the house. Thankfully, the back porch light reached the area, giving me enough light. I sat down in the corner of the patio sofa, crossing my legs under me. I pointed for him to stand near the wicker patio chair across from me. As he walked over, I opened my sketchbook and turned to the first clean page. I opened my box of chalk-like pastels before looking up to meet his eyes.

"Who are you?" I asked. That was all he needed.

His name was George McFee. As I listened to the story of his life over the next couple of hours, I drew his portrait in my sketchbook. I drew his face. Minus the gash in his throat. It took time; he began talking about his family. His daughter Rose, she was only six when he died. His wife Charlotte and how much he missed her. He'd lived in Brooklyn in the 1920's and had made the mistake of working with the mafia. He told me all the horrible things he did while trying to support his family. Some of it was pretty gruesome. Eventually, he went on the run. They caught up with him here. His own boss killed him and left his body in the lake. I ignored that part for now.

My head was starting to ache, his memories from his life started pouring into my mind. I pushed them aside and focused. I asked if his body had been found. He said it was. He was buried in St Michael Cemetery.

"Do you want to see Rose and Charlotte again?" I kept my voice polite as my head began throbbing in time with my pulse.

George pressed his lips together and nodded.

"Then why are you still here?" I asked, feeling wetness dripping onto my upper lip. I needed to help him faster. He was staying too close for too long.

"I don't think I'm going to where they are," he told me honestly, his eyes filling with pain.

My own heart ached for him; I could feel how much he wanted to see his family again. I wiped at my nose, blood smearing across my hand.

"Do you regret the things you did?" I asked, gently keeping the urgency from my voice.

"Yes, more than anything."

I barely heard him over the blood rushing through my ears. I felt more blood dripping from my nose.

"George, if there is a God, do you really think he would punish you for something you regret so much?"

He was quiet for a while. Just sitting, not speaking, not moving. I waited, trying to be patient as my head throbbed and my nose began to bleed even more.

Finally, he nodded. He looked into my eyes and smiled.

"What's your name?" he asked.

I smiled in understanding. "Alexis."

He gave me a smile full of joy. "Thank you, Alexis." I watched as his body disappeared slowly.

"You're welcome, George."

When he was finally gone, I took my first full breath in what felt like forever. I rubbed my hand over my forehead, my head throbbing. Footsteps had me looking up. Rory was there holding out a red handkerchief. I took it gratefully and put it against my nose. Rory took a seat across from me, a strange look on his face. I tilted my head back and closed my eyes. My head was killing me, and my stomach churned. In short, I felt like shit.

"I have never seen anything like that."

I brought my head up so I could look at him. He was looking out on the lake.

"All the other times I've seen were horrible," he said. "Claire was always screaming, shaking, blood pouring." He turned back to me, his eyes meeting mine. "Why was this different?"

Claire was my Aunt. She died when she was eight years old.

"Depends on the ghost, their memories, how close they are to you, if they're angry or not. You have to keep them away from you. They don't normally try to jump you," I explained, pulling the handkerchief from my face.

I picked up my sketchbook, and on the facing page, I wrote a large paragraph summing up the life and death of George McFee with his birth and death year at the bottom of his portrait.

"How did you learn to do that?" he asked, watching my face.

I knew that one day he would ask that question. I know I should tell him, but I was exhausted, and I didn't want to have the long drawn out conversation it would need.

"I'll tell you someday," I began, letting exhaustion into my voice. "Just not today."

Rory met my eyes and gave me an understanding smile. He gestured to the sketchbook in my hands. I handed it over to him without thought.

"You keep a record of them?" he asked, surprise in his voice.

I nodded, feeling my heartache.

"Some of them haven't been found. I figured someone should remember them." I looked out over the water, listening to it lap at the dock. "How long have I been out here?"

Rory was flipping through my sketchbook as he answered. "A couple hours."

I sighed and rubbed my eyes. I turned my mind back to one of my big worries.

"What did you tell Tara?"

16

Rory sighed closing the book. He raised his head and met my eyes.

"I told her it was none of her business." He handed me back my sketchbook before resting his elbows on his knees.

"How long do you think we can keep it from her?" I asked.

I really didn't want to deal with Tara thinking I'm crazy. I've done it at school and dealt with it at home. I really didn't want to go through that again, if I could help it.

"If you want to tell her, tell her. I can't make that choice for you. But she's at her mom's every other week, it should make it easier," he said.

Rory was right, but I had one big question that nagged at me. If the Sight was always passed down through the women in the family, why didn't Tara have it?

"Okay, kid, you've got school tomorrow. Get up to bed."

I picked up my supplies and headed inside. A light shut off above me, drawing my eye. Tara was stepping away from the window. I sighed. Great.

CHAPTER 2

I felt the blade as it sliced across my throat, hot liquid poured down the front of my suit. NO! I couldn't breathe; everything was getting dark. Terror ripped through me. My Charlotte, my Rose! I was sinking into the dark...

I WOKE UP GASPING, my heart slamming in my chest. Still mostly asleep, I scrambled back until my back hit the wall. Pain knifed through my body, stealing my breath and waking me up instantly. I froze, still gasping. I searched the room looking for movement. When I found nothing, I took deep breaths and tried to calm myself down. I pulled my knees up to my chest and wrapped my arms around them. What the hell had that nightmare been about? I couldn't remember the details, only that my throat was cut before I woke up.

I held myself until I could finally calm down. I hate when this happens. George's death was hanging around in the back of my mind. It happened after every ghost I talked to.

I ran my hand through my hair and looked at the alarm clock. It was 6 am. I had finally gotten to sleep after midnight--six hours of sleep were the best I ever managed. Knowing I wasn't going back to sleep, I got out of bed and headed to the bathroom. Only to find the door shut. I gave a light knock in case the door was only closed.

"I'm in here!" Tara's shrill voice was loud through the door.

Okay, I'll wait.

I went back to my bedroom, leaving the door open to keep an eye on the door. I made my bed and pulled my clothes together for the day. I folded my PE clothes and stuffed them into my messenger bag along with my new sneakers. Still, no Tara. Sighing, I headed downstairs in my pajamas and went to the kitchen. I finished making my lunch, took it upstairs, and put it in my bag. Still no Tara.

I looked at the clock; it was 6:30, I needed to get in the shower. I grabbed my bathroom kit and walked into the hall. This time I knocked harder on the door. The door opened to Tara, dressed, with a makeup brush in her hand. Was she doing her makeup? Really?

"I need to take a shower," I told her calmly.

Tara waved her hand at me.

"Then you need to take one at night. I'm doing my makeup," she told me, her voice condescending.

My temper sparked.

"You can do makeup in your room. I can only shower in there," I pointed out, managing to keep my voice calm.

Tara snorted at me and tried to close the door.

Oh hell no.

I jammed my shoulder hard against door. Tara lost her grip, the momentum slamming the door into the wall. She gaped at me.

I kept my calm as I walked past her toward the shower. "Now, you have a choice, Tara." I dropped my flannel bottoms and underwear. "I'm taking a shower, then I'm going to use the toilet." I pulled off my shirt, dropping it to the floor. I opened the shower and stepped in. "You can either stay and continue to do your makeup while I do that. Or you can go into your bedroom to finish." I turned the hot water on, adjusted the temperature, then turned the shower on.

Tara huffed and slammed the door behind her. I smiled, enjoying my little victory.

I took a minute to let the water run over my bruises, easing the tightness in my back. I washed up quickly, making sure to use Tara's conditioner on my hair since I didn't have any of my own yet. I pulled a towel off the glass door of the shower before I did my usual morning routine, and then went back in my room. It took only 10 minutes, not bad. I quickly dried off, grabbed my clothes, and got ready.

I ended up wearing my favorite pair of blue boot-cut jeans, a gray V-neck, long sleeved shirt along with my usual black army boots. I took the time to pull on my worn black grommet belt. My long, curly, copper hair was back in a ponytail reaching my mid back. My heart shaped face, I thought, was pretty but nothing spectacular. My skin was porcelain pale like most redheads. But my eyes were pretty unusual. My eyes were a mix of dark green and light green, with gold flecks mixed in. Next to my pale skin, they really popped. My makeup was natural; only eyeshadow, black eyeliner, and mascara. A redhead never left the house without mascara and sunscreen on.

I checked the time as I finished rubbing in the sunscreen; 7:15. Thankfully, I still had time for breakfast. I grabbed my wallet off the desk, tucked it into my back-right pocket, and my cell phone into my bra. I grabbed my black leather jacket and my messenger bag, then hurried downstairs. I dumped them on the couch and went over to the kitchen.

I was eating a bowl of cereal when Tara showed up. She looked like she just stepped out of a magazine. Her straight blonde hair was down to her shoulders. Her makeup was heavy for my taste, but it was well done. She wore a pink sweater that reached her mid-thigh, and black leggings that disappeared into tan knee-high, lace up boots. She carried a white infinity scarf and a tan leather purse that I swear said Dolce and Gabbana. Did she go to all this trouble for school? I don't get it. It's school, not a photo shoot. I liked to look good, but I wasn't going to bend over backwards to do it.

I went back to my cereal.

"You're going to have to park on the street," Tara said, breaking the silence.

I took my bowl and rinsed it out in the sink before turning back to her.

Tara's eyes ran over my clothes. Her mouth opened like she wanted to say something. I looked down at my clothes, too, thinking I'd spilled milk on my shirt. Nope, clean. I looked back to Tara, an eyebrow raised.

Tara gave me a tense smile. "The spots in the student lot are assigned at the beginning of the year."

I shrugged. Parking on the street didn't bother me.

"Got any suggestions?" I asked, hoping to ease the tension in the room.

She tilted her head, her eyes narrowed. She seemed to be thinking.

"I'd try by the tennis courts on Douglas. They're probably your best chance." With that, Tara picked up her bag and headed out the door.

I sighed. I don't think Tara liked me. Oh well.

I pulled on my jacket and bag. Then I was out the door and headed across town. I took a deep, tired breath. It was the first day at a new school. Again. I wasn't too worried about other people. I usually ended up in the library looking for a good book. However, this year I would be here all year. I could actually make a friend, maybe actually keep one. That would be new. I hadn't been able to keep a friend since I was twelve years old and Mom lost the house.

It didn't take me long to reach the school. I shut off the navigation on my phone and found Douglas Street. Tara was right; I was able to park right next to the tennis courts, only half a block from what looked like the library. I parked, grabbed my stuff, pulled out my map and started walking. Yeah, it was the library.

Finding the mark for my locker, I started walking. The hallways were already full of people, some of whom started staring. I chalked it up to the red hair. It always drew attention. I found my locker right next to a tall boy digging through his own locker. I ignored him and dropped my bag onto the cement. I felt eyes on me as I spun the dial. I knew he was staring. The twisted side of me was tempted to turn and stare right back, but I held back the impulse.

"You're new," he stated cheerfully, his voice rich and smooth to my ears, like honey.

After I had gotten the locker open, I turned and had to look up. He was a head taller than me, my head just reached his shoulders. He was wearing a pair of old jeans, a blue shirt, and a neon green hoodie. When I met his eyes, chocolate was smiling down at me. Something about his smile was infectious. I had to stop myself from smiling back. I vaguely registered his square jaw, wide full lips, and a straight nose. His hair was buzzed down on the sides but left long on top of his head. It wasn't too long, but long enough that I could tell he hadn't bothered combing it this morning. But what struck me was the color- -it was blue, a deep bright blue. It surprised me enough that it took me a second to answer.

"Yeah." I turned back to putting my gym clothes and sneakers into the locker, planning to come back before gym.

"Is that your real hair color?"

I sighed. I hated that question, but at least he wasn't asking if the carpet matched the drapes.

I closed my locker before turning back to him as I pulled out my schedule and map.

He stuffed a book into his backpack before leaning over towards me. "Cause mine's not," he stage-whispered.

This time I did smile.

"Yeah, it's my natural hair color," I answered, running my eyes over his hair. "I kind of like yours, though."

He waved his hand as he closed his locker. "It's not done yet, I'm adding in some darker blue streaks." He shrugged on his book bag, a lazy smile still on his face. "I'm going for a Cookie Monster thing."

"I'm going to call you Cookie Monster from now on, you realize that, right?" I gave him my smart-ass smile. Impish, my Dad had once called it.

His face lit up with a big smile.

"Hey, I like that." He snapped his fingers and pointed at me. "But I get to call you Red. Deal?"

"Deal." I waited for a beat before adding. "That's way better than Pippi Longstocking."

His eyes went wide as he opened his mouth.

"Too late, you only get one." I chuckled as his face fell with disappointment.

"Ugh... fine."

A loud bell rang through the halls.

"That's the first bell," he announced, walking backward down the hallway. "I'll see ya later, Red." He turned and hurried down the hall before I could say anything.

He didn't seem so bad. Maybe it wouldn't be that hard making friends.

I looked at my schedule on my map and started moving. Thankfully, the hallways were wide, so there wasn't a crush as everyone hurried to class. AP World Civilizations was in the 300 building, which luckily wasn't far. Finding the room, I walked into the classroom and found a desk in the middle, against the right wall. It was warm in here, so I took off the jacket and hung it on the back of my chair. People were whispering and staring again. Oh, the joys of being the new girl. I pulled out a notebook and pen and just started doodling.

It wasn't long before the teacher came in. Mr. Matthews was in his fifties, tall, thin and with a head of white hair. He put down his bag at his desk and moved to the podium, his eyes searching the class. He smiled when he spotted me.

"We have a new student today, Alexis Delaney," he announced with a booming voice.

Everyone in class looked at me. I gave a small smile and a short wave.

Mr. Matthews pulled a textbook off his desk and passed it to the girl at the top of the row. Everyone in the row then passed it back till it reached me. "There is a quiz every Friday on the chapter. I expect you to catch up."

Then class began. I mostly ended up taking notes off the power point projection. All in all, Mr. Matthews seemed rather nice. Class went quickly, and soon I was on my way to English.

I walked into another classroom; this time a small woman was at a desk in the back of the room. She waved me over as I walked in. She was as tall as I was, with a pregnant belly.

"You must be Alexis." Her voice was soft, her face sweet. "I'm Mrs. Hayes. Welcome to my class. We're reading Romeo and Juliet right now."

I resisted the urge to groan as she pulled a book off her desk and handed it to me.

"Here's your copy. I hope you'll enjoy this class."

I thanked her and headed to find an empty desk. The whispering and staring started again. I was already tired of it. Annoyed, I pulled out my notebook again and started doodling. The rest of my classes went exactly the same way. Nothing interesting happened the rest of the morning. Until my AP Chemistry class.

The Chemistry classroom was really the lab. It had tall counters sticking out from the edge of the walls instead of desks, with tall metal stools to sit on.

Mr. Turner was a tall man, probably nearer forty than thirty. His blond hair resembled straw. He had a pleasant face, but his large nose took center stage.

"Alexis, I imagine," Mr. Turner said, not even looking up from his papers. He picked up a textbook and handed it to me. "We move fast in this class, so you better catch up." Then he looked up at the other kids, who were all settling down, looking for something.

"Hey, Red!"

I turned my head immediately to find Cookie Monster waving his hand from the second table against the left wall.

"Mr. Turner, we'll take her." The other boys at the table look up surprised.

"It seems Isaac is willing to accept you into their group." Mr. Turner gestured for me to move along.

As I walked over, I thought I was seeing double for a minute. The boy sitting next to Cookie Monster had the same face, only his hair was black, straight, and reached his jawline. He was just as tall as Cookie Monster, and his long sleeved, black shirt was tight against the muscles in his arms and chest. He was leaning against the table on his elbows, a silver pendant in the shape of a dragon dangled from around his neck. Cookie Monster and his twin were damn good looking.

"Hey, Cookie Monster." I smiled as I put my bag on the floor.

The twin brother laughed, turning to his brother. "Cookie Monster I like it," he said, teasing his brother and enjoying himself. His voice was smooth, yet smoky. The mix was surprising and attention getting all at once.

The twin looked over at me still smiling. "I'm Ethan, and thank you. You've just made my day."

"No problem," I smirked back at him.

"Like you needed something else to torture Isaac with." The boy to my left said, his voice a quiet timber. He had been hunched over the table, his nose in his textbook, when I walked up, so I hadn't gotten a good look at him. He was cute--high cheekbones and angled jaw. His chestnut hair was short but had a wave to it that looked completely natural. He had emerald green eyes behind black-rimmed glasses. He was leaner than the other boys, but his shoulders were still broad with some muscle to it. His baggy shirt spelled out the word "nerdy" with elements from the periodic table. I instantly loved it.

He turned those green eyes on me. "I'm Miles." His fingers began tapping on the table in quick staccato rhythm. He seemed tense introducing himself.

"I'm Alexis." I gave him a friendly smile before reaching down into my bag and pulling out my notebook.

"You're the new girl. I wouldn't have expected you to take a hard class like this," Miles said, his voice flat.

I went still, my pen still in my hand. Isaac rolled his eyes. Ethan shook his head laughing softly.

"Ah man, Miles. You need to work on talking to girls," Ethan chided.

"And people in general," Isaac added, sighing in frustration.

Miles looked over at the twins.

"What?" he asked, his brow drawn down, his eyes confused.

Did he really not realize he had just insulted me? I ran my eyes over him again. Judging by the confused look on his face, he didn't.

"I was in AP Chemistry at my old school. I can keep up." I told him, grinning to let the others know I wasn't insulted.

Mr. Turner called for everyone's attention. I turned on the stool toward the front of the class.

I was taking notes when I heard Miles whisper behind me.

"What did I say?"

I held back my smile and kept writing. Miles really didn't seem to understand.

"You basically implied you think she's stupid," Isaac whispered back.

This didn't sound like the first time the others had to explain something like this to Miles. There was a long silence. I could practically hear the gears turning in Miles' head.

"That's not what I meant." Miles' voice was even quieter this time.

I ignored them as I listened to the instructions for the lab half of the class. Apparently, we were separating hydrogen and oxygen from water with electrolysis. I remembered this experiment from my last school.

Mr. Turner set us loose. The boys began setting up the experiment when I had a thought.

"Hold on, are we using distilled water, or do we need to add sodium hydroxide?" I asked, wondering if I missed something.

Miles' brows went up for a second, then he gave me a small smile.

"Distilled water," he answered. Ethan and Isaac burst out laughing.

"And you were worried she couldn't keep up," Isaac said, taunting Miles.

Miles' ears grew red, his cheeks pink.

"Actually, I did this lab three weeks ago at my old school," I said, smiling. "So, technically you guys are behind me."

The twins laughed. They kept teasing Miles through the rest of the class.

I HAD JUST thrown my jacket back on and picked up my bag when Ethan stepped in close to me. He wrapped his arm around my back, his hand on my shoulder.

"You have so made my week today, Beautiful," he told me emphatically.

I raised an eyebrow at his choice of words. Was he calling me beautiful or saying showing up Miles was beautiful?

While I was wondering, he continued. "You need to sit with us at lunch." His voice had gone soft and smoky; it was toe curling.

Suddenly Ethan stumbled forward. He went a couple steps and turned, glaring at Isaac who now stood by me, his arm hanging around my neck.

"No flirting with Red," he declared firmly, pointing at his brother. He leaned in close and whispered loudly, "Ethan is a huge flirt. Don't fall for his evil ways."

Ethan smiled and spread his arms out to his sides palms up.

"I can't help that I'm the better looking one, brother," he taunted, walking backwards towards the door.

"And he's so humble, too," I said with fake awe.

The guys burst out laughing, even Miles was grinning.

"Yeah, you're coming to lunch with us," Isaac announced, using his arm to pull me out the door and into the hallway.

Ethan dropped back to walk next to me. Between them both, I was feeling short. Miles brought up the back, staying close enough to hear.

"Where did you move from, anyway?"

"California. I got here yesterday," I told them, trying not to wince. Isaac's arm had moved from around my neck to the back of my shoulders right over a bunch of bruises. I was about to take his arm off me when Miles spoke up behind me.

"Isaac, she just met you. Stop hanging on her or you are going to make her uncomfortable." Miles warned, he sounded distracted. Isaac winced and pulled his arm from around me.

"Sorry, Red," he whispered.

"No worries." I smiled up at him. Isaac was fun; there was no other way to describe him. He was just fun.

"You don't want to be under there anyway, he has PE before Chemistry," Miles called from behind us.

I burst out laughing as Isaac turned to punch Miles in the shoulder. Miles took it, looking unrepentant.

"Hey! I'm not that smelly," Isaac insisted with pride.

"You're at the center of all the hot gossip running around the school right now," Ethan chimed in, changing the subject as he winked at a cute blond girl as we walked past. "The rumor mill is going crazy."

We turned down another hall and past a courtyard between four of the buildings.

"Oh yeah? What have they come up with?" I asked, actually curious.

He tucked his hair behind both of his ears as we walked, showing five silver hoops running up his right earlobe.

"The usual, you were in juvenile hall, you were expelled, drugs." Ethan shrugged. "Nothing original." He raised an eyebrow at me before adding, "There is contemplation floating around about whether your hair color is real or not. And whether or not you have a soul."

I groaned and rolled my eyes.

"Those aren't new," I told them as we went down a few cement steps. We'd reached the area outside the cafeteria. It was set up like the other courtyard and had metal tables everywhere. Everyone seemed to stay outside even with the overcast sky. The guys stopped at an empty four-sided metal picnic table. The boys sat down, Isaac and Ethan sharing a bench, Miles on the bench to the left of them.

"I hate those questions, "I said as I sat down on my own bench next to Isaac. I opened my bag to pull out my lunch.

"I can understand why." Miles' voice was polite while he narrowed his eyes at Ethan. Ethan held his hands in front of him palms out.

"Hey, just repeating what I heard." Ethan turned toward me as he opened his book bag. "So how do you usually handle those?"

I was still digging in my bag when I answered.

"I usually say 'yes, the color is real'." I looked at the boys. "For the other one, I smile sweetly, look innocent and say, 'No I don't have a soul, can I have yours?'" They burst out laughing. "That usually shuts them up."

"Yeah, that'll do it."

Ethan was the first to stop laughing. The guys started opening their lunch bags. Miles stopped and looked at me quizzically.

"Why would you answer them at all?"

I gave a half shrug as I opened my lunch bag.

"Most people aren't expecting me to answer, or they're just asking to mess with me. So, when I say all that, they look scared and walk away." I pulled out my water bottle and pointed with it. "They tend not to ask again after that."

The guys chuckled. Isaac leaned into Ethan.

"Can we keep her?" Isaac asked, smiling over at me. I winked at him while opening my bottle of water.

"Sounds good to me," Ethan replied, frowning at the bag of chips in his hand.

"What sounds good?"

A rich baritone voice came from behind Miles. I looked up. A rather tall boy was standing there, a backpack over his shoulder. He looked like your boy next door, but with model good looks. His high cheekbones and sharp chin belonged in a magazine. His sandy blonde hair was close to his head. His buttoned long-sleeved shirt was blue and untucked over gray pants. His clothes didn't hide his muscles; the guy must have to work out pretty seriously for that body. I suddenly felt the need to work my ass off in gym class later. Those blue eyes went to me, his face puzzled as he reached the table.

"Keeping Beautiful here," Ethan explained looking at his sandwich. Ethan put his lunch back in his bag and put it down in front of Isaac, then took Isaac's lunch bag. "Mom gave me your tuna again."

"Yay, tuna." Isaac opened his bag happily making me smile.

The blonde boy sat on the bench next to Miles; he reached over the table and held out his hand.

"I'm Asher."

I shook his hand. "Alexis."

"Nice to meet you."

He seemed to just accept that I was here and staying. I liked that about him instantly.

"So, you're up for adoption, huh?"

I held my hands out palms up. "I guess so."

He gave me a warm smile as he pulled out his lunch bag. It was a good smile; it belonged in a toothpaste ad. I had to stop myself from giggling at the thought.

"Don't let the manner-less twins scare you off." Asher pulled a sandwich out of the bag. "We're not too bad."

"Something tells me she doesn't scare easy," Miles said with a small smile before taking another bite of his sandwich.

Ethan and Isaac shared mischievous grins.

"How long have you guys known each other?" I asked.

Asher tilted his head his eyes unfocused. "Since forever, we all grew up on the same block." He answered, gesturing at the guys. "It's always been the twins, Miles, me and Zeke. Well, then Zeke and Miles moved."

"Where is Zeke by the way?" Miles asked, pushing his glasses up again. Everyone shrugged.

"I was stuck fixing a carburetor someone else fucked up."

The deep, gravelly voice came from behind me, making me jump. I turned on the bench and looked up and up. He was giant, and not just his height. A black motorcycle jacket encased his broad shoulders. I could see a black thermal underneath that was tight against the muscles on his chest. When I finally saw his face, I had to stop my mouth from dropping. Oh, shit. He had a striking face only much rougher and way scarier. His black hair wasn't very long, but it was rumpled like he ran his hands through it often. His wide cheekbones and strong jaw made his face attractive, but a much rougher and scarier kind of attractive. I was vaguely aware that black scruff covered the lower half of his face. Hell, he looked like someone you wouldn't want to run into in a dark alley.

His sharp blue eyes were running over me, his expression

confused. He stepped around my side of the table and loomed over the empty bench. From the corner of my eye, I noticed the metal chain from his wallet going from his hip to his back pocket. He was frowning down at me, looking intimidating as hell.

"Who the hell are you?" he demanded, his voice hard.

I was about to snap back at him when I noticed the bags under his eyes.

"Zeke, you're being rude," Miles shot back at him, his voice had a bite to it.

Zeke winced and ran a hand through his short hair.

"Sorry, I'm just tired," he offered in a normal tone. He dropped his bag and took the empty bench. His knees bumped my legs under the table, so I scooted over, giving him more room.

"Hi tired, I'm Alexis." I smiled at him, hoping a corny joke would cheer him up or at least make him less grumpy.

He snorted quietly, one corner of his mouth twitching as he opened his bag and pulled out his lunch bag.

"Zeke," he mumbled before turning to the table and opening his lunch.

Ethan's phone vibrated. Ethan picked it up, looked at it and started smiling.

"Late night at the garage?" Miles asked, putting his trash in his lunch bag.

Zeke nodded. "Yeah, and I have the physics test this Friday. Mr. Turner's really up my ass-"

"That's what she said," Isaac and I interrupted at the same time.

We looked at each other, both surprised, then broke out giggling. There were a couple of other laughs around the table. Asher shook his head smiling. Ethan laughed as he was texting. Zeke just ran his eyes over me like he was trying to figure me out.

"Great, Isaac has corrupted her," Asher observed, his voice laughing.

"Nope, sorry, hon, I came prepackaged this way." I gave him my smart-ass smile.

Miles started talking to Zeke about some Trig homework. I kind of blocked them out. I watched Ethan texting someone. Then I looked around the table at the guys. Each of them was good looking in their own way and nice. Well, Zeke was a bit grumpy, but they seemed kind of fun. To be honest, I wanted to keep them.

"So, is this like the hot guy table at this school or what?" I asked when there was a lull, eyeing each of them in turn again. I suddenly had all five pairs of eyes on me. "No seriously, you're all ripped. Even Miles over there, though he's trying to hide it with a shirt that's too big."

"Oh, well, we all work out together." Asher offered.

Ethan lifted his head from his phone.

"Isaac's in Mixed Martial Arts training, so we all end up sparring with him. And if we are going to spar with him, we need to make him work for it."

"So, you all basically do MMA training?" I asked, looking at each of them.

"Yeah, I guess we do," Ethan answered for everyone. "But Isaac's the only one who does any actual matches."

I looked over at Isaac who was throwing his trash into his lunch bag.

"What's your win to loss record?" I was going to be nosey, this sounded interesting. Isaac gave me a big warm smile.

"I have four wins to three losses right now. But I can't fight again for a while," Isaac admitted. "I got a concussion a few weeks back, and our Mom won't let me get back in the ring for a few months."

"He's grounded for letting someone knock his head around. He can't go back until he learns how not to do that," Ethan said in a stage whisper across the table.

I chuckled as Isaac smacked his brother upside the head.

"Thanks, brother." Isaac's sarcasm was thick, his cheeks tinged a light pink. Ethan just smiled at him.

I leaned across the table towards Ethan. "Got any video?"

Isaac groaned as the others chuckled.

Ethan was beaming as he got up and came around the table to sit next to me. He brought up a video of the match as he explained who

Isaac's opponent was. I watched as the match began. Isaac started out on solid ground, but then it started going downhill. It ended when Isaac took a knee to the face that ended the match. I looked at Isaac, wincing. His face was red, and his mouth pursed together.

"Ouch." It was all I could think to say. Then I looked back at Ethan. "Now show me a win." Isaac just shook his head at me as I got Ethan to show me all Isaac's matches and filling me in on who he was fighting at the time. Isaac ignored me and his brother as we huddled around Ethan's phone. Everyone else went back to talking about schoolwork and upcoming tests. Eventually, Isaac checked his cell phone.

"Guys!" he all but shouted across the table. Everyone stopped talking and looked at him.

"Lunch break is almost over. I make a motion to keep Red," Isaac announced to everyone.

A motion to keep me?

"Seconded," Ethan spoke up.

I raised my eyebrows, they were actually voting.

"Third," Miles added quietly.

"Motion carried," Asher announced, pulling his cell phone out of his pocket. "You're stuck with us now, sweetie. Phone numbers."

I smirked at them. Suckers, they were the ones stuck with me.

Everyone dug into their pockets pulling out their phones. I followed suit.

Isaac took my phone and handed it down to Miles. "Do that thing where you share contacts, so it doesn't take forever."

Miles pressed some buttons on his phone then picked up my phone. I grabbed my lunch bag full of trash and got up.

"I'm hitting the trash can, anyone want me to take theirs, too?" I asked, watching as they all added my number to their phones. Every one of them held up their lunch bags. I rolled my eyes and took them to the trashcan. I skirted around a group of people and threw away the bags. I was on my way back when I almost ran into Tara.

"What are you doing here?" she demanded, her voice hushed.

I pointed at the garbage can.

"Throwing stuff away," I answered matter-of-factly.

Tara ran a hand down her hair, her eyes darting around us.

"I don't want people to know we're related." She hissed at me before looking over her shoulder at her group of friends. No one was paying attention.

"Fine by me." I walked off, heading back to the guys' table.

I have to admit, it hurt a little that Tara would feel that way; a *very* little part. As I was walking away, my twisted side really wanted to turn around, wave, and say loudly 'Goodbye cousin Tara.' However, I had to live with her, so I kept a lid on the impulse.

I was almost past the group when someone stepped in front of me. A boy with blonde hair and brown eyes with a nice face. His smile was friendly, but something about it rubbed me wrong.

"You're the new girl, aren't you?"

Before I could answer, he wrapped his arm around my shoulders and pulled me into a different group of people across from Tara's friends.

"I'm Jason, that's Hale, that's Brendon." He went around the group introducing names, but all I could focus on was the arm grinding into my bruises. I tried to step away, but he moved his arm to around my waist and yanked me back, his grip tightening.

Yeah, no, that's not happening.

My face went blank as I looked him dead in the eye.

"Get your arm off me before I break it," I said very calmly. I didn't like anyone I didn't know grabbing me. The twins had been a surprising exception.

His smile disappeared and then reappeared as he ran his eyes over my body.

"Tell me, honey, does the carpet match the drapes?" he asked. The guys in the group laughed.

Oh, you asshole. I warned him.

I have attended a lot of different schools in the last five years, not all of them in good neighborhoods. After one horrifying incident, I took a self-defense class and a little kick-boxing in LA. My focus was getting out of holds.

I reached across my body with my left hand and grabbed hold of his thumb. I broke his grip and spun around him, taking his thumb with me so that when I stopped, his arm was in a lock behind his back.

"First, when a girl says let go, you let go. Second, don't be such an asshole," I all but growled at him.

He winced before I gave him a shove; he stumbled into the other gaping boys. Other people around the courtyard were laughing and hooting. I didn't really care. Watching Jason, I backed away several steps. When I was sure he wasn't coming after me, I turned and smacked into a brick wall.

Surprised, I started to stumble. Big hands caught me by my arms, keeping me on my feet. I looked up to find Zeke glaring at the guy who grabbed me. His face was like stone, his jaw clenched, and his eyes were starting to burn. I looked around him to see that the other guys had also gotten up and had only been a few steps behind Zeke. None of them looked happy, even Miles.

My heart melted in my chest. Had they been coming to help me? It was so sweet that I didn't quite know what to do or say.

Jason was steady on his feet again. He was cursing, calling me a bitch--among other things.

Miles' face went cold as he took a step towards Jason. Isaac grabbed hold of him, stopping him.

Oh, this could be bad. I had to diffuse the situation.

"Hi, guys," I said cheerfully, as if I was running into them in the hall. I had five pairs of eyes on me instantly. Their faces began relaxing back to normal.

"Did you guys finish with my phone?" I asked, stepping back out of Zeke's hands. Not one bit intimidated by Zeke's size. Sure, really, I only just reach the middle of his chest. The guy was, just, huge.

"Yeah, Miles finished," Zeke answered his shoulders relaxing.

That seemed to be the signal for the others to relax as well. I stepped around Zeke and headed back toward the table, acting as if nothing had happened. The boys followed me. I picked up my cell phone and was putting it into the inside pocket of my jacket when Ethan pointed at Isaac.

"Remind me never to piss her off," Ethan announced. As the guys were laughing, the bell rang. I grabbed my bag and pulled out my map. The locker room wasn't that far away. That's when it hit me.

"Shit." I closed my bag and began to take off.

"What's wrong?" Miles called after me. I turned and walked backward down the hall.

"I forgot my gym clothes in my locker." I waved at them. "I'll talk to you guys later." I turned and ran. Thankfully, my locker wasn't far, and I was soon on my way to the locker room.

I got to my locker and changed in a stall to keep anyone from seeing my back.

Gym was the usual boring stuff. I was back in my clothes and hurrying across campus to my art class when I heard a shout.

"Alexis!" a baritone called down the hall. I stopped and looked around to find Asher moving through the crowded hall towards me.

"Hey, what class are you going to?" I asked as we started walking again.

Asher winced.

"Art." He shifted his bag on his shoulders.

"Me too." I raised an eyebrow at him "Do you not like Art class?" He was looking over his shoulder as if expecting to get ambushed any minute.

"No, it's the way to Art class I don't like." We dodged around a couple making out in the middle of the hallway.

"Why's that?"

Suddenly, I felt that familiar chill down my neck, only this time, it was painful. I took a deep breath and looked around trying to spot the pissed off ghost.

"There's a girl that walks by here and always has to stop to talk to me. She's really pushy. She's always trying to get me to do school stuff I don't want to do, you know, like the student council." Asher explained.

As he kept talking, I found her. She was about 100 feet ahead near a cement pathway to the other buildings. Her long blonde hair was pulled back with braids. Her big blue eyes were watching the living. She wore bell-bottoms and a peasant blouse.

My chest ached all the way from here.

Some ghosts were stronger than others, especially if they are pissed off. This girl didn't want to be dead. I could feel from this far away. She was pissed off to a level I have never seen. I didn't want to get closer, but we had to pass her to get to class.

"Hell, maybe she'll back off if I'm walking with you." I nodded as if I'd been listening.

"No problem, chick deterrent mode activated," I continued, hoping I kept the strain from my voice.

As we got closer to the ghost, my head started to pound. I could actually feel the waves of hatred from her. We were just about to pass her when a familiar voice called for Asher. Asher stopped dead in his tracks, his eyes closed. I looked around us to find Tara coming up the path towards us. Even though my head was pounding, I laughed. Tara was the pushy girl.

Tara's smile drooped a bit when she saw me standing next to Asher. But she pepped it right back up when she got closer.

"Asher, I see you've met my cousin Lexie," Tara began, surprising me, even through the pounding headache.

The dead girl had stepped closer to me, making it feel like a knife was being driven into my chest. Breathing was getting harder. I felt like shit but I had no other excuse for what I said next.

"I thought you didn't want anyone to know we're related?"

Tara's eyes threw sparks at me before turning pleasant again.

The ghost started circling us. No one else felt a thing.

"Oh, don't be ridiculous, Lexie." Tara chided, then turned her attention to Asher. "Asher, we really need your help on the home-coming board."

At that point, I tuned her out. The ghost was behind me again, reaching out. My head felt like it was in a vise as Tara prattled on. I started hearing my pulse in my ears and wanted to throw up. We needed to move or I was going to be sick.

I reached out and grabbed Asher's arm, tugging him in the direction we were going. When we started walking, I let go, but Tara kept pace next to him. Unfortunately, so did the dead girl. I focused on moving and not listening to the memories of her life that kept trying to push into my head.

I turned my head enough to look the ghost in the eye. Her eyes went wide--she realized I could see her. Her eyes narrowed as she reached for my face. I mouthed the word no, feeling it with everything inside me. I shoved the ghost back, her eyes furious. I turned back to the others; no one noticed anything odd. Tara had pulled Asher to a stop, so I stopped too.

I felt the pressure in my face, then the drip onto my upper lip. Silently cursing, I pinched my nose closed. Tara was still talking. I was done. I wasn't going to just stand here and let the bitch of a ghost hurt me. But I couldn't leave Asher to Tara. Before I could decide what to do, Asher looked over at me. His eyes went wide.

"Oh man, Alexis." He pulled his backpack around and pulled out one of those small tissue packages. He tore out a few and handed them to me.

I put them to my nose and stopped pinching.

"Are you alright?" He actually sounded concerned. He swung his backpack back around his back and took my arm.

He turned to Tara and said, "We got to take care of this, Tara. I'll think about it." He gave me a small tug as we walked quickly away.

Tara mumbled under her breath. She was not happy. I didn't really care; my headache was disappearing the farther away from the ghost we got.

When we got out of sight, we slowed down. Asher didn't look so worried now; he looked like he was holding back a laugh.

"Did you just give yourself a bloody nose to get us away from her?" He let go of my arm as we continued down another hallway.

"I'm not that good," I said in a nasally voice. Asher's smile faded away, he looked worried again.

"Are you okay?"

I nodded, waving my other hand.

"Yeah, it just happens sometimes," I hedged. It's not like I could tell him the truth. I pulled the tissues away and pressed a clean spot back against my nose. Since we had gotten away from the ghost, it should stop quickly.

"I don't care if it wasn't on purpose." He looked at me, his blue eyes sparkling. "That was the best save ever." I nodded, agreeing with him. At least my bloody nose was good for something.

My nose had stopped bleeding by the time we reached class. I threw the tissue away and went to the sink. I used a wet paper towel to wipe off my fingers and under my nose. I turned to Asher who nodded.

"You got it all," he reassured me. Asher led me to a table with four other people around it.

"Hey everyone, this is Alexis. It's her first day," Asher announced as I sat down.

Everyone nodded or waved at me, but ultimately went back to whatever they were doing. Class started, and the teacher did what was the usual for today--announce me as a new student as I smile and wave. Then we got down to business.

Mrs. Archer had set up a bowl of fruit at each table and wanted everyone to draw it. Asher showed me where the supplies were. I picked up a pack of oil pastels that had all the colors I wanted. Then I went back and went to work. I'll admit, I kind of ignored everyone around me, including Asher, as I worked with the pastels. I was absently wiping my hand on my jeans again, cleaning my fingers, when Mrs. Archer looked over my shoulder.

"Oh, well done Alexis," Mrs. Archer exclaimed loudly. Every head came up. I don't think she meant to get everyone's attention; she just seemed excited. "I love that you used the pastels here, you're the first one to touch them in ages." She pointed to the background of gray and streaks of white. "Beautiful blending, you have some talent here, missy."

I felt my face turn red as I bent back over my drawing. Asher leaned over and looked at my drawing.

"That is cool," he said. I felt my face grow hotter.

"Oh, now you blush," Asher said, sitting up straight. "You put a linebacker in an arm lock, with everyone in school watching without a problem. But someone says you drew something pretty, and you blush." I lifted my left hand and flipped him off. Asher just chuckled.

My face finally cooled down by the time he spoke again.

"So, Tara Delaney is your cousin?"

"Yep."

"She calls you Lexie?"

"Yeah, my Dad used to call me Lexie, it just sort of stuck. I always liked it," I explained, focusing on what I was doing.

"Did she really not want anyone to know you two were related?" he asked, using an eraser on part of his page.

"That's what she said to me at lunch," I answered absently. I was focusing on a part of the bowl that wasn't looking right. It was the shading; it was off. I focused on trying to fix it.

"And you're okay with that?" he asked, then grumbled and reached for the eraser again.

I shrugged.

"If that's what she wants, then fine, it doesn't really bother me." I cursed; I'd messed up the shading even more. "Before yesterday, I hadn't seen Tara in five years, so it's not like we grew up together or anything."

"Then why did she announce it to me?" he asked absently.

I looked up from my drawing long enough to glance at him. He was concentrating on his drawing, the tip of his tongue between his teeth. It was adorable, so I was smiling when I went back to my drawing.

"She has a crush on you," I informed him.

I watched his head pop up out of the corner of my eye.

"Why do you say that?" he asked doubtfully.

I stopped drawing so I could explain it to him.

"She stops you every day, right?"

He nodded.

"Asks you to do stuff that would make you spend time with her?" His eyebrows rose. "Does she play with her hair around you? Does she find a reason to touch you?"

His cheeks were starting to turn pink when he bent down to focus on his drawing.

"She does all of those things," he mumbled.

I went back to my work. How can guys be so clueless?

"That's flirting," I told him simply. I started working on the light spot on the apple. I was almost done with it when Asher grabbed my attention again.

"I still don't understand why she told me you two were related if she said she wanted to keep it a secret."

I stopped blending to answer.

"She probably saw that I was sitting with you guys at lunch, and then I was walking with you to class," I explained before going back to my drawing. "She probably thought I'd be her way in."

Asher snorted. "That's not right."

I shrugged, wiping my hands off on my jeans. "That's the way the world works," I muttered, going back to work.

It was a while later when I spoke back up. "If you want to date her, you can, you know." I felt like I had to make it clear that I didn't really expect him to pick a friendship with me over dating Tara. I personally didn't see a problem with both, but I doubt Tara would see it that way.

"No thank you, I don't like people who use other people." he answered, surprising me.

Tara was a cute girl who liked him; that was usually enough for most guys. Huh. I'd never seen that before.

It wasn't long after that that he dropped his drawing pad onto the table.

"That's it. I give up," he declared as he pulled out his cell phone. It made me curious; I reached for his drawing. He slammed his hand down on it and eyed me. "Don't even think about it."

"Oh, come on, it can't be that bad," I offered, trying to reassure him.

His blue eyes had a small sparkle in them as he looked down at me. That's when I really noticed his eyes. They were a mix of dark blues and lighter blues, with white flecks here and there. He really had ocean eyes.

"Oh, it is," he assured me, his voice overly dramatic.

I bit back a smile.

"I can help you get better," I offered, now dying to see his drawing.

Asher chuckled. "There's no getting better for me Lexie, I can't draw," he admitted, his tone light.

"Then why are you taking art if you don't want to get better at it?" I was curious now.

"It was the only elective class that had room in seventh period." He shrugged looking back down at his cell phone.

I kept eyeing the back of his drawing. I'd go back to my drawing, but soon I was looking at the back of his again. I did this several times. I saw him grin down at his phone out of the corner of my eye.

"It's just driving you crazy, isn't it?"

"Yeah, a little bit," I said honestly.

He lifted his head and smiled down at me. He reached out and flipped the paper over. It was awful. The bowl was lopsided, the fruit out of proportion. On the edge of the bowl was a stick figure leaping to his death, then another one falling onto a big splat on the tabletop.

I had to bite my bottom lip hard to stop myself from giggling. When I had control of myself, I pointed at the stick figures. "I like the little guy."

He laughed at me, shaking his head.

"Do you want any help?" I asked.

He shook his head still smiling. "I've accepted that I'm no artist, Lexie," he said, his hand going to his chest. "I've made peace with it."

I smiled and went back to my drawing. Soon, I noticed him texting under the table. I didn't think much of it. He was done with his drawing while I was still adding layers to the grapes.

When Mrs. Archer let us go for the day, I was more than ready to go. I was walking down the hall with Asher when I spotted Zeke and Ethan walking towards us.

Zeke didn't have to dodge around people; he was big enough that everyone just got out of his way. But I don't think he realized it. He didn't seem to notice people moving away from him.

They met us in the middle of the hallway. As Ethan and Asher talked about their homework, Zeke's eyes were on my face, his brow drew down. He reached out and swiped at my jaw with a calloused finger. He showed me his thumb; it had red pastel on it. I shrugged.

"Is this paint or blood?" he asked, his deep voice demanding an answer.

Ethan and Asher stopped talking.

"Oil pastel, actually," I answered him cheerfully, refusing to be intimidated. Zeke's face relaxed as he wiped the color off on his black jeans.

"Yeah, she got all the blood off earlier," Asher told him absently waving his hand. "Hey guys, did you know Lexie's an artist?"

Isaac stepped up to my right and rested an elbow lightly on my shoulder.

"We're calling her Lexie now?" Isaac asked, looking around the group.

I looked up at him and gave a half shrug. "That's what my family has always called me unless I was in deep shit," I offered.

Isaac smiled down at me.

"She can draw?" Ethan asked, bringing us back on topic.

I got the feeling they were trying to not address the mention of blood.

"What blood?" Zeke asked, his gaze going to Asher. Asher ignored him as he snatched my drawing from my hand and offered it up to everyone.

"Hey, Red, that's really great," Isaac spoke loudly.

I think they were irritating Zeke on purpose by not answering his question. I was mostly sure I was safe from Zeke's wrath, but the boys probably weren't. On the other hand, it might be fun to push Zeke's buttons.

"It's not really good." I decided to go for it. "I still have to add some texture to the orange and the shading is completely messed up."

"What blood did she wash off, Asher?" Zeke asked again, his voice getting louder.

Isaac's head went up this time, his eyes darting from Zeke to me.

"What are you talking about, Lexie? This is pretty great," Ethan continued, taking it from Asher and rolling it up. "In fact, I'm keeping it." He tucked it under his arm and made to walk off with it.

I darted across the group and snatched it out from under his arm.

"No, you aren't! It's going in the trash."

I was back in my spot by the time Ethan spun around with fake shock on his face. Miles walked up to stand on the other side of Asher filling in the circle. His hair was wet, and he was just putting his glasses back on.

"So, where are we going for homework today?" Miles asked us.

Asher took the picture from me again and opened it so Miles could see.

"Look what Lexie can do." Asher's voice gushed with pride.

Miles looked over my picture smiling.

"That's really good Alexis. You should enter something in the fair this year," Miles said, shifting his bag on his shoulder.

"Is there a competition or something?" I've never put my art into a competition before.

Miles nodded, his emerald eyes meeting mine.

"They have a cash prize for first place."

"If someone doesn't tell me why she had blood on her I'm going to stuff someone in a locker," Zeke growled loudly, his eyes heating up, his hands clenching into fists. We were really getting to him.

Miles raised an eyebrow at me questioningly; I winked at him.

"The only one that would fit is Alexis, and I doubt you'd even consider it." Miles chimed in, a smile teasing at the corners of his mouth.

"Hey Beautiful, can you draw me a dragon with this stuff?" Ethan asked me, his eyes full of mischief.

"Ah, guys, I think he's going to blow." Isaac cautioned beside me.

"Sure, what kind do you want? Asian, Celtic?" I asked, rolling up my picture again.

"No, seriously guys," Isaac warned us again, his voice getting higher. I kept my eyes off Zeke and focused on Ethan.

"I think Asian, but with black and red colors," Ethan said before looking over at Zeke. His smile got bigger. I figured we'd irritated Zeke long enough.

I looked up at Zeke and almost stepped back. His face was hard, his jaw clenched. His hands were in tight fists against his sides.

"Don't get your panties in a bunch," I teased him, meeting his gaze. The other guys laughed. "I got a bloody nose on the way to Art class."

Zeke seemed to relax all at once; his jaw unclenched, and he stopped frowning. All in all, he stopped looking scarier than his usually scary self.

He looked over at Asher.

"Rumor is, Jason's girlfriend is pissed as hell and looking for Lexie," Zeke announced.

"Shit. Asher is out for homework." Isaac groaned.

"Why's that?" I asked.

"Jason's dating my sister," Asher explained with a sigh. "Let's hit Miles' house." Miles raised an eyebrow at Asher.

"Don't you have football practice?" Isaac asked from across the circle.

Asher snorted. "I'm skipping today."

"Coach Jones isn't going to like that," Miles pointed out.

"What is he going to do, not play me Friday?" Asher snapped his fingers, fake disappointment all over his face. "Aw, darn." Isaac and Ethan chuckled.

"My Mom is having the floors waxed today, so I'm not allowed back in the house until at least six tonight," Miles announced as he scratched his nose. "How about your house, Zeke?"

Zeke shook his head. "Nah, Aunt Silvia is working the night shift at the diner, she's sleeping right now." He nodded toward Isaac.

"Nope," Ethan and Isaac answered at the same time. Isaac explained. "There's a lot of activity at the house right now."

Everyone seemed to accept that as if it made complete sense.

"I can ask my Uncle Rory if you guys can come over to his house," I offered, already pulling my cell phone out of my pocket. "But my cousin might be there."

"Who's your cousin?" Ethan asked, tucking his black hair back behind his ears.

"Tara Delaney," Asher said with a groan. Everyone winced, and a couple cursed. Asher snapped his fingers, his face lighting up. "No, wait. The student council is meeting today, those meetings last until like six."

There were rounds of thank God, and that's a relief from the guys as I was texting Rory.

Alexis: Rory? I made some friends today at school. Can they come over to do homework?

I didn't have to wait long for an answer.

Rory: Hey, how was school today? Any problems with the campus?

I felt all five guys trying to read over my shoulder. I bit my lip, cringing at Rory's question. I pulled my cell phone a little closer to my chest. The guys started talking about homework.

Alexis: One nosebleed, otherwise it's fine. Can my friends come over?

Rory: How many? And, are they boys or girls?

Alexis: Five boys. But they are really nice and have been looking out for me today.

It wasn't technically lying.

My phone rang. I winced, it was Rory.

All eyes went to me as conversations stopped.

"Hi, Rory."

"You want to take five boys to the house without me there?" His voice was very precise, as if he wanted to be very clear.

"Yeah. They offered to help me catch up in my classes," I offered, lying my ass off.

Rory was silent so long I thought he hung up. I heard him sigh.

"If it were Tara asking, I'd say no, but I trust you not to do anything stupid," Rory admitted. I tried not to show how much that affected me by looking down at the ground between everyone.

"Are they with you now?"

"Yep."

"Put me on speaker." Rory demanded.

I looked up at the guys who were watching me. I pulled to phone away from my ear.

"Rory wants to talk you guys first," I told them matter-of-factly and hit the speaker button.

"Rory, you're on speaker."

"Before you go anywhere with my niece I want names, full legal names," Rory demanded. They all hesitated. I looked to Isaac trying to be encouraging. They started around the circle.

"Isaac Turner."

"Ezekiel Blackthorn."

"Ethan Turner."

"Miles Huntington."

"Asher Westfell."

They all waited in silence as we heard typing. I suddenly got an idea of what Rory was doing.

"Rory you're not-"

"Damn right I am." His voice was harsh. "You've had enough shit happen to you, so I'm going to make sure nothing else happens." I fought back tears as his words hit me right in the heart. No one really cared in a long time, not since Dad died.

"Rory." I swallowed hard. "You're still on speaker phone."

There was silence.

"Yeah, sorry." He took a deep breath and let it out. "Okay, you boys check out. No priors, no complaints. But, I have a rule that if you break, I will bring down hell on your heads."

I looked around the group I saw mostly raised eyebrows, a couple open mouths. Zeke, however, looked like he expected this.

Rory continued. "No boys upstairs. There is no give on this. If you go upstairs, you will never set foot back in my house again. Does everyone understand?"

A round of yes and yes sirs went up. The boys were taking Rory seriously.

"Lexie, if there isn't enough food in the house to feed them, order some pizzas or something. There is money in the emergency jar on my dresser." He took a deep breath. "I have to go, I'll see ya later." Rory hung up. I tucked my phone back into my jacket in the tense silence.

"How did your uncle know we don't have records?" Miles asked, his eyebrow raised.

"He's a cop." They all seemed to accept that and understand Rory a bit more. "Come on, guys, let's get out of here." I looked around the now empty hall; everyone else seemed to have gone home.

"Yeah, let's not run into Tara." Asher reminded them, which got everyone moving.

I gave everyone my address before we split up. I walked back to my Blazer and unlocked it. I was just climbing in when a car went by with Isaac half hanging out the window, waving. I shook my head and waved back. Isaac was nuts.

CHAPTER 3

*E*ven though I was one of the last to leave, I was the first to arrive at the house. I grabbed my bag and unlocked the door. The house was quiet. I had just finished taking off my shoes when someone knocked. I opened the door to find Miles standing there, his fingers tapping on his book bag strap.

"Come on in." I opened the door and let Miles close it behind him. He stepped just past the door his eyes running all over the great room. I went to the kitchen and pulled out a water bottle. "Want some water?"

"Yes, please," he answered as he headed over to the dining table I pulled out several cold bottles and brought them over to the table.

Miles finally looked at me. "About what I said in Chemistry, I wasn't trying to say you weren't smart," he said, his cheeks and ears turning pink. "Things don't always come out right when I talk to girls. Or people in general." His fingers started tapping against his leg. "Ethan and Isaac say that I have terminal foot in mouth disease."

I smiled; I couldn't help it, he was so sweet, trying to apologize and say the right thing.

"Don't worry about it, Miles, I figured you didn't mean it that way." I kept my voice light since he seemed so nervous.

His shoulders seemed to relax a little as he grinned.

"Is that why you haven't really been talking to me?" I asked him.

"Well, I don't usually talk a lot, but I also didn't want to insult you again." He admitted.

I didn't like that he censored himself around me. I don't mind the occasional rude comment, as long as it wasn't on purpose.

"How about you talk like you usually do, and if you do say something rude, I'll tell you," I offered. Miles smiled at me.

"I'd appreciate it." The loud roar of an engine started out in the street. "And there's Zeke." The roaring got louder; I'd take his word for it.

"Can you let the others in? I'm going to pop upstairs real quick."

"Sure."

I picked up my shoes on my way up the stairs. I was in my bedroom when the loud engine sound shut off. I peeked out my blinds just in time to see Zeke climbing off a motorcycle. I wondered what kind it was. I undid my belt and dropped that onto my desk. I also put my boots away and pulled my hair off my neck into a messy bun high on the back of my head. I heard the door open and close downstairs a couple times.

As I was pulling my cell phone out of my jacket, it vibrated. I checked my messages.

Isaac: Bringing food, what do you want on your sandwich?

I smiled to myself as I texted back what I liked. I got a winking smiley face back. I tucked my cell phone into my bra and headed downstairs.

Zeke and Asher were looking out the French glass doors toward the lake. Miles was already at the table pulling out books. I was walking across the room with my book bag when Zeke turned around spotting me.

"I think I know whose house we're hanging at this summer," Zeke announced walking back to the table.

"Miles' house does have a pool," Asher reminded him as he kept looking outside.

"Yeah, but that's a lake back there. It's better than a pool." Zeke argued his point as he sat down and began pulling books out.

"We have to get her uncle to trust us first." Miles pointed out as he opened his Trig textbook.

"We will." Asher sounded confident as he came toward the table. "We're likable."

I smiled to myself. They were definitely that.

"Ethan and Isaac stopped to pick up food, so we should probably start without them," I told them, starting to pull out my own books.

"Good, I'm starving," Asher said, rubbing his belly.

"Next time just say so, we have food here," I said as I got up and went into the kitchen.

I opened the pantry and pulled out a couple bags of chips and a box of crackers. I put those on the table; the boys snatched them up like they were priceless.

"Thank you," they all managed to say before stuffing their mouths. I raised both eyebrows at them.

"Guys eat a lot," Asher explained before eating another chip.

"We require a lot of fuel," Zeke added after he swallowed his food. Miles opened up the crackers and ate like he was starving.

"How much do you guys eat?" I asked, sitting down next to Miles with my leg tucked under me.

"Varies, but generally 3 meals a day and constant snacking all the time," Zeke answered between bites. Asher nodded with his mouth full. Even Miles confirmed with a nod, his mouth also full.

"Damn," I said, "so if I go for a chip, I might lose a finger?"

The guys paused.

"We share; you just have to speak up fast before the food is gone," Asher explained.

Everyone offered their bags of chips or crackers. I smiled and shook my head.

"Just wondering if I had to watch my fingers."

There was a knock on the door. I hurried over to answer it. Ethan and Isaac's arms were full of plastic grocery bags.

"Scoot Beautiful, these are heavy," Ethan grunted. I moved out of the way to hold the door open. Isaac came in behind his brother, his arms just as full with groceries plus their book bags.

"I thought you guys were bringing food?" Asher called over. Isaac snorted.

"This is food dumb ass." The boys dropped the bags onto the table. Everyone opened the bags; deli sandwiches were pulled out and passed around.

Miles kept looking, even after he got his sandwich.

"Did Alexis get one?" he asked, standing up and looking through another bag.

"No, I didn't get the girl anything." Isaac's sarcasm was so thick you could practically taste it. He opened the bag still in his hand and pulled out a sandwich. His voice was back to normal when he spoke to me. "I got you your turkey on sourdough with veggies, Red."

"Thank you."

"Happy to."

Isaac and Ethan proceeded to dump the rest of the bags onto the table. There were candy bars, chips, and several sodas. I sat back down next to Miles and looked over the pile.

"Okay, if I ate like this all the time I'd be a blimp," I announced in awe.

Zeke's eyes ran over me quickly.

"You're tiny. We're not." He stated matter-of-factly before opening his Trig book.

"Mm. Before I forget, everyone owes me ten bucks each." Ethan announced to the room as he sat in the chair to my right. Everyone pulled out their wallets. I was pulling cash out of my wallet when Ethan added. "Except Beautiful, it's her first day with us." No one argued as they tossed their money down onto the pile. Ethan was picking it up when I noticed someone had thrown a twenty in. I smirked but kept my mouth shut.

Everyone ate while we worked through our homework. I ate half my sandwich and wrapped it up for later. I had just finished reading my World Civ chapter when I noticed Zeke rubbing his eyes with one hand. He kept blinking hard as if trying to stay awake.

"Zeke? You want some coffee?" I asked, breaking the silence in the room. Zeke's eyes met mine, the corner of his lip twitching.

"What he needs is a nap." Miles looked up, pushing his glasses back up his nose. "You've been working late every night the past week."

Zeke ran his fingers through his hair as he answered. "The garage has been slammed lately, but we're finally caught up. I have the next couple days off." He turned back to me. "I would love any kind of coffee you have." I was about to get up when Ethan put his hand on my shoulder stopping me.

"Man, go take a nap on the couch, I don't think I'd even trust you driving right now." Ethan's voice was worried.

Zeke refused. As he was defending himself, Miles looked over at Zeke's homework. His hand darted out, snagging Zeke's notebook.

"Zeke, you multiplied four by two and came up with nine," Miles told him plainly, looking at him over his glasses. "There's no point in doing homework if your brain is too tired to think."

Zeke glared at him halfheartedly, and then he gave a big sigh. He looked over at me.

"Care if I crash on the couch?" he asked, resigned.

"Go for it."

He nodded his thanks and got to his feet. He was passing the table when Miles picked up his homework list.

"I'll do the rest of your homework," Miles told him as if this happened all the time.

"Don't do Physics, you suck at Physics," Zeke called from the living room before he dropped onto the couch.

I leaned over to Miles.

"Do you really suck at Physics?" I whispered. Miles shook his head.

"Not really, I just do it to mess with him," he said.

I snickered quietly as I turned back to my books and pulled out my Algebra. I was just starting the first problem when I heard a soft snore coming from the living room. I couldn't stop the smile that spread across my lips; it was kind of cute. Poor Zeke must really be exhausted. I pushed those thoughts to the back of my mind as I focused on my homework.

At some point, everyone had put their phones on the table. The boys kept getting texts, which they ignored, but Ethan's kept vibrating. After what had to be the 20th time in five minutes, the guys all groaned and glared at him.

"For the love of God, man, make them stop," Asher pleaded, his face in his hands. Ethan just grinned and picked up the cell phone.

"Them?" I asked. Asher nodded.

"Girls. I honestly think Ethan's cell phone number is on the wall in the girl's bathroom," Isaac chimed in. I couldn't help but chuckle at the image he had created. Ethan waved his hand dismissively.

"You're just jealous I'm the better-looking twin," Ethan said.

All the guys groaned.

"Shut the damn thing off before I do it for you," Asher threatened across the table. Ethan gave a suffering sigh and then turned off his phone. We got back to work.

AN HOUR AND A HALF LATER, I closed my chemistry book and rubbed my temples.

"You okay, Ally girl?" Asher asked, looking up from his own book.

I smiled at the nickname. "Brain full," I said in my most suffering voice.

He smiled and closed his book, too.

"Yeah, I'm done for the day, too." Asher looked down the table. Everyone else started closing books.

"What about Zeke's homework?" I asked Miles.

"I have it done, except for Physics." Miles adjusted his glasses as he looked at the group. "Who's waking Zeke up?" Everyone immediately pointed at me.

Surprised, I stammered. "W-What? Why me?"

"We have a theory that if you, a girl, wake him up, he might not wake up swinging punches," Miles explained, putting his books away. The others nodded in agreement. Apparently, they wanted to experiment with Zeke.

"Just touch his shoulder and back away fast," Isaac advised, stretching his arms above his head. I got to my feet and pointed at them.

"Fine, but if he hits me, I'm coming after all of you," I warned before walking across the great room.

Zeke seemed dead to the world. His large frame took up the entire couch. One muscled arm was over his eyes blocking out the light. I debated the best way to wake him up. I decided to try saying his name first.

"Zeke," I called in a soft voice. Nothing, he didn't even budge. "Zeke," I called louder in a singsong voice.

He mumbled something in his sleep and shifted onto his side, facing the back of the couch. I took a second to look at him. He was the most relaxed I'd seen him. He didn't look so big and intimidating right now. I debated my next move. Isaac said touch his shoulder and back away. I looked behind me to find the guys standing a couple feet from me. Everyone seemed to be enjoying themselves. Screw this. I really didn't want to get hit.

I quickly put my hand on his shoulder and hip, then gave Zeke a hard shove. He rolled off the couch and landed on the floor with a big thud. The guys burst out laughing behind me. Zeke sat up half way, holding himself up on one arm. His blue eyes were wild as he looked around. When he saw me, he figured it out.

"Why the hell did you do that?" he shouted, getting to his feet.

I pointed behind me to the other guys who were laughing hysterically.

"They were making me wake you up," I explained with a shit-eating grin on my face. "They also said you usually woke up swinging."

Zeke's gaze went to the guys; Ethan was doubled over holding his stomach.

"I didn't want to take the chance of getting hit," I said.

Zeke's gaze came back to me; he rubbed a hand along his jaw.

"Good call." He agreed. Then he turned to the others. "You chicken shits! Next time, one of you have the balls to wake me up." That sent the guys into another round of laughter.

I rolled my eyes as Zeke walked around the couch.

"Miles finished your homework." I began, not bothering to wait till the guys calmed down. "All that's left is Physics."

Zeke nodded as he stretched his arms over his head. His shirt rode up, showing off a bit of his skin. I turned away and headed for the kitchen phone, trying hard not to think about that glimpse of hard abs.

"I'm ordering dinner. Does anyone want to stay?"

"Yes," they all said at once. I had to bite back a smile. I found the menu for the pizza place.

"What kind do you guys want?" I asked, bringing the cordless phone to the dining room where they were all sitting while Zeke did his homework.

Everyone shot off something different; I had to slow them down. Nevertheless, the order turned out to be four pizzas, all with different toppings.

After I ordered, I went into Rory's bedroom and found the jar. I took the amount I needed, stuffed it into my pocket then came back out. I sat down next to Asher, putting my feet on the chair and wrapping my arms around my knees as everyone started talking about the coming football game and how close homecoming was. Ethan and Isaac talked about dates for the dance. While Zeke asked why they even wanted to go. I joined in the conversation whenever I felt like it.

It was easy hanging out with the guys. They were fun and nice. I don't know how else to describe it; we all seemed to fit like puzzle pieces. At least I hoped I fit.

Before I could start worrying about it, the front door opened. I looked over my shoulder, fearing Tara had come home. Instead, Rory stepped through the door in his street clothes, carrying several plastic bags. His eyes swept over the group then rested on me. I smiled at him, letting him know I was fine.

"Hey, Rory, I already ordered pizza." The guys stopped talking; it was suddenly awkward.

"Tara's eating over at her Mom's tonight," Rory announced as he walked to the kitchen and put his bags down on the counter before coming over to the table.

"Hello boys," he greeted, not exactly cheerful. There was a round of hellos. He looked me dead in the eye. "Anyone go upstairs?"

"Nope," I answered. "We've been doing homework. Zeke's just finishing Physics." Rory's eyes went to Zeke since he was the only one with books still out. He nodded again. He took a deep breath.

"I remember Physics, it was a bitch." Everyone chuckled. "So, who's who here?" Rory smiled. It felt like the room exhaled as everyone introduced themselves to Rory. He sat down and started talking to the guys. No interrogating. Just talking, learning about them and their hobbies. Asher played sports, Ethan was in a rock band, Isaac liked skateboarding and MMA fighting, Miles liked to mess with computers, and Zeke worked at a mechanic's garage.

By the time the pizza got there, everyone was laughing at a story Isaac was telling. Asher went with me to the door and helped carry the pizzas. Ethan ran into the kitchen and brought out plates. I brought out drinks and napkins. Everyone ate and talked. It felt good. All of it felt natural like we'd been doing it for years.

When dinner was over, the boys cleaned up while Rory pulled me aside.

"Nosebleed, fill me in." It was clear he wasn't kidding. We were in the corner of the dining room, and the guys were cleaning up in the kitchen.

"It was on my way to Art class," I began, whispering, crossing my arms over my chest. "There's a really pissed off girl along that path. From the looks of it, she's from the 60s. She was probably stabbed in the chest, maybe the lung." I kept it short and to the point. I didn't want the guys to overhear us. Speaking of the guys, I looked over Rory's shoulder to see them all cleaning up. However, Miles kept sneaking glances our way.

"Do you need to go back tonight and deal with her?"

I looked back to Rory. I shook my head immediately. "Some ghosts want help, others want to cause as much suffering as they can. She's the latter."

Rory sighed, rubbing the back of his neck.

"I'll try to find another way to that class tomorrow," I said. "I'll avoid her, it should be fine."

"If you say so," he agreed. "But if it gets worse let me know."

I nodded. A quick check-in was all Rory wanted. That I could handle.

Rory turned and walked to the kitchen.

"Anyone see the football game yesterday?" he asked. Everyone shook their heads except Asher. "Come on, I've got it recorded."

I smiled to myself as we all moved to the living room. Rory took the armchair near the door; Asher sat in the one to the left of the couch. Ethan and Miles sat on the floor. Zeke sat at the corner of the couch while I sat on the other side. Isaac nudged my shoulder.

"Scoot over, Red, you're the only one safe from him right now," Isaac stage whispered.

"Damn right she is," Zeke mumbled.

I scooted over and sat in the middle. Isaac wasn't as big as Asher or Zeke, but he took enough space that my shoulder was pressing against Zeke's arm.

Everyone was debating about what football player was better when Zeke lifted his arm and rested along the back of the couch. I went still then I peeked at him out of the corner of my eye. He was leaning his head on his fist, his elbow on the arm of the couch, his eyes on the screen. It didn't seem like he was hitting on me; just getting comfortable.

I looked up and realized the motion had caught Rory's eye too. He looked at Zeke's arm a long time, then he went back to watching the game, probably coming to the same conclusion I did. Ethan turned around to look at me, then scooted back and leaned against my legs, his hair covering my knees.

As we watched the game, I realized I was running my fingers through Ethan's soft, thick hair. He didn't seem to mind, so I kept doing it. Then the twisted side of me wondered what he would look like with braids. I smiled to myself as I slowly put braids in his hair. It was thick enough that when I started at the top, he didn't even notice it. Soon I had the top of his head covered in braids. Then I sat back and looked around for something else to do.

I was looking at the boys on the floor, wondering how much it would cost to buy some bean bags when Rory seemed to read my mind.

"If this becomes a regular thing, we're going to have to get another couch," Rory announced. The guys chuckled.

"We usually end up changing houses every day," Asher offered, then tilted his head. "But this summer you might be stuck with us." Rory chuckled.

It was around 7:30 when he paused the game. He turned to everyone, looking serious.

"Look boys, I know I probably seem a bit overprotective of Lexie," he began, the tension seeming to run out of his shoulders. "But she's my only niece. And I'll be damned if I'll allow anything else to happen to her."

I felt eyes on me, thanks, Rory. That's not going to cause any questions. No, not a one.

Rory continued. "You're good kids. So, you boys are welcome here anytime. And I'll rest easier if you guys keep an eye on her at school." Almost all the guys nodded. Ethan and Isaac exchanged smirks.

"I can take care of myself, Rory." I managed to say through clenched teeth.

"I know that, but having some backup never hurts," he told me before speaking to the group again. "Alright boys, it's getting late, and Lexie still has some physical therapy to do," Rory announced.

I groaned, closing my eyes. Physical therapy, my ass. I had to lay down with ice on my back.

No one else grumbled as they all started getting to their feet. Ethan reached up to run his hand through his hair, his fingers caught.

"What the..." I couldn't hold it. I burst out laughing. So did Zeke and Isaac who had watched me the whole time. Asher turned, a big smile making its way across his face.

"Aw. You look so adorable, Ethania," Asher taunted. Ethan was grumbling as he began pulling out the braids. The other guys chimed in with their taunts as Ethan tried to find the rest of the braids. Giving up, he got to his feet as the boys kept taunting him. He turned and glared at me with his dark eyes. I just kept giggling.

"Oh, Beautiful, this means war." He pointed at me, his face pink.

"Bring it," I challenged.

His eyes narrowed his broad lips half grinned at me. "Oh, I will."

Everyone said goodnight and thanked Rory for dinner. When they were gone, the house suddenly seemed quieter. Rory turned to me.

"That's a good bunch of boys."

"I like 'em." I shrugged, looking back to the TV. Reality set back in. "It'd be nice if they stick around."

"What do you mean?" he asked, his head resting on his hand, his elbow on the arm of the chair.

"You know what's going to happen," I told him my voice resigned. "They'll be my friends until I can't hide the Sight anymore. Then poof, they'll be gone." It had happened time and time again. At every school I'd ever gone to. I would make friends, and it'd be great. Until they caught me talking to a ghost they couldn't see, or my nose bleeds one time too many. If they find out, they leave. Some believed me, some thought I was lying, other people thought I was crazy. The rest thought I was a freak. It always happened. It was only a matter of time.

"You just met those boys today, and you're already thinking of them not being your friends anymore?" Rory pointed out frowning at me. "You can't go through life thinking everyone is going to leave you, Lexie."

I shrugged at him.

"Haven't been wrong yet," I pointed out.

Rory sighed deeply.

"Those boys might surprise you," He said.

I gave him a small smile. I hope they did. I pushed it to the back of my mind, not wanting to deal with it right now.

"Can I take a shower before we do the ice? I want to avoid Tara in the morning."

"Yeah, hurry up, though."

I got to my feet and hustled up the stairs. I grabbed my jammies and went into the bathroom. Before stepping into the tub, I turned in front of the mirror and looked at my back. Long strips of blood blisters covered my back with black and deep purple mixing along the strips of red and in other places. I sighed; with my pale skin, when I bruised, I bruised badly. The image of my Mom's face as she came at me flashed through my mind. I pushed it away quickly, not wanting to remember.

I took a long hot shower and got into my Star Wars jammy bottoms and a black cami. Then I trudged downstairs. I laid down on the couch with my cell phone in my hand. Rory put a towel on my back then the ice. At first, I hissed at the weight, but when the cold finally seeped through, it felt great. I had my head turned toward the TV with the game playing.

"How long?" I asked, already hating this position.

"20 minutes," Rory answered, putting a timer in front of me.

"No, how many more days do I have to do this for?"

Rory sighed. "A couple more weeks, then we'll mix in heat if the bruising isn't healing."

I groaned miserably.

Memories of my mother coming at me flashed through my mind, the feel of the belt hitting me. I pushed the memories away, focusing on the TV. It was constant--memories coming to the surface from that night, me pushing it away again. I really hated this.

I was vaguely aware when Tara came home. That is until she started demanding answers from me.

"What were you doing, talking to Asher Westfell?" Tara snapped above me. All I could see of her was her black leggings.

"I was making friends," I pointed out like it was obvious. "And you know, walking to class."

"You embarrassed me in front of him!" she accused me.

The timer went off. I sat up and picked up the ice packs.

"I'm confused, Tara." I looked up at her my brow drawn in mock confusion. "Didn't you tell me an hour before that you didn't want anyone to know we're related?" Rory's head turned as he frowned at

61

Tara. "Then you see me walking to class with Asher, and all of a sudden I'm cousin Lexie?"

"Tara is that true? Did you say that to her?" Rory asked his voice hard.

Tara turned and whined at Rory. "She's not going to be popular, Dad. She's already got the most popular girl in school gunning for her." Tara turned back to me and narrowed her eyes. "She twisted Jason Miller's arm behind his back, then shoved him in front of everyone." Tara tattled.

Fair enough, I tattled on her first. Rory turned his frown onto me.

"Explain." He demanded.

I sighed.

"This guy, Jason, wrapped his arm around me, I told him to let go," I explained, keeping it simple. "Instead, he wrapped his arm around my waist and asked me if the curtains matched the drapes."

Rory's face became hard.

I continued. "So, I broke his hold and did an arm-lock on the guy. I told him he was being an ass and pushed him into his friends." Rory's frown had disappeared as I spoke. Now he was smiling.

"Good girl," he told me.

I winked at him. He went back to watching football.

"Dad!" Tara scoffed.

Rory looked up at her blankly. "I'm not going to punish her for defending herself," he told her plainly. "She told him to let go, he didn't. So, she made him. Perfectly justified."

Tara's mouth dropped, then she turned back to me her eyes calculating.

"Dad, she tried to stop me from talking to Asher today," Tara complained, all but stomping her foot in her tantrum. "We were standing there talking, and she tugged him to start walking. I had to tug him to stop. Then she gave herself a bloody nose to get me away from him."

I looked over at Rory and met his gaze. He inclined his head towards me; he understood what happened.

"The nosebleed wasn't about you, Tara," he told her, turning back to the football game. "Lexie has always gotten a lot of nosebleeds."

Tara looked at him like he was insane. Then she crossed her arms and glared at me. She seemed determined to get me in trouble for something. "She's hanging out with a bunch of boys. One of them is Zeke Blackthorn. That really scary guy, he's a total bully."

Rory shrugged. "He didn't seem so bad," Rory said absently.

I winced. Tara's eyes went wide.

"You met him?" she asked, stunned.

Rory didn't notice the can of worms he had opened.

"Yeah, I met all of them. They were nice kids," he said dismissively, still watching the game.

Tara looked at me, her eyes wide.

"Asher Westfell was here?"

"Yeah, we all had dinner." I got up and took the ice packs to the freezer to put them away for tomorrow. I turned and found Tara blocking my way out of the kitchen.

"You have to tell me when Asher is here." She actually ordered me.

I scoffed at her. "I'm not going to help set you up with my friend."

Her mouth pinched, and her eyes narrowed.

"Your friend?" She huffed. "You're just the new girl, Alexis. Soon enough they won't even be talking to you."

That hurt, I admit it, it really hurt. Because she was probably right. Even if they did want to be my friends, when they found out about the Sight, they'd be gone anyway.

"Night, Tara." I walked around her and went upstairs. I turned off my light then climbed into bed, miserable.

Tara's comment shook me. I was just wondering if they'd even talk to me tomorrow when my phone vibrated on the desk. I reached over and picked it up.

Zeke: Why do you have physical therapy?

That was it; no hi or how are you. Straight to the point Zeke. I didn't want to tell him. Especially after Tara had rattled me. So, I asked him something I doubt he'd answer.

Alexis: Why do you wake up swinging?

He was silent so long that I thought he'd never answer. Then my phone vibrated again.

Zeke: Not every family is a good family.

My heart sank. I knew exactly what he was saying. Just because someone is your parent doesn't mean they give a damn. Hell, my own mother couldn't care less about me. I was invisible as long as I was able to keep food on the table. And when I couldn't... I pushed those memories away as another text message came in.

Zeke: Why do you have physical therapy?

I bit my lip trying to decide how to answer. I wasn't going to lie; he'd been honest with me.

Alexis: Not every family is a good family.

I thought that would be the end of it, but my phone vibrated again.

Zeke: That's why you moved into your uncle's.

It wasn't a question, not really. So, I didn't answer. He sent another text.

Zeke: Are you okay?

I bit my lip; his simple question shook my control. I took a deep breath to stop the tears from falling. I didn't want to deal with it, not yet. So again, I was honest but vague.

Alexis: I'm alive.

Zeke: Some days alive is the best you get. But, there's always tomorrow.

I smiled at that. Underneath the rough and scary, Zeke had a soft spot somewhere.

Zeke: Night.

Alexis: Night.

CHAPTER 4

I woke up twice that night, both times with nightmares. So, when the alarm went off, I wasn't happy. At least I got to sleep in an extra half hour since I showered last night. I got out of bed slowly, my back stiff. I rubbed my eyes; I felt like I hadn't slept at all. I got up and headed to the bathroom. Surprisingly, Tara wasn't in it this morning. I opened the medicine cabinet and found a small bottle of Ibuprofen. I took two, and then quickly washed my face. After brushing my teeth, I took the bottle with me. By the way my back felt, I was going to need it.

Now more awake, I dressed the way I felt today; dark boot-cut jeans, an olive long sleeve, thin sweater with a black cami on underneath. The neckline on the sweater was low enough that the cami kept the girls covered. I brushed my hair, leaving it down and only pulling the front back into a small clip at the back of my head. I did my usual sunscreen and makeup, then I grabbed my jacket, making sure I had my wallet, cell phone, and keys before heading downstairs. Thankfully, I found a metal travel mug. I turned the coffee maker on and made my lunch.

My cell phone vibrated in my bra. I pulled it out to find a text from Miles.

Miles: Picking up coffee today, what would you like?

I texted back, smiling; it looks like Tara was wrong about them. My mood lifted from dour to just tired.

Alexis: Mocha with two espresso shots, please.

I had stronger coffee coming. That alone, got me out the door. That and the coffee in my hand. By the time I reached the school, I had already downed half of my coffee. I finished it before I even reached my locker. I turned the corner and there they were, all five of them, waiting for me. Ethan in all black again, Asher looking classic in another button-down shirt and wool coat, Zeke wearing his black clothes, wallet chain and his motorcycle jacket, Isaac in his blue hoodie, gray jeans, and white shirt. I spotted Miles. Sweet, wonderful Miles in a grey hoodie and a t-shirt with a chemical compound written across his chest, and who also had my coffee in his hand. I made a beeline for him.

"Morning," he greeted me cheerfully, handing over my coffee. I took it and hugged him tight. His body became rigid, his hands hovering over my back uncertainly.

"You are my hero for the day." My voice was muffled; my face was in his grey hoodie on his shoulder. He smelled like wintergreen.

"Um, no problem...?" Miles' voice trailed off.

I felt him looking to the guys for help. I smiled, gave him one last squeeze, then stepped back.

"Hell, if coffee is all it takes for a hug, I call tomorrow," Isaac said, raising his hand. A few of them chuckled at Isaac. I ignored it and went to open my locker. With how my back felt today, I wasn't going to be lugging all my books around all day.

"You okay, Red? You look as bad as Zeke did yesterday," Isaac said.

I waved his concern away, still not awake as I put my bag on the ground and pulled out my Chemistry book.

"I'm fine, just had nightmares all night," I said absently before I took another deep drink of coffee and put the book in the locker. I was debating my World Civ. book when Asher spoke up.

"Jessica's on the warpath today," he warned, stepping up to the other side of my locker. I ignored it and put my World Civ book in the locker, too. That should make my bag light enough for me today. I also put the empty travel mug in for good measure.

"What is she bitching about?" I asked as I closed the locker, turned and realized they all looked serious.

"Jessica's the most popular girl in school for some reason," Isaac explained. Asher nodded and met my eyes.

"She believes some bullshit story Jason came up with about you hitting on him." Asher continued, holding my gaze, "I explained to her what really happened, but brain power was never my sister's strong suit." He scratched his jaw as he continued. "She can destroy your reputation here before you even have one."

I snorted.

"I don't really give a shit what people think about me," I told him bluntly, I really was too tired for drama this morning. I took a drink of coffee before gesturing around the circle. "Does my reputation really matter to you guys?"

They all shook their heads; the twins were smiling. Zeke did his almost smile thing.

"We thought you might," Miles chimed in. "She might make it harder for you to get along with girls."

I sighed trying to find a way to explain how I felt about this.

"If the girls here are so spineless that they can't think for themselves, I don't want them as friends," I told them bluntly. I gestured at them again. "Besides, I've got you guys. I'm good." All the guys smiled; Zeke smirked.

"See? This is why we kept you. You think like a guy," Ethan declared, wrapping his arm around my back jarring me. I winced as he hit a particularly nasty bruise on my back--my hands actually shook from the pain. I just smiled back at him, hoping no one had noticed.

The bell rang, and the group split up. I couldn't move yet, I had to give my back a minute. I was looking at the ground focusing on breathing when a pair of motorcycle boots came into view. I bit the bullet and looked up. Zeke's eyes ran over my face, accessing.

"You okay?" he asked. His eyes bore into mine demanding an answer. I put on my best smile.

"Peachy." I lied.

He looked at the lockers over my head.

"The twins are affectionate with everyone," he began, tilting his head down, meeting my eyes. "If you don't want them touching you, you just need to speak up." I felt my eyes widen, was he serious?

"I have never had a problem speaking up in my life," I told him honestly. "You should have seen some of the notes from teachers in grades school. 'Motormouth' was mentioned, often."

The corner of his mouth twitched. "Just checking." He ran his eyes over me again before taking off down the hall.

Zeke had noticed the wince. Damn, he was observant. I needed to be more careful around him, and right now, I was too tired to figure it how. God, it was too early for drama.

I WAS on my way to Algebra 2, and my mind was finally awake, though my body was still tired. I was going to make it through the day and take a nap this afternoon. Hell, maybe I could bribe one of the guys to do my homework.

I had put Asher's warning out of my mind and was simply walking down the hall when a shout rang out. Then another.

"Hey, new girl!"

That had to be me. I turned to find a tall girl with the same blonde hair as Asher striding toward me with fire in her eyes. I sighed, reminded myself about my temper, and waited. People backed up creating a ring around us. Jessica was pretty but had on too much bubblegum-pink lip gloss. She was wearing a white crop top even though it was cold this morning. Her big, gold hoop earrings shined at me. She stopped within a few feet of me, towering over me. Two of her friends were standing on either side of her. Oooh. A show of force. I barely managed to keep my face straight.

"Yes?" I asked, keeping it polite. Her eyes flared at me.

"Keep your hands off my boyfriend, bitch," she spat. I really wasn't in the mood to deal with this.

"Your boyfriend put his hands on me, and I made him stop." I shrugged, feeling my hair slide down my shoulder. "Tell your boyfriend to keep his hands to himself, and we won't have a problem," I added, again, my voice reasonable.

Jessica took a step forward, and I swear, she did a head bob.

"Jason told me what happened. How you came up to him, flirting and touching him." She ran her eyes over me then back to my face. "Acting like a slut...." This was Asher's sister, so I tried again to make her understand.

"Asher was there, ask him what happened," I said, but she was coming at me hard. Yelling, getting in my face. Yeah, I wasn't going to back down and crawl away. And to be honest, it seemed like that was what she expected. I was very aware of the surrounding crowd; I even saw a few cell phones out filming. Great.

"He's lying to cover for you," she snarled.

All right, I had enough. I opened my arms to her, palms up.

"Then what the hell do you want?" I asked, more of my anger slipping through the more I spoke. "Asher told you what happened, I told you what happened. You don't believe it." I shook my head not caring that I was almost shouting now. She needed to learn that she wasn't scaring me, and I had to make her realize it "What are you hoping to do, coming at me like this? What? Do you want a fight? Fine," I stated.

I put my bag down and pulled off my jacket, which I dropped onto my book bag. I stepped closer to her, waiting. Jessica's eyes grew wide; had no one done this before? Had no one ever just pushed back? Then she looked pissed as she stepped back away from me.

"I'm going to make your life here hell," she snarled. I felt my face go blank, my eyes go dead.

"You don't know a damn thing about me, Jessica." My voice was flat and honest as I kept eye contact with her. I pushed it; I had to make her understand something very simple. "You don't intimidate me, and you sure as hell don't scare me." Her eyes flashed at me, I continued. "So, knock yourself out. It's not going to make a bit of difference to me."

She pursed her lips before storming off, her heels clicking down the hallway. The crowd parted for her in stunned silence.

When she was gone, I turned my back, bent over, picked up my jacket and book bag. The circle was starting to break up since there wasn't going to be a show. It was quick and bloodless, the way I preferred it. I just hoped Jessica got the message; if you come at me I won't back down.

I straightened up and sighed. Zeke was leaning against the wall with Asher standing next to him. Both were watching me. I felt awkward walking up to them- after all, I did just tell Asher's sister to pretty much fuck off. Though Asher had the biggest smile I'd ever seen.

"That was beautiful," Asher told me happily. "I've wanted to see Jessica taken down a peg for a long time."

"Happy to help." Surprised, I didn't know what else to say.

"I've got ten on it being on Youtube before the end of the day," Zeke said, an actual grin spreading across his face.

"I'm not stupid enough to take that bet," Asher said.

I shook my head; I didn't know what to think about that. I looked up at Asher.

"Do you think that will be the end of it?"

Asher tilted his head, thinking. "I don't think she'll come at you directly like that again." He was smiling again. "No one's ever stood up to her before. But we probably haven't heard the end of this."

"Oh well, let her knock herself out," I said as the late bell rang overhead. "See you guys at lunch." I waved to them before heading off to class.

I figured that the rest of the day would go back to normal. However, halfway through Algebra people were showing phones to each other and sending looks my way. Damn, Zeke had been right. It hadn't even been an hour, and it looked like the video had gone viral through the school. I ignored it the best I could; it wasn't easy.

The quiet girl with brown hair that sat to my right leaned over.

"Did you really stand up to Jessica?" She whispered.

I looked up from my book at her. Her brown hair was straight to her shoulders. She had a sweet face that was clear of makeup. Her fingers were twisting in her lap like she was anxious about something.

"I just made a couple things clear to her, that's all," I whispered back, keeping my voice friendly. She smiled and it changed her face completely. She was pretty, but you wouldn't know it since she kept hiding in her hair.

"Wish I could have done that when she came at me," she mumbled, picking up her pen.

Jessica went after this girl too? It got me curious.

"She goes after girls like that a lot?"

She nodded, sucking on her lower lip. "All the time," she said quietly.

I snorted at that; Jessica wasn't a pissed off girlfriend, she was a drama queen.

"She even goes after some of the boys sometimes."

That really caught my attention. I abandoned my class work and focused on her.

"Goes after them how? Yelling, screaming?"

The girl nodded her eyes unfocused for a couple seconds.

"That and she'll slap them. Once, I saw her slap her brother across the face during lunch."

I'm pretty sure my eyebrows disappeared into my hairline. I reassessed. Jessica wasn't a drama queen; she was a fucking bully who used drama as an excuse. Then why didn't she hit the other girls? I knew the answer before I finished asking myself the question. Because they could hit her back. That fucking bitch. My temper surged. She hit guys because they couldn't hit her back without getting in deep shit.

I looked over at the girl next to me and smiled. I held out my hand to her.

"I'm Alexis."

The girl's eyes lit up as she shook my hand. "I'm Laura."

Her hand shook a little in mine. She seemed very nervous, even timid. Jessica going after her was ridiculous. I tore a piece of paper off the corner of my page. I wrote my number down and handed it to her.

"If she comes after you again call me, and I'll take care of it." I didn't even have to think about it. It was clear to me this girl was too shy and timid to stand up for herself. "Or you know, if you're bored or something." Laura's face lit up; when she smiled, she was even prettier.

"Okay."

Soon algebra was over, I said goodbye to Laura and headed toward Chemistry. That's when it hit me. Did I just make another friend? I was going over the conversation in my head as I moved through the halls. I decided that I had. I was smiling as I walked into class.

The boys had already beaten me to the table. They were leaning forward, looking at Isaac's cell phone. My smile disappeared. As I stepped up to the counter, I heard my own voice coming from the phone.

"I see you've heard," I announced, mildly annoyed. Isaac was beaming, Ethan laughing. Miles was his usual quiet self.

"Heard, seen, and watched about a dozen times," Isaac answered joyfully. "That was the best thing I've seen in years."

"You did handle her rather brilliantly," Miles said.

I sat on my stool and dropped my bag. Then curiosity had me asking.

"What do you mean?"

Miles adjusted his glasses before answering. "Jessica relies on fear to get what she wants. You telling her she doesn't scare you took away any power she felt she had."

I thought about it for a minute. Was he right? Is that what happened? Looking back at the whole scene with that in mind, I realized he was right.

"That wasn't my plan," I explained. "I was just telling her the truth."

A smile made its way across his face, turning his cute face handsome. His emerald eyes sparkling. He really should smile more.

"And that's why it was epic."

I shook my head not knowing what to say as I heard Isaac playing the video again.

"Oh, this is my favorite part." Isaac said gleefully.

The teacher clapped his hands, getting everyone's attention, and then class started. Miles ended up taking Ethan and Isaac's cell phones so they would stop watching the video.

AFTER CLASS, Miles handed them back, making them promise not to use them in class. Both boys grumbled an agreement.

We were talking about Ethan's band practice that night when we reached the courtyard in front of the cafeteria. It was jam-packed with other students.

"What the hell?" Ethan asked, looking at the crowd.

"Is our table even open?" Isaac asked, shading his eyes. He pointed. "Yep, there's Zeke and Asher. They've managed to hold the table."

It wasn't hard to see Zeke and Asher; they towered over everyone else in the courtyard. We headed into the crowd. We eventually ended up going single file; Isaac in front, me in the middle, and Ethan taking up the back. It took a while, but we finally arrived at the table. Zeke and Asher moved their bags so everyone could sit down. I shared a bench with Miles, Zeke was on the bench to my left. Asher shared across from me with Ethan and Isaac having their own bench.

"What's with the crush?" I asked, pulling my lunch from my bag.

"That's your fault," Asher said, getting his own lunch out. "After you told off Jessica this morning, everyone's here hoping to see more."

I rolled my eyes and opened my lunch bag. "That's not going to happen."

"We know that, but they don't." Isaac said before biting into his sandwich.

We did our best to ignore the crush around us. But every once in a while, someone would try to pass someone else, and one of us would get bumped. I was in the middle of telling them about meeting Laura when someone knocked into Asher again, making him spill water down his shirt. I was fed up.

"Let's go eat somewhere else, guys. This is ridiculous," I said.

Everyone agreed and gathered their stuff.

Asher stood up straight and looked over the crowd. He pointed in a direction.

"That's the fastest way out," he announced. We all started moving, again single file. Somehow, the crowd had gotten worse. I reached out and grabbed a handful of Ethan's jacket, trying not to lose them. Ethan reached back, took my hand, his rings biting into my fingers as he kept pulling me through the crowd. When we finally got free, he let go.

"Next time, we need to put her in the middle," he said to the guys. "We almost lost her in the crowd."

Everyone looked at me.

"It's not my fault I'm short," I told them simply, stepping further away from the crush.

"At least you've got the cute thing workin' for ya," Isaac said.

"Damn right I do," I said, my head held high.

The guys were laughing as we started walking down the hall.

"Where are we going?" Ethan asked as he pulled his sandwich from his bag and started eating it.

"How about the library?" Miles suggested.

"We can just walk and eat?" Asher offered.

"Who wants to walk and eat?" Ethan asked.

Four of us raised our hands.

"Majority rules, we walk," Ethan declared.

I pulled out my water bottle and took a drink.

"So, how did this voting thing start?" I asked, looking down the line as we walked shoulder to shoulder down the mostly empty hallway.

"I think when we were eight," Isaac answered. "We all kept wanting to do different stuff, and we'd get into fights over It."

"When we broke a vase at Asher's, his mom made voting a rule for us." Zeke shrugged. "We've been doing it ever since."

"Aw, I need to see kid photos of you guys. I bet you all were adorable," I said, unable to help smiling at them.

To my astonishment, every one of them blushed a bit. Oh, this was going to be fun.

"No, never, not in a million years." Zeke denied me immediately.

I was so going to find those photos. I snickered. "Oh, I so am."

"Anyway, what's the plan for homework tonight?" Asher asked, changing the subject, his cheeks still pink.

"Not my place, Sylvia is still sleeping," Zeke said. "Miles?"

"Still decorating," Miles answered. "Asher?"

"Jessica has girls coming over," Asher said. "Ethan?"

"Not if you actually want to get work done," Isaac said "Lexie?"

"Tara is very aware that Asher was over there last night, so, she'll be around," I warned them. "If you can deal with her?"

Everyone groaned.

"There's always the county library?" Miles offered.

"I call library," Isaac said. Everyone agreed.

"Good, because we have a Chemistry test tomorrow, and I've had about a day and a half to study for it," I complained. "Oh, and Algebra and World Civ."

The guys winced in sympathy.

"Chemistry isn't bad, it's a ten-question quiz and they're the ones from the back of the book," Miles reassured me.

"What about English?" Asher asked looking down the line at me.

"We're reading Romeo and Juliet," I grumbled. "I understand it's a masterpiece of theater and everything. But please knock me out for that class." The guys chuckled.

"Wait a minute, I thought all girls liked those tragic love stories?" Isaac asked as we turned down another hall.

"I guess I'm weird." I shrugged. "I prefer a good happy ending to a story, there are enough tragic ones in real life."

"That makes sense." Miles said.

"What's the training schedule look like this weekend?" Zeke asked. Isaac emptied his water bottle.

"I've got training tonight at seven, then Sunday. If any of you are joining me...?" Isaac asked.

"I'll take Sunday with you," Zeke said. Isaac nodded.

"I'll take tonight," Ethan chimed in. "We just need to get our home-work done first."

We turned another corner and were walking by a group of girls; they were giggling and pointing at us. I ignored it. They were prob-ably checking out the guys.

"I heard she's already slept with half the football team," I heard whispered from their group. "What a slut."

I doubted anyone else heard it, so I ignored it and kept walking It was clear Jessica was working the gossip mill. But even I thought that was fast.

However, Asher stopped and turned around. The others stopped a second later.

"What?" the others asked, confused as to why he stopped.

Asher looked at me, his eyebrow raised, asking without words if I had heard them.

"I heard," I told him simply, then started walking again. The guys followed.

"That doesn't bother you?" Asher asked, like he found it hard to believe.

"What did we miss?" Ethan asked, looking down the line at both of us.

"Those girls back there were calling her, well, names," Asher informed them, his eyes going to Miles.

"They were saying I'm a slut." I supplied, dropping my trash into a trash can as we walked by.

Zeke cursed under his breath.

"And that doesn't bother you?" Asher asked, obviously finding it hard to believe.

"I know I'm not a slut, you guys know I'm not a slut." I shrugged and tried to explain. "Those girls don't mean anything to me, so why would I care what they think?"

"Those kinds of rumors can bring out some pervy guys," Zeke warned.

"Then they'll be really disappointed." I said, chuckling, my twisted side finding the situation funny. A couple of them chuckled, too. Zeke was frowning. I rolled my eyes as the sixth-period bell rang.

"I'll see you guys at the library; I'll see you in seventh period, Asher," I called over my shoulder. I heard several see you laters.

GYM WAS NORMAL, except the line for the stalls were so long that I said fuck it and changed by my locker. With my hair down, no one noticed my bruises. Yay, for thick hair! I made sure to stuff some tissues into my pocket before I left the locker room foreseeing a nosebleed coming. I really needed to find a better way to art class. I met up with Asher, and I asked him.

"Is there another way to art class?"

He frowned and shook his head. "Not that I've found, and believe me I've tried," he said.

Great. Daily torture. I sighed.

"Have you tried just telling her no?" I asked as we headed down the path.

Asher started rubbing the back of his neck. "I don't want to be rude.

I rolled my eyes.

"It's not rude to tell her you're not interested in doing those activities she wants you to do," I offered. "If it was me having this problem, would you think I was being rude by just telling some guy that I didn't want to join some club of his?" I stopped talking; it was up to him how he wanted to deal with Tara. I was just along for the ride.

We headed down the walkway, Asher looking around for Tara, and I looked around for ghost girl. That familiar chill went down my neck, only this time it was like a finger touch running down my skin. The pain hit me hard and fast, driving the air from my lungs and forcing me to stop. Ghost girl was walking down the path toward me, a strange grin on her face. My hand went to my throbbing chest. I glanced to Asher, he hadn't noticed because he had spotted Tara.

My heart raced as he took a deep breath and started forward again. I followed.

"Please don't leave me alone with her," he said out of the corner of his mouth.

My head was pounding as ghost girl followed Tara.

"You got it," I answered, hiding the pain from my voice. By the time we reached Tara, my stomach was rolling. What the fuck? Had ghost girl been feeding off someone? How did she have this much energy today?

I concentrated on breathing through the pain.

"Asher, hi!" Tara greeted cheerfully. Her eyes darted to me then back to Asher. She began pulling pieces of paper out of her binder. "I brought you copies of the plans for homecoming, I would really like your opinion-"

"Tara, I'm sorry, but I'm not going to help with any of this stuff," Asher told her, surprising me.

I might have looked at him, but I was too busy trying to breathe around the hot burning spike that felt like it was being driven through my chest right over my heart. Ghost girl stood across from me, her memories starting to pour through my head. I saw her death in my mind, my heart grew heavy. I felt the pressure in my face a second before the first drip on my upper lip. Absently, I reached into my pocket and pulled out my tissues. I put them to my nose, hoping we could go soon.

"I'm just really swamped with football and work right now. Not to mention homework." Asher was explaining to Tara when ghost girl reached out and touched my neck.

Pain tore through me like lightning, from neck to toes. I glared at her with everything I had. I mouthed no at her. She was pushed back instantly, the nerve pain easing up, allowing me to take a more normal breath again. Ghost girl was pale, her skin shining as if she was sweating. She kept backing up. She had nothing left.

I blinked hard, becoming more aware of what was going on. Tara was glaring at me before she smiled up at Asher.

"Alright, I understand. You're too busy to help now." Tara gave him big eyes and a small smile.

Shit, was she going to cry? Oh nope, she was pulling the girl card, looking sweet and hurt.

"Maybe you could help with Winter Formal and Prom next semester?" she asked.

Before he could answer, Asher looked over to me, his brow drew down as he frowned.

"Lexie? Is your nose bleeding again?" he asked, his voice filled with concern. My head still pounding, I nodded. He ran his eyes over me, his face worried. He reached out and took my arm.

"Come on, let's get you cleaned up." He gave me a small nudge to get me moving. "I'll think about next semester, Tara," he called over his shoulder, his gaze still on me as we passed by girl ghost.

I felt a surge of blood and cursed as I pinched my nose shut. I walked faster, trying to get away so the burning pain in my chest would stop. By the time we turned the corner, my tissues were soaked. Seeing this, Asher pulled his little pack of tissues out of his bag and handed them to me. I added some to my nose. The further away from the dead girl we got, the less my nose bled.

"Seriously Lexie, what's with your nose?" he asked, still frowning.

I tried to figure an excuse that would explain this.

"It's kind of a medical thing," I hedged, checking to see if my nose had stopped bleeding. Thankfully it had.

Once in the class room, I went straight to the sink, Asher one-step behind me.

"What kind of medical thing?" he asked, grabbing a dry paper towel and handing it to me.

"It's nothing serious. It just gives me nosebleeds and makes me sick once in a while." Warming up to the lie I was creating, I though this might just work. Asher frowned at me then backed off the subject as we went to our table.

During the whole hour of class, Asher thankfully seemed to forget about my nosebleed. I tried to help him with his drawing of a vase but he always ended up drawing stick men leaping to their deaths. I eventually gave up.

CHAPTER 5

efore heading to the library, I stopped at a gas station for a big bottle of water and a couple of those tissue packs. I needed to stop using Asher's tissues. I made sure to text Rory telling him where I would be.

The county library wasn't a huge library, but it looked big to me. The building's outside walls were made of river stone, and near the entrance was a sign that said, 'no climbing.' It made me grin.

I walked into the big room, noticing that there were comfy armchairs here and there, scattered into corners, creating reading nooks. It didn't really look like a library. If it weren't for the book-shelves, it would look like a coffee house. It was big and cozy all at the same time.

I spotted the guys at one of the bigger tables and headed over. Isaac sat at one end of the table, Ethan and Miles sat on one side, Zeke on the other. I sat across from Miles next to Zeke and started pulling out my books.

"Heard you got another nosebleed today," Zeke announced in his gravelly voice. I narrowed my eyes at him. "Asher said it's some kind of medical thing." He looked over at me, his eyes demanding answers.

"You guys gossip just as much as girls do," I shot back as I opened my World Civ notes to study. Isaac and Ethan chuckled. Miles adjusted his glasses and ran his eyes over me. Before he could ask me any questions, I changed the subject. "How is it you guys can stay out late on school nights?"

They all looked at each other for a second before looking back down at their books.

"Asher's dad is usually out of town on business," Miles began, his fingers tapping out a staccato rhythm again. "Right now, my mother is on a redecorating spree, so, she doesn't want me in the way." He shrugged, all but burying his nose in his textbook. That didn't seem right to me, but before I could even think to ask, Ethan spoke up.

"We can't do anything we want, our mom's a teacher at the grade school, and she's usually stuck grading papers after school. We always have to check in, but she knows our friends and knows that we're not interested in doing anything too stupid." Isaac nodded in agreement. They didn't mention their dad, and I decided not to ask.

"My Aunt Sylvia works nights at the diner in town." Zeke shrugged as he turned a page in his Physics book "As long as I check in and stay out of trouble she pretty much lets me do what I want."

Everyone was avoiding looking at me. That's when I understood -- they didn't usually have anyone at home most of the time. They stayed together all evening to keep each other company. I felt the wall I kept around my heart crack a little more. Shit.

"Feel free to come over anytime, guys," I said, keeping my voice light. "It'll annoy the crap out of Tara." Chuckles ran around the table.

We all got to work studying. I focused on my World Civ. for the first hour. I had moved on to Chemistry when I noticed Ethan shifting out of the corner of my eye, wincing. I looked up from my book and watched him trying to stretch his lower back while staying in his chair.

"Ethan, are you okay?" I asked.

He was still grimacing when he answered.

"Yeah, I just..." He closed his eyes, grunting in pain.

Isaac's head snapped up, his face serious. He ran his eyes over his brother like he was examining him.

"It's just an old back injury," Ethan said. He looked down at his bag on the floor and scowled at it. He closed his eyes and sighed, sounding resigned. "Brother, could you-"

He didn't even have to finish his sentence. Isaac reached down, picked up Ethan's bag and put it on the table for him.

"Thanks." Ethan opened a pocket on his bag and pulled out a water bottle followed by a prescription bottle. He poured out one large white pill, then swallowed it quickly. "Oh, Ibuprofen, how I love you," he grumbled as he put the bottle back into his bag. He pushed his bag into the middle of the table.

What did he do to his back? For once, I wasn't going to ask; Ethan didn't seem okay with the situation. He went back to his homework. I went back to my chemistry.

"Muscle spasms?" Isaac asked quietly.

"It's fine." Ethan all but growled at his brother.

"You're not going to training tonight." Isaac's voice was firm. It was strange coming from Isaac.

"It'll be fine," Ethan hissed at his brother. "I just forgot to take my noon pill." Isaac dropped it.

It was a while later when Asher showed up, freshly showered. He dropped into the chair at the end to my right.

"How did practice go?" I asked, opening my math book.

"Fine, coach was angry I skipped yesterday," Asher informed us as he pulled one of his books out. "He made me run more suicides as punishment, and it wiped me out. What did I miss?"

"Oh, nothing much. The guys were just telling me all your most embarrassing secrets," I told him, my voice sincere.

His head shot up, looking around the group with wide eyes. The other guys snickered. Asher narrowed his eyes at me playfully

"They wouldn't, I have too much dirt on them," he assured me before he opened his book.

"Okay, you and me, we need to talk soon," I told him earnestly. Asher smiled then everyone got back to work.

A half hour later, I was in the middle of my Algebra home-work when I felt it. That damn chill down my neck. I lifted my head slowly and looked around. There was a dead woman walking down an aisle of books, looking at them sadly. I could almost see the waves of distress rolling off her. I didn't want to help her. But as she came closer, I felt her emotions running through her. Grief, loss, and confusion poured over me. She didn't know she was dead. My head started to ache. I couldn't *not* help her.

Fuck.

I put my pen down and made a show of stretching my arms.

"I'm going to stretch my legs, maybe find a book to take home," I told the guys as I got out of my chair. No one asked questions as I moved off into the shelves. The closer I got to her the more my head throbbed. I was guessing she died from head trauma. I met her halfway down an aisle.

"I see you," I whispered to her.

She turned to me, relief sweeping over her face.

"Thank goodness," she said, her eyes running over the shelves. "No one seems to be listening to me."

The pain in my head spiked, making my stomach roll. I gestured further into the stacks and stepped around her. I stuck my hand out as the world spun. I blinked hard and focused on getting further out of sight. When I found a corner, I took a step back from her and the world stopped spinning. Definitely head trauma.

I looked up at the woman; she seemed sweet. She looked like she was in her thirties when she died. Her brown hair up in a messy bun held together with pencils. She wore a long, dark, tweed skirt, and a blue cable knit sweater with a white blouse on underneath. The peter pan collar showing over the sweater.

"What's your name? Who are you?" I asked as my head began to throb with my pulse. She licked her lips before answering.

"I'm Lily Mason. I'm the librarian here, but no one seems to be listening to me," she told me before pointing at a section of books. "Non-fiction isn't supposed to be back here, it's supposed to be on the east wall. And..." She began listing off the changes that had occurred since her death. She really had no idea she was dead. Fuck.

I sat down in an armchair and pulled the tissues from my pocket.

"Tell me about yourself," I asked, my head already throbbing.

Lilly Mason told me everything. She told me about her love for books, how she wanted nothing more than to sit and read for hours uninterrupted. She told me about her dreams of making this library the best in the area. That was all she wanted, she didn't care if she had a family or kids. Just her books.

I listened to her for as long as I could. My head felt like it was raw, all her memories were pouring in. I had been holding tissues to my nose for 15 minutes when I couldn't take it anymore.

"Lilly, honey, you're dead," I told her in a nasally voice. She looked surprised, and then quickly shook her head.

"No, I'm not, I'm here trying to get things done," she insisted.

I resisted the urge to groan, my stomach was rolling, I didn't have much time left. I pointed to a book someone had left on a table.

"Grab that book," I ordered. The pain wasn't with my pulse anymore; it was constant.

Lilly went to the table and tried to pick up the book. Her hand passed right through it. She looked up at me stunned. My heart ached for her, but I was running out of time here.

"Your body is gone, honey, but you don't have to be stuck here." She looked like she was going to cry. My stomach rolled. Ugh, I was going to need a trash bag. "Lilly." I got her attention, tears were falling down her face. "I don't know what's in the next part, but everyone I've ever seen cross had a look of pure joy on their face," I explained. I had to close my eyes as the world spun.

"Really?" Lilly's voice shook with uncertainty.

Oh, please God, crossover, please. I swallowed hard as I opened my eyes and met hers. I felt more blood began pouring from my nose; I grabbed more tissue trying to save my sweater.

"Really," I told her, my voice muffled behind my hand. "If there is a heaven, Lilly, wouldn't yours be better than this? With books you could actually read, touch, and smell?"

She nodded, her eyes eager. "How?" she asked.

My head spiked, my vision fading for a moment.

"Just let go of this world," I explained, my voice soft and muffled. "You're the one keeping yourself here."

She nodded before looking around the library one more time. Tears were still falling down her cheeks as she started to disappear.

"Thank you," she whispered just before she was gone.

As soon as she finished fading away, I ran. I didn't have time to walk. I ran through the isles, my stomach already rebelling. Not yet, not yet, not yet. I ran into the alcove with the bathroom doors, barely noticing that the guys spotted me diving through the door. I ran to the closest stall, dropped to my knees and threw up. I was sick over and over. Blood streaming into the bowl from my nose, eyes streaming with tears. My head exploding. The world spun as I tried to breathe between bouts of sickness. Finally, I had nothing left. I held my hair back in one hand and fumbled for the toilet paper with the other.

When I was sure I wasn't throwing up again, I flushed the toilet and sat back on my butt, my back against the stall wall. I held more tissue to my nose and used my other hand to clean up my face. I felt weak, drained, and wobbly. So, I just sat there focusing on breathing as my stomach stopped cramping. I had to keep changing out my tissues; my nose didn't want to stop bleeding. I was there a long time.

When my nose finally stopped bleeding, I threw the bloody tissues into the toilet and slowly got to my feet. I went to the sink, washed my hands and looked in the mirror. My already pale skin looked even whiter, my skin clammy. Dry blood had crusted around my mouth and chin. A few drops stained my sweater. Great. Feeling shaky, I washed my face and used the paper towels to dry. I felt weak, like one breeze would knock me over. I knew I needed to go home. What was I going to tell the guys? Food poisoning would work, right? People get food poisoning all the time. Right?

I took a shaky breath and headed back out into the library. I felt the guy's eyes on me instantly. I walked with my eyes on the floor, the shelves--anywhere but at them. When I reached the table, they didn't waste time.

"Red, you look like shit," Isaac informed me.

"You okay, Beautiful?" Ethan sounded worried.

"What happened?" Zeke demanded.

"Are you feeling alright?" Miles asked gently.

"Did you have another nosebleed?" Asher asked directly.

I shook my head as I started packing up.

"Nah, I'm fine, I must have got a bad burrito at the quick stop," I told them, keeping my voice impassive, though I couldn't even look at them when I said it. "I'm not feeling well, so I'm going to head home." I took my jacket off the back of my chair and pulled it on, swallowing against another wave of nausea. I noticed they were watching me like hawks. Miles' face was suspicious as his gaze ran over me.

"I can drive you home, Red." Isaac offered, already getting out of his chair. Ethan was nodding in agreement. I waved for him to sit back down.

"No, it's fine, you have training tonight. Besides, I'll probably be fine now after puking my guts out." I picked up my bag before anyone else could offer to drive me. "I'll see you guys tomorrow." I turned and walked away. I was only a few feet away when I heard them talking.

"Did anyone else notice the blood on her sweater?" Miles asked, his voice quiet. The others say they did. How much longer was I going to be able to hide this?

When I got back to the house, I never even made it upstairs, I reached the couch and dropped.

IN WHAT FELT like a second later, Rory was shaking me awake. Ugh, nooo.

"Huh?" I asked, sitting up still half asleep. Rory's hands grabbed my face and forced me to look at him. He was trying to open one of my eyelids when I finally woke up. "I'm fine! I'm fine!" I snapped at him. My head throbbed, and my stomach churned with the motion. It was a heartbeat before his hands let go of my face. I blinked my eyes open; the living room was dark except for one lamp.

"What happened?" Rory demanded his face hard. "Tara's upstairs swearing you came home drunk and passed out on the couch."

I snorted and immediately regretted it. My face ached. I lay back down with my eyes open so Rory wouldn't freak out again.

"I ran into that girl ghost again today, she was being a real bitch, too," I told him, rubbing the bridge of my nose. "Then we all went to the library, and I ran into a dead woman there." I groaned as I sat back up putting my feet on the floor. "I helped her move on, got a really bad bloody nose and got sick."

Rory turned until he was sitting normally on the couch next to me.

"How did you cover for that?" he asked.

I smiled painfully. "I told them I ate a bad burrito from the quick mart." Rory snorted at that. "Asher was asking about the bloody noses today, I told him it's a medical condition that crops up now and then."

"You think that was a good idea?" His voice was full of doubt.

I rubbed my fingers against my forehead trying to ease the pain.

"It's better than the truth," I told him honestly. "This way they'll at least hang around a while longer."

"Lexie," Rory began in his lecturing voice, but before he could get started, there was a knock on the door. Rory frowned at me before he got up and answered it.

"I bring chicken soup!"

My head snapped up so fast I got dizzy. Ethan was standing in the doorway. A big plastic tub in his hands with DVD cases on top. "And movies with minimal gore,"

Rory smirked and gestured for him to come in. Ethan tossed the movies to me and then headed into the kitchen

"What are you doing here?" I had never been more surprised in my life. Ethan was banging some pots and pans in the kitchen.

"Beautiful is sick, we make Beautiful better," he told me, his smooth voice calling from the kitchen.

Rory was still smirking when I looked over at him not knowing what to do. "It's what friends do Lexie," he said gently.

I couldn't wrap my head around the fact Ethan was here.

"What about training?" I asked.

Ethan came back over and held out the videos for me to pick one. "Isaac said he could spar with one of the other fighters tonight." He shook the videos in front of me to get me to pick. I picked a superhero movie.

As he went to put the movie on there was another knock on the door. Rory's brow furrowed as he got up and answered it. Miles was standing there with a plastic bag in his hand. His ears went pink as he held it up.

"I brought some medicine that might help Alexis feel better," Miles offered uncertainly. Rory smiled a big smile and gestured for him to come in. Miles made a beeline for me; he sat down to my right and dug into the bag. "Are you still nauseous?" he asked, pulling out a white box, which he started to open.

"Um, a little, just when I move too fast," I told him, still in shock to see them. Miles pulled out a round tablet still in its wrapper. He handed it to me.

"Chew that, it'll stop the nausea," Miles ordered.

Miles ordered me!

Still in shock, I opened it and chewed it. It tasted like cherries. I was still looking at them like they were from another planet when there was another knock on the door. Rory started chuckling as he got up again to answer. Asher was there with a big plastic bag in his hand. I only saw him walk in because Miles was asking if I had any other symptoms.

"A headache, body ache," I answered bewildered. Miles pulled out a bottle of painkillers and began to open it. That's when a big, fluffy, emerald green blanket landed in my lap. Asher dropped down next to me. I looked at him, confused, and up an edge of the blanket. He shrugged.

"When my sister is sick, she uses a big, fuzzy blanket." Asher gestured at my blanket-covered lap. "So, you get a big, fuzzy blanket."

My mouth dropped open to say something, but nothing came out. I was still trying to grasp this. The guys were here? There was another knock on the door while I was still looking like a stranded fish. Rory was laughing as he leaned his head back.

"Come on in," Rory shouted, enjoying himself way too much. I turned to see Zeke closing the door behind him a couple grocery bags in his hands. He opened them and began listing what he brought absently.

"I've brought different kinds of clear sodas and some crackers." He didn't even bother to look at me he just headed into the kitchen area. Ethan turned and spotted Asher.

"Spot stealer," Ethan accused before heading back toward the kitchen. Asher just smiled at him. I finally found my voice.

"What are you guys doing here?" I all but shouted; I was really out of my depth here. They were really here.

"It's what we do when one of us is sick," Ethan called from the kitchen.

"We show up and bring you things to make you feel better." Miles said, adjusting his glasses.

"We bring movies and blankets to keep the sick one on the couch, and if it's Zeke, we all sit on him to keep him there," Asher added, like this was perfectly normal behavior.

"I heard that," Zeke shot back from the kitchen.

"We bring Mom's chicken noodle soup, which is the best thing in the world," Ethan informed me as he came around the couch. He handed a bowl to me carefully which Asher took so that Miles could hand me the painkillers.

"And we keep you company," Zeke announced as he stepped around the couch and handed me a glass of gold liquid.

I looked around at them all, completely and utterly dumbfounded. They came because I was sick, and they wanted to make me feel better? It was that simple for them. I felt a whole section of that wall around my heart crumble. Emotions tore through me as I looked at Rory speechless, tears filling my eyes. Rory just smiled understandingly at me. Tara saved me from embarrassing myself by coming downstairs.

"What's with all the noise...?" Tara's irritated voice trailed off.

I quickly took the Tylenol, using the soda to wash it down--more to give me a moment to compose myself than for the actual pain.

Asher took my glass and handed me the bowl of soup. He was pointedly not looking up at the stairs where I assume Tara was standing.

"What is everyone doing here?" Tara asked, her voice suddenly becoming friendly.

"Beautiful is sick, so we're here to smother her back to health," Ethan declared before turning and sitting on the floor between Miles and me. Zeke took the armchair on the left. Ethan's hand touched my shoe, then he looked down at my feet.

"You're still wearing shoes?" Ethan groaned. I didn't even get to answer. Ethan started taking my boots off. Ethan tossed them over to Zeke, who caught them and set them on the floor.

"We have a strict no-shoes-when-you're-sick rule," Asher pointed out, stretching his arm across the back of the couch.

"I-I see that," I stuttered, still in a daze.

Out of the corner of my eye, I saw Tara walk slowly to the bottom of the stairs.

"We also have a pajama policy," Asher informed me, his gaze ran over my sweater coming back to my face. "But we'll let you slide since it looks like you just came home and passed out."

"I just got her up a minute before you boys started showing up," Rory admitted smiling.

Asher nodded, then looked back at the television. Ethan hit the play button.

"Hey, I brought that big tub of soup from our house if anyone's hungry." Ethan waved his hand toward the kitchen.

"We ate at the diner after Lexie took off," Asher admitted before looking down at me and frowning. "Eat your soup, woman."

I gave him a small smile and started eating. It really was amazing chicken soup.

"In that case, I'm getting a bowl," Rory announced as he got to his feet, Tara followed him to the kitchen.

I took a second to look around at them all. I was sick, they thought with food poisoning, so they came to keep me company and take care of me.

"You guys are pretty amazing, you know," I told them honestly. I'm glad I kept my voice from cracking. Most of them shrugged, a couple waved a hand dismissively as they watched the start of the movie.

"We're family, it's what we do," Miles told me absently. They really didn't know just how incredible that was to me. I ate my soup, covered in my blanket, surrounded by people that actually seemed to care about me. It wasn't long before I fell asleep again.

CHAPTER 6

$\mathcal{I}$ woke up the next morning still on the couch. I groggily looked around until I found my cell phone on the coffee table. I shut off the alarm as soon as possible. I sat up and put my feet on the floor, then rubbed my hands over my face. I tried to remember what happened after I ate that awesome soup. I remembered everyone talking, and that was it. I must have passed back out. I vaguely recalled snuggling into someone's shoulder. I hope I didn't drool on them. Those guys were incredible, and they really didn't even know it. I wanted to do something to thank them.

I quickly made a group text asking them all for coffee orders before heading upstairs and taking a shower. I had just put on my usual black underwear and bra when my phone started vibrating. I picked it up to find the drink orders coming in. Then it occurred to me; I didn't know where to meet them.

Alexis: Where do you guys want to meet this morning?

Miles: Where do you park? You'll need help to carry.

Alexis: I can manage, just where do you guys want to meet?

Zeke: At your locker?

Asher: How about our usual table?

Alexis: I vote table!

Isaac: Locker!

Ethan: I don't care.

The conversation went on like that till I finally called it.

Alexis: I'm bringing coffee to the table! Now, if you don't mind, I'd like to put some pants on.

There was a long silence. I was about to put my phone down when it vibrated again.

Ethan: Beautiful wins, because she's pantless.

Asher: Yeah, pantless girls always win.

Zeke: Agreed.

Isaac: You cheat, Red.

Miles: Ignore us and get dressed, please.

I smiled to myself and pulled on my dark boot-cut blue jeans, gray v-neck shirt, and a royal purple plaid that I left unbuttoned. I did my usual morning routine and put my hair back in a loose braid. I pulled on my jacket, making sure I had everything. I made my lunch, grabbed my bag, and was out the door early.

I picked up the coffees and was extremely grateful the coffee drive through had good holders. I was carrying in my bag and the coffee when I realized I could see my breath, it was so cold this morning. I was surprised to find Miles, Asher, and Zeke were already there at the table.

"Morning." I put the coffees on the table and pointed out what was what.

"How are you feeling this morning?" Miles asked as he looked through the coffee's finding his.

"I got eight hours of sleep, I'm the best ever," I told them cheerfully. It was true; I usually never felt this good in the morning. Hell, my coffee was even decaf.

"Good, you look a lot better this morning," Asher said as he picked up his coffee.

"Thanks for coming over to take care of me, guys." I felt my face turn red as I kept my eyes on my coffee. "You didn't have to, but I really appreciate it," I forced myself to admit to them. I cleared my throat before changing the subject as fast as possible. "So, how annoying was Tara?"

Zeke and Miles chuckled. Asher groaned. I looked up to see his face pained.

"She kept trying to get Asher to talk to her," Zeke answered me, a smirk on his face. "He answered her, but he kept his answers short."

"Then one of us would change the subject or ask Asher something," Miles admitted, smiling his small smile.

"I suffered for you, Ally," Asher declared, pointing at me. I walked over and hugged him around the waist. He gave me a squeeze. Vanilla and cinnamon filled my nose.

"Hence the coffee." I stepped back smiling. He was smiling back at me when a blur bashed into me.

"Red!" Isaac shouted as he practically tackled me. I would have fallen if it weren't for Isaac lifting me up around the waist and swinging me in a circle. I barely managed to save my coffee. Isaac put me back down, his arms moving up to a hug. "Sorry, I wasn't there last night. How are you feeling?"

I hugged his arm across my chest, smiling. Isaac was so sweet. Ethan strolled up at a normal pace.

"Much better, thanks." I leaned my head back against his shoulder. "Asher was just telling me about Tara last night." I felt Isaac laugh as he gave me a squeeze before letting go.

"Oh yeah, Tara wasn't happy," Ethan said as he stepped around me to grab his coffee.

"She probably thinks you're trying to steal him away, especially after you fell asleep last night," Isaac said, smiling as he drank his coffee.

"What do you mean?" I asked, looking around the group, my heart racing. Did I say something weird in my sleep?

"After you fell asleep on the couch, you kind of ended up sleeping against Asher's shoulder," Miles informed me before taking a sip of his coffee. I let out the breath I had been holding. Snuggling Asher in my sleep, that I could deal with. I looked over at Asher who looked a bit uncomfortable.

"Did I drool?" I asked him seriously. A couple of them chuckled.

"No drool," Asher assured me.

"Tara really didn't look happy when we left," Zeke informed me smirking.

I sighed. There was going to be backlash from this. Oh well, nothing to be done about it now.

"I'll deal with it later." The morning bell rang. "See you guys at lunch," I called over my shoulder as I headed toward class.

MY DAY WENT on as usual, though there were more whispers and insults as I walked through the halls today. When Chemistry was finally over, I was more than ready to call it a day.

We were talking about the chemistry test as we reached our usual table. Asher was just getting there himself.

"So how did you guys do on your tests?" Asher asked as he sat down next to Ethan on the bench to my left. Isaac sat next to me, our backs towards Jason and his friends.

"I'm sure I did alright," Miles mumbled. Isaac laughed.

"You were done with that test in ten minutes; you spent the rest of the time rechecking everything," Isaac said. Miles' ears went pink as he shrugged.

"How about you, Ally girl?" Asher asked, pulling out his lunch bag.

"I think I passed, and with only two days to study, I'll take it," I told him emphatically as I pulled out my own lunch. "In fact, I did so well I'm thinking about ditching the rest of the day. Any takers?"

"If you ditch they call your house," Zeke announced as he dropped onto the empty bench across from us.

"Every time?"

He nodded as he pulled out his own lunch.

I cursed, it would have been nice to avoid increasingly-bitchy ghost girl today.

"You don't want to get grounded this weekend," Ethan informed me. "My band's playing at Vegabond on Saturday night."

"Vegabond?"

Ethan nodded, then seemed to realize I didn't know what he was talking about.

"It's a club in Dulcet that lets the 16 to 20 crowd in on Saturday night," Ethan explained, opening his water bottle. "There isn't much to do around here for us, so they let us in on Saturdays so we have something to do besides party. They always have live music those days."

"Sometimes the music is pretty good," Isaac admitted before biting into his sandwich.

It did sound like fun. Ethan leaned forward and gave me serious eye contact.

"You have to come, you don't get a choice, he ordered. I held back a smile.

"Of course, I'm going. I want to see your band play," I said. I really wanted to hear that smoky voice of his sing.

"What else are we doing this weekend?" Zeke asked before biting into his sandwich.

Miles raised a finger before he finished swallowing his food.

"There's a small meteor shower coming in tonight that I wanted to see," Miles announced.

"Care if I come with you? I've never seen a meteor shower." I said, not wanting to bother Miles.

"That's perfect," he told me, a small smile on his face. "Because I was going to ask to use your dock to watch it tonight."

I smiled at him and took a drink of water.

"I'm working tonight," Zeke announced, everyone groaned. Zeke shrugged. "If I work tonight, I'll get tomorrow night off, and I can go with to see Ethan's band."

"Well, that's okay then," Ethan said, finishing his sandwich.

"I'm working Sunday and Saturday morning," Asher said. No one seemed to groan at this; apparently, only working nights was groan worthy.

"Where do you work?" I asked, putting my trash in my bag.

"I work at the indoor rock climbing center here in town." Asher pointed at me. "You should come by Sunday; I'll give you a free lesson."

"Sounds good to me."

"Yeah, you'll probably end up rock climbing with us this summer anyway," Isaac told me matter-of-factly. "Might as well start learning."

"I'll give it a shot."

The guys smiled, Zeke smirked.

"The meteor shower comes in around nine tonight, so what do you guys want to do until then?" Miles asked.

"I'll be back from the game by nine," Asher said before taking another drink of water.

"You guys can just come over. We can watch movies and have dinner," I suggested, putting the lid on my water bottle.

"Sounds good to me." Miles agreed.

"Me too," Isaac said.

"Me three." Ethan chimed in.

Asher rolled his eyes at them before meeting mine.

"I'll be there latish, away-game tonight." Asher said.

"I'll save you a plate," I offered.

He gave me that big, handsome smile.

We went on to debate what movies to watch tonight. I was insisting on Monty Python and the Holy Grail when my cell phone rang. Curious, I pulled it out and answered.

"Hello."

"Alexis, this is Laura," a girl's soft voice said in my ear.

"Hey Laura, how are you?" I asked, completely surprised by the call. I just saw her in math a couple hours ago.

"Remember when you told me to call you if Jessica Westfell went after another girl?" Laura's voice was anxious and getting louder.

"Yeah, what's going on?" I asked, my voice hard. The boys stopped talking, all their attention switching to me.

"She's got a freshmen girl cornered in the bathroom. She's just tearing into her." Laura's voice was getting panicky. I got up and grabbed my bag.

"Which bathroom?" I asked, swinging my bag over my shoulder.

"The girls' out by the quad at the 200 building." I knew that bathroom.

"I'll be there in a second." I hung up the phone and pointed at Asher. "Your sister's about to get her ass kicked," I warned him, my voice hard.

I took off at a jog, the boys caught up quickly. They had longer legs.

"What's going on, Ally?"

I turned a corner, and ran down the hall, the boys kept pace.

"Jessica has a freshman cornered in the bathroom," I snapped over my shoulder as we passed the 100 building.

"Is she hitting her?" Isaac asked, not even breathing hard.

"If she is, she's going to get hit back in a minute," I warned Asher as we reached the hallway I wanted. Laura was standing outside the bathroom door pacing. When she saw me jogging towards her, her face relaxed with relief.

"Thank God, none of the other girls will do anything! They're just watching," Laura yelled to me, her hands shaking.

I didn't bother to stop jogging; I dropped my bag as I headed for the door. The bathroom was almost packed. I shoved the door open and started elbowing my way through the crowd. I wasn't gentle about it. I finally reached the edge of the girls. Jessica towered over a girl not much bigger than me. The girl stood cornered against the wall and the closed door of the handicap stall. She was sobbing, her face red.

"You're a complete waste of space," Jessica sneered. "You might as well just kill yourself and get it over with."

Oh, hell no!

Furious, I strode across the pink tiled bathroom and grabbed Jessica by the back of the neck. I didn't stop moving until I had her pretty face pinned against the pink tiled wall. She tried to push off the wall, but I pressed my weight against her back, keeping her there. I took a deep breath and managed to find my calm--barely. I looked over to the crying girl and gave her a friendly smile.

"Hi Sweetie, I'm Alexis." I kept my voice cheerful and friendly. Like I wasn't pinning a bitch to the wall. Jessica's hands reached back to claw at my hands; I barely noticed. "I want you to walk outside," I told the girl. "There is a girl named Laura waiting with my five friends. I need you to tell the tall blonde guy what happened today and what Jessica said to you. Okay, sweetie?"

The girl's eyes were wide as she nodded. She quickly grabbed her bag and hurried through the crowd and out the door. That's when my voice changed.

"What the fuck is the matter with you people?" I shouted, anger boiling through my veins. "You just fucking stand there as she's terrorizing someone? That's fucked up to a level I've never seen." The girls in the crowd shifted, some of them blushed, and some looked ashamed. "Get the fuck out of here!" The girls started heading out the bathroom door.

When the bathroom was empty, I turned to Jessica. "I'm going to let you go, and I'll step away," I told her calmly. Then I did as I said. I took a couple steps back from Jessica, staying in a defensive stance. Jessica pushed herself off the wall and turned her face red.

"You fucking bitch-"

"No honey, you're the fucking bitch in this scenario," I snapped, my voice hard. "You had her cornered in a bathroom telling her to kill herself." I spelled it out clearly for her so there would be no way she couldn't understand. "I don't know what your fucking damage is but you need to fucking deal with it and stop taking it out on other people." She looked at me like I was a bug under her shoe.

"It's none of your business what I do," she snarled, stepping up to me.

Oh yeah, this was going to get ugly. I stepped up to her until I was in her face, too; I was aching to hit her. Her eyes went wide for a second.

"You're right, it's not, until you start taking it out on other people." I pointed to the corner where she had the younger girl cornered. "That was sick and fucked up." I kept eye contact with her. My voice growing hot with my temper. "You pull that shit again, we'll be back here again. Just you and me. Do you understand?"

I waited a couple heartbeats before I stepped back and away from her, not turning my back. I needed to get away from her or I would smash her face into the mirror. Jessica laughed.

"What are you going to do? Tell everyone to find you if I misbehave?" she taunted, her voice condescending.

I smiled coldly at her.

"If I have to, yeah." I pointed to the corner. "To prevent this type of shit, I'll be happy to." I turned to walk away.

I was almost to the door when she spoke up again.

"Stay the fuck away from my brother," Jessica warned me.

I stopped and bit my lower lip trying to keep my cool. I turned back to Jessica who was still glaring at me.

"Oh yeah, speaking of your brother." I began, feeling my voice going cold. "If you ever hit Asher across the face again, I'll hit you." Her eyebrows went up in surprise. "Just so we're clear." The sound of the bathroom door opened; I heard big feet on the tile.

"What the hell Jess? How could you do that to someone?" Asher was yelling across the bathroom.

I turned and walked out the bathroom door, leaving Asher to deal with his sister. The boys were still waiting outside. Laura and the girl were still there. The girl had calmed down and was wiping her face with tissues. Asher's no doubt.

"You okay?" I asked her, not quite knowing what to say. I deal with the dead not really the living.

She nodded, taking a deep breath. "Thank you."

I felt my face turn red, and I knew the guys noticed.

"No problem." I looked over to Laura, her arm around the girl. "Do you know who her usual targets are?"

"Yeah, she makes the rounds with the same people," Laura informed, me adjusting her glasses.

"Can you get my number to them please?" I asked, taking the plunge. I wasn't going to hurt Jessica unless she started hitting people. But I wasn't going to sit idly by like those bitches in the bathroom. I fucking couldn't.

A smile spread across Laura's face turning her pretty again.

"Yeah, I can do that." She looked down at the smaller girl. "Come on, I'll take you home," Laura said to the younger girl who just nodded, her eyes glazed over. I watched Laura walk her around the corner before going to pick up my bag.

"Lexie, you're bleeding," Zeke pointed out.

I looked down to see the backs of my hands covered in scratches from Jessica's nails. I pulled out some tissues from my bag and wiped the blood away as my adrenaline rush disappeared. My hands were shaking as I tossed away the tissues. That's when I looked up, my face warm.

"Beautiful, we heard you yelling at those girls from out here," Ethan began a huge smile spreading across his face. "That was awesome."

I felt my face start to turn red.

"I really wish we had a camera in there; that would have been great to have on video." Isaac sighed wistfully.

My face grew hotter.

"Talking to Jessica without a crowd was a great idea," Miles said, his eyes running over me.

My face was burning as I looked around for anything else to talk about.

"You're blushing," Zeke stated, a smirk spreading across his face. All four of them were smiling.

"Alexis blushes when someone compliments her about something she's done," Miles observed, his head tilting.

"Oh, a new game." Isaac's voice was entirely too happy about this.

"This is going to be fun," Ethan added, his eyes sparkling.

I was saved by the bell for sixth period. I just turned and walked away, my face
in fire.

THE REST of school went as expected. For gym class, I didn't bother changing in a stall again. No one really looks around in the locker anyway. It's kind of an unspoken rule.

I was on my way to art class, grateful that without Asher or Tara here today I wouldn't have to stop near the dead girl. Just a quick walk by; it should be a piece of cake.

I was just stepping out onto the pathway when it hit me. Pain shot through my body, sharp and stabbing in the middle of my chest. I gasped, almost stumbling. I had to stop for a minute just to get used to the feeling. My head was throbbing as I looked up. Ghost girl was standing in the middle of the path, feet apart, her head tilted. The grin on her face sent fear through me. Where the hell did she get this kind of power from? She couldn't get this much power from pulling energy from the students at the school. So, where the fuck was she getting it from?

I started forward, her rage like a wall in front of me. I began to push through it; it was like wading through waist-deep mud. My head throbbed; I felt the blood on my lip. I pressed my tissues to my nose, my heart racing. The closer I got to her, the more she pressed in on me. Her memories started slipping through my mind threatening to push me out. Terror, raw and consuming, ripped through me. I stopped pushing; I stepped back. Then kept going. I turned away from the dead girl and got the hell out of there. I wasn't going to make it to art class today. I couldn't get past the dead girl without risking her jumping me.

I pulled out my cell phone and headed straight to my truck as fast as I could without drawing attention. My hand was shaking as I held the tissues to my nose.

"You should be in class," Rory answered.

I looked behind me, checking to see if Bitch Ghost was following. She wasn't. My heart was still racing.

"We have a fucking problem," I snapped, my voice shaking.

"What's wrong? What happened?" Rory demanded, his voice hard.

"Somehow ghost bitch got a whole lot of fucking juice." I spotted my Blazer as I passed the library. "I can't get past her to get to art class without her jumping me."

"Get your ass home now," Rory ordered. I reached my truck and opened the door.

"Already headed there." I climbed in, my hands still shaking, my stomach in a knot of fear. I didn't want to get jumped; I didn't want to die. "I don't know how to deal with her, Rory," I admitted, shutting my door. I sat in my truck and was terrified for my life.

"Go home, do some research. Look for a way to...deal with the problem."

The way he phrased it told me he wasn't alone. I was nodding emphatically as I answered.

"Yeah, sounds good. Research. I'll look for a way to get rid of her." I hung up the phone, my chest tight. I knew Bitch Ghost wasn't around, so it was all me. FUCK!

I took a deep calming breath as I buckled my seat belt. I can figure this out. Yeah, I can figure this out. I swallowed hard as I started the truck. Just because every other woman in my family died from getting jumped didn't mean I was going to.

I pulled out onto the street and headed home. I kept taking deep meditative breaths, reminding myself to slow down and brea... stop sign! Shit, I missed it. I checked my mirrors and saw no one else on the road. Thank God. I focused completely on driving home. I made sure to stop at every stop sign; I obeyed every law.

When I pulled up to the house, I hurried. I shut off the truck, grabbed my bag, and ran to the door. When I got there, I realized I had left my keys in the truck. I growled at myself and ran back. When I finally got inside, I ran straight into the kitchen and grabbed the salt shaker. I opened it, poured it onto the counter and began to rub it onto my skin. I don't know why I did this. I wasn't being possessed or jumped. But I wanted the salt on me anyway. I slipped some into all my jean pockets. I sprinkled some in my hair, even went so far as to slip a little in the cups of my bra.

Once I knew I was covered, I finally started to calm down. Taking deep calming breaths, I just pushed the rest of the salt from the counter into the trash and then put the lid back on the shaker. I walked back to the door, my mind a bit clearer now that I was calming down. I grabbed my bags and headed up to my room. I dropped my stuff and started my computer. Still taking deep calming breaths. As soon as I could, I started looking for ways to get rid of a ghost in a public space.

It was a couple of hours later when I heard someone knocking on the door. Curious, I went downstairs and answered. Miles, Isaac, and Ethan were all standing there, their arms full of stuff. Shit, I had totally forgotten that the guys were coming over.

"Hey Beautiful, will you please tell my brother he's a tool?" Ethan asked as he walked into the house with a guitar case across his back. Isaac was a step behind him with plastic grocery bags and video games in his hands.

"Red wouldn't do that would you, Red?" Isaac asked, heading towards the couch.

"You're a tool," I announced, smirking. Ethan and Miles burst out laughing.

I looked at Ethan. "Why is he a tool?"

Miles stepped into the house, a brown cardboard box in his arms

"Because he still listens to country music," Ethan replied, looking at his brother like Isaac had disappointed him. I laughed as I closed the door. When I turned around, Miles' gaze ran over my face.

"Are you alright, Alexis?" he asked. "You look paler than usual."

"Oh, yeah, I just had to kill a spider upstairs." I lied hoping they'd buy the girly thing.

"You're afraid of spiders?" Isaac asked, his face stunned. "I thought you didn't scare easy, Red."

I ignored Isaac and tried to look into the box Miles was holding.

"What did you bring?" I asked.

Miles tilted the box, so I could see inside. I saw wires and controllers.

"A PS4, we're gaming tonight." Miles smiled at me before heading to the TV to set it up.

Video games? I never really played them before. But if that was what the guys wanted to do, I'd give it a shot.

AN HOUR LATER... Oh my, God, this is so fucking awesome! How the hell didn't I know how fun video games were? I was so focused on making my character beat Isaac's to a pulp that I didn't notice when Rory came home.

"Lexie!" Rory's shout finally got my attention.

I looked up at him, wincing. My character promptly died on screen. Isaac raised his arms in victory.

"Hell yeah!" Isaac shouted.

"You technically didn't win, Rory got her attention. So, no win," Miles informed us.

I looked at Isaac and taunted him. "Ha Ha."

I turned back to Rory who had an odd look on his face; it was half angry and half "what am I going to do with you?" look. It was an odd look.

I got to my feet and handed my controller to Ethan. "I've got something for you upstairs, Rory."

He nodded, his eyes on the boy's playing their game.

I stepped around Miles and headed upstairs. I went to my desk and tapped my computer to get it to wake up. Rory close the door behind me. I tucked one leg under me and sat down in my desk chair. "Okay, I've found a couple things that might get rid of Bitch Ghost." I showed him the store I found online. "Something called tar water. It's supposed to pretty much keep malevolent spirits or things away." I turned back to Rory who sat on my bed. "But it's back ordered for two months, at least. Apparently, the tar this person uses isn't that easy to get anymore."

Rory pulled out his wallet and handed me a credit card.

"Order it anyway. That will come in handy."

I quickly ordered the tar-water and handed the credit card back. "The second thing is really just information." I turned towards him again. "I came across a website about natural barriers, which everyone has. It basically says the more energy thrown at you, the more these barriers degrade." I shook my head, I wasn't even sure I was getting accurate information. "From that, I had a thought. What if Bitch Ghost isn't getting more juice? But it just seems like it because my barriers are degrading?" It made sense to me, but I really needed a second opinion.

Rory thought about it for a few moments.

"That sounds possible," he agreed as he narrowed his eyes at me. "What can you do to get your barriers back up?"

I shrugged; he wasn't going to like it.

"Pretty much stay away from anything that can throw energy at me." I sighed. "I have to stay away from her for a while. Which shouldn't be hard since it's the weekend. If I can stay away from the dead for a couple days, it should help bring up my barriers." I hope. I wasn't a hundred percent on it. But it's the only thing I've found so far. Rory looked me in the eye, his face stern. "No dead this weekend. You hear me? I don't care if they are in the house," he ordered. "No dead. Understand?"

I nodded. "I understand." Then pushed my luck a bit. "Can I still hang out with the guys? Ethan's band is playing in Dulcet tomorrow night. And Asher wanted to give me a rock climbing lesson at that indoor center on 5th." I gave him my sweetest, please let me do this face.

Rory snorted.

"Yes, but you see a ghost, you go the other way," he declared.

I saluted him.

"Aye, aye, Captain."

He shook his, head laughing. "You're such a smart-ass."

A COUPLE HOURS LATER, Rory was out picking up dinner from the local Italian restaurant when I gave up trying to beat Miles at the racing game. I went to the kitchen to grab a bottle of water and noticed Ethan out back on the patio. He had his guitar out and looked to be writing down notes. Curious, I grabbed a couple water bottles and slipped out back. Oh, it was chilly out here. Ethan didn't seem to notice it as he frowned down at his notebook, bobbing his head to notes only he could hear. I smiled, watching his mouth moving, singing silently. I stepped into his view, and his head snapped up. His chocolate eyes found me as he gave me a half grin.

"Caught me, huh?" Ethan sighed, putting his guitar on the seat next to him. I walked over and handed him a bottle of water.

"Do you ever stop working?" I asked, sitting down across the patio coffee table from him. He shook his head.

"On music? Never. You can always do better." He leaned forward one elbow on his knee as he reached for his notebook.

"What are you working on?" I asked, leaning forward, trying to take a peek. He snatched his notebook up fast.

"Just some song," he mumbled, his cheeks tinting pink.

I smiled; it was so cute when the guys blushed.

"It's not really that good," he said.

I settled into the corner of the patio sofa, making myself comfy.

"How long have you been working on it?"

Ethan opened his bottle of water and took a drink before answering.

"Six months," he told me, looking everywhere but at me. Some of his hair came out from behind his ear, hiding one eye from me.

I raised an eyebrow at him. Six months and he was still working on it?

"Can I hear it?"

He looked up at me with a deer-in--headlights look on his face. He swallowed hard. I had never seen Ethan look insecure about something, but I was sure I was seeing it now.

"I still don't think it's very good," he said, shaking his head. It was strange seeing him like this, he always seemed so confident. Then again, everyone had something that meant a lot to them. I had my art, and Ethan apparently had his music.

"Are you nervous about tomorrow night?" I asked before taking a drink of my water.

He nodded, his gaze on the patio cement. "Yeah, it's our first 'bigger than what we've been playing' venue," Ethan admitted as he began to twirl one of his silver rings. "There's a lot riding on tomorrow." He licked his lips as he looked out at the water again. He was really anxious.

"Are you playing your band's songs or covers?" I asked, hoping that if I got him talking, he'd relax enough to tell me about his music.

He looked back over at me that half smile on his face.

"We're still doing covers, some Breaking Benjamin, some Seether, some other hard rock." His eyes started to sparkle a little. "It depends on where we are playing, really. Eventually, we'll figure out our own music, but for now..." he said with a shrug. As he kept talking he got more animated, his eyes lit up, and his face relaxed. It made me want to hear more.

"Tell me about your band."

That was all it took.

He told me about his band mates, what they each had a talent for. Ethan's was guitar and singing. I could see that with just his speaking voice. He was worried about writing songs, even though they were still playing covers. We talked about all of it. And through every word and gesture, I saw how much he truly loved music. How passionate he was about the right tone for a song, the right notes.

When he finally relaxed enough, I asked him, "Can you play something for me? A cover you guys play?" I didn't really want to wait until tomorrow to hear him sing.

"Beautiful..." he began, groaning.

"I'm going to hear you tomorrow anyway." I shrugged and looked out at the water, acting like I wasn't as interested as I was. He thought about it for a few heartbeats then sighed. He reached over and picked up his guitar.

"One song." He told me firmly, his cheeks turning pink.

He settled and took a deep breath, his eyes on the table between us. He started playing. I recognized this song; Breaking Benjamin's Give Me a Sign. I was smiling as he played. Then he sang, and my mouth dropped. I barely managed to cover it by playing with my lower lip. His voice was amazing. That smooth, smoky voice went a little low, rolling over my ears and making my toes actually curl. He slowed the tempo down by just half a beat so he could use his voice in the best way.

I won't lie; his singing mesmerized me. All I could do was sit and listen. When he was done he put his guitar back in the case, his face was red as he avoided looking at me. I closed my mouth and dropped my hand.

"Ethan." My voice was soft simply because I was still trying to think after hearing him sing.

Ethan finally looked over to me. His body tense again.

"You could sing the worst songs ever written." I said, "and they will line up around the block to hear you sing it." I met those warm eyes and told him the truth. "Ethan, your voice is fucking toe-curling. You're going to make it in music with a band or without. It doesn't matter."

Ethan smiled at me a little uncertainly. "You really think so?"

I nodded emphatically. "Oh yeah. You're going to be phenomenal." I took a deep drink to cover how much that voice had affected me. Seriously, I wanted to roll around in silk sheets with that voice.

"Thanks, Beautiful." Ethan's voice was steady again, sounding more like himself. "I really needed to hear that today."

"I will listen to you sing anytime," I assured. I let him get back to work, then headed inside to try again at beating Miles.

WHEN RORY CAME BACK, everyone came to the table to eat. I got tense when Isaac went to use the saltshaker and found it empty. Rory shot me a knowing look. I played it off as one of those things that just happens. Everyone bought it, and the conversation went on as usual.

Miles told Rory about the meteor shower tonight. How he hoped Rory wouldn't mind if we used the dock out back to watch it. Rory smiled and told him to come over anytime. Tara called Rory asking to spend the night at a friend's house. Rory said yes. Soon after, I got a text from Asher. He was going to take a shower before coming over because he, and I quote, 'stinks to high heaven.'

We were playing video games again, this time with Rory taking a turn, when Zeke texted Isaac to bring him food at work. I made Zeke up a plate, and the twins headed off to deliver.

It was getting close to nine when Miles and I headed out to the back and sat on the dock. Asher had finally made it over. Apparently, they won the game. Rory was asking Asher about it as he ate the dinner I kept for him. So, it was just Miles and me out on the dock looking up at the sky. It was freezing; I could see my breath. I really needed to start wearing hoodies under my leather jacket. I was sitting with my head tilted up, looking at the stars when Miles broke the silence.

"Do you know anything about astronomy?" he asked. I heard his fingers tapping in that staccato rhythm against the dock. Poor Miles, he always seemed so uncomfortable around me.

"I know our solar system, and that our galaxy is called the Milky Way. I know what a light year is," I began, searching my brain for any information. "And that there are other galaxies out there. That's about it."

"It's pretty cool if you think about it," he began, his voice warming from polite to friendly. "Our galaxy is one million light years across, and we have photos that prove there are other galaxies out there." I saw him adjust his glasses out of the corner of his eye. "The closest galaxy is Andromeda, and that is 2.5 million light years away."

I whistled.

"That's big." I said.

He chuckled. "It's enormous; the space out there could be infinite," he said. I looked over at him to see him smiling; he kept looking up as he lifted his hand. He held his forefinger and thumb barely apart. "And we're just this little dot in all of that."

I looked back up at the sky trying to imagine all that distance out there.

"That sounds really lonely when you think about it," I admitted quietly. Getting a crick in my neck, I laid down on the dock. I crossed my arms under my head.

"Well, statistically, there has to be other life out there somewhere." Miles shrugged. "It's probably really, really far away, but it's probable."

We were quiet for a while as I thought about that. More life out there, a different species of thinking beings. And probably more dead to see. I smiled at myself, imagining trying to move on an alien's soul.

Miles gave up and lay down next to me on the dock, tucking one arm behind his head.

"Did you know," he said, "that since the stars are so far away, that by the time the light reaches us the star has been dead for years?" Mile's soft voice turned silky, I'd never heard his voice like this before. It was soothing, and at the same time made me want to bite my lip. Yeah, a good voice does something for me, so sue me.

I was thinking about what he said, though, all those stars out there were dead?

"Well, when you say it like that, it's not so pretty anymore," I said, my voice quiet.

"Why's that?"

"It kind of takes something away from it. Knowing that they're dead." I kept my voice soft, not really knowing why.

"Nothing lasts forever, Alexis," he told me softly.

"Don't I know it," I whispered under my breath, looking at a big clump of stars across the sky.

"What do you mean?"

There was something about Miles and that voice; he soothed something ragged inside me. I felt calm, peaceful, laying here next to him on the dock. It's the only reason I answered at all.

"People." I licked my lips. "People don't last forever. They either die or just leave."

We were quiet for a while.

"Does that take away from the time you had with them?" he asked, his voice still a silky timber.

"Doesn't it? You know it's going to end, so what's the point if it's not going to last?" I had to bite my tongue to keep control of the emotions this conversation was bringing to the surface.

"Just because something will end, doesn't mean you can't enjoy it while it lasts, Alexis" Miles gestured toward the stars. "Most, if not all, of those stars are already dead. Does that mean I shouldn't look at them? That I shouldn't enjoy the fact they existed?"

I don't think we were talking about the stars anymore. I was fighting back tears, so I bit down on my bottom lip hard. It didn't work.

He continued. "If I did that, then those stars would have lived and died without anyone appreciating them." He sighed. "And that would be a travesty."

We laid there quietly as I thought about what he said. I was expecting the guys to leave me if--or when--they found out about the Sight. I worried about it every night before I went to sleep. It was in the back of my mind when I was with them. It shadowed everything we did together, all the fun we had together. It was always there. Maybe Miles was right. Yeah, the guys might bail on me in the end. But that didn't mean I couldn't enjoy their friendships while I had them, I just couldn't let them in too far.

I gave Miles a small nudge in the arm with my elbow.

"You're pretty smart, you know that?" I kept my voice light and soft. I saw him smile out of the corner of my eye.

"Book smart, yes, but people smart? Not always." He scratched his nose. "That perspective just sounded very familiar to me."

"Who did you get your answer from?" I asked, looking over at him.

He smiled a bit. "Several Psychology textbooks," he admitted, his ears getting pink. I chuckled quietly as I looked back up at the sky. I felt him shrug next to me. "A friend was having a hard time, and I needed some way to help."

"You went and found one."

"Yes." He took a deep breath before continuing. "There is usually an answer out there to any question you could have. You just have to know how to find them, or where to find them."

I smiled to myself.

"So you memorized the textbooks?"

He snorted. "Not intentionally," he said, his voice still silky soft as it slid through my ear. "If I read something or see something, I can just remember it perfectly."

"A photographic memory?"

"For places and things, yes. For books, if I read them, I remember every word and can access that information at any time." His voice lowered to a whisper, "It's kind of weird."

I felt a large chunk of the wall around my heart crumble as I smiled to myself. Miles didn't know what weird was.

"Not weird, Miles. Unique," I whispered back to him. "You are unique, and that's not a bad thing in a world full of carbon copies."

We were quiet for a while.

"Thank you, Lexie."

"Thank you, Miles."

We were still laying there in comfortable silence when the back door opened. I didn't bother sitting up to see who it was. Big feet walking on the dock made the planks move underneath me. I knew it was the guys.

"Did we miss it?" Isaac asked, sitting down behind us.

"Not yet, it's not an exact science with meteor showers," Miles said as he lifted his arm and checked his watch. "They should be getting close, though."

Someone sat behind me. I tilted my head to see Asher upside down. I gave him a smile then looked back up at the sky. It wasn't long before I felt fingers playing with my hair. I smiled, knowing it was Asher. A streak of light ran across the sky.

"Here we go," Miles announced.

I kept my eyes on the sky as I blew into my hands.

"Where are your gloves, Beautiful?" Ethan asked from behind Asher.

"I didn't know I needed to have any," I answered honestly. I was from California--this was winter weather to me, not fall.

"I'm buying you some gloves." Ethan sighed.

I smiled to myself as I watched more lights streak across the sky. I knew hanging out with the guys would end, but I decided to enjoy it while it lasted. We sat there in silence watching the meteor shower late into the night.

CHAPTER 7

" $\mathscr{L}$ exie."

"Hmm?"

"Lexie, wake up."

Rory's voice brought me out of my comfy sleep. I opened my eyes to find Rory standing in my bedroom doorway. He was grinning down at me.

"The boys are downstairs, they're going hiking. Something about scouting out new rock climbing spots."

I rubbed my eyes and stretched on my side. That sounded pretty fun to me.

"Tell them I'll be down in like, ten minutes."

I put my feet on the floor and ran my hands through my hair. It was a mess; I had forgotten to put it back in a braid last night. Rory shut the door as he left. I went to my closet and found a pair of old blue jeans and an old faded, black Aerosmith shirt. I pulled on an old pair of boots and grabbed a hoodie. I was heading down the stairs trying to pull my hair back when I heard laughing.

"Damn, Red, you've got serious bed hair." Isaac's voice was cheerful this morning, and loud. It was too early for this. I stuck my tongue out at him as I finally tied my hair back. I looked over at Zeke, Ethan, and

Miles. Oh yeah, Asher was working this morning. Everyone was wearing old faded clothes for the hike.

"Before we go anywhere you need to feed me," I warned them grumpily.

"We're picking up coffee and breakfast on the way." Ethan was practically bouncing on his toes. I was pretty sure he already had his coffee this morning. I shrugged, and we headed for the door.

"Hold on!" Rory shouted. We all turned and watched Rory walk out of the kitchen. "What path are you hiking? How far are you going? And when will you be back?"

Zeke answered all Rory's questions, then we were all piled into the back of Zeke's old '97 black Jeep Cherokee. Soon I was happily downing my breakfast sandwich.

"So, why didn't I get any warning about this morning?" I asked before taking a deep drink of my coffee.

"I thought someone had already told you," Miles admitted before biting into his sandwich.

"I told Ethan to do it." Isaac said.

"You did not. You said you were going to tell her," Ethan shot back. Isaac gave Ethan a shove which knocked him into me. I saved my coffee, barely. Ethan shoved him back.

"No fighting with her right next to you!" Zeke barked at them over his shoulder.

The twins stopped instantly. Isaac leaned around Ethan and looked at me.

"Sorry, Red," Isaac offered.

I glared at him.

"You're lucky you didn't kill my coffee," I told him in a menacing voice. The guys chuckled.

Soon we were pulling off the road to a marked trail ahead. When I climbed out, some of the guys were already opening the back of the Jeep. Zeke pulled out a big pack and pulled it on; he clipped the straps across his chest. The straps didn't look comfortable, they were a little tight against his chest.

"Shit, I'm going to need a new pack this summer," Zeke grumbled as Ethan pulled on his own pack.

"Good, then I can have your old one," Isaac chimed in.

I just shook my head at them.

It wasn't long before we were walking along the trail. The woods were beautiful, full of reds, oranges, and yellows. There was even some green here and there from the pines. I wish I had thought to bring my sketchbook. Then again, the guys probably wouldn't have stopped long enough to let me draw, anyway.

"I'm going to have to come back out here with my sketchbook," I announced. My fingers were actually twitching to use my pastels.

"Not alone," Zeke called back from the front of our line.

I rolled my eyes.

Over the next couple hours, the guys told me about their rock climbing trips over the years. Isaac told me a story about Ethan losing his grip, dropping and swinging right into the rock face. That set Ethan off on a story about Zeke grabbing a weak ledge, the ledge crumbled, and he dropped eight feet to the ground. Zeke only admitted that it hurt. The boys explained how rock climbing worked, what kind of stone you want to find, and what happens if you make a bad decision. You drop, and if you had a bad anchor or belay, you die. This did not deter me a bit in wanting to try it. Eventually, we reached a rock face that ran a few hundred feet up to the top.

"Wow, that's high," I said lamely.

"That's kinda the point." Zeke chuckled before turning to the other guys. They began talking about possible routes, and hand holds; whether there were any cracks for hand holds.

The more they talked, the more I started to see the rock face the way they did. It was a challenge. I decided then and there that I was rock climbing with them this summer--well, if they were still around.

At some point, Isaac stepped away from the guys as Zeke was pointing out an overhang on the left that Asher might want to try climbing. Isaac began climbing up the wall without any gear. He was about eight feet up when I started to get worried. If an eight-foot fall hurt Zeke, then it'd hurt Isaac, too.

"Um, guys? Isaac's climbing." I actually pointed at Isaac's back.

Everyone looked up and cursed. Well, except Miles. Miles never cursed.

"Isaac, get your ass back down here!" Zeke barked, his voice hard, his face pissed.

Isaac waved a hand dismissively at us. He climbed another few feet, my heart started racing.

"Isaac! You have no gear on! Get your ass down!" Ethan shouted, his face stormy.

"It's an easy climb!" Isaac called down to us. He moved to the left towards the overhang.

"Don't even think about it, Isaac!" Miles shouted, his voice turning cold. Miles, mild and sweet Miles, was getting angry too.

"I'm going after him," Zeke growled. The guys stepped in front of him.

"You can't get him down without gear, Zeke," Miles said, his voice so cold it sent shivers down my spine. "It's not like you can carry him down."

Isaac had reached the overhang; he was looking for a handhold when I got an idea.

"I'll get him," I told them quietly, my eyes still on Isaac. I knew they were looking at me. They probably thought I was crazy.

"You're not touching that wall, Lexie," Zeke growled.

I smiled wickedly.

"It'll only take a few feet," I reassured him before I stepped closer to the wall. "Hey, Isaac. I'm coming up!" I shouted. The boys went still behind me.

"No, you're not, Red!" Isaac shouted from above, his head now turned toward me. I stepped up to the wall and looked for a handhold.

"You said it's an easy climb!" I shouted back innocently. "If that's true, then I can probably do it." I found a hold and grabbed it, my fingertips scraping against the stone. I put my foot on another ledge, and boosted myself up. I looked for more holds.

"Someone fucking stop her!" Isaac shouted, his voice demanding. I found another hold and another spot for my foot and lifted myself up.

"I'm not going to piss off Beautiful," Ethan answered Isaac, realizing what I was doing. I moved up another hold.

"Zeke!" Isaac shouted. I couldn't tell, but I think he was coming closer.

"I've learned that Lexie is stubborn. If she wants to hurt herself that's on her," Zeke declared his voice, indifferent. I smiled to myself.

"Miles, damn it!" Isaac shouted. I looked up to watch him making his way back along the route he'd taken.

"I don't go around grabbing girls, especially without permission," Miles shot back.

I smiled at the wall as I hoisted myself up a little more. I didn't know how high I was, but I trusted that if I were getting past the guys' reach, they would grab me off the wall. I found another handhold and pulled myself up.

"Lexie." Ethan coughed. He was telling me not to go any higher.

I nodded my head, so they knew I heard. I was pretending to look for another handhold when I heard Isaac cursing. I looked up to see him making his way down the rock face.

"Don't you dare move an inch, Red," Isaac growled as he found hand holds that brought him down beside me.

"But I thought it was an easy climb?" I asked, pretending to be confused. His face was furious as he reached a hand out to my back.

"It's not!" he snapped, looking down at where I was on the wall. He seemed to realize I wasn't that far off the ground because he started climbing down again. "Don't you fucking move."

I kept still as I watched Isaac climb down the last 6 feet or so. He dropped to the ground and looked up at me. His hands wrapped around to my hips, his fingers biting into my skin.

"Come down a bit so I can get you," he ordered his voice boiling. Oh boy, Isaac was pissed.

I reached down with my left foot and started feeling along till I found that foothold I used before. Finally finding it, I moved my foot and hand at the same time, hitting both holds right. I looked for the next foot and hand holds, then moved onto those. Isaac's hands slid up to my waist before he pulled me off the wall and against his chest. I was dangling for a moment before he put me down on my feet.

He turned me roughly towards him and got in my face.

"Don't you ever fucking do that again." He growled, pointing at me. "You don't have any gear on; you've never even had a lesson!" He took a breath then growled at me again. "You understand?!"

I swallowed hard at the anger on his face; I nodded.

Satisfied that he got the answer he wanted, he turned on the guys. "What the hell were you guys thinking? You just let her start climbing?!"

All the guys shrugged.

"Lexie is going to do what Lexie is going to do," Zeke explained calmly, his arms crossed over his chest.

"Yeah, we can't stop her if she wants to do something," Ethan added, looking innocent.

Miles just shook his head.

"Next time stop her!" Isaac shouted, though the volume of his voice was starting to lower as he calmed down. Isaac reached back and wrapped a hand around my arm. "Come on, Red, you're staying next to me so I can keep an eye on you," he grumbled, giving me a tug as he began walking back down the trail.

When Isaac's back was turned, Zeke gave me a thumbs up, Ethan grinned at me, and Miles started laughing quietly. I winked at them as I followed Isaac, trying my best not to smile.

ONE OF THE guys gave me a bottle of water as we headed back down the trail. We were maybe halfway back when that chill down my neck. Really? Fucking really? I'm out in the fucking woods and of course there's going to be a ghost. I sighed as I looked around for it. I spotted her watching us on the trail. She had long blonde hair, blue eyes. She was wearing a bloody, flannel shirt and slashed jeans. She was screaming at us.

"Come on! Can't one of you find me?" she was crying as she

pushed her bloody hair out of her face. Any annoyance I had disappeared as I watched her.

Shit.

"Hey guys, I've got to...you know, find a tree," I announced, my eyes on the ghost. The twins chuckled. Everyone stopped walking.

"Go a hundred feet off trail," Zeke informed me as he took off his pack.

"How does a girl do that in the woods, by the way?" Ethan asked curiously.

I laughed as the other boys groaned.

"I'm not going to explain it to you." I shot over my shoulder as I headed off trail.

I made eye contact with the woman and tilted my head that she should follow me. Her eyes grew wide before she followed. My head started throbbing. My body felt torn up across my chest, my head felt crushed. I don't know how she died, but it wasn't easy. I walked until the others were out of earshot before turning to her.

"Who are you?"

The relief on her face was so great that my own head spun. Shit, she was way too close. My head started throbbing.

"My name's Karen Malone; I just want someone to find my body," she told me in a rush before continuing. "A bear got me a couple weeks ago, I think, and no one has found me. Please help me."

I was afraid of that. I had the guys with me now; I couldn't go body hunting. Could I?

"How far away is your body?" I asked, debating.

"Not even half a mile, I'm maybe 150 feet off the trail," she assured me.

Fuck. I was going to do this. I knew I was.

"You're going to have to show me." And I was going to have to come up with some reason to get the guys in her direction.

"I will. It's just right at the next trail split, then a little further."

"Okay, let's go. I'll think of something to tell the guys." I mumbled heading back toward the trail.

"Thank you so much, you have no idea what this means to me," she said.

"Oh, I do, that's why I'm doing it," I whispered, sighing before stepping out onto the trail.

Everyone got up, and we started walking again. Karen stayed next to me the whole time. She told me about her life. She had been a university student, here on a little weekend vacation when she somehow got between a bear and its cub. The bear didn't like that. Then she told me about her family. She was an only child; her parents were still alive and would be devastated if she wasn't found. She just wanted them to know what happened to her. I nodded along, trying to keep up with the guy's conversation and Karen's chatter. My head was throbbing; Karen's memories started slipping in.

It was an hour before we reached the trail split.

"Here! We need to go right," Karen announced anxiously. My mind raced to find some reason to go down the other trail, anything besides, 'hey, there's a dead body this way we need to find'. Otherwise, this girl's soul won't move on. I finally just settled on curiosity.

"Hey, what's this way?" I asked, stepping down the right side of the split. The boys stopped. Zeke pulled out the map and checked the trail.

"That connects to a longer trail around the mountain."

I looked over my shoulder at the guys.

"Let's check it out," I offered lightly. Come on guys, this ghost is killing me. "We won't go too far."

All the boys shrugged, and we headed down the trail. Yay for being the only girl in a group of boys! When you wanted to check something out, they were willing to go with you. We started walking again, the boys talking back and forth. I couldn't focus on their conversation now, my head was throbbing in time with my pulse, and there was that pressure in my face. I had tissues out and against my nose before the others noticed. Come on Karen, where's your body. This fucking hurts.

It was fifteen minutes later when Karen ran ahead of me and pointed off into the trees.

"I'm just off the trail here." Her voice was desperate. Shit. I waited until I was next to Karen to stop.

"Sorry guys, I need to go again," I announced, hating to use the excuse.

The guys groaned.

"Hey," I said to them, "I got that tiny girl bladder. It's not my fault."

A couple of them chuckled as I followed Karen off the trail. My stomach was starting to churn; blood was still coming out my nose. I still followed Karen. The smell hit me first, rotting, sweet and thick on my tongue. I had another ten feet to go to reach Karen. As I got closer the smell got worse, I tried not to think about what I was smelling. When I reached Karen's body, I braced myself and looked down. She was destroyed. Her body was bloated, black liquid seeping from what was left of her abdomen. Her face was utterly ravaged; her skull was exposed, her jaw broken. Karen came too close. Her memories of being mauled poured over me. Her pain, her fear, the feeling of her death. I was going to be sick.

"Thank you," she said to me as I turned and started puking.

The boys must have heard me because my name was being called. I couldn't answer as I threw up again. I felt Karen move on. Yay, great for her. I was too focused on breathing between puking to care. Hands grabbed me; someone pushed and held my hair back from my face.

"We've got you, Beautiful." Ethan's voice was to my right. An arm wrapped around my waist and forced me to move away from the body. They thought that was what was making me sick. Oh, if only. But it was nice of them to try.

It wasn't long until I finally stopped puking. When I stood up straight, a wave of dizziness washed over me. The twin's hands steadied me, till it passed. I wiped a shaking hand across my mouth. Isaac handed me my dropped water bottle, and I started washing my mouth out. I was on my third rinse when someone mentioned calling the police.

"Call Rory," I managed to say, my voice shaking. I reached into my back pocket and held out my phone. Someone took it from me. My head was killing me too much to care who right now.

"I'll call him. Get her back on the trail," Zeke ordered as he swiped his finger across my phone. Ethan and Isaac each had a death grip on one of my hands as they walked me back to the trail. They let go when we were out of the brush.

"Red, your nose is bleeding," Isaac told me. I pulled more tissues from my pocket and pressed them against my nose. My headache was starting to ease up when Zeke and Miles came back down to the trail.

"Rory wants to meet us at the trail head," Zeke said as they reached us. Everyone got to their feet. Miles' eyes went to the tissues in my hand, he frowned. I just turned away and headed down the trail after Isaac. I really didn't want to answer questions right now.

An hour later, I was sitting in the front seat of Rory's truck, a blanket around my shoulders. I didn't understand why I needed a blanket, but Miles had been insistent. He muttered something about shock before walking away from me. There was an ambulance; someone from the forestry service had shown up along with several other cops. Rory was standing at the door, blocking my view of everything happening at the trail head.

"Lexie, what the hell happened?" Rory asked, his eyes narrowing on my face.

"A dead girl found me," I admitted quietly. Rory cursed. "She begged me to find her body so her parents would know what happened to her."

Rory shook his head at me, his brow drawing down.

"Lexie, your heart's too big for your own good," he said. "You said no ghosts for the weekend, now here we are with a dead body."

"I was in the woods hiking with the guys," I pointed out. "How was I supposed to know there would be a soul out here?"

Rory sighed, frowning again. "What did you tell the boys?" he asked.

I smirked up at him. "I said I was curious about a trail, and we walked down it for a bit. Then I said I had to pee." I shrugged. "Karen Malone led me right to her body."

Rory nodded.

"Uh-huh. Now, why did you start puking?"

I wrinkled my nose at him. He was way too observant.

"She was standing too close; her death memories kind of filled my head," I admitted.

Rory sighed and stepped back so I could get out of the truck. Apparently, he got the information he wanted. "Zeke's going to take you guys home. I want you resting for the rest of the day."

"Can I still go watch Ethan's band play?" I asked, my voice close to pleading. Rory snorted.

"Yes, you can." Rory waved Zeke over. "Take her home and make sure she gets some rest even if you have to sit on her."

Damn it, Zeke would actually make me rest. Zeke smirked at me, he was enjoying this entirely too much. I glared at Rory who just smiled down at me; he knew exactly what he just did. Zeke reached out, took my arm, and tugged me towards the others at his Jeep. That was low, Rory, real low.

ZEKE DIDN'T SIT on me, but the twins might as well have. Isaac and Ethan snuggled up next to me on the couch and wouldn't let me get up until they had to leave. Isaac wanted to get some things done before heading out to the club tonight and Ethan had to go set up. Miles was quiet all afternoon, typing away on his cell phone with a frown on his face until he headed home soon after the twins. Zeke refused to leave until Rory was back. When Rory walked in with a pizza in his hand, his eyes found me on the couch and Zeke in one of the armchairs. I glared at Rory. He burst out laughing. Zeke headed home to take a shower and change before we headed out to the club.

I ate dinner quickly, then headed upstairs. I took a shower and went into my bedroom to get ready. I turned on my computer and started listening to my favorite going-out songs as I got ready. I walked to the closet and threw it open. What to wear? I smirked at myself. I pulled on a pair of black boot-cut jeans, a black scoop-neck shirt, and my trusty black combat boots. It was going to be hot in the club so I might as well dress for it. I was doing my makeup when there was a knock on the door.

"Come on in." I focused on my eyeliner and didn't look behind me.

"I heard you're going out tonight with your friends." Tara's voice stunned me.

I finished with making my eyeliner darker than usual before turning around and answering.

"Yeah, Ethan's band is playing tonight." I watched Tara as she looked around my room. There wasn't much to see; I didn't have any pictures or posters to put up. Tara seemed to want to ask me something, but she was stalling. When she stayed silent, I started on my eye shadow, giving myself smoky eyes for the night. I finished one eye and was doing the other when I got tired of waiting for Tara to ask her questions. "What do you want to ask, Tara?"

She gave a soft sigh. "I was just wondering where you and your friends were going," Tara asked, without making it sound like a question.

I shrugged. "I don't know; they're driving tonight," I said. I didn't want Tara to show up and ruin Asher's time tonight. But I also didn't want to tell her I didn't want her to go. I was putting on my mascara when Tara spoke again.

"Lexie, I like Asher. I think we could be good together if we had a chance to get to know each other." Tara's voice was honest and vulnerable. It was weird.

I sighed as I finished with my lashes and turned around.

"Honey, Asher's not looking for a girlfriend right now," I tried to explain gently. "He's having trouble with his sister; he's always busy with work and football." I wanted to get her to understand. "He doesn't have time for a girlfriend right now."

Tara was looking at the floor for a while. I felt bad having to tell her, but I didn't know what else to do. I checked the time. I needed to hurry; the guys would be here in a few minutes.

I was pulling out my deep red lipstick when Tara caught my attention again.

"But he has time to go out with you?" She snapped bitterly.

I raised an eyebrow at her. "A friend that is a girl is not a girlfriend, Tara," I told her patiently. "I require a lot less time and effort." I snorted. "Besides, I think the guys sometimes forget I'm a girl." I put on my lipstick; it was a good deep red, with a bit of dark to it. Combined with my hair and skin, it looked great.

There was a knock on the front door. I turned to find Tara still in my room. Hell, I had to give her something. "If you want my advice with Asher...ease back until at least football ends. Don't flirt with him. Just, try to get to know him as a friend."

"Lexie, the boys are here!" Rory called up the stairs. Tara had a strange expression on her face like I had said something offensive. Ah hell, I give up. I put my wallet in my back pocket and my cell phone in my inside jacket pocket. I gestured for Tara to leave my room before me. She stopped outside in the hall.

"I've never been friends with a guy before," she said, sounding confused.

Shit.

"Guys are fun, I'll tell you all about it tomorrow if you like. But right now I have to go," I told her, gently closing the door behind me. She looked thoughtful as she nodded and disappeared into her room. I let out a breath. That was weird.

I hurried downstairs and found Isaac, Miles, and Zeke waiting. Isaac was wearing blue jeans, a black and white shirt with some graphic I couldn't make out. Along with his trusted blue hoodie. Miles was wearing his usual jeans and a black shirt with an extremely complex equation written across his chest in white, along with his green hoodie. Zeke just looked like Zeke--black jeans, black shirt, motorcycle boots. Though his hair was still wet from his shower.

I narrowed my eyes at him.

"Did you even change your clothes?" I asked doubtfully. He smirked as he looked down at his outfit.

"Yeah, these are clean," he simply said.

I couldn't help but grin.

I looked at Rory to find him frowning at me.

"What's my curfew?" I asked, wondering what the frown was for. Rory sighed.

"Midnight." Rory looked at the boys. "Keep an eye on her for me."

The guys nodded. I rolled my eyes.

Then we were out the door and in Zeke's Jeep. I could have gone around to the other side, but I wanted to play with Asher, so I opened his door and climbed over him to the other side. Isaac followed me. While Asher just laughed as I crawled over him, he groaned under Isaac's weight.

"Hell, Isaac, how much do you weigh?" Asher groaned. Isaac sat up in the middle.

"165 and it's all muscle, baby." Isaac chuckled.

"That's right, sweetie, you own it," I told him, my voice proud. The boys laughed.

As we headed out to Dulcet, I told Asher about Tara asking about where we were going. I also told him I advised her to back off, at least until after football. He said he was getting me a present. I asked for rock climbing lessons. His eyes lit up as he agreed.

The radio was starting to go to static so instead of interrupting Zeke and Miles conversation I slipped off my seat belt, wedged myself between the front seats, and played with the knobs until I found one that worked. It wasn't until I was sliding back that I realized I had just shoved my breasts practically into Miles' face. I winced as I sat up.

"Sorry Miles."

"I'll live." He assured me.

I burst out giggling as the others looked at me questioningly. I only shrugged and refused to answer.

Soon enough we were at Vegabond. We climbed out and got in line. The club was a big warehouse-like building, not as big as the clubs in the city but it looked like it would work for a town this size. I followed Zeke after I paid my cover. I was surprised the club was so packed. I quickly snagged Zeke's belt so I wouldn't get lost in the crowd. He reached behind him, took my hand in his and pulled me with him through the crowd. I felt a hand snag my other wrist. I looked behind me to find Isaac holding my other wrist.

Zeke somehow managed to find five spots at the bar. I believe glaring was involved on his part. I hopped onto my bar stool and ordered a soda. It was warm in here, so I took off my jacket and slipped it under my butt. I watched Isaac disappear into the crowd. Asher leaned over to me.

"I heard about today," he said, his ocean eyes met mine. "Good thinking getting Isaac to come down."

My face warmed under his gaze.

"I'm just glad it worked," I told him before turning to pay for my soda. I turned back and took a sip.

The band walking out onto stage cut off all other conversation. Ethan was in his usual all black, only tonight he wore a black tank top. It must be hot under the lights. My stomach was in knots for him. I bit the corner of my lip, nervous. The band got into position, and Ethan took the microphone.

"He's nervous," Asher commented.

I nodded and leaned over to him.

"Yeah, but once they hear him sing, the crowd will go crazy," I said. Asher nodded.

Then they started to play. The crowd cheered; they recognized this song. I watched the girls around me as Ethan began to sing. Jaws dropped, toes curled, and absolute devotion was created. It was everything I thought it would be. I all but jumped up and down on my stool in happiness. Zeke looked down at me like I had lost my mind. I crooked a finger at him. He leaned down so I could talk into his ear over the music.

"Look at the girls' faces."

Zeke straightened and looked around. Zeke smirked. He saw it too. They were into the second song when everyone started swaying on the dance floor. Zeke got my attention and gestured for me to stay here. I rolled my eyes at him. He shook his head and walked into the crowd. Everyone was dancing in the middle of the club, and I was tired of sitting still. Ethan's voice was rolling through the bar, and it made me want to move. I tapped Asher's shoulder; he leaned down to hear me.

"You're dancing with me," I told him flat out, no question about it. I wanted to dance, and Asher was stuck with me. He smiled down at me, and we headed out into the crowd as a fast, hard beat started up.

I danced with Asher, moving with the music. Though I made sure not to get too close, after all, I wasn't dating the guy. The dance floor was crowded, and soon enough, Asher saw someone he wanted to talk too. He leaned down and told me he was leaving. I nodded and kept dancing. I looked back over to the guys and found only Zeke and Miles still standing there. I caught Zeke's eye. I crooked a finger at him; asking him to come dance with me. He shook his head and mouthed the word no. I looked over at Miles and crooked a finger at him. He also shook his head as he gave me a warm smile. I shrugged and went back to dancing surrounded by people.

A hand moved around my waist, a body pressed against my back. I pulled the arm off and turned around. Wow. He was cute. A head taller than me, he had broad shoulders and great eyes. I dropped his arm and raised an eyebrow at him. He gave me a smile; it made me smile back. So, I danced with the guy, not the way he wanted me to. I didn't even know him. We danced until the band needed a break. He smiled down at me and held out his hand.

"I'm Markus. I go to Dulcet High School here."

I shook his hand and smiled.

"I'm Alexis, I go to Spring Mountain."

"I've never seen you here before," he said in the quiet of the club.

"I just moved to town this week," I admitted.

He nodded, then he pulled out a flask and took a drink. That was ballsy, drinking in the only bar around that would let in underage kids. He was going to get himself kicked out. He held it out to me, offering me some. I shook my head. He put the cap back on and put it back in his pocket.

I looked over to see Zeke talking to a tall girl with purple hair, and Miles was on a couch talking to a couple guys I recognized from school. I had no clue where Isaac or Asher had gone. Club music blasted through the speakers. Markus gestured, asking me to dance. I nodded. I wanted to dance, and he seemed okay. Though I didn't like the drinking here.

We danced to the club music, jumping with the crowd. Then a slow song came on. Markus had taken another hit from his flask when he reached out and pulled me closer. What the hell, why not? No one else was going to dance with me. I kept my body from pressing against his as we danced. Thankfully, the band came out, and they started up again. I stepped back away from Markus, turned and watched Ethan start to sing again. Damn that boy was good.

I was swaying to the music when Markus pressed his body up against me again, his arm going around my waist, again. Okay, he's not getting it. I pulled his arm off and turned around again. I shook my head. He gave me a nasty look and waved at me dismissively before going deeper into the crowd.

At least he got the message. I headed off the dance floor back to where my jacket was and waited to order a bottle of water.

"Hey, Red." Isaac popped up beside me making me jump. He ran his eyes over me. His question clear on his face. "You okay?"

"Yeah," I gestured over my shoulder at the dance floor. "I just got rid of some touchy guy on the dance floor. For a second, I thought you were him."

Isaac frowned and turned, resting his back against the bar. I ordered water from the bartender. When I finished paying, I turned to see Isaac watching the dance floor. I nudged his shoulder.

"Which one?" he asked.

I rolled my eyes.

"Don't worry about it. I already took care of it." I opened my water bottle and turned around to stand next to him. "Where have you been?"

Isaac grinned, his gaze still on the dance floor.

"I saw a girl I know from school; she's always had a boyfriend, though." He gestured toward a table near the door to the bar. I saw a couple blonde girls and didn't know which one he was talking about. "I heard a rumor this week that she was single now, so I'm taking a shot."

"Next slow song Ethan does get her on the dance floor," I offered. "Ethan's voice will do most of the work for you."

Isaac's face spread into a wicked grin.

"You're a genius, Red." Isaac turned to the bartender and ordered a couple sodas. "Now we need to find you someone."

"Got any friends that we don't hang out with?" I asked, only half kidding. I missed having a boyfriend, someone who made my heart race and my stomach flutter. Isaac seemed to be actually considering it.

He winced. "Nah, no one good enough for you, Red." Isaac paid the bartender and picked up the sodas.

"Aw, thanks, Cookie Monster." I smiled over at him.

He winked at me before heading off towards the booth with the blondes. I sat down on my jacket and watched Ethan perform. Any sign of nerves seemed to have vanished once they started playing. My phone vibrated in my back pocket. I pulled it out and checked it.

Asher: Where are you?

Alexis: At the bar. Where you all left me.

I smirked as I hit send, the guys really had kind of ditched me, but I couldn't blame them. There were girls here that they could hit on, and I wasn't one of them. My phone vibrated again.

Asher: I'm sending a friend your way, I'm sitting with a bunch of couples, and he's the odd guy out.

Alexis: Are you trying to hook me up?

Asher: Not really, all the girly giggling is irritating him. So, I told him to find you. The least girly girl I know.

There were only a couple seconds before my phone vibrated again.

Asher: And if you two hit it off, would that be so bad? Let me know what you think when he gets there.

I shook my head and smiled at my phone. Asher, what am I going to do with you?

"Sorry, are you Lexie?" A husky male voice rolled over my ears from my right. I looked up and had to stop my mouth from dropping. He was so freaking cute. His strong chin accented his angled jaw. Coupled with high cheekbones it gave him a boyish charm that made my heart race. His brown hair was a little long on top and kind of sticking up all over the place. He was wearing a gray Henley long-sleeve shirt with a couple buttons undone. The guy had muscle, not like Zeke, but it was there. I vaguely realized this because I was still looking at those dark blue eyes. Damn.

It was only a couple heartbeats before I pulled myself together and answered him.

"That's me." I gave him my best smile. "And your Asher's friend?"

He nodded and pulled a sleeve further up his forearm.

"Yeah, I'm Dylan." His husky voice was like fog and chocolate in my ears. It was so unfair. I gestured for him take the stool to my right.

"Have a seat. Just give me a second, Asher wanted me to text him when you got here."

He sat down and ordered a soda while I texted Asher back.

Alexis: He's here. You are the best friend ever!

I quickly put my phone away and started talking to Dylan.

"So, you're the other odd man out tonight, huh?" I offered, trying to get him talking.

He chuckled, as he paid for his soda.

"I guess so." He looked down at me his gaze measuring. "Though I don't remember seeing you around before."

"I moved here this week." I shrugged turning a bit on my stool, so I didn't have to keep turning my neck. "So, how do you know Asher? And if you have any embarrassing stories from his childhood, don't hold back on the details."

He burst out laughing; it was a good laugh. One you'd hear and look around for whoever it belonged to.

"We've played football together since we were kids. Well, till my family moved over here." He was still smiling as he turned on his stool toward me. "I do have some stories, but he has just as much on me, so stories are a no-go."

I gave an exaggerated sigh.

"I'm never going to hear anything good," I grumbled.

He chuckled.

"So, what do you do for fun around here?" I asked.

He thought about it for a couple heartbeats. "Outdoor stuff, really; hiking, skiing, climbing. We're a very outdoorsy area." His eyes ran over my face. "You are going need to invest in sunscreen this summer."

I laughed. "Are you kidding? I'm going to be buying it by the case." I told him matter-of-factly. "Or maybe the flat, which do you think will get me the better price?"

He had a great smile.

"Probably the flat, but then you have to store it all," he pointed out before taking a drink.

"Ah, good point. The case it is."

He smiled again and started talking. We talked about his surfing trips to Hawaii with his family. Music, school; we even talked about my artwork. Everything I learned about him I liked. We had talked for a good hour before he gestured to the dance floor.

"Want to dance?" he asked awkwardly, rubbing the back of his neck. It was so fucking cute.

"Sure, let's go."

I hopped off the stool as he stood up. He was a head taller than me. Perfect height for dancing. He took my hand, which of course immediately started tingling, and led me through the crowd to a spot on the dance floor. We just got there when the band changed into a slow song. We both started laughing.

I gestured back at the bar. "Want an out?" I offered, still laughing.

He smirked down at me and shook his head. He used my hand to pull me closer. One of his hands went to my lower back while mine disappeared into his.

"I think we'll survive." He bent his head down a little so I could hear him better, his chin brushing the back of my jaw. "Besides, with our luck, when we got back to the bar, it'd change back."

"Then if we came back out, it'd go back to a slow one." I snickered. He chuckled in my ear. My heart was racing, my back and hand tingling from his touch.

He sighed. "Yeah, better to just ride it out."

I smiled and tried not to get too close to him. I didn't want to scare him off. We had a few heartbeats of silence; I wanted to keep him talking. I couldn't seem to get enough of that voice.

"So, what is it about surfing that you like?"

"Hmm." His voice was low in my ear.

Oh, shit. My stomach did that low flip as goose bumps ran over my arms and down my back. I hoped he didn't notice.

"It's quiet, peaceful. When you're out there, it's just you and your board looking for the next wave." His voice poured into my ear.

I bit my bottom lip. That was not fair.

"Yeah, just you, your board and the sharks that want to eat you," I pointed out, trying to distract myself.

He chuckled in my ear making me smile.

"Sharks don't really want to eat you," he said. I could hear his smile in his voice. "When there is an attack it's usually because the shark thought the surfer was a seal." His chest brushed against mine. Did he step closer? Yes. Yes, he did. I couldn't stop smiling as I kept my gaze on his chest. "You should try surfing sometime, it's fun."

"Nu-uh, I have this rule. Don't go where I'm not at the top of the food chain," I told him seriously.

He chuckled in my ear. He moved our hands to rest on his chest. I bit my lip again, my stomach doing a different kind of hard flip low in my belly. Okay, yeah. I missed having a boyfriend.

"Sweetie, you're so small you're not at the top of the food chain now," he said.

I burst out laughing; my face grew warm.

"A bunch of us go out the coast in the summer," he continued, "it's all arranged by the town. There are chaperones, separate hotel rooms for girls and guys. You should come." He was talking like we were going to still see each other in the summer. I wasn't going to count on that, but it wouldn't be so bad if he were right.

"Promise I'll come back?" I asked, completely serious. He chuckled. "Yes."

"With all my limbs attached?"

He kept laughing.

"Yes, with all your limbs attached." He assured me, still laughing.

"What about toes? We haven't talked about toes?"

He laughed even harder, pulling me against him more. He rested his forehead on my shoulder as he continued to crack up.

"It's a legitimate concern of mine; I like my fingers and toes." I continued, smiling.

I noticed Asher out of the corner of my eye. I turned my head to see him on the dance floor with a leggy brunette. When his eyes met mine, he smirked at me. I winked across the dance floor at him. When Dylan lifted his head, his face was pink from laughing. His deep blue eyes met mine.

"I promise I will personally guard your limbs, your fingers, and your little toes." He assured me sweetly. I felt myself melt a bit, okay more than a bit.

"Okay, I'll see what I can do." I agreed.

The slow song stopped. I stepped back and let go. A faster song started. Dylan leaned down to my ear again.

"I need to use the restroom, I'll be right back."

I nodded. "I'm getting water, do you want one?" I felt him nod against my cheek.

We split up on the dance floor, he headed to the restroom. Apparently, the restroom was in the back-right corner of the same wall as the bar. I walked to the bar with a big stupid grin on my face. Dylan was pretty damn cute; he was nice and had a damn good voice. I reminded myself not to get too excited about it. Nothing would probably come from it.

The bar was busy, so it took a bit to get two bottles of water. I had put my wallet away and was picking up the water bottles when a hand ran from my back down to my ass. I dropped the bottles, took the hand off of me and spun around. Markus was crowding close to me. I threw his arm at him; he didn't seem to notice.

"Hey baby, miss me yet?" His voice was slurred his eyes running over me. Ew, just ew.

"Back the fuck off," I told him clearly, my voice hard.

"Don't be like that." He put one arm on each side of me, resting on

135

the bar, his whiskey breath in my face making my stomach roll. "I'll treat you better than that other guy ever could."

That's it. I was done.

"Back the fuck off!" I repeated myself louder this time as I shoved him away from me. He moved back a step. He really was much bigger than me, after all. I only wanted him to back up.

His face twisted. "Fucking cock teasing bitch," he spat out.

His hands shot out, hitting me in the middle of my chest hard. I fell backward, my back slammed into the edge of the bar. Agony ripped through me as I dropped hard on my right side and hip. My eyes watered from the fire running through my back. I gasped for air. My body shaking from the hit to my spine. A big black blur hit Markus across the face; he went down hard. Zeke was on him again in a heart-beat. I was trying to relearn to breathe as Zeke pounded his fist into Markus repeatedly. I couldn't move, not yet. My back was still trying to kill me. I kept taking deep breaths trying to get through the pain. Zeke kept wailing on Markus.

"You think you could put your hands on her? You fucking piece of shit!" Zeke was shouting, among other things.

By the time I could move, Miles was kneeling next to me, his face worried. His eyes running over me, looking for any sign of injury. I waved him off and sat up. Miles helped pull me to my feet. It fucking hurt. I watched Zeke still hitting Markus.

Before I could start worrying, Asher and Isaac bolted out of the crowd and grabbed Zeke's arms. They pulled him away from Markus. Zeke struck out with a boot nailing Markus in the gut before he was out of range.

Miles picked up Zeke's jacket and handed me mine. He gently wrapped an arm around my back, his hand was warm against my ribs. I was still trying to process what had just happened. Zeke had just beaten Markus to a bloody pulp. Yeah, the guy hurt me. And yeah, I kind of liked that he was now unconscious on the floor. But I didn't like that Zeke was still fighting Asher and Isaac as they pulled him through the stunned crowd. That was starting to scare me. This wasn't the controlled Zeke that I knew.

Miles gently helped get me moving through the crowd, my back still throbbing; it hurt to just breathe from it. But we needed to go now. So I moved, following in the wake of the other guys. We stepped outside into the quiet of the parking lot. Zeke was still cursing, he wanted to go back in there and finish the guy off.

"Are you okay?" Miles asked, probably not for the first time, his emerald eyes ran over my face again. "What happened?"

"That guy grabbed my ass and blocked me against the bar," I explained, watching the guys pin Zeke against the Jeep, his arms behind his back. They weren't hurting him; it looked like they were only holding him until he calmed down. "I told him to back off, and he didn't, so I pushed him," I admitted as we started walking towards the Jeep. "He shoved me back, my back hit the bar. I hit the floor."

Miles frowned as he watched how carefully I was walking. I took a deep breath and forced myself to walk normally. It fucking hurt.

"Do you want me to take a look?" Miles asked, his voice warm and silky again.

"No, no, I'll be fine. He just knocked the wind out of me." I really didn't want any of them to see my back, especially right now. We needed Zeke to calm down, not go on a killing spree.

By the time we reached the Jeep, the pain had mostly faded from my back, and I was walking normally again. Isaac and Asher were taking turns trying to calm Zeke down. Zeke was still cursing and talking about ripping that guy's head off.

"Ally, are you alright?" Asher asked, still pinning Zeke to the Jeep.

"Yeah, I'm okay," I answered, distracted as I watched them hold Zeke calmly. I bit the corner of my bottom lip.

"Someone want to tell us what the hell happened?" Isaac shot over his shoulder, his face red as he struggled to hold Zeke in place.

Miles repeated what I told him. This just had Zeke straining against the others again.

Isaac looked over at Asher. "How'd you know someone hurt her?" Isaac grunted.

Zeke gave a jerk, the boys were forced to adjust their grip and slam him against the Jeep. It rocked with the force of they put behind it.

"Nothing else gets Zeke this pissed off," Asher hissed, using his body weight against Zeke's shoulder. Asher looked at me over his shoulder and tilted his head towards the Jeep. "Go ahead and get in the Jeep, this might take a while," he managed to say between clenched teeth.

"Jeep's locked." Isaac groaned. The boys cursed, well, except for Miles. Asher gave Isaac a look. Isaac immediately began shaking his head.

"Nuh-uh, no way," Isaac declared. "I'm not looking for keys near his junk with him this pissed off."

"Miles?" Asher called over his shoulder.

"I'm with Isaac on this one. I think we should wait until he calms down," Miles admitted.

I rolled my eyes and handed Miles my jacket.

"I'll do it," I announced, stepping closer to Zeke.

"He usually keeps them in his right pocket," Miles said. I stepped up behind Zeke and touched his back lightly. He jerked hard against the guys.

"It's Lexie!" They all snapped at him. Zeke seemed to hear them and stopped jerking.

"Zeke, it's just me," I told him calmly. His head turned trying to see me over his shoulder, but he couldn't, I was too short with Isaac's shoulder in the way. I ran my hand over his back so he could feel where I was. I stepped closer biting my lower lip again. Please don't hit me. Please don't hit me. "I'm just looking for the keys to the Jeep. The guys want to get out of the cold."

He seemed to hear me because he stopped fighting the boys. Feeling more confident that he knew I was there, I stepped closer, slipping in a bit between Isaac and Zeke. I ran my hand along the hard line of Zeke's waist to his right front pocket. I reached into his pocket and felt around for the keys. During my fumbling, I felt something else besides keys, but I was trying to ignore that. My fingers snagged the key chain and pulled the keys out. Zeke was completely still, his forehead on the roof of the Jeep. He was taking deep, even breaths and slowly letting them out.

138

Miles walked me to the other side of the car; my eyes never left Zeke.

"Get in the car, Lexie," Miles told me gently, his voice firm. "He's going to need a few minutes."

I slid into the back seat. Miles got into the front, started the car and started the heater for me. Then he was out again shutting the door behind him. The guys were talking to Zeke, telling him repeatedly that I was fine. That I just had the wind knocked out of me. I winced at my lie. My hands were still shaking from hitting the bar, but there was no way I could tell them that. Not with Zeke this angry.

It was a while before Zeke was allowed to step back from the Jeep. I bit the corner of my lip as he began pacing in the parking lot. The guys watched him silently. Eventually, everyone got into the Jeep. Miles took the driver seat; Zeke took the front. Asher and Isaac slipped in back with me. Zeke's eyes ran over me once before he looked out the windshield, his jaw clenching.

This was all my fault. I shouldn't have danced with someone I didn't know. I should have stayed next to one of them all night after dancing with that asshole on the dance floor.

The ride back to Spring Mountain was tense and quiet. Zeke's gaze never left the road the whole way back. Shit. He knew it was my fault, my chest tightened till it was getting hard to breathe.

When the guys dropped me off Asher reminded me about my lesson with him in the morning as I was getting out. The boys said goodnight, Zeke didn't say a word to me. My stomach was in knots as I walked up to the front door. The guys waited until I was inside before driving off.

Well, I royally fucked that up.

CHAPTER 8

*I*n the morning, my mind was still on last night. How pissed off Zeke had gotten, how it was my fault. I even sent Zeke an apology text as soon as I woke up. I got no response. So, when I headed over to the indoor rock-climbing center, I wasn't in the best mood. Asher had said dress to climb. I was wearing black, capri yoga pants, a sports bra, a navy blue t-shirt, and an old pair of black sneakers.

I walked into the center and found Asher immediately behind the counter. He was wearing a bright blue tank shirt that showed off the muscles in his arms and chest. And brought out the blue in his eyes. When he spotted me, his smile reached his eyes.

"Ally girl, you ready to climb?" he asked, coming around the counter to meet me.

I gave him the best smile I could manage and shrugged. His smile disappeared; his brow drew down.

"What's wrong? Do you not want a lesson today?"

"No, I do, I'm just still a little grumpy about last night," I admitted, I really did want to learn how to climb, but I just couldn't seem to focus this morning.

Asher crooked his finger at me; I walked to the counter.

"What size shoe do you wear?"

"Eight."

Asher disappeared behind the counter and came back with a pair of shoes in his hand. He walked around the counter and led me to a set of benches. He gestured for me to sit. I did.

"That fight wasn't entirely about you, Ally," Asher began, gesturing for me to take off my shoes.

I bent down and untied them as he kept talking.

"You know Zeke has a temper, and he's usually very good at controlling it."

I nodded as I pulled my shoes off. He handed me the pair in his hands; they had very thin hard bottoms.

"Zeke has what's called a trigger, he has a couple."

I stopped putting on the shoes to look at him. He looked like he was trying to decide something.

"But one of his biggest ones is a guy hitting a girl. He sees that, and he loses all control." He rubbed the back of his neck as he continued. "It would have happened even if Zeke had never met you before. He would have knocked the guy out and backed off. But Zeke knows you, so, it set him off in a big way."

"He wouldn't even look at me in the car last night." I reminded him, feeling ridiculously girly at the moment.

"After he gets triggered, he doesn't look at anyone, he doesn't talk to anyone until he's ready. He has a really hard time afterward." He eyes narrowed on my face. "He doesn't blame you for what happened, Ally. No one does. That guy had it coming."

I smiled at that, I agreed completely. Okay, it wasn't completely my fault. I could deal with that.

"Any other triggers I should avoid?" I asked.

Asher sighed and thought about it while I put on the shoes he gave me.

"Yeah, don't come up behind him and touch his back," he said.

I winced; I had done that last night, too.

Asher noticed.

"It's really not as bad as the hitting trigger; he only jumps and spins around."

"Okay, no touching his back," I assured him. "Anything else?"

"Besides waking him up? Nothing you need to know about." Asher hedged.

I raised an eyebrow to let him know I noticed.

He gave me a half grin; he was keeping his mouth shut.

I took a deep breath and let it out feeling much better.

"Okay. Now show me how not to kill myself."

OVER THE NEXT COUPLE HOURS, Asher taught me about anchors, belays, and the safety equipment needed to rock climb. He taught me several knots and drilled me on them relentlessly. Soon enough, I was in a harness and trying to climb the 5.7 wall; the "beginner's wall", he said. Beginners wall, my ass. The wall went up forty feet. I was climbing alone since Asher was down below acting as my belayer, holding the slack from my line in case I fell. The center wasn't busy today, so I was alone half way up when I had to stop for a second.

"Are you sure this is the beginner's wall?" I shot down at him, holding tight to my handholds.

Asher chuckled at me.

"The expert wall is sixty feet high, with a lot of angles and over-hangs," Asher shouted up at me.

I groaned at what he was describing.

"Ease up on your grip, Ally girl, you only want enough pressure to keep you there."

I immediately loosened my death grip on the hard handholds. I started moving again, finding handholds that were comfortable for me to grab and pulling myself up. I climbed several more feet, my arms starting to burn. I paused again and made the mistake of looking down. My head spun at the distance to the mat. I looked back at the wall, trying to forget how high I was.

"Remind me again, what happens if I fall?" I called down, really needing the reminder.

"In here, I have the other end of the rope through a clamp on my harness; I've been pulling off the slack from your rope. You fall, my weight will counter yours, lifting me up and bringing you to a stop," he reassured me. "I'm not going to drop you, Ally."

I nodded, as I started moving again.

"Use your legs to move your weight, not your arms!" he shouted up at me a few minutes later.

I nodded and did what he said. I was almost there. My arms and legs were shaking as I finally reached to top. I smacked it like Asher had told me to. Then I had to get down.

"Asher! How the fuck do I get down?" I called, looking down at him. He gave me that big smile of his.

Shit.

"You're going to drop," he told me.

My stomach knotted hard.

"You need to practice falling anyway."

I bit my lower lip, my arms were shaking, and I was going to lose my grip soon anyway.

"You sure?" I asked. I'd seen other people in the center drop that way, it did look kind of fun.

"Yeah, I've got you. Now drop."

I took a deep breath for courage and let go. I dropped. My stomach jumped into my throat as I sped towards the mats. Only, I wasn't going as fast as I thought I would.

When I stopped, I looked down to see that Asher had been pulled about five feet up the wall, his grip on my rope tight. I watched as he let out his end of the line, slowly bringing him to the floor. I spun around, my back to the wall. Asher's arms worked as he lowered me slowly. When my feet touched the mat, I looked up at the wall, grinning from ear to ear. That was awesome.

"Still want to go climbing with us this summer?" Asher asked, pulling my attention from the wall. He started unhooking himself from his harness.

"Oh, hell yeah," I said emphatically.

Asher chuckled as he dropped his harness and reached out to unhook mine.

"You're going to need a lot of practice if you want to go climbing with us." Asher began letting go of my harness so I could pull it off my lower body. "We're talking a couple times a week to practice, more if you're really into it."

"I'll talk to Rory about it. I'm pretty sure he'll let me," I said.

Asher picked up the harnesses and led the way back to the benches in the front of the building. I was pulling off my shoes when he handed me a bottle of water. I opened it and took a big drink. I finished taking my shoes off and looked over at him.

"So, how long have you been rock climbing?" I asked.

"Since forever. My dad used to take me every chance he got." Asher shrugged, opening his water bottle. "We don't really go anymore."

I finished pulling on my shoe.

"Sorry." I didn't mean to bring up a sore subject.

He winked at me, letting me know it was okay.

"So, is this what you want to do when you finish school? Be a climbing instructor?"

"No, I love my hobby, but I don't want it to become my job." He turned towards me, his legs straddling the bench.

I started pulling on my other shoe.

"So, what do you want to do?" I asked, genuinely curious.

"My dad wants me to get a football scholarship, get to the NFL, the whole nine yards." His voice was resigned, like he accepted that this is what he was going to do.

This kind of irked me.

"That's what your dad wants, what do you want?"

I finished tying my shoe and turned on the bench towards him.

Asher sighed as he started peeling the label off his bottle. He was looking everywhere but at me. He knew what he wanted to do; he just didn't want to admit it.

"If I tell you mine, will you tell me yours?" I asked, hoping this would get him to talk.

Asher grinned at me.

"Okay, you first," Asher stated, leaning forward.

Shit. I groaned as I felt my face turning red. That really got his attention.

"Oh, this is going to be good," he said, still grinning.

I wrinkled my nose at him before looking at the bench between us.

"It's a little different," I told him gathering my courage. "I want to be a tattoo artist." I peeked up at him.

His eyebrows had shot up; the surprise on his face was clear as day. Then the eyebrows came down, and he seemed to think about it.

"You are a really good artist," he admitted. "You're better than good. But that's just my opinion. You know, the guy who can't draw?"

I smiled gratefully; he wasn't going to make fun of me. I wasn't insecure about much, but becoming a tattoo artist was one of them. My face was still burning when I pointed at him.

"Your turn," I stated.

"I would honestly like to be a chef," Asher admitted, his face wincing.

"Then do that," I said simply.

His eyes grew darker as his frown came back.

"I can't, my Dad-"

"Are you going to do what your Dad wants your whole life? Or are you going to wait until you're in your 40's or 50's, and he dies before you do what makes you happy?" I asked, looking him in the eye. "That would be half your life, gone. Fifty years is a long time to be unhappy." I shrugged backing off; I couldn't make Asher's choices for him. I only wanted Asher to be happy, and it didn't seem like football was going to do it. "Just promise me you'll think about it?"

Asher's gaze ran over my face before he nodded. Then he leaned forward smirking at me. Uh-oh.

"It looked like it went pretty well with Dylan last night," he offered.

I eyed him suspiciously.

"Maybe."

"Just maybe? Not yes?" he asked, smiling entirely too much; he knew something or heard something.

145

"You boys gossip just as much as girls do." I tossed one of the shoes at him.

He chuckled, catching it against his chest.

"Come on, Ally, I sent the guy over to you," he pointed out. "I should get some details."

I sighed, he was right. If I had sent a girl over to meet him, I'd want details too.

"Yeah, we had fun," I admitted. "He's nice, he got my sense of humor right away, and it doesn't hurt that he's a hottie." And that voice was killer, but there was no way I was going to admit that to Asher. "It was great, until I got shoved into the bar and whisked outside without a word."

Asher smiled. "He called me last night wondering what happened. He, apparently, only saw the last part with Miles taking you outside and a bloody, unconscious guy on the floor." Asher took a drink before continuing. "Dylan ended up taking the guy to the hospital; he had a broken nose, a concussion, and a cracked jaw."

I groaned and closed my eyes. Zeke had really lost control last night.

"Let me guess, he didn't ask for my number."

Asher snorted. "Actually, he did."

I raised an eyebrow. Really? Dylan asked for my number? After that?

"Seriously?" I had to ask, just to be sure I heard him right.

Asher nodded.

"I had to explain who Zeke was first, but he asked for your number." He ran his eyes over my face. "Should I give it to him?"

I felt my face start to turn pink.

"Yeah, give him my number." I gave a half shrug. "Just because he gets it doesn't mean he'll call, Asher."

Asher pulled out his cell phone, grinning. He typed a text message and sent it.

"I bet he'll call as soon as he has it," he stated.

I laughed at that.

"I'll take that bet, another free lesson if I win," I offered. I pulled my cell from my bra and set it on the bench between us.

"Deal." Asher gestured toward the phone. "Give him five minutes."

"Agreed."

Asher sat there watching the phone and looking at the clock. He was frowning more as time went by. We waited five minutes before Asher cursed. I snickered at him.

"Told ya." I said, taunting him before picking up my phone and putting it back in my bra.

"He'll call, Ally, maybe not right now. But I'm pretty sure he'll call," Asher said.

I started laughing. Asher the matchmaker.

"If he does, I'll let you know. If he doesn't, you'll never hear the end of this," I promised.

Asher groaned.

I left soon after that; another client of Asher's had an appointment. I walked away wondering if Dylan would really call today. Probably not, but it would be nice.

WHEN I GOT HOME, I told Rory that I wanted to take climbing lessons so I could go climbing with the guys this summer. Rory smiled and agreed. It was weird asking for something and getting it. I walked upstairs and took a shower. I pulled on comfy boot-cut blue jeans, a black cami, and a big, over-sized, gray and black sweater. The neck hung off my shoulder, but since I was at home, it didn't matter. I spent the rest of the day on the Internet looking for ways to deal with Bitch Ghost at school tomorrow. It was around nine when my phone vibrated. It wasn't Dylan.

Miles: Has anyone heard from Zeke today?

I was looking down at my phone as the others answered.

Asher: No.

Ethan: Nope.

Isaac: He didn't show up for training.

Alexis: Me neither.

There was a heartbeat of time as I wondered what was going on, and then my phone was vibrating.

Miles: That's not good.

Isaac: He's working tonight.

Asher: Someone needs to get over there and talk to him.

Ethan: Beautiful, can you head over and talk to Zeke?

Asher: Are you sure that's a good idea?

Miles: That's a brilliant idea.

Alexis: What's going on guys?

There was a pause as I waited for an answer.

Asher: After Zeke is triggered, we usually hear from him the next day.

Miles: We need someone to get him to talk tonight, and you're the best option.

Isaac: You he won't hit or shove out the door.

Ethan: Pick up some fast food and take it over to the garage. Show him the bag, and he'll let you in the door.

Asher: Ask him why no one has heard from him.

Isaac: Yes! Feed the beast, it soothes him. But don't give him the bag until you're inside.

Alexis: Send me the address, tell me what he likes, and I'll head over.

They sent over the address and the burger joint in town that Zeke loved. I pulled my jacket on and headed downstairs.

Rory and Tara were in the living room. I tucked my phone away inside my jacket as I went to Rory.

"Rory, can I go out for a bit?"

Rory looked up at me a frown on his face.

"It's a school night," he said, eyeing what I was wearing. "Where do you want to go?"

"Zeke hasn't talked to anyone today, the guys asked me to take him some food and get him talking." I shrugged, not really understanding how I'd be able to help, but willing to try.

Rory's frown disappeared.

"Yeah go on, but be back before eleven," he told me, already going back to watching television.

I was out the door when Tara started screaming about letting me go out on a school night.

I winced and pushed it out of my mind. I drove to the burger joint and got what the boys told me to pick up. A triple bacon cheeseburger and large fries. The damn burger was huge.

I followed the navigation on my phone till I reached a mechanics shop. It was a two-bay shop, both bay doors closed, though I could see the light was on. Zeke's Jeep was parked to the side out front. This must be the place.

I grabbed Zeke's food and hurried to the door. I gave a few hard knocks and waited. It didn't take long for him to answer. When the dented metal door opened, Zeke looked down at me confused.

"Lexie?" he said like he didn't quite believe I was here.

I looked at his face and started to worry. His eyes were bloodshot, the bags under his eyes dark. It didn't look like he had even gone to sleep last night. The guys were right; something was wrong.

"Quick, let me in, it's freezing out here," I demanded as I pushed my way into the garage office. Zeke took a step to the side as I closed the door behind me with a slam. I was in! I held the greasy bag out to him. "I brought food." His brow drew down as he frowned at me. He took the bag and opened it. He sighed then closed the bag and looked down at me.

"The guys sent you," he stated simply. "You shouldn't be here, Lexie."

He turned and walked through a door and into the garage. Was he still wearing the same clothes from last night? With Zeke's wardrobe, it was hard to tell, but I think I was right. I followed a few steps behind him, really getting worried now. There were two cars sitting in the bays, both with their hoods up. Zeke went to the sink near the door and began washing his hands.

"Why's that?" I asked, watching him clean as much of the grease off his hands as he could. He worked on cars so much; parts of his hands have permanently stained the color of engine grease. I noticed the bruises and cuts on his knuckles from last night. "Because you're at work?"

He shook his head, his shoulders tense as he dried his hands. He tossed the towel in the garbage and picked up the bag again. He was walking toward the second bay before I tried again.

"Why haven't you talked to anyone today?"

He dropped the bag on the worktable then leaned on his hands against the surface.

"Because no one should be around me," he growled over his shoulder at me before he looked back down at the table. "Least of all you."

I stepped around what looked like a hoist to stand closer.

"What are you talking about?"

He stared at the pegboard in front of him as if it had the answer to every question he ever wanted to ask.

"I have my father's temper, Lexie." He was looking down at the worktable again shaking his head slowly. "I shouldn't be around people; I shouldn't be around you." His voice was honest. Like he really believed the bullshit he was saying.

"This is about the fight last night?" I asked keeping my voice soft. I watched his back as his body tensed up even more.

"I shouldn't have lost control like that," he bit out, a fist banging on the table. "Not with you that close."

Was he pissed at himself because he thought he could have hurt me? That's what it seemed like. That wall around my heart lost a large chunk right there in that garage. Zeke might be terrifying as hell at times and intimidating to a scary degree. But I had no doubt in my mind that he would never hurt me. But I wasn't the one who needed to be convinced.

"Zeke, I'm the reason you lost it," I told him, my voice serious. "That guy shoved me into the bar-"

"I know, but I overreacted." His voice was hard, his jaw clenched. His hand shook as he ran it through his hair. "I saw you hit the bar. I saw your face, and I fucking lost it."

My heart ached, he was so furious with himself.

"I thought he really hurt you, Lexie, "he continued, "and you only got the wind knocked out of you."

Fuck. This was my fault; if I hadn't lied about how much I was hurt, Zeke wouldn't be torturing himself right now. I was going to show him my back. I knew I was. He was trying to tell me that he didn't trust himself around me, that he was dangerous to me. And I couldn't let him think that.

"Zeke, that guy hurt me-"

"I know he did, but-"

"No, Zeke," I said, my voice hard. "He really fucking hurt me." My heart slammed in my chest as he finally looked at me. I watched two different emotions fighting it out in those sky-blue eyes. I held his gaze refusing to look away. I pulled off my jacket and dropped it to the floor. I reached for my sweater, glad I was wearing a cami underneath.

"Lexie, stop, what are you...?" Zeke turned to stop me.

I pulled off my sweater and dropped it onto my jacket. His voice trailed off as he saw I was still dressed. If I weren't so tense, I would have laughed at the stunned look on his face. I collected my hair in my right hand, and I gestured for him to come closer with my left.

"Take a look."

He was frowning. It felt like he was walking in slow motion around me. I heard my pulse in my ears; my chest was tight as I waited. When he saw my back he cursed, and everything seemed to come back to normal speed.

"Baby, what the hell happened to you?" he asked, , his voice just barely there, just a breath. I felt a rough fingertip trace from my neck to my shoulder. "These aren't fucking new."

My eyes were on the far wall.

"My mother beat the shit out of me. It's why I'm here with Rory," I told him, trying to keep my voice matter of fact. "It doesn't even hurt unless I get hit in the back." I turned around and looked up at his face. His eyes had changed from self-hating to wanting to rip someone apart.

"He shoved me into the bar, Zeke," I pointed out trying to keep the topic on him, not me. "That look you saw? I was in a lot of pain. You saw it, recognized it, and reacted to it."

I shrugged as I was turning around and picking up my sweater feeling entirely too naked in front of him, and it had nothing to do with what I was wearing. I pulled it on and looked back up at him, his eyes still looking to hit something

"So, you have a dark side, Zeke, welcome to the world." I kept my voice matter of fact. "You're not the only one with a temper."

He looked like he was finally listening to me.

"A guy tried to hurt me once; I got away." I licked my lips before continuing. "Then I came back with a short crowbar." The corner of his mouth twitched. I smiled, still pleased with myself even a year later. "His jaw was wired shut for a few months." I gestured around at the world in general. "Everyone has a dark side, Zeke; the key is not to let it make you its bitch."

He snorted at me once and gave me that half grin of his. The tightness in my chest finally eased up so I could take a deep breath again.

"And I think you do a pretty good job of that, Zeke."

He took a deep breath and let it out slowly. His gaze still on my face, I could almost see his gears working.

"Come here." He reached out, wrapped his big hand around the back of my neck and pulled me to him. I rested my head on his chest and wrapped my arms around his waist. I took a deep breath of leather and engine grease as he gently wrapped his other arm around my shoulders. He had never hugged me before. I liked it. His fingers massaged my neck gently.

"I still want that guy's name," he mumbled under his breath.

I smiled against his shirt. I was tempted to give it to him.

CHAPTER 9

I overslept the next morning. I only had time to throw on what I wore to the garage last night. Then I had my bag and I was out the door. And of course, today it's pouring down rain. I was almost soaked through by the time I reached my class. First period was halfway over when I walked into class. I mouthed a sorry to Mr. Matthews and took my seat as fast as possible. He only gave me the stink eye. After class, I was headed to English when my cell phone vibrated.

Miles: Are you coming to school today?

I was texting back that I had overslept when someone whistled at me.

"Hey, red, you wanna come over to my house later?" some guy called out to me. I hit send on my text and flipped him off without looking at him or even stopping my stride. It was still pouring down, and I had to leave the hallway to get to English. I tucked my phone away and ran for it. I was soaked again by the time I reached class.

After English, I headed out into the hall and had to cross a court-yard. My hair was soaked by the time I got across. I gave up on being dry as I headed toward my next class. Zeke and Asher spotted me in the hallway then headed my way. I smiled. Knowing I was going to see them between classes always made my morning. Zeke's eyes ran over my clothes, an eyebrow raised.

"Weren't you wearing that last night?" he asked, his voice cautious.

"Ally, are you doing the walk of shame?" Asher teased, his blue eyes sparkling.

"No." I chuckled. "I'm doing the walk of 'oh shit, oh shit, I forgot to turn on my alarm clock.'" The guys chuckled. "I didn't even have time to brush my teeth or do my makeup." Asher's eyes ran over my face.

"You look pretty," he said with an exaggerated smile.

"I look like a drowned rat," I said to him, not buying it for a second.

"But a pretty drowned rat," he offered.

Zeke and I burst out laughing. Asher smiled normally and swung his bag around so he could reach it. "I can't help with makeup, but I can help with your teeth." He pulled out a pack of gum and handed it to me. I promptly popped a couple pieces into my mouth.

"Thank you so much, Asher, you are seriously my hero for the day," I said emphatically. Asher puffed up his chest.

"Hero for the day, I like it," he said in a superhero voice.

Zeke's big hand came down on Asher's shoulder.

"Come on, hero, I've got Trig, and you have Gym," Zeke reminded him; Asher sulked as he walked away. I was still laughing on my way to Algebra, I got soaked through again but this time I cared less.

The rest of the day went on like normal a few girls made insults to which I flipped them off. Otherwise, it was my usual. It was after Chemistry as we were walking towards the cafeteria when Zeke and Asher met us halfway to the cafeteria.

"Don't bother heading that way, this whole side is packed," Asher announced meeting us in the hallway.

"Why this time?" I asked in my suffering voice.

"Because of you and Jessica on Friday." Zeke pointed at me. I cursed.

"I still need to hit the cafeteria. I didn't have time to make lunch today," I grumbled. Isaac swung his bag around and dug into it. He pulled out a sack lunch and handed it to me.

"I'm not taking your lunch, Isaac."

Isaac snorted. "That's second lunch. I can grab something from a vending machine later," Isaac admitted pulling out another lunch bag. I raised an eyebrow.

"Second lunch, like a hobbit?" I asked, wondering if they would get the reference. All the guys chuckled.

"Guys eat a lot," Asher reminded me. I shook my head at the bag in my hand. Yeah, I was finally getting that.

"Wait, are we just going to ignore the fact she just made a Hobbit reference?" Miles asked, raising his hand. He narrowed his eyes at me. "Which is better? Book or movie?"

"Book," I answered immediately. Miles looked impressed.

I looked over at Isaac. "Thank you, Isaac."

He winked at me as we started walking down the hall and away from the cafeteria. Everyone pulled out their bags and started eating as we walked.

"Yay, I got tuna. I got tuna," Isaac sang to himself as he opened his first lunch, making me smile.

"Well, the rumor mill is going crazy from Saturday night," Ethan announced. I cringed.

"About how awesome you guys played?" I offered, hoping that was where this was going. Ethan chuckled.

"Oh no." Ethan shook his head then pointed at Zeke and me. "That Zeke and you are a thing, and he kicked someone's ass for hitting on you." He was enjoying this way too much. I groaned. Zeke cursed. Miles and the twins burst out laughing.

"Didn't anyone notice me being shoved first?" I asked, pleading for Ethan to give me some good news.

"Amazingly, that didn't make the rounds," Ethan admitted.

"I'm never going to get a date," I grumbled. Most of the boys burst out laughing. I fought the urge to smack each of them.

"Dylan hasn't called yet?" Asher asked before taking a drink of water.

"Nope." I playfully glared at him. Asher winced.

"As much as I love torturing you," Ethan admitted as he tried to stop laughing. "I know some girls that can spread the truth around, if you want?" I threw my arm around Ethan's waist and squeezed.

"Please, please, pretty please?" I begged, trying to look cute. Ethan chuckled at my antics.

"Okay, okay, I'll get on it tonight," Ethan promised. We turned down an empty hall. This side of campus seemed to be deserted today.

"I don't know guys." Zeke began with a mischievous light in his eye. "Do we really want Lexie dating?"

My mouth dropped as the guys hemmed and hawed.

"Don't you fucking dare," I growled at them. The boys burst out laughing again. Ethan wrapped his arm around me.

"Don't worry, Beautiful, I'm on it," he said me before letting go. I shook my head at them.

"Where are we going tonight for homework?" Isaac asked the group.

"Jessica's not going to be home tonight, she's staying overnight at a friend's house." Asher offered.

Everyone was debating as we turned a corner. Pain tore through me as Bitch Ghost slammed into me. I stumbled, catching myself against the lockers. I rested my weight against the metal, having a hard time staying upright. My chest felt like a red-hot metal stake had been driven into it, making it hard to breathe. The ghost rolled over my mind like a black fog, trying to take control. I pushed back. No, this was my body. Fuck off! She poured her memories into my mind trying to drive me out with her pain. My head felt like it was exploding, my chest burned. I pushed back with my own memories, throwing them at her as if they were grenades. She backed away enough for me to gain some control over my body again. I couldn't beat her; she had too much juice. I could only hold her at a stand-still.

Fear shot through me as I opened my eyes. I was vaguely aware that I was sitting on the cement against the lockers, blood pouring from my nose. Zeke was yelling at me, his hands cupping my face, lifting so he could look at me.

"Lexie! Lexie!" he barked, demanding an answer. "Come on baby, don't do this to me."

Another hand pushed the hair out of my face. My body was completely limp. I only had minor control for now. Someone said hospital. No! Panic ripped through me. I had to tell them what to do, Bitch Ghost pushing down on me already. I only had a few moments of control left.

"No... hospital... Rory... home..." That was all I could manage before the bitch slammed down on me again and I had to focus on fighting her off. Her darkness crashed down on me, and I fought back with light, then my temper finally caught up, turning the light red. During all of this, I was aware of what was going on in the world. But it was very far away, like a dream you can't recall when you wake up.

Zeke pulled my cell phone out of my jacket and handed it off. He was shouting instructions to the others as he pulled me into his arms, lifting me as if I weighed nothing. He held me against his chest as he ran. My body was screaming at me every; nerve on fire as Bitch Ghost pushed back again trying to use pain to get me to stop fighting. I gave a little ground just enough so she'd feel the pain herself. She retreated a bit, letting me swim back to the surface.

My entire body was shaking as Zeke slid into the backseat of a car. He kept me in his lap as others were shouting. I heard Rory's voice. Relief poured through me. Rory! My vision swam, as the bitch hit me with everything at the same time, like a tidal wave crashing down on me. I was drowning.

Everything went black.

I CAME-TO GASPING. Deep dragging breaths as if I had actually stopped breathing. I couldn't open my eyes; I didn't understand what was happening. Very hot water rained down on me. Something hard was rubbing down my arms, my legs; something was rubbing on my scalp. I kept hearing my name but I couldn't move, couldn't answer, not yet. It took me several moments of breathing before I could grasp what was happening. Someone had me in their arms against their chest, my face was resting on a shirt, and they were standing under the spray from a shower. Hands were rubbing stuff against my skin, into my scalp; it felt like it had been hurting for some time.

"I'm back," I rasped out, too quiet to be heard over the shower. I swallowed then tried again, using what energy I had. "I'm back." I could only manage a whisper. That was it; it was all I could say.

"She's awake," a rich baritone announced from behind me. I knew that voice, I couldn't think through the pain to remember. Different sounds of relief were loud in my ears. I was shaking, freezing. The water felt too hot, but I was craving it. My head was throbbing so much it made my vision fade in and out, my stomach churned.

"Let me get in there." A few heartbeats later, a hot hand cupped my chin. "Show me your eyes, Lexie." I knew that voice, that was Rory. I didn't want to open my eyes; it would hurt. I tried to turn away into whoever had me; they were so warm.

"Lexie, now!" Rory shouted, hurting my ears; I whimpered, turning my head back. I used everything I had left to open my eyes. My vision swam, like looking up through water from the bottom of a pool. My teeth clattered. Rory's face was a big blur. The blur was coming closer. Then bright light stabbed through my head. I wanted to scream, but I could only whimper and cry. When the stabbing light went away, I buried my face against whoever held me, my forehead met warm skin, I smelled leather and engine grease. I knew that smell. Voices were loud and muffled.

"No bleed this time."

"She's freezing cold," a deep, gravelly voice vibrated through me. Zeke? I whimpered as the sound hurt my ears.

"Can you stand hotter water?"

Everything was so loud. I wanted to cover my ears, but my body wouldn't listen. All I could do was whimper. There was a movement against my forehead, and the water got hotter.

Something warm pressed into my hair. Everything faded away, and I slipped blissfully into unconsciousness.

I SLOWLY WOKE up to a dark room. A bone-deep ache was everywhere, even the bottom of my feet. Seriously, why did the bottom of my feet hurt? My head ached too much to try to figure it out. I braced myself and sat up slowly. I was gasping in pain when I finally managed it. There was movement in the dark.

"I'm turning on a lamp, Lexie." Rory's voice came from somewhere in the room.

I closed my eyes and saw the light from behind my eyelids. I slowly opened my eyes. A little bit at a time, it took a while. When my eyes finally adjusted, I found Rory, sitting on the edge of the bed watching me closely. I tried to speak, but my throat was dry. Rory reached over to the nightstand and handed me a glass of water. I took it, drinking down half of it. Rory handed me some pills; I didn't ask I just took them. I hurt too much to care. It took me a couple minutes before I looked around; I was in a queen-sized bed with a blue and green plaid comforter. There was a mahogany dresser with a TV on it.

"Where?" I asked, my voice so small. It was how I felt. Like one strong breeze, and I'd blow away.

"You're in my room; it was the closest to the front door." Rory kept his voice to a whisper. I was going through my memories, trying to remember how I got home. Then I remembered--the guys, Bitch Ghost, Zeke's eyes as he held my face, the others' panicked voices in the car.

"The guys saw everything, didn't they?" I asked, already knowing the answer. Praying he'd tell me differently.

"Yeah."

Panic gripped me, my stomach knotted. Oh God, they saw it all. I used a shaking hand to push my hair out of the way.

"Did you tell them?" I asked, my voice shaking. Please tell me you didn't, please tell me you lied your ass off.

"Just the basics, that you see the dead, that the Sight runs in the family," Rory answered me.

My stomach dropped, my chest aching.

"I wanted to leave the details to you."

I closed my eyes, tears pouring down my face.

It happened; it really happened. A week, it took one fucking week for them to find out.

I pulled my knees to my chest; I rested my forehead on them and covered my head with my arms as I cried. It was over. They knew I was a freak; they were gone. They'd never speak to me again. I started sobbing, my heart breaking. Every fear I had over the last week crashed down on me, making my chest so tight it was hard to breathe. I cared about them, I don't know how it happened, but I did. I cared about them. I sobbed knowing it was over. I was alone, all over again. I was the fucking freak again. I sobbed as my world crashed around me. I was alone again. I'm a freak; I'll always be alone. Arms wrapped around me and rocked me as I broke apart.

"Lexie, you're not a freak, honey. And you're not alone," Rory whispered into my hair. I hadn't even realized I spoke out loud.

I shook my head. I didn't care. It was over.

"They're gone." I gasped as everything poured out of me. I had nothing left. I didn't have any more fight. I was done. My heart was a raw and aching pit inside my chest. Just let the fucking dead have me, this hurt too much. I can't take this anymore.

I vaguely realized that Rory's arms were gone, but I didn't care. I rocked myself back and forth, sobbing.

Rory's voice said something, but I was too miserable to listen. Hands touched me, arms wrapped around me. I smelled vanilla and leather.

"Lexie, stop fucking crying," a deep voice growled.

"Ally, you need to calm down," a rich voice followed.

My head shot up, my heart stopped. Asher and Zeke were there.

"W-w-what?" I stammered, not understanding what I was seeing. "You're.... here..."

Asher reached out and brushed the hair from my face, while Zeke wiped the tears from my cheek. Zeke looked pissed off, and Asher's face was pale and drawn. I didn't understand. They were here? The tightness in my chest eased, I could breathe a little easier. Tears were running down my face as I stared at them uncomprehending. I was still crying, but I had stopped sobbing.

"Okay, boys back outside," Rory ordered. The guys looked like they wanted to argue but they obeyed. Rory shut the door behind them. He came back and sat in front of me again. I was still staring after the boys. They were still here? What? I looked to Rory, not understanding.

"They were all here as long as they could be," Rory said gently.

"All of them?" I asked softly. I couldn't wrap my head around it. All of them had been here? They had stayed?

Rory nodded, then proceeded to talk slowly and clearly.

"Those boys carried you home bloody, unconscious, and turning blue." Rory's haunted eyes met mine again. "Then they refused to leave you." Rory reached over, pulled out some tissues, and handed them to me. I sat there numb. "The others would still be here but Mile's and Isaac's parents called them home, Ethan had band practice." Rory reached out and brushed more of my hair away from my face. "They only felt like they could leave because Asher and Zeke were here."

"They all stayed?" I asked, my voice shaky, thin. I saw them; I knew they were outside the bedroom door. It was just so hard to believe. No one ever stayed.

Rory held my chin in his fingers and looked into my eyes.

"Those boys saved your life," he told me clearly. "I wasn't going to make it to you in time; I had to give them instructions on the phone, Lexie."

I blinked at him, my mind starting to work again. Slowly, but it was working.

"The salt? The shower?" I asked, needing confirmation.

Rory nodded. "All the boys. I got here just as you woke up," he explained. "The boys took turns holding you in that shower for over an hour trying to get your body temperature up. The others refused to leave the bathroom." Rory's thumbs wiped the moisture from my cheeks. His eyes still looking into mine, willing me to understand. "Those boys aren't going anywhere, Lexie. Stop expecting them to."

When what he was saying finally starting to sink in, I swallowed hard and nodded. Satisfied I got the message, Rory let go of my face. I used my tissues to wipe my nose. The boys really didn't leave me. They were still here, some had to go home, but they had been here. They still wanted me around. That last chunk of the wall around my heart crumble into dust. They weren't leaving. I fought back tears again as warmth filled my chest. I took me a while to remember what this feeling was. It was love, I felt loved, cared about. For the first time in years. Oh fuck, I need to stop crying. I took several deep breaths as I struggled to get myself under control.

I looked down at my clothes to distract myself. I was still wearing my cami that I wore under my sweater and my underwear. Towels and blankets surrounded me. My skin was raw and gritty, I needed a shower.

"Zeke knows about my back, but did anyone else see?" I asked It seemed stupid right now, but I wanted to know.

"If they did, I'm sure questions would have been asked," Rory reassured me.

I nodded, licking my lips.

"What time is it?" I asked, running a hand down my arm wiping the salt off my skin.

Rory checked his watch. "7:45."

"Where's Tara?" I sighed wearily.

"I told her to sleep at her mom's tonight." Rory's voice was understanding. "She still doesn't know about this, and I'd like to keep it that way as long as possible."

"Sounds like a plan," I agreed, especially if Tara was what I suspected.

Rory pulled me into a hug; I rested my head on his chest as he held me.

"We almost lost you, kid." His voice shook; I wrapped my arms around his waist and squeezed back. That feeling of being loved washed over me again. Oh, this feeling was going to take some getting used to.

"I'm not going anywhere," I whispered back. I hoped I wasn't lying. "I'm too stubborn." I felt him snort.

"I brought you some clothes from your room, they're on the dresser," Rory told me as he let me go. He brushed my hair off my face again. "Let's get you out there before those boys decide to break down the door."

I huffed at that. Then thought about it. Yeah, that sounded like something Zeke might do.

Rory got up and held out his hand. I took a deep breath for courage and took it. He helped pull me to my feet. My whole body throbbed with the sudden movement, and then a bone-deep ache settled in. Even my fucking feet hated me. Rory held on as I walked slowly towards the dresser. Once he knew I wasn't going to fall, he walked out the door, closing it behind him. I bit back a groan as I took my clothes off, every movement making me hurt more. I pulled on the black underwear, loose white t-shirt, and black sweatpants. I took a second to look in the mirror; I wasn't surprised to see I looked like shit. My hair was a tangled mess and had chunks of salt here and there. My face was even paler than usual, my eyes were red from crying, and I had bags under my eyes. Screw it. I almost died. I can look like shit.

I slowly walked to the bedroom door and opened it. Asher and Zeke were waiting a few feet from the door. At the sight of them, I started crying again. They really were here.

"I told you to stop crying, Lexie," Zeke growled, his face hard. I huffed at him as I wiped my cheek.

"Happy crying this time." I bit my bottom lip and looked up at them. "You guys are still here."

Asher looked at me like something hurt as he stepped forward and gently pulled me against him. One of his arms wrapped around my back, the other cradling the back of my head pressing my cheek to the middle of his chest. I wrapped my arms around his waist. It was an amazing hug, full of warmth and caring. Tears kept falling as I breathed in his cinnamon and vanilla scent.

"Did you really think you could get rid of us that easy?" Asher asked, his voice thick. He leaned down, putting his face in my hair. "You're stuck with us, Ally," he whispered to me. I sniffed and nodded against his chest. I think I was starting to believe it.

Asher held me long enough that Zeke tapped his shoulder.

"No, you held her the longest in the shower. Now it's my turn." Asher at snapped at him before pushing his face further into my hair. "Text the other guys. It'll help with the wait," he mumbled at Zeke. I vaguely heard Rory in the kitchen doing something. Asher was still holding on.

"Lexie, look over here for a second," Zeke asked, in his usual 'it's not really a request' voice. I opened my eyes. He was holding his phone up; there was the distinct sound of a picture being taken. The shit head.

"Zeke, I look like shit," I groaned, wiping more tears away. The corner of his mouth twitched as he focused on doing something with his phone.

"The guys wanted proof you were alive and awake." He looked up his eyes meeting mine. "I put 'Getting suffocated by Asher' in the text, just so you know."

I snorted as I began rubbing Asher's lower back.

"Ally girl, you scared the hell out of me," Asher whispered into my hair.

"I didn't mean to." Asher grunted before giving me a small squeeze and letting go. He stepped back, and Zeke stepped forward immediately. His hard eyes softened as they ran over my face. He bent down to pick me up, one arm under my butt the other lightly across my back. My arms moved around his neck, my face finding a spot between his neck and shoulder. I took a deep breath of leather and engine grease. I had never had a hug like it in my life.

"You didn't leave," I whispered as my tears fell against his skin.

"I'm not going anywhere, baby," he whispered back, his gravelly voice rough. He took a deep breath and let it out slowly. "Never stop breathing on me again," he whispered in my ear as he rested his cheek against mine. I smiled into his neck. "You hear me?"

"I hear ya," I whispered back, it was muffled, but I was sure he heard me because his arms tightened around me.

"I hate to interrupt, but she needs to eat, or she's going to crash," Rory announced from the dining room.

I thought Zeke would put me down, but instead he walked into the dining area, carrying me; holding onto me as long as he could. He gave me one last squeeze before setting me down in a chair. I turned in my chair, wiping my tears off my face. Then I saw the huge plate of food Rory had set out. A big, thick steak with a pile of potatoes, and a small amount of green beans. My stomach growled. I started digging into the food, my body craving it.

"Ally usually eats a quarter of that; can she really finish it all?" Asher asked, sounding genuinely curious. I didn't bother answering. I needed to get the food down, or I'd be in real big trouble.

"Just watch, during after-burn you use a lot of energy, especially stored fat. I bet you she's a couple pounds lighter than she was this morning," Rory explained.

Feeling a little stronger, I stopped eating long enough to be a smart ass.

"Yeah, it's the best diet in the world," I told them with fake enthusiasm before taking another bite of potatoes. My joke fell flat; Rory glared at me.

"It would be if not for the threat of becoming a vegetable, or oh yeah, death," he said sarcastically, though his voice was hard. He really didn't like my joke.

The boys watched in stunned silence as I finished off the plate of food--it didn't take long. I pushed the plate away and leaned back, my stomach very full.

"That was so good," I announced.

"Asher cooked, I only bought the groceries," Rory admitted gesturing to Asher. I turned to Asher whose cheeks were turning a tinge pink.

"Really?"

Asher nodded, one hand rubbing the back of his neck.

I turned to Rory. "Can we keep him? Please?" I asked, sounding entirely serious. Which I was. That was the best meal I'd had in years.

Rory rolled his eyes at me. There was a knock at the front door. Frowning, Rory got to his feet and answered.

"Where is she?" A honey like voice demanded. I turned a little in my chair to see Isaac darting past Rory and towards me. I balled up and covered my head with my arms.

"Gently, gently, gently," I whimpered painfully, almost squeaking. When I wasn't pounced on, I peeked out of my arms to see Asher had intercepted Isaac; Zeke was halfway out of his chair as if Asher had just been faster.

"Easy, she's sore." Asher's voice was soft but firm.

Isaac's eyes were running over me, his pale face serious as he nodded. He knocked Asher's hand away as he came toward me again. He knelt down on the floor and wrapped his arms around me, knees and all. It was a couple minutes before he shifted, lifting me and putting me in his lap on the floor. My head against his chest, my legs draped over one of his. Tears were falling again as I wrapped my arms around his neck.

"You came back," I whispered, not quite realizing I spoke out loud. He squeezed me tighter.

"No shit." he whispered, his voice thick. He just held me against him as if he could keep all the bad things away as long as I was with him. It felt really fucking good. It was a while before he spoke to me again.

"You scared the shit out of me, Red," Isaac growled against my hair. "You ever do that again I'm going to smack you silly." One hand cupped my face, his thumb caressing my cheekbone. It was comforting.

"Sorry, Cookie Monster."

"Shh, I'm still mad at you."

Isaac was still holding me when there was another knock on the door. Isaac turned me in his arms as Rory opened the door. Ethan's eyes went straight to me as he strode through the great room. Isaac intervened this time.

"Soft hands, brother, soft hands."

Without stopping, Ethan nodded that he understood without. He held out a hand, I took it. He pulled me to my feet, wrapped his arms around my waist and pulled me to him. One arm running up my spine, his hand around the back of my neck. My nose bumped his collarbone; I lifted my chin to his shoulder for comfort. I wrapped my arms around his shoulders holding him. Tears were falling again.

"Should I even bother closing the door this time?" Rory asked the room.

"Probably not, I bet Miles is on the way over here," Isaac offered, his voice strained.

"You really came back," I whispered starting to believe that they weren't leaving me.

Ethan dropped his forehead to my shoulder and took slow deep breaths.

"Always," he whispered back, his voice shaking. His spicy cologne filled my nose as he actually shook in my arms. I felt tears fall on my skin that weren't mine. I held his shoulders tighter and pressed my body completely against his, from chest to knee. His hands kept flexing against me, as if he wanted to squeeze tighter but was stopping himself. I moved one hand around the back of his neck and stroked it, trying to comfort him.

"I'm okay, I'm here. I'm fine," I kept whispering. My heart ached. Ethan and Isaac's reactions were intense. Like they were in a terrifying nightmare, but now they were awake and trying to reassure themselves it was all a dream. I didn't understand how to make it better. So, I just held him against me.

I spotted Rory out of the corner of my eye standing at the table; he was watching Ethan hold me with a hard look on his face. Asher leaned toward him and said something I couldn't hear. Rory's face softened, then quickly his face was full of understanding.

"Why didn't you tell us?" Ethan asked, his voice not like himself. I swallowed hard.

"I didn't want you to think I was a freak," I whispered.

"That was dumb, Beautiful, very dumb."

I smiled into his hair. He was starting to sound like himself again.

"How was band practice?" I asked.

He barked a laugh once against my shoulder. "Shitty, beyond shitty. They wanted to kick me out I was so bad." He took a steady breath. "I told them to fuck off."

I wiped my tears from my cheek. There was another knock on the door.

"Can I come in?" Miles asked. Rory must have left the door open this time.

"Will you just get in here?" Isaac groaned at him.

Ethan pulled back from me wiping at his face before joining the others at the table.

I turned around to find Miles standing behind me. For once, he didn't hesitate. He wrapped an arm around my shoulders and pulled me to him, his other hand cupping my neck his thumb resting in front of my ear. He held my cheek against his collarbone, my forehead against his neck. I took a deep breath of his wintergreen scent and let it out. His body was relaxed against mine.

"You're really here." I couldn't seem to stop saying that to them.

"As long as you want me," he whispered back to me, his voice had that silky note to it. I was crying again. "Is this why you expect people to leave you?"

I bit my lip before answering.

"After they find out, they leave." My voice was a bit steadier but still shaky.

"Not anymore."

I smiled into his shirt, soaking it with my tears.

"You know, I thought you had a brain tumor," he said. He sounded so relieved that I snorted into his shoulder.

"I'm sorry." I swallowed hard before trying to make it easier on him. "And you thought you were weird."

He snorted and held me a little tighter.

"Unique, Lexie, unique. Remember?" he whispered back to me.

I gave a small nod, my face rubbing against his hoodie. I was vaguely aware of the others in the room.

"How'd you get out of the house?" Ethan asked, from behind me.

"Snuck out," Isaac answered.

"I thought I saw Mom's car out there. She's going to be pissed."

"Miles probably snuck out, too," Isaac pointed out.

"But he didn't steal his mom's car," Ethan replied.

"Are you sure you're okay?" Miles asked, his voice concerned. "Do you taste anything strange? Are you numb anywhere? Has your vision changed?"

I smiled into his chest. He'd been looking up the symptoms of a brain bleed.

"I'm okay, Miles, just hurting and tired," I whispered to him.

"Do you need anything? I can have a doctor here in fifteen minutes."

I squeezed him a little tighter. That was Miles, always looking to make things better.

"Hey, why didn't you warn Miles to go easy?" Isaac accused someone.

"It's Miles," several voices answered at once.

I smiled against Miles' hoodie again. It wasn't much longer before Miles started to get tense against me. I let him go then and stepped back. His ears were pink as he adjusted his glasses, looking everywhere but at me. That only lasted a moment before his eyes were running over me assessing.

"So, can you please explain what's going on?" Miles asked politely.

I nodded and walked back to the table. I sat down between Asher and Isaac. I looked around the table, still amazed that they were there. I was tired, wrung out. But they were there, so I started talking.

"I've been seeing the dead since I was a kid. I remember seeing my first ghost at 5 years old." I kept my eyes on the table as I laid it out for them. "It's usually not like this. A ghost will find me or run into me. Some need someone to listen, they tell their story to me. Others just need to be convinced that they don't belong here anymore. And some just don't realize they're dead."

I paused and looked up, meeting Rory's eyes.

"And then there is the kind that wants to watch the world burn.

169

They're angry. They want to cause as much pain and damage as possible." My voice cracked, I swallowed hard.

Rory got up and walked into the kitchen then brought me out a bottle of water. I smiled my thanks. I tried to open it, but my hands were shaking again. Asher took the bottle from me, opened it then handed it back. I thanked him and took a deep drink before continuing.

"All ghosts will interact with their surroundings, the sound of footsteps when no one is there. An empty chair rocking. But the other kind..." I was looking down at the table again. "They are the ones that scratch, bite, and try to jump into your body and take it over. They're the ones they make horror movies about." I looked around the group feeling naked. I've never had to tell anyone outside the family about this, they never stuck around long enough. This was going to be harder than I thought "Is that what happened today? You got jumped?" Ethan asked, his face turning dark.

I met his eyes and nodded, then explained, my gaze on the middle of the table again.

"On my first day, I saw a dead girl at the school, judging from her clothes I'd say she was from the 60s. She is so angry that she's dead that she wants to tear into everyone around her. Make them suffer like she is." I shook my head as I remembered her. "When they get like that, I just stay the hell away."

I looked around at the guys again, then settled my eyes on Rory. "I don't know if there is a way to help them, to stop them or even how to get rid of them." There. I finally admitted to Rory how little I actually knew. My lungs were tight as my eyes filled with tears again. A storm of emotions raced through me. I was ashamed that I didn't know the answer that I knew I should. I was embarrassed that it's taken me this long to admit it. But connecting all of that was this deep feeling of helplessness. I didn't know what I was doing. I'd been winging it for so long that I've never had the chance to figure it out.

I bit my bottom lip, using the pain to chase back the tears. I really needed to stop fucking crying. It worked. I took a shaky breath and let it out slow.

"If you saw her that day, why didn't she jump you then?" Asher asked, his face neutral.

"She tried a little, she reached out, and I told her no," I explained, my voice stronger now that I was back on a topic I knew something about. "You can keep them out, by putting your energy into saying no. By simply meaning it. But if they have more juice, they can keep trying." I took a drink of water before continuing. "The first day, she used everything she had and only managed to give me a nosebleed."

Asher frowned at me.

"That's why you've been getting nosebleeds at school? This ghost is attacking you? Every day?" Isaac asked, looking disturbed by the news.

I nodded and then tried to explain "In this case, yes, though a ghost doesn't have to be attacking me. I usually get a small one just by being near a ghost for a while, it happens all the time."

"Hold it," Zeke growled, his eyes on my face. "The library?"

"Yeah," I said, "there was a dead woman in the stacks. Two ghosts in one day and the physical side-effects get worse."

"I think I know the answer to this but, the hike?" Ethan asked, rubbing his fingers over his eyes.

I bit the corner of my bottom lip before answering.

"Yeah, Karen Malone only wanted her body found," I admitted.

"You weren't sick because of the body, were you?" Miles asked, his face blank.

"That had two parts. She walked with us for a while so she could show me where her body was."

"How long?" Isaac asked, his arms crossed over his chest.

"Since the first time I supposedly had to find a tree, till we found her," I admitted, wincing. Rory frowned.

"How long was that boys?" Rory demanded.

Oh, come on, I almost died today. Didn't that give me a 'don't get chewed out' pass?

"Forty-five minutes to an hour," Asher offered.

Rory's eyes bored into mine. I swallowed hard.

"God damn it, Lexie!" Rory shouted at me. "You can't fucking expose yourself to the dead for that long!"

"She stayed back, mostly," I raced to explain. "I only had a nose-bleed for the last ten minutes."

Rory ran his hands through his hair, clearly pissed with me. But he was quiet, so I continued.

"At the end, when we found her body she stood too close and the memories of how she died kind of poured into my head. I felt every-thing that she did when she died." The guys cursed, Miles clenched his jaw. "I usually can keep that from happening, but I was distracted at the time."

I looked back at the guys and went back to what I was trying to tell them before. "Basically, I get nosebleeds two ways: The first is just by being around a ghost. It also depends on how old the ghost is; the older they are, the more juice they have. The more juice, the faster I have a bloody nose." I took another drink before continuing. "But the angry ones like to do it on purpose."

I wasn't explaining this very well. So I tried again. "All the angry ones want is to hurt someone, most of the time. They can barely manage it on a normal person. It takes everything out of them." I swal-lowed trying to get rid of the knot in my throat. "Then here I come, a person sensitive to the dead, which means they don't use as much energy to hurt me as they would a normal person." I shrugged and summed up. "I'm a shiny new toy to play with."

There were curses all around the table. Ethan's eyes were stormy; his face dark, Isaac was frowning. Miles' eyes were unfocused. Asher seemed bewildered. And Zeke, Zeke was glaring at the table, his face hard, jaw clenched. The effect was scary. His blue eyes met mine; he was shaken. He blinked, and it was gone so fast I started doubting I saw it at all. His face was like stone again.

"Let's go back to this afternoon," Rory said, breaking the tense silence. "I know she kept you from getting to your last class on Friday. You did some research and had that theory about barriers."

"Yeah, and I was wrong. She's getting more juice from some-where," I admitted freely. I fucked up, and I had no clue what to do.

"How?" Rory asked.

I scoffed out a laugh. "I have no fucking idea," I said wearily, keeping my gaze on Rory. "She shouldn't have been able to. She bulldozed me," I explained, my voice becoming hard. "She took control hard and fast."

"Is that why you dropped like that? She took control?" Miles asked.

"Sort of, I reacted fast enough that she couldn't take full control. She had control of my body; I had control of my mind. We were both too busy attacking each other for either of us to use my body." I answered him before turning back to Rory. "I realized pretty damn quickly that I couldn't knock her out of me. I managed to get the upper hand long enough to get a few words out." My eyes moved to Zeke, met his gaze then back to Rory's. "After that, I could only hold her off. She realized that I was stalling. She slammed down on me and knocked me out. The last thing I remember is the backseat of a car."

"If she knocked you out, then why didn't she take control of your body?" Miles asked, pushing his glasses back onto his nose.

"She couldn't, I was still in my body, and my body was out cold. So, she did the only thing she could." I looked at Rory hesitating.

"She tried to kill her," Rory told them for me, his face dark.

Curses sounded around the table. Isaac rested his hands on his head, his fingers pressing into his scalp. Ethan was twirling one of the rings on his fingers, Asher began rubbing his neck, Miles' fingers were tapping, and Zeke was running his hand through his hair. They all looked upset or pissed to some degree; Miles' face was blank.

Rory looked around the table at the guys. "She would have died if you guys weren't there, if you hadn't listened to her." Rory swallowed hard. "Someone would have called an ambulance; she would have gone to the hospital and died. It would have looked like an aneurysm."

I watched his hands shaking. He was remembering Claire. He couldn't take this right now, not after today.

"Rory," I called my voice soft. "I got this now, it's okay to take a walk."

Rory met my eyes, his brown eyes brimming with tears. He nodded, got up and walked out the back door. I waited until I knew he was away from the house. I looked around the table as they looked at me questioningly. "That's how my Aunt Claire died," I explained. "She was eight years old."

Soft curses came from them. I leaned forward, resting my forearms on the table determined to get it out. "So, if you're unconscious and you have a dead person's soul inside trying to kill you, the only thing you can do is get them out." I looked around at their faces, trying to judge how they were taking this. I didn't get much. "Hot water keeps your temperature from dropping, while scrubbing with salt forces the ghost to leave."

"Why salt?" Miles asked, his eyes calculating.

"It's a pure mineral, I'm guessing. It's the only thing my family has found that keeps the dead away." I bit my lower lip hard before looking up at them. "Rory told me you guys were the ones who got me in the shower, started scrubbing with salt." I looked around the table meeting each pair of eyes. "Thank you, you guys saved my life."

A tense moment followed. No one knew what to say. So naturally, I had to be a smart ass. I pretended to look confused. "Who's the butt guy? Cause I've got, like, road rash on my ass."

Everyone burst out laughing; it was a little desperate, slightly hysterical but exactly what we needed. Miles was the first to pull it together.

"You don't really, right?" Miles asked, actually looking concerned. I shook my head as another round of laughter went up, this time at Miles. When we all settled down, I grinned at them.

"So, that's everything. You now know all my deep dark secrets," I told them, half joking, but mostly feeling naked in front of them. I really didn't like feeling this vulnerable; it made me twitchy.

"Seems to me..." Miles began, drawing everyone's attention by pulling his cell phone out. "We need to find something that will keep a ghost from touching you. Correct?"

I smirked at his choice of words.

"Yes, I need a ghost condom," I told him in my most serious voice. I burst out giggling at myself as the boys groaned, a couple of them chuckled. Miles' ears turned red. I liked being a smart ass.

"Oh, Red. That was bad," Isaac told me still laughing.

I shrugged as I stopped laughing and was serious again.

"I don't know if there is anything like that," I admitted, looking down at the middle of the table again. "I've never really had a chance to do any research. Not with..." I stopped myself before I told them about my mother. I looked up to find almost all the guys were looking at their phones. Thankfully, no one had noticed.

"You were just trying to survive, Lexie," Miles said absently, tapping away at his phone. "Just surviving isn't good enough, we want you to thrive." Several sounds of agreement, including a grunt or two came from around the table.

I couldn't stop staring at them. They weren't leaving. I had a problem; it was freaky and weird. Instead of walking away, they were trying to find an answer. They were fucking amazing. I felt that feeling again in my chest again, that feeling of being cared about. It was really going to take time to get used to it.

I picked up my phone and started looking, too. A while later, Rory came back inside and asked what we were all doing. Miles was explaining when Asher interrupted.

"Okay, I've got one." He didn't bother looking up from his phone. "Rosemary. It says it's a banishing herb."

"How is she going to use that?" Miles asked, pushing his glasses back up his nose.

"Maybe she could wear it," Asher offered, his eyes still on his screen.

"Anise can work too... oh wait that can be toxic." Isaac's voice started happy but then slid into grumpy.

"Yeah, we're trying to keep her alive," Zeke grumbled.

"I found something, but it's for the house," Ethan announced, hesitating.

I looked up at him and nodded, encouraging him to continue.

He looked back down at his phone and read out loud. "Growing Betony around your house will help keep evil and malicious entities out."

"Guess we're getting some Betony," Rory declared. "That'll have to wait till spring, though."

I looked up and found him looking through his own phone. It went on like that for over several hours--the boys calling out what they found and debating the best way to use it. It was near 11 when Rory called it and sent the boys home. I gave them each their own hug, thanking them again for saving my ass. Then they were gone. Rory let me go to bed, for once, without icing my back.

CHAPTER 10

I bolted up in my bed heart racing. Gasping as my head throbbed. That fucking chill running down my neck. Fear tightened my chest as I snapped awake.

"Shit, fuck, shit, fuck," I cursed, my eyes closed tight against the pain. "Claire that better be you," I snarled out to the room.

"Yeah, sorry," a girl's voice replied. "I felt you in trouble today."

Claire must have backed up because the pain went down to manageable. I opened my eyes and turned on the lamp on my desk. I looked at my Aunt Claire from across the room. The 8-year-old was dressed in a pair of jeans with a hole in one knee, and a Care Bears t-shirt from the 80s. Her face was sweet with her dark red braids down to her shoulders. Her green eyes smiled at me. I put my feet on the floor and rubbed the sleep from my eyes.

"Yeah, I got jumped today." My voice was still sleepy. "By a ghost that shouldn't have had that much juice."

I saw Claire's "bad news face", the one every 8-year-old has when they don't want to tell you something. Her nose scrunched, her mouth twisted, and she squirmed.

"What?" I asked immediately.

Claire's shoulders lifted as if she took a breath, even though she couldn't.

"I was out of town looking for someone to help you. Someone gifted." She shrugged and dug her shoe into the floor. "I taught you everything I could years ago, but it's not enough." Claire wasn't too far away for me to feel her emotions. She felt so guilty for not being able to help more. I couldn't have that.

"Claire, without you I would have died or gone insane by now," I told her honestly. "You have saved my life, a lot."

She looked up at me, her eyebrows raised, looking hopeful.

"Really?"

I snorted. "Really." I got the smile I loved to see from her; it made her whole face shine.

"Well, I finally found one, someone who can help," she announced.

Everything was silent. It didn't quite compute in my head for a full minute.

"Seriously?"

She nodded, her braids bobbing.

"Who? Where?" I couldn't even form a complete sentence.

"She has a shop in Bridgeport, it's a couple towns away, around the mountain."

I got up, tore into my bag and pulled out a notebook and pen. Claire gave me the name of the shop and the address.

"She's a witch, so she's used to working with, well, the living. But she could hear me a bit," she explained. "She might not be able to, you know, give you lessons like I did. But she's a good place to start."

I was so happy I could have kissed her, if she had a body and all.

"Claire, this is great news," I said. "What was with the bad news face?"

Claire started playing with one of her braids. "The dead here are weird, angry, they're not right," she told me. I raised an eyebrow.

"There are always some angry ones," I offered, though my stomach was knotting.

She shook her head; she looked scared.

"Not like this. Ghosts have more juice than they should. Like, even the newly dead. There's a whole lot of energy floating around, just waiting to be picked up." She twirled her braid in her fingers. "The whole area is...wrong. It scares me." Her eyes met mine. "The other dead here scare me; I don't think I can be around them, not until it's fixed."

I nodded, suddenly very eager to get Claire out of town. How the hell was I going to fix this? Where the hell was I going to start? I couldn't have Claire scared all the time.

"Okay, stay out of town. Keep your head down."

Claire waved her hand dismissively.

"I'll just go to the cemetery, the dead never go there," she said. "And that way, if you need me, you can find me."

It's strange but true, the cemetery was always empty of the dead. When I had too many encounters with ghosts in the past, I would drive to a cemetery and sleep in the back of the blazer. There was still a sleeping bag and pillow in there.

"Sounds good to me." I noticed the way she was edging towards the wall, a small smile on her face.

"Are you going to pop in on Rory?"

She smiled like the little kid she was. "Yeah, just want to mess with him a bit. I'm thinking the butter dish this time. I'll see you later, stay safe."

"You too." I shut off the light and climbed back into bed. My head wouldn't shut off. What the hell would give the dead that much juice? What can warp the dead? And why the hell was there energy just lying around to be picked up? And how the hell was I supposed to fix it?

I wasn't going to sleep. I got up, turned on my laptop, and spent the next five hours trying to find some explanation as to why the dead would be acting so strange. I looked for every variation on the Sight, every religion I could, every culture I found. When my alarm went off, I still had nothing.

I took a quick shower and got dressed for the day. I dressed for my mood. My favorite old pair of boot-cut blue jeans. A loose black, v-neck, boyfriend shirt tucked into the front of my pants, and a green and gold plaid, long-sleeved shirt left unbuttoned. I pulled the front half of my hair back into a small clip to keep it off my face and said fuck the rest.

I heard Rory shouting downstairs about his losing his keys as I was putting on my belt. It made me smile. That was Claire's favorite trick, hiding his keys in weird places.

I made sure to pick up coffee on my way to school, four espresso shots this time. The barista had looked at me like I was nuts. I didn't care; I needed caffeine. It was overcast today; big thick gray clouds hung low over the town. Please don't rain on me again; in this shirt, it would be hard to hide it if I was cold. Some blue Honda parked in my spot so I had to park on a side street a block from the school. I didn't really care; I had coffee.

I was drinking that coffee when I turned the corner into the hall and found Zeke and Asher waiting for me at my locker. Zeke in his usual black. Asher wore a button-down shirt again--but today it was open, showing a white t-shirt underneath--and his tan cargo pants and a blue hoodie. Overnight it had really started to sink in that they weren't going anywhere. A small part of me thought they were nuts, the rest of me was just grateful.

"Hey," I greeted them, yawning. I was trying to open my locker for the third time when Zeke stepped up behind me, reached around and grabbed the dial.

"What's the combo?" he barked at me, but I felt numb enough that I didn't care. I gave it to him.

"Ally girl, didn't you get any sleep last night?" Asher asked, coming over to lean against Isaac's locker. As Zeke was opening my locker, he stood close enough that I felt his body heat.

"Man, you're like a furnace." I don't know why I said it, but since I did, I didn't really care. Zeke finished opening my locker for me and moved to my left to lean against the locker next to mine. I felt both of them examining my face.

"About 3 hours, after-burn sleep doesn't count as rest," I answered Asher bluntly. Then I tried for cheerful. "No rest for the ones who see dead people." Yeah, that fell flat.

I looked at my bag, the coffee in my hand, then at the books.

Figuring out what I was going to do was taking longer than I liked to admit. I finally handed Asher my coffee and started loading my books into my bag. "I saw my Aunt Claire last night," I told them, my voice matter-of-fact. "She said the dead in town aren't right, something is wrong with them. Other ghosts are also getting extra juice that's just floating around out there to be picked up."

I closed my locker. Then looked up at them, Asher looked surprised. Zeke's brow had drawn down. Then I realized I hadn't told them that Claire was a ghost. I waved my hand dismissively. "Oh yeah, Claire's a ghost, she's been helping me since I was 8. She's honestly the only reason I'm alive today. Don't tell Rory." I stopped talking and took a long drink of coffee. Zeke raised an eyebrow before looking at Asher.

"She sounds drunk," Asher told Zeke. "You know, like her filter is shut off."

Zeke smiled wickedly. "We can ask whatever we want," he said.

They both looked very happy with the idea. I swallowed my drink and continued.

"Anyway, it scared Claire, so she's going to hide out where there aren't any other ghosts. Ya know, the cemetery." I took another drink.

"There aren't any ghosts at the cemetery?" Asher asked. "That's weird."

"Why is that weird? You don't see people in the cemetery so why would the dead want to be there?" I asked as if it were obvious.

I took another drink. I was halfway through my giant coffee. My brain was starting to wake up; I blinked and looked up at them. "Coffee is cure for no filter, so if you have questions ask them now," I warned, my voice turning singsong. Yeah, I was extremely tired.

"What do you really think of my sister Jessica?" Asher asked his face excited. I blew a raspberry.

"Bully, bitch, and a drama queen. I would have told you that normally." They both started laughing as I took a long drink of coffee. It was finally starting to kick in, though I still couldn't really control my mouth.

"What's your favorite kind of food?" Zeke asked grinning.

"Chinese."

"What's your favorite color?" Asher asked. I took another drink and gestured to my clothes.

"Take a guess."

"What, green or black?" Zeke asked.

"Both." Finally, the coffee kicked in, and my brain woke up. It was like I was in a haze and now everything was sharp. All my gears were finally moving again. I blinked hard a couple times and looked up at the boys. "And you're out of time." The boys burst out laughing again.

"What did we miss?"

I turned to see Isaac and Ethan joining us. Ethan in all black again, with his silver hoops in his ear. Isaac wore a bright blue hoodie today, orange shirt, and dark blue jeans.

"Apparently when Lexie gets really, really tired her filter shuts off," Asher announced, holding back another laugh.

"We've been asking her questions the last couple of minutes," Zeke chimed in.

"Ooh! I want in on this!" Isaac got excited.

"Too late, my coffee kicked in."

His smiled dropped.

"Oh, that's not fair," Isaac whined.

"Before I forget," Asher tapped my shoulder. "I picked this up this morning." He handed me a little brown bottle labeled rosemary oil.

"Asher, you are my hero for the day, and if it works, you'll be for the week, maybe month, possibly year," I told him happily as I opened the bottle. There was a plastic ball for rolling just like on a perfume bottle. I quickly rolled a bit on my wrists, on both sides of my neck. Then for an extra measure, I pulled out the neck of my shirt and rolled some between my breasts right over my heart. I knew I was kind of flashing the guys, but I was wearing a bra. I was covered.

While I was doing that, a guy was walking by watching me, slowing down the more he looked. "Keep walking," I snapped at him as I pulled the bottle out and readjusted my shirt. The guys burst out laughing, and the guy hurried off.

"That... uh... was quite a sight there, Lexie," Ethan said, smiling.

"That was a good view, but I think Zeke got a better one," Isaac replied.

I stopped to think about that. Zeke was two heads taller than I was; I reached the middle of his chest. And he was standing right next to me, towering over me. Then again, Asher was a head and a half taller than I was.

"Yeah, a great view," Zeke admitted.

I looked up at Asher, whose cheeks were slightly pink. Asher had a great view too. I sighed. I know I should be embarrassed; a normal girl would be blushing like hell right now. But I have nice breasts. Anyway, it was kind of nice to see that they remembered I was a girl every once in a while.

I clapped once.

"Okay, let's stop talking about my breasts."

"You guys were talking about her chest?" Miles asked, his face full of disbelief, as he walked up to fill in the circle.

"Not anymore," Ethan answered.

I was looking closely at Miles. His hair didn't look like it was combed; he had big bags under his eyes. He was also wearing a collared shirt, buttoned all the way up.

"Miles, are you okay?" I asked, worrying more the longer I looked at him.

Miles' mouth made a tense line before answering.

"You guys know how hard I sleep, right?"

"Yeah, you work until you pass out," Asher said.

"Well, I woke up last night to my room freezing cold, as in 'ice actually forming on the windows cold'," Miles said.

My heart dropped. I was afraid I knew where he was going with this.

He stepped in closer to us and lowered his voice. "Then something was choking me. Really choking me." Miles undid the top two buttons of his shirt and it aside. Five bruised smudges in the shape of finger-tips wrapped around his throat.

My stomach knotted as fear raced through me. That wasn't possi-ble; ghosts didn't leave their haunting grounds. They couldn't jump from place to place. Claire was an exception because she was psychic when she was alive. But I doubt Bitch Ghost was. Seeing those smudges on Miles' neck terrified me, not for myself but for the guys. Deep inside, something ignited and began a slow burn.

"I was about to pass out," he continued, "when it finally let go. And my room smelled like patchouli."

I kept my face completely calm; there was no reason to freak the guys out.

I held out the bottle of oil.

"Let's have everyone put this on," I suggested; my voice light like it wasn't a big deal. "And let's have everyone sleepover at my house tonight. Just to be safe." I was going to stick those guys in a salt circle so fast their heads were going to spin. Rory too, if I had to.

"You sure that's a good idea?" Isaac asked, rolling the oil along his neck.

Yes! Can't you see I'm freaking out here?

I nodded, keeping up my fake calm.

"Yeah, I think all of us in the same house would be the best option," Asher said, handing me back the oil after everyone was done. I took it and tucked it into my pocket.

"Is Rory going to be cool with this?" Ethan asked.

No! He's going to kill me, bring me back and kill me again. Having guys over was one thing, having them sleep over was entirely another.

"Oh yeah, I'll explain what's happening. He'll agree once he knows what's going on." I lied through my teeth. Hell, he might if he lets me explain anything at all before he strangles me.

The first bell rang. Quickly, I said, "Bring pillows, sleeping bags, jammies and clothes for tomorrow. Alright?" I waited until everyone agreed to spend the night at Rory's house.

Everyone headed to class except Zeke and Miles who were both watching me with a strange look on their faces. I picked up my bag and walked around the corner. In the exact opposite direction of my class. I all but ran across campus. I had to find a way to protect the guys; I couldn't let them get hurt because of me. How the fuck did she change locations? Fuck! She should have popped back to the campus yesterday, drained as a fucking dead battery. What the fuck is going on?! I don't know what the fuck to do! This shouldn't be happening! When I figure out how, I'm going to rip that ghost to shreds. By the time I reached the edge of campus, my chest was tight, and it was a little hard to breathe.

"Lexie!"

I looked over my shoulder to see Zeke striding towards me, his face was determined. I don't remember my train of thought, but I knew that Zeke would stop me from leaving, and I had to go. We needed answers.

I turned away from him and ran across the street. Zeke's boots speed up behind me. My heart slammed against my ribs as I jumped onto the curb in front of me and kept going. I spotted my Blazer at the end of the block and pumped my arms harder. I was halfway there before Zeke caught me. A thick arm snagged me around the waist. I was yanked off my feet, my butt slamming into his stomach, my back against his chest. I pushed my weight forward trying to make him drop me when his other arm wrapped around my chest. His arm between my breasts, his hand on my right shoulder pinning me back against his chest. I swung my legs around, cursing at him. It did nothing; he was as steady as a rock.

"Let me go!" I snarled through my teeth. I lifted my legs as high as I could and threw them out, trying to knock him off balance. He budged, barely.

"When you calm down," he said calmly.

I didn't want calm. I wasn't calm so how could he be calm?! I yanked at his arm across my chest, using everything I had.

"I have to go!" I yelled, swinging my legs again, hoping to get one of his legs. He dodged and lifted me higher, taking my shorter legs out of range. My head tilted back, my face was looking up at the sky.

"You have to stop freaking out," he growled against my neck.

"I will scream Zeke, I swear to God!" I warned him, trying to slam my head against his, hoping to stun him.

He pressed his face against my neck dodging me.

185

"Go ahead. I think they'll believe me over you right now, anyway."
His voice never lost that annoying calm.

"You have no idea what's going on!" I shouted, hitting my fists
against his hold.

"You're freaking out. That's what's going on."

"Of course, I'm freaking out! I don't know what the fuck to do!" I
yelled vehemently. I stopped fighting Zeke and covered my face with
shaking hands. Out of breath, I rubbed my hands down my face then
resting them against his arm across my chest.

"You have no idea how bad this is," I told him, tears running down
my face and past my earlobes. "Miles got hurt! That shouldn't have
happened. They aren't supposed to change locations like that." I took a
deep breath, trying to calm down; it was all I could do, being
completely pinned against him. "Claire is scared of the other ghosts in
town, something is fucking with them. There is energy flying everywhere." I took another breath, my voice getting quieter. "I'm in over
my head, and I'm taking you guys with me."

That was it; I was out of fight. I hung limply in Zeke's arms, my
hands resting against his forearm.

"I'm guessing it's Miles getting hurt that's bothering you the most?"
Zeke asked.

I nodded, the back of my head rubbing against his shoulder, tears
still falling as I looked up at the gray sky.

"It happened to him, it can happen to you and the others." I took a
shaking breath. "I can't let that happen, not because of me."

He was silent for a heartbeat.

"Baby, this isn't your fault." His voice was gentle. The scruff on his
face rubbed on my neck as he spoke. "Miles didn't get hurt because
of you."

I shook my head, he was wrong. Miles did get hurt, it's all my fault.

"Yes, he did. If I wasn't here, none of you would be in danger,"
I said.

"Did you send the ghost over to Miles' house? Are you the one who
amped up the power to the dead in town?" he asked me, his voice soft
and full of understanding.

I sniffed and wiped my tears away from my face. "No."

"Then you aren't the one who caused it," he pointed out logically. "Whatever this is, it was happening before you even got here."

I was quiet for several minutes, going over what he said in my mind. Zeke stood like a rock, waiting patiently in the middle of the sidewalk. Was he right? I know I didn't cause the energy floating around. And I knew I didn't send Bitch Ghost over to Miles. And.... Claire did say the whole area is wrong, and I've only been here for a few days. I cursed. Zeke was right; I wasn't the one who hurt Miles. I hadn't started this. But I sure as hell was going to end it. I swallowed hard, took a big calming breath, and let it out. Then, as usual, I was a smart ass.

"Well, if you're going to bring logic into it," I said. I was starting to feel better than I had since getting jumped. I was going to find whoever hurt Miles and beat them into the bedrock. Magically speaking... maybe physically, you know, if it was possible.

Zeke smiled against my neck. He slowly lowered me to the ground, he removed the arm across my chest then let go of my waist. I turned around looking up at him. His face was soft, his eyes understanding as they met mine.

"How did you know I was leaving?" I asked.

Zeke's mouth made that half grin. He reached out and started brushing my crazy hair away from my face.

"It's what I would do," he admitted. "If someone hurt someone I cared about, I'd make a plan, find who did it, and tear them apart.". His eyes unfocused as he thought about it for a second. "Sometimes I skip the planning part."

"I was thinking more about protecting you guys, finding answers," I told him. "Then tearing Bitch Ghost apart."

Zeke smiled down at me. He reached out and lifted my chin with a finger, his thumb on the middle of my chin grazing my bottom lip.

"There's my girl." he said quietly.

I raised an eyebrow at him as he dropped his hand.

"What?"

"You've been looking entirely too scared since yesterday," He said, his smirk back. "You've got that fire back in your eyes." Stepping back, he rubbed his thumb against his jeans. "You look more like you again."

It was strange; I felt more like me again. Was forgetting myself a side effect of getting jumped? I never really thought about it.

"How did you know I was freaking out?" I asked, picking my book bag up from where I dropped it.

"I didn't, Miles did. He said you were way too calm and way too cheerful." He picked up his bag from the sidewalk. "He knew I was going to follow to see if you actually went to class, and he warned me you might be having a freak-out. Well, he said panic attack."

I snorted at him, shaking my head. Miles was way too observant.

His eyes met mine again. "Did you really think you could outrun me?"

I sighed but reluctantly admitted the truth "Wasn't much thinking involved."

He grunted before his face turned serious.

"I take it you have a plan?" he asked.

I nodded. "Claire gave me a lead on someone who might be able to help me. She runs a store over in Bridgeport."

Zeke took a slow deep breath, running his hand through his hair for a couple seconds. Then he dropped his arm.

"Then let's go," he said.

Wait. What? He wanted to come? I didn't want to bother any of them with this.

"You don't need to come, it's a store. I shouldn't have a problem," I said, trying to reassure him, but he ignored.

He grabbed my hand and gave me a tug to get me moving towards the Blazer.

"You're not going anywhere alone," he ordered. "Until that ghost is dealt with, I want one of us with you as much as possible."

He seemed to think on what he just said.

"Well, not in the bathroom," he amended, "but someone is standing outside the door. Yeah, that's happening."

I laughed, hoping he was kidding; he gave my hand a squeeze as we walked to my truck.

BEFORE LEAVING TOWN, I stopped and picked up some money from Rory's emergency jar. If this woman had anything to protect the guys, I was buying it. I'd make it up to Rory later.

Two towns over in the mountains turned out to be an hour and a half on curving roads. We talked about the music we each liked as we fought over the radio. I demanded that he listen to a few girly pop songs just to mess with him. He bitched and complained the whole time as if it was killing him.

It wasn't until I had to pull over because I was laughing so hard that he realized I was messing with him.

"That's cruel, Lexie, real cruel." He sounded angry, but he was still smirking.

I pulled back onto the two-lane road, unrepentant.

We talked about school, his work at the garage, and the guys. He was in the middle of telling me a story about Ethan and a blonde chick when we reached Bridgeport.

Bridgeport was bigger than Spring Mountain, about double the size. I handed Zeke the address, and he looked up the directions to the store. It wasn't long before we parked in the gravel parking lot in front of a cute building that looked like a small cabin, complete with front porch. I got out and walked around the truck, my stomach in knots.

Zeke was a comforting presence next to me. Okay, yeah, I was glad he came along. I bit the corner of my lower lip before walking up the steps.

Wind chimes were tinkling in the small breeze as I opened the half glass door with an "open" sign hanging from it. I stepped in and looked around. Shelves were everywhere, packed full of all sorts of things; crystals, small statues, books, you name it, and it was here. The store felt cramped simply by all the shelves. Lavender tickled my nose as I walked to the counter, behind the counter was even more shelves, but these were stuffed with jars of all sizes. And they reached the ceiling.

I was looking at a ladder that hooked to a rail in front of the shelves when someone stepped out from behind a cloth curtain in the back of the shop. She was stunning, skin the color of mocha. Clear and flawless. I instantly wanted to ask what skin care products she used and go buy them for myself. I pushed that thought away and focused. She had high cheekbones, a small chin, and big silvery eyes. Her hair hung to her shoulders, a mass of brown, spiral curls. She was wearing a loose purple sweater and white skirt. Her eyes ran over me, accessing. I got the distinct impression she was seeing more than just the surface. She started to frown then quickly covered it with a welcoming smile.

"Welcome to Serenity. Is there anything I can help you with?" She stepped forward, her hands clasped in front of her. I felt Zeke step closer behind me, his presence, well, reassuring.

"Claire sent me." I said.

Her smile disappeared; her eyes ran over me again. When she met my eyes her eyebrows drew down, her mouth pursed.

"You're in trouble, girl," she announced, her voice matter-of-fact. "You're about running on empty, and that is not a good place to be."

She gestured for us to follow before turning around and heading back through the curtain. "Come on, we can talk back here."

I followed her behind the curtain; she led us down a short hallway into a small kitchen in the back.

She gestured toward the two-seater table. "Have a seat."

I looked at Zeke as he settled himself, leaning against the right wall a couple feet from the table. I sat down in the chair closest to him and watched the woman put a teakettle on the stove. When she turned back, she was frowning again as she joined me at the table.

"You must be Alexis." She gave me a small smile. "I'm Serena. I know a little of what I could get from Claire." Her eyes narrowed on my face. "Now, you tell me; what have you been dealing with?"

That was all it took. Once I started talking, I couldn't seem to stop.

I told her everything, from my first ghost at five, to Claire protecting me all the way up to this morning. It took a while.

During that time, the tea kettle whistled. She poured three mugs of tea, handed two to us, and sat down with hers, all the while still listening intently.

By the end, my voice was rough; I sipped my now cold tea and waited.

She looked at me, her face full of sympathy.

"Alexis, from what you're telling me...you don't have the Sight," she said.

My world stopped, my heart gave a hard thump. This had come out of nowhere; out of any scenario I could imagine, this one never came to mind. She didn't believe me; I had to make her believe me. She was the only lead I had.

"I see the dead," I stated clearly, my mind racing.

She waved her hand as she finished sipping her tea.

"Oh, I don't doubt that at all." She put her cup down. Her eyes met mine assessing me. "The dead find you, yes?"

I nodded.

"They can try to possess you, hurt you and you can push them back. Like you did at school that first day, right?" she asked.

I nodded again, having no clue where she was going with this.

Her face was soft as she continued. "Those with the Sight are only witnesses. They are Seers, they see what is really there. You see everything and interact with the dead."

For some reason, her words filled me with dread. Interacting with the dead didn't seem good, or healthy, or anywhere close to normal. I focused on what she was saying.

"You're a Necromancer, Alexis."

My mind went blank, I had no clue what the hell that was.

"A what now?"

Her face was patient as she explained. "A Necromancer, you can control the dead." She picked up her tea and brought it to her mouth. "And a natural talent, too. That is incredibly rare." She said before taking a sip.

191

I was already shaking my head.

"I can't control any of it. They control my life, if I sleep, if I can even function..." I trailed off not knowing what else to say.

Her silver eyes were full of understanding as she put down her mug.

"That's because you are still growing into your abilities," she told me gently. "This gift you have hasn't even finished growing to its full potential."

"You mean it's going to get worse?" I asked, not wanting to believe it.

Serena shook her head gently.

"Not worse, just more. You'll see more, new and different things."

Her eyes ran over me again.

"It'll scare the heck out of you whenever you see something new." She smiled gently. "When that happens, you need to figure out what you saw. The more you see, the more you learn, the more you'll be able to protect yourself." Her mouth pressed into a tight line. "And for that, you'll need control."

Her eyes shifted to Zeke. "Your friends had the right idea; finding charms, herbs, stones, even incantations that will keep the dead away are exactly what you need right now." She shook her head. "You have very thin natural barriers as it is and they are completely down, your resources are non-existent. You're one soul away from death right now."

The leather of Zeke's motorcycle jacket creak as he shifted. I latched onto what she had said.

"I read about barriers, but I don't think I really understand it," I admitted.

She smiled at me. She seemed happy to get a question out of me.

"Have you noticed that sometimes, you can be around one kind of spirit longer than a different kind? That the more dead you see, the faster they affect you?"

"Yeah," I said slowly. I had actually noticed that over the years. When it got too much, I'd go sleep at a cemetery.

"That's your natural barrier wearing down." She swallowed and tried to explain. "It's like a sea wall. The energy of the spirits are the waves, wearing down your barriers. And the older the spirit, or the angrier, the harder the waves hit the wall, tearing it down faster."

"So, the more juice they have, the faster they'll tear through her barriers?" Zeke asked, speaking up for the first time.

Serena nodded before turning back to me.

"You have to take care of yourself to keep your barriers strong, especially you, Lexie. That means getting at least 8 hours of sleep, eating right, exercising." Her voice grew stern. "These are not options for you; you have to do this if you want to survive."

If she was trying to scare me, she'd be happy to know she did. My gut was knotted and my heart racing.

Her hand reached out and took mine. "But none of this explains why you're in constant pain right now. Show me your back," she ordered softly. It was very clear to me that I wasn't going to get a choice in this.

I sighed and took off my jacket, then my plaid. Serena got up and walked around the table to stand directly behind me. I pulled up the back of my shirt, fighting off memories.

"Did you do this to her?" Serena hissed.

"Fuck no!" Zeke snapped.

"It was my mother," I shot back to her over my shoulder; I didn't like her accusing Zeke.

I turned my gaze back to the table. I felt small, smooth fingertips on my back and instantly knew it was Serena.

"This might also explain why you're having so much trouble." Serena walked around the table and sat back in her chair. I let my shirt fall back down. "Repressed emotions will tear you apart just as easily as a spirit will."

"I haven't exactly had time to process anything." I couldn't keep the sarcasm from my voice. I changed the subject before she could push further. "How can a ghost leave their haunting grounds?"

Serena blinked at me.

"They don't."

"This one did," I said.

I explained about Miles and the choking.

Serena's brow furrowed. "If she had enough energy, she could hitchhike." She looked back at me. "Attach herself to someone and ride along with them. If she had a whole lot more, she could direct a person towards where she wanted...then walk up to the door?" She shrugged at me looking uncertain.

"This ghost had more juice than she should have," I told her. "And from what Claire told me, she wasn't the only one in town. She also said there is a lot of energy floating around, waiting to be picked up."

Serena tilted her head back her features blank while I continued my questions.

"What does that mean? Is something happening? Does it happen sometimes then settles down?" I asked.

Serena's lips pursed. "It means someone is messing with things that should be left alone. They are messing with the natural order on some level," she told me, her eyes on the table. "Someone is behind it, and you'll need to find out whom." She sighed, her hands smoothing the tablecloth. "I'm sorry Alexis; the dead really aren't my field. I specialize with the living."

She licked her lips before meeting my eyes again. "This is your field, so it's your responsibility to fix it. You need to find a way to take control of your gifts, and I don't know how to help you." Her eyes narrowed at me as if something had just occurred to her. "But I might be able to point you in the right direction."

I nodded; I'll take anything I could get.

"What about my friends?" I asked. "Is there anything that can protect them from the dead right now?" I couldn't help the small bit of anxiety in my voice.

"That I can help you with," she said, her eyes full of sympathy.

Over the next hour, we collected stones, charms, jewelry, herbal oils, and even a couple of books from around the shop. An herbal ointment for my bruises, a salt scrub that would remove any hitch-hiking ghosts, and the instructions on how to make it all myself.

Serena told me not to get close to a ghost for at least three days to give my mind some rest, six for complete recovery. Zeke enthusiastically agreed.

Serena refused to charge me for everything. When I objected, she waved her hand at me.

"Oh honey, most of my business is done online. I mostly deal in special herbs, soaps, candles. I don't even really need this inventory anymore."

I had to fight the urge to hug her. It was so much stuff that Zeke had to make two trips to the truck. We were standing on the front porch saying goodbye as Zeke was taking out the last box when Serena pointed at Zeke.

"That boy has been through hell," Serena whispered.

I looked over at Zeke putting the box in the back of the truck.

"How do you know?" I asked.

Serena smiled sadly.

"His aura, it's scarred." She squinted at him. "But healed, mostly." She turned to me. "It's one of my gifts. I can see to the heart of the person through their aura."

I raised an eyebrow. "What does that mean?"

"He's built a wall around himself so thick it's hard for anything to get through." She was looking at Zeke again as he pulled his cell phone out and answered. "It looks like he's almost closed himself off. But there is still a crack he's left open." She made a humph noise. "If anyone gets in and hurts him, it'll be devastating." She looked at me. "Keep an eye on him." She ran her gaze over me her eyes unfocused. "You'll have that scarring too if you don't deal with your emotions about your mother. Or the other thing." Serena's eyes focused again.

I blinked at her. Then I realized what she was talking about. My shoulders tensed.

"That was a year ago, I've dealt with it," I told her, not understanding where she was going with it. I'm over it; I've moved on, why was she bringing this up now?

"You think you have, but now you're quicker to respond with anger. With violence."

I bit the inside of my lip. She was right, but I really didn't want to admit it.

"You've been closing yourself off over the last year, Lexie, trying not to feel." She leaned in and made eye contact with me again. "Deal with it. Or scar."

My lungs felt stiff as I nodded. Mental note: Deal with your shit.

Zeke walked to the base of the stairs and stopped still talking on the phone.

"I can't tell you how grateful I am for all this, you have no idea," I said to her, changing the subject.

Serena smiled sweetly.

"Oh yes, I do. I was once where you are." Her eyes ran over me as she smiled. "Well, not exactly. But everyone starts somewhere." She held out a slip of paper, it was an address.

"This is in case you need more help than I have given you. It's in case of an emergency. It's a Catholic church in Boulder, Colorado. Ask for Father Francis; tell him you see the dead. You'll have to prove it, which isn't hard; there's a spirit always hanging around him. He might be able to give you a little more oomph against the dead and worse things."

"Thank you so much," I thanked her again; I couldn't seem to stop. For the first time in my life, I had hope that I might be able to control this. I just needed the right information.

"Do your research; find a way to control this. No spirits for 6 days," she told me seriously, then smiled. "And come back if you need any advice."

I agreed that I would and walked to Zeke on the stairs; he was still on the phone. He turned and headed toward the truck still talking.

"No, Isaac, we're not going after the Bitch Ghost. Lexie had a lead, and we followed it. We'll be back soon." His gaze went to me. "And pick up Lexie's homework from her teachers, mine too." Zeke was quiet; I could hear Isaac bitching from here. "Do it."

He hung up and tucked his phone away. "The guys just realized we were missing."

I winced. After yesterday, they must be pissed.

We climbed into the truck and buckled up.

"They thought we were going after Bitch Ghost, and they wanted a piece of the action," he said.

I burst out laughing. I couldn't really blame them; someone hurt Miles, and they wanted to return the favor.

I pulled out of the parking lot and headed toward the highway. It wasn't long before Zeke pointed out the window.

"Let's get some food."

I looked over, it was a sandwich shop, and we'd have to get out.

"Let's just hit a drive through," I offered. I wanted to get back to the others as fast as possible.

Zeke's jaw clenched.

"Drive thru is crap, she said you needed to eat healthy, right?" He pointed toward the sandwich shop. "So, we're eating healthy. Pull over." His tone was clear; he meant business.

A little twisted part of me wanted to keep driving just to see what he would do, but I kept a lid on it and pulled into the parking lot of the shop. We were waiting in line, deciding what to order when I got another wicked idea. I looked up at Zeke and smiled sweetly.

"You know, if I'm stuck eating a salad, you're not going to be eating a foot-long sub in front of me, right?"

His eyebrows almost disappeared into his hairline. He gestured at himself, his face almost desperate.

"But... man... hungry... need lots of fuel," he stuttered, looking horrified.

I changed tactics.

"Are you really going to make me watch you eat a huge sandwich full of meat and cheese, while I'm stuck with a salad?" I asked. I made my eyes big, and my bottom lip began to pout. I hadn't even started with the lip trembling yet when his eyes narrowed at me, and he cursed.

"You cheat, Lexie," he growled.

I smiled happily to myself. If I had to suffer, it wasn't going to be alone.

I ended up with a tuna salad, Zeke a 6-inch turkey sandwich and a garden salad. He grumbled the whole time. It was so worth pulling the pout. While we ate, , I told him about the priest that she wanted me to see if I couldn't manage on my own.

We were on our way back out to the Blazer when Zeke took my arm and pulled me to the passenger side door. He opened the door and held out his hand.

"Give me the keys and get in." His tone told me not to argue.

I did anyway.

"I can drive."

"You were almost falling asleep over lunch, you're not driving," he said, flicking his fingers towards his palm. "Keys."

I shook my head. This was fun.

His eyes narrowed on me.

"Give me the keys or I'll grill you about your back."

Suddenly it was less fun. I pressed my lips together hard and handed the keys over.

"You cheat, Zeke," I grumbled.

Zeke had a satisfied smirk on his face.

"You started it. Now get your exhausted little ass in the truck."

I ENDED up falling asleep on the way back to Spring Mountain. I don't even remember leaving Bridgeport. I didn't wake up until a hand was shaking my shoulder.

"Lexie, come on, we've got shit to do." Zeke's voice wasn't gentle, but it wasn't too harsh either.

I groaned and opened my eyes. I was instantly confused. I remembered Bridgeport, lunch; I remembered talking to Zeke about going to my house. Why the hell were we sitting in a cemetery?

Zeke had parked the Blazer facing the front of a red truck. Two cars were parked behind it, one of them familiar.

"What are we doing here?" I asked him, sounding grumpy.

Zeke took the keys out of the ignition and put them in his pocket.

"Time for a meeting," he explained, like that would make sense to me.

Before I could ask, he was out of the truck, the door closing behind him. Confused, I opened the door and slid out to the gravel.

All cemeteries looked alike to me. Lots of green grass, some trees, and lots of headstones. That's about it.

I walked around the front of the Blazer and followed him. When we passed the cab of the red truck, I saw the other guys. Asher and Isaac were sitting on the tailgate, their backs to us. Miles and Ethan stood across from them, leaning on the hood of a green sedan. They all turned as we walked up to join them.

"Zeke, what are we doing here?" Asher asked. "We were all supposed to meet at Ally's."

"Yeah, what's going on?" Ethan asked, his dark eyes bouncing between Zeke and me.

I pointed to Zeke; I wasn't taking the blame for this.

"Where were you guys today?" Miles asked, his fingers dancing on his thigh.

"Lexie," Zeke gave me that stern stare. "Tell them what we found out."

"Fine, but why do we have to do this here?" I asked, a little frustrated.

"We'll get to that," he assured me.

I sighed, then turned to the guys and explained some of what we learned. I started with why I left school today, that a ghost leaving their haunting grounds shouldn't be able to happen. How the ghost could hitchhike onto someone and leave their haunts if they had enough energy. And we knew Bitch Ghost had more juice than she should. I told them about Serena and about the books, stones, and charms that she gave me to help us. I stopped before I got to the more personal stuff.

"Tell them all of it, Lexie," Zeke ordered me when I hesitated.

I met his eyes and tried to tell him "no" without a word. I didn't want to scare the guys, or worse, give them something else to worry about. I just wanted to get those charms on them, put them in a circle and keep them out of it from now on.

"We don't lie to each other Lexie," Zeke said coldly, "we don't even have secrets from each other. They need to know what's going on."

When I still hesitated, his eyes narrowed.

"You tell them or I will," he said

Completely irritated with Zeke, I turned back to the guys and told them what Zeke wanted. Everything. How I didn't have the Sight, I was a Necromancer. I explained what that meant. I explained what barriers were, and that mine were down now. That I wasn't supposed to interact with the dead for three to six days to let my mind heal. How since my natural barriers were so thin I had no choice but to take care of myself to keep my barriers up. How Serena said that someone was messing with something they shouldn't; they were messing with the dead here. This was giving the ghosts in the area extra juice. That it was my responsibility since it's my area of talent.

I was telling them everything, showing everything. I was vulnerable again, and I didn't like it. My temper was getting the better of me. So when I finished, I glared at Zeke. "Is there anything else, or should I tell them my bra size too?"

I noticed Ethan's eyebrows go up out of the corner of my eye. The corner of Zeke's mouth dropped a bit. His eyes slightly narrowed at me.

"If what you're saying is true, "Miles spoke up, "then we can't go to Lexie's,"

"That's what I was thinking." Zeke agreed.

"What? Why?" I asked, surprised. "If we explain to Rory what's going on, he'll be okay with you guys staying over. A salt circle, and everyone is safe for the night."

"But will Rory and Tara be willing to sleep in this salt circle too?" Miles asked, his brow drawn together.

I stopped to think about it. Shit. I wanted to argue, but he had a point. I doubt I could get Rory to sleep on the floor in a salt circle. Let alone explain it to Tara.

"Tara doesn't know," I admitted to them.

One of Miles' eyebrows arched.

"But it runs in your family through the women, right?" Miles asked slowly, as if making sure he wasn't going to insult me.

"Yep."

"But Tara doesn't have it?" he asked again.

"Nope." I met his eyes, trying to let him know my suspicions without telling him.

"So, Tara isn't-" Asher began.

"Rory and I have a 'don't ask, don't tell' policy about Tara's lack of abilities," I explained. "He wants to keep her in the dark." I looked back to Miles. "So, no, Tara wouldn't be sleeping in the circle." My head was starting to hurt, not from a ghost just from everything going on.

"If Bitch Ghost is after us specifically, then we can't bring that to Rory and your cousin," Asher said, bringing us back on topic.

"Why the hell didn't I think of that?" I cursed in a whisper at myself, my eyes closed.

"You haven't been sleeping, Red. Your brain's not at hundred percent right now." Isaac hopped off the tailgate and wrapped his arm around me. His body warmth felt really good right now, comforting. I sighed and let myself lean against him a little, breathing in his lime smell. I think I was starting to understand why the twins were so affectionate. Touching and being touched by someone who cared felt pretty good.

"We need to go somewhere with enough room for a circle and no other people," Isaac announced. He looked to Zeke. "What about your house?"

Zeke shook his head.

"Not enough room, unless you want to be in a tent." Zeke said.

"You all know you're coming to my house," Miles announced, his voice chiding them.

Everyone looked at him. He sighed wearily. "Mom left for a spa in the Hamptons or Fiji, somewhere, and won't be back for a week at least. We can sleep in the living room. It's big enough." Miles' voice was stern. His body tense. He didn't seem very happy about it.

Isaac leaned across the circle and staged whispered. "Can we make smores in the fireplace again?"

"Yes, we can make smores," Miles' said, his voice sounding resigned.

Isaac let go of me and did a dance. Miles gave him a half smile, his body relaxing a little.

Why didn't Miles want anyone over?

"All right, let's get our stuff and meet at Miles' house for the night," Zeke announced to everyone and then pointed to Asher. "Can you give me a lift back to my bike?"

"No problem," Asher said.

Zeke took my keys out of his pocket and handed them over.

"Let's all try to get there before dark," Zeke suggested.

I snorted and shot him a look.

"Yeah, easy for you to say. You're not the one who has to go back to an armed, overprotective uncle and ask to stay overnight, without a parent, with a group of boys that I met last week."

Asher's eyebrows were in his hair, his mouth open as if to say something. Ethan's face was twisted in a grimace as he scratched his neck, Isaac was making an ouch face, Zeke cringed. And Miles simply looked concerned.

"Yeah, that's a tough one, Red," Isaac admitted.

"That's going to be a long conversation," Asher added.

"I'm sure he'll understand," Miles said calmly.

"That conversation is going to suck," Ethan added honestly.

"You'll make it before dark, when you're 18... maybe," Zeke predicted.

I looked at them all and had an idea.

"You guys could come help me explain?" I offered in my sweet voice. They all scattered. Isaac went so far as to dive through a window to get into their car.

"Ugh, I hate you guys!" I shouted.

They were laughing as they started driving off.

CHAPTER 11

$\mathcal{I}$t actually didn't go as badly as I feared. Rory listened--after yelling at me for skipping school, of course. I told him everything; I didn't hold back a bit. When I was done, my voice was getting hoarse. I told him that if he really wanted to keep Tara in the dark and safe, then I had to go stay somewhere where the guys and I could sleep in a salt circle. He agreed I couldn't do it here. When I explained about Miles, how I was afraid the other guys were being targeted, he understood why I ditched school. He even agreed that I needed to stay with the boys.

It only took 4 hours to convince him.

Asher texted me once, asking if I wanted them to pick up anything. I told them to get a shit ton of salt and a few jewelry-making kits. I got a picture 15 minutes later. It was of Asher pushing a grocery cart loaded with round salt containers and Isaac sitting in the basket, his arms wide. It looked like they bought out the store. It made me laugh, so I showed Rory. Even he smiled.

In the end, he told me I had to check in and ice my back every night. I packed a bag and headed out to the address Miles texted to me.

It was almost dark when I left Rory's house. I headed east out of town on the highway until I reached the right number in front of a paved road. I turned onto the driveway and followed it. It ran back through the woods, curving here and there. It was a good 5 minutes before I reached the front gate. River-stone walls disappeared to the right and left of the metal gate. What the hell? Was Miles rich? Sure that I was in the wrong place, I reached out and hit the button on the call box. There was a buzz then nothing. I was about to hit it again when the speaker crackled.

"Hey Red, you look good on camera," Isaac's voice came through the box.

I looked up and found the camera. Then I promptly flipped it off.

He laughed. "Aw, so adorable."

I rolled my eyes as the gate started moving. When it was open enough, I drove through and continued to follow the driveway.

When I finally saw the house, my mouth actually dropped. The house was enormous. The house stretched out on top of the hill. Three stories of gray stone. Ivy clinging to the walls. The front yard was huge, cleared of trees, with a thick carpet of green grass stretching down the hill. The river stone wall ran around the yard and disappeared from view around the house.

I pulled into the big, circular driveway in front of the door. The other cars told me the guys were already here. This place was massive I really didn't want to think about the electricity bill for a house this big. I got out of the truck, grabbing my backpack, my clothes bag, and my old sleeping bag. I'd have to come back for the other stuff.

I was walking up to the double front door when it opened. Miles came out followed closely by Asher and Ethan. Miles stepped to the side letting the other guys pass.

"Zeke said there are boxes?" Asher asked.

"In the back of the Blazer," I told him gratefully.

I watched Miles as I walked towards him. He was barefoot; his collared shirt now unbuttoned showing the white undershirt beneath. His hands were in the pockets of his tan jeans. His eyes were on the ground, his shoulders tense. My stomach knotted. Miles was rather reserved, and here we all were, taking over his house.

"I'm so sorry about this, Miles. I know you're probably uncomfortable with all of us here," I began, trying to apologize.

His head came up, and those beautiful, dark green eyes met mine.

"I'm not uncomfortable because you guys are here," he said, his voice sincere.

The knots in my stomach eased. But I still didn't understand why he was so tense. I chewed on the corner of my lip, trying to figure it out.

"Is it because I'm a girl? I promise I will keep my hands to myself.... unless I need to smack Ethan, or Zeke, or Isaac.... okay I reserve smacking privileges," I told him seriously.

Miles gave me a small chuckle and smiled.

"It has nothing to do with you being a girl," he reassured me as he began shifting his weight from one foot to the other then back again. "I just don't like being here at the house."

Surprised, I was about to ask why when Ethan and Asher walked between us. They were arguing about something being fair or not. After they passed, Miles gestured towards the door. I headed inside, and he followed. I stepped into the foyer and froze. The foyer was big; the ceiling was twenty feet high. With exposed dark wooden beams. A large staircase went to the second story in front of me. Paintings lined the staircase all the way up. The whole place screamed classic and beautiful. I wanted to appreciate it, but all I could see was all the expensive, breakable things around the house.

"Miles you're rich, huh?" I asked, still looking around at all the potential collateral damage. When he didn't answer, I turned to him. Miles' ears had turned pink.

"Well, yes," he said, his voice uncertain.

I nodded.

"Does your family have a lot of breakable priceless things, like Ming vases? Stuff like that?" I asked, really hoping he'd say no.

His eyes ran over me, his gaze questioning.

"I believe so." His voice was flat.

I nodded. Shit.

"I think we might want to put anything like that away. We are expecting a ghost to come and be pissed that she can't reach us, remember?" I said, my smile strained. "We don't want her to start destroying any priceless heirlooms."

Miles blinked a couple times then stared at my face for a few heartbeats before he gave me a wide smile.

"That's a good idea, Lexie." His eyes were warm on mine, and an odd look crossed his face. It was only there for a couple seconds and then it was gone. He walked away through the open French doors on the left where I could hear the other guys.

"Guys, we have work to do before we eat," he announced.

It took a little over an hour with all of us working together to hide away all the priceless pieces of art. After we were done, we headed into the kitchen to reheat the Chinese food Asher and Isaac had picked up on their way in.

"You are the best guys ever. I swear," I managed to say around a mouth full of General Tso's chicken.

The guys thought me talking with my mouth full was cute. They thought it was hilarious when I stole someone's egg roll. Being the only girl in a group of guys had its benefits. Zeke had made a point to put a big helping of stir-fry veggies on my plate. I made a face at him but ate it anyway. I had just thrown a fortune cookie to Asher when Miles pulled out his phone.

"Lexie, Rory says to pick up your phone," he called across the long table.

I groaned as I got up and walked down the long hall that ran the length of the house. Seriously, this place was huge. I picked up my cell phone in the living room. I was just walking back into the dining room when I read Rory's text message.

Rory: Send a picture of you with ice packs on your back or you will be grounded for a month after this.

My heart sank. I didn't bother sitting down.

Alexis: Rory, please don't make me. The guys don't even know about my back. I hate the way it makes me feel.

It wasn't long before I got a text back.

Rory: I'm sorry hon, but you have to. Doctor's orders. Zeke knows. He'll help you.

I was still standing behind Isaac's chair trying to decide if getting grounded for a month was worth it when Zeke pulled out his cell phone and checked it. My stomach knotted as I waited. Zeke looked up and met my eyes.

"Lexie."

His voice was understanding, but his face was hard. He wasn't going to let me get out of this. Fucking traitor.

"You know you have to," he said.

The room grew silent; I shook my head at Zeke telling him I didn't want to.

His jaw clenched. "Miles, do you have any ice packs?" His eyes never left mine.

I closed my eyes, my face warming.

"Uh, yes. I have a couple in the freezer, but I also keep a lot of frozen veggies around," Miles answered uncertainly.

I turned around and started walking out of the dining room.

"Lexie," Zeke called me, his voice hard this time.

I stopped and took a deep breath.

"I'm just changing," I told him calmly over my shoulder. "I'll meet you in the living room."

I walked out, my hands in tight fists. I wanted to hit Rory right now, hell, I wanted to hit Zeke for this. I went to my bag of clothes by the stairs. I knelt down and was pulling out my black sweats and a gray cami for sleeping when Ethan stepped up behind me.

"Lexie, what's going on?" he asked.

I shook my head too angry to speak. No point, they were going to see everything anyway. I grabbed a hair tie and got to my feet.

Ethan's dark eyes ran over my face, his brow furrowed. "Talk to me." His smoky voice was low, almost toe curling.

"Physical therapy," I said through clenched teeth.

I stepped around him and walked down the long hall again towards the bathroom. The guy's voices came from the kitchen asking

Zeke what we were doing with the ice. He told them to ask me. Asshole. I shut and locked the door behind me. I was cursing Zeke and Rory the whole time I was changing. I couldn't have just kept one fucking thing to myself, could I? Nope, everyone had to know everything. I put my hair back in a loose braid that hit the bottom of my ribs. No point in hiding them now.

It wasn't really about the boys seeing my back, I knew that. That was just my excuse. I didn't want to lay there and remember. I didn't want to answer questions as those memories washed over me, over and over again. I took several deep breaths before I found my calm again. It was a fragile calm, but it was the only kind I had. This was going to happen, and there was nothing I could do about it. Except maybe punch Zeke and take the grounding. No use stalling, Zeke would probably just break down the door anyway, the shit head.

I took a deep breath for calm and opened the bathroom door. My stomach rolled as I walked into the living room. Everyone's eyes were instantly on me. I crossed my arms over my stomach as my face started to burn. The guys were spread around the room, and everyone but Zeke looked tense. Ethan's face was dark, his eyes never leaving me. I glared at Zeke. He stood by the coffee table where he piled the ice packs and frozen veggies. He gestured to the couch to the right. My hands started shaking. At least this time I'd be comfortable, and Zeke could get a good picture for Rory.

"What's with the ice? And why does she have physical therapy?" Ethan demanded, his voice low and boiling with its usual smoothness. It would have sent shivers down my back if I wasn't already breaking out in a cold sweat.

"Someone needs to start talking because she's as white as snow right now," Asher demanded, his voice hard.

I took a deep breath and swallowed hard. I kept my eyes on the floor as I walked to the couch. I stepped past Zeke, refusing to look at him. My fists were clenched, aching to take a swing at him for making me do this. I laid face down on the couch, looking toward the back cushions. They all stepped closer. I bit the corner of my lip trying to keep myself from moving.

When they saw my back, I knew it instantly. Curses went around the room. I closed my eyes. My face burned so hot I thought it might actually burn through the leather.

"What the fuck?"

"Son of a-"

"Who the hell did that to you?"

Why didn't Zeke put the goddamn ice on already?

Someone moved my braid from my back. A towel covered me from neck to butt.

"I want a goddamn answer," Ethan said quietly, his voice no longer smooth but almost rough.

I heard his voice moving as he walked behind the couch. I felt the ice packs being placed. I wished Zeke would just fucking hurry up. This was a nightmare. My arms started shaking now as he continued to place the packs.

"We all want an answer," Asher snapped.

Leather squeaked above me. I opened my eyes to see Ethan standing there, his hands gripping the cushions until his knuckles turned white. His dark eyes were storming as Zeke put another ice pack on my back. I closed my eyes again. I curled my fingers until my nails bit into my palms and pressed hard.

"I don't want to talk about it," I told them, my voice dead. Another round of curses went up. Zeke put the last pack on. My stomach rolled, chills ran up and down my body. Memories of my mother coming at me poured from the back of my mind. I tried to push them back, but this time they weren't going so easily. I focused on staying still, waiting for him to take the fucking picture.

"Beautiful," Ethan called his voice scorching but gentle at the same time. "You have to tell us who did this to you."

"Why?" My voice was deadpan. My stomach stopped rolling, it was like a rock in my belly. Hard and unmoving. I felt the way she yanked me from my bed, screaming at me. I was feeling it all again. The first hit of the belt, the next and the next. I bit my lip stopping myself from making a sound.

"So we can fucking tear them apart," Isaac's voice came from near my head, bringing me back to the present.

"I'm actually on board with that," Miles' voice came from near my feet.

My breathing was shaky as I realized they were standing there looking down on my back, surrounding me, seeing everything. The memories kept coming along with the memory of what it felt like when she dropped the belt and started punching and kicking me. The bite of the engagement ring my Dad had given her. Her cursing at me because I was a freak, a demon child. I could hear my heartbeat in my ears as I focused on trying to remember where I was.

"Did you take the picture, Zeke?" I asked, my voice weak. Images kept flooding through my mind, over and over. My entire body started shaking. It wouldn't stop.

"After twenty minutes," he answered.

I didn't have fucking twenty minutes of this in me. At that moment I hated Rory, I hated Zeke. I desperately needed everyone to just leave me alone so I could push these memories away. I felt her pulling my hair again, the hard, thin carpet under my face as I hit the floor.

"How did this happen?" Miles tried asking gently.

"When did this happen?" Isaac chimed in.

They kept going like that until I wanted to scream. I couldn't stay here like this. I can't keep listening to them while I felt the sting of the belt over and over. Did they have to keep fucking asking?! Did they have to know about this too?! Can't I keep one thing to myself?! They already knew everything. Why the hell did they have to have this one too!

I heard the dull thud of fist meeting skin. I felt the hits as she kept swinging into me. I was taking fast, deep breaths as I felt my mom's foot coming down on my back, again and again. I couldn't stand it anymore. The questions; the memories. It was too fucking much. I pushed myself off the couch, red hot anger rolling through me.

"Fuck you, fuck you, fuck you, fuck you, and fuck you!" I started out whispering, my voice rising with every word until I was shouting as I got to my feet. I felt my body shaking, and I didn't try to hide it.

They backed up a step, all of them surprised.

"Can't you back the fuck off?" My entire core was rock hard now, my body rigid. I clenched my fists and started storming off toward the foyer, but I turned around after a couple steps. "You know everything about me! Every one of my dark little secrets!" I shouted, unable to control myself anymore. They were seeing too much, finding too much. Eventually, they'd see something they didn't like, and that would be it. They needed to stop!

"You want to hear all about one of the most horrible events in my life?" I continued, "Like it's so easy to fucking talk about?" I crossed my trembling arms over my chest and glared at them. "Let's talk about your horrible life events huh?! Let's see how easy it is."

They seemed to not know how to answer, so I got the ball rolling. I glared at Zeke.

"Why does Zeke wake up swinging? Why does Miles hate being in his house? Ethan and Isaac, what are yours? Asher?" I asked them, knowing I wouldn't get an answer.

When no one volunteered to go, I glared at each of them. "Not so fucking easy, is it? And that's with you knowing everything about me. Now imagine sharing everything about yourself with someone who asks for everything and tells you nothing." My voice was shaking now, and I didn't care. I turned to storm off. A big calloused hand grabbed my arm yanking me to a stop.

"Lexie, you have to-" Zeke began.

My temper sparked, I turned around and shoved against his chest making him back up a step. I was on the edge of my control, and I was doing everything I could to not punch Zeke across the jaw. My eyes started to fill with tears, and I didn't care.

"I don't have to do anything!" I shouted as I pushed again, needing to get him away from me.

He backed up again, his arms up, his palms towards me.

I bent down grabbed an ice bag and straightened, tears were running down my face.

"Fuck Rory and fuck you, Zeke, for being on Rory's side." I threw the ice pack at him. He caught it against his chest. His face was completely dumbfounded.

"You're supposed to be my friend, not Rory's!"

My whole body was shaking as I strode away, furious at him.

I stormed through the house until I found the French doors that went out back. I slammed them shut behind me. The huge yard was dark, with small lights around the path and the pool. The cool fall breeze started cooling my body down as I strode across the stone walkway out to the other end of the pool. I walked as far as I could to be away from the guys and not be on the grass. I was fuming, shaking; my gut was feeling like a stone. I sat sideways in one of the wooden lounge chaises near the end of the pool, my back to the house. I looked at the tree line as I tried to calm down. It took a long time.

I COULDN'T TELL how long I had been sitting out here. At some point, I had pulled my knees against my chest, wrapped my arms around them. It was cold out here, but I wasn't ready to go back in yet. I had embarrassed myself, completely lost control. I had yelled at all of them, for what? Not telling me about their own trauma? For wanting to know who hurt me so they could tear into them? What the fuck was wrong with me? Of all people, I should know how hard talking about your own crap is. The guys were just being protective and well, guys. They always had to fix things.

I rested my chin against my knees, watching the trees move in the breeze. I wasn't a problem they could fix. They couldn't stop the memories from tearing me apart. I wanted to go home, I didn't want to go back in there and face them.

Oh, wait I can't go home; we still had Bitch Ghost to deal with. And we had those charms and stones to go over. I should go in. They would still want to know and still ask their questions. Why did I have to fucking lose it in front of them like that?

I was going around and around in circles when a jacket dropped onto my shoulders. I jumped. I looked up in time to watch Miles come around the lounge chair and sit down beside me. He rested his elbows on his knees, leaning forward, his eyes on the tree line.

I put my jacket on, grateful he thought to bring it out. I didn't know what to say to him after my screaming fit inside. My face burned as I thought about what happened in there. I started trying to figure out what to say to him. But I kept coming up with nothing.

"You're right," he simply said, breaking the silence.

Surprised, I looked at his profile. That was so not what I was expecting.

"We do know everything about you, at least the big things," he said. "And we never told you any of our stuff. We shouldn't be asking that of you."

I watched his throat work as he swallowed.

"My Dad used to beat my mom in this house."

A heavy weight settled in my heart. I was such an asshole. He was giving me exactly what I asked for. A horrible life event. I tried to stop him.

"Miles you don't-"

"Yes, I do," he said, interrupting me and meeting my eyes.

His sweet face was earnest, determined. His gaze held mine for several heartbeats before he looked out at the trees again. He licked his lips before continuing, his voice quiet.

"My Dad would come home in a rage over something, usually to do with the shipping business. He'd start criticizing my mother, calling her names. He spoke to her in such a horrible way that I can't even begin to repeat it to you." He looked down at the stone patio, the muscles in his jaw clenching. "I still have trouble when guys talk to a girl that way."

He took a deep breath and let it out as he moved on.

"He'd have a few drinks and start hitting her. I heard everything, saw everything, every time."

His hands clenched into fists between his knees. I reached over, took his hand, and wrapped it in mine on the top of his thigh. He sat up his shoulders tense, his hand was stiff in mine. He slowly relaxed and continued.

"I tried to get between them, but he'd just knock me out of the way and keep going. Till finally one day, I bought a video camera. I filmed him beating her. I wanted to take it to the police, but my mother asked me not to. I gave the video to my mother, and she got a lawyer." He was shaking his head, his mouth a hard line. "I'm pretty sure my mother blackmailed him because he left, he's working at the offices in New York. But they are still married, and he's still putting money into her accounts and mine."

He gestured at the back yard. "I hate living here because I still see my Mother getting beaten. I still hear her screaming for him to stop. All over the house. I usually stay at one of the other guys' houses, Isaac and Ethan's mom never minds if I come over and stay the night."

My stomach dropped. And here we were, all staying in this house that was still haunting him.

"We don't have to stay here, Miles, we can figure something else out," I offered. We couldn't stay here if being here was hurting him.

He gave me a small half grin, his warm eyes meeting mine. "It's easier with other people here." His thumb started making small circles on the back of one of my knuckles. "You guys keep my mind off it, you distract me."

I leaned against his arm and rested my head on his shoulder trying to think of a way to make it better. Miles was such a sweet guy; he didn't deserve to live in a house he hated. But what could I do to make him not hate it so much?

We were quiet for a while.

"Maybe we need to make good memories here for you," I said, hoping I wasn't pushing too far. "We can all spend more time over here. Help override the bad with the good. Fill this place with fun, games, laughing, and the occasional food fight."

He was quiet so long that I was sure I'd overstepped, that I had insulted him or something. I was about to apologize when he finally answered.

"That's a good idea, Lexie."

We sat in comfortable silence, listening to the water lap at the edge of the pool. It was my turn, I knew it was. But Miles wasn't going to push if I didn't want to talk about it. I took a deep breath for courage, and I began.

"My Dad was a firefighter; he died when I was 12." I kept my cheek against Miles' shoulder, watching the trees dancing in the breeze. My voice was quiet. "After the funeral, my Mom started drinking. A little at first, then it got worse and worse. Eventually, she lost her nursing job, and we soon lost the house."

Once I started talking, I couldn't seem to stop. It was as if I needed to get it all out for once.

"She sold Dad's new pickup, bought an old trailer, and we left town. We'd go to a new town, she'd get a job waiting tables or something, and she'd do really well for a month or two."

Miles squeezed my hand. I rubbed my cheek against his hoodie before settling again. Wintergreen filled my nose.

"Then she'd start drinking on the weekends, then at night, then all the time. Over the years, she started doing drugs. A little at first, then that went on just like the drinking. She'd be so wasted she'd lose her job. Since I turned sixteen, I always had to keep a part-time job just to keep us going. Then suddenly she'd decide we needed to move and start over again." I tried to keep my voice calm, but my voice was cracking. "And it would all start over again. We did that again and again."

I took a deep shuddering breath; Miles was a warm, soothing presence beside me. I don't know what it was about him, but something about him made me feel calm.

"I was sleeping in my bed when she came home drunk and high as hell. She yanked me out of bed, screaming that I was a devil child, that I was a demon. She had found one of my dad's old belts and had it in her hand." I looked down at Miles hand in mine as I remembered everything again. "She started swinging and swinging. When the buckle broke off, she used her fists, then her feet. She stomped the hell out of me. I didn't even realize I was screaming until the cops broke in the door and dragged her out." I looked back out at the trees. "I was taken to the hospital, Rory was called, and he agreed with the social worker to take me in. I took care of the trailer, putting it in a storage yard for her for when she gets out. And I started driving, I got here the next day." That was it. That was everything.

"Why do you hate having your back iced so much?" he asked, his voice silky soft. It melted away any resistance I had.

"Because I have to lay there, with no distractions, while I remember her coming at me. I feel it all over again," I told him honestly. "It's like it's happening all over again and again while I lay there. For those twenty minutes, I'm in hell."

Miles leaned his head against mine.

"Lexie, that's a flashback," he said, his voice still that silky timber that soothed my ears. "It happens when you've experienced trauma."

I nodded against his shoulder.

"I figured it was something like that," I admitted quietly.

He squeezed my hand gently, his thumb still making small circles on my skin.

"Does it happen any other time?"

I shook my head, staying quiet.

"Have you told Rory?"

"No."

"You probably should. He wouldn't want you to keep getting triggered like that every day."

"I can usually get through it. It's just, you guys were asking me those questions," I explained. "I couldn't focus on pushing it away, I couldn't..."

Miles rubbed his cheek against the top of my head. We were quiet for a while.

"How did you know I wasn't just mad at Zeke for bossing me around?" I asked, getting a big whiff of wintergreen.

"I saw your face when you got up. You weren't mad, Lexie. You were terrified and trying to get away," he whispered, his voice understanding. "After I realized what was happening, it wasn't hard to theorize from there that you were triggered and probably having a flashback."

We were quiet for a while.

"I'm sorry your mother is the way she is," he whispered down to me.

I smiled sadly.

"I'm sorry your Dad is an abusive dick."

He laughed softly.

I heard small voices coming from Miles' back pocket. Another voice shushed someone else. I lifted my head and narrowed my eyes at Miles.

"Is your cell phone on speaker?" I asked very clearly.

Miles' face was apologetic as his ears turned red.

"It was the only way I could get the others to agree to send only one of us out," he quickly explained. "They all wanted to come out and talk to you, but Zeke and I thought that would be too much."

I gaped at him, stunned.

"They were all stressing out," he continued, "wanting to find out what happened to you. Ethan mentioned shaking it out of you, and Zeke almost slugged him for it." He shrugged, watching me cringe. "I thought this might be better."

I looked out at the trees and counted to ten. Strangely, I wasn't mad; it had been easier to tell one person than all of them at once. And now I didn't have to repeat myself. But it did irritate the hell out of me.

I let go of Miles' hand and reached behind him. He stiffened as I reached his back pocket and pulled the phone out. Sure enough, it was on speaker to Isaac.

"You guys are such assholes," I spoke into the phone. "Sending sweet Miles out here to get me to talk. That is so low," I told them while smiling. "You all suck."

I pulled back my arm and chucked the phone into the pool.

Miles' mouth was open as he watched it sink.

"Lexie, that was my phone; I love my phone," he whined, his face pained.

I wrapped my arm around his and rested my chin against his shoulder, watching him watch his phone sink.

"Then you shouldn't have used it for the others to eavesdrop on us," I told him simply.

He glanced down to see me smiling against his shoulder.

"You're rich, you can afford another one."

He smiled down at me, and we both started laughing.

CHAPTER 12

*I*t wasn't long before we headed inside. Everyone was sitting in the living room. They all looked up, with varying levels of concern. I walked around the room, smacking each of them on the back of the head.

"Didn't anyone ever tell you it's rude to listen in on other people's conversations?" I said through my teeth as I popped each of them.

"Ow," Ethan said.

"She hit me." Isaac declared, pointing a finger at me.

"She hit all of us." Zeke pointed out, rubbing the back of his head.

Asher was the only one who didn't complain, he nodded his head knowing he deserved it.

"She didn't hit Miles," Isaac said.

"No, she didn't, but I do need a new phone now," Miles announced, sitting on the couch next to Ethan.

I sat down cross-legged on the floor at the end of the coffee table.

Asher raised an eyebrow. "What happened to it?" he asked.

Miles half grinned at him. "She threw it in the pool."

The guys smiled at that.

"Maybe you should get one of those waterproof ones," Isaac suggested to Miles. "You know, just in case."

"There will be no repeat of that," I said, pointing at all of them. "That was rude and invasive. If I don't want to tell you something, then respect that. I'll tell you when I'm ready."

Mumbled apologies ran through the room, so I let it drop.

"Lexie, you still need to ice your back," Zeke tired again.

All the other guys groaned, glaring at him. Asher threw a decorative pillow at his head.

"You seriously did not just say that?" Ethan moaned, his hand over his eyes. The silver rings on his fingers catching the light.

"Zeke, you need to stop while you're ahead, man," Isaac advised.

"Even I know that was a stupid thing to say," Miles mumbled.

I took a moment to think about it. Zeke was right; I still needed to ice my back. It always felt better afterward, no matter how much it sucked during. If they could just not distract me, I could get through it.

"Go get the ice," I agreed, resigned. Zeke got up as the others protested.

"You don't have to stay in that position, Ally," Asher told me. "We can just take the picture, and you can get up."

"You shouldn't have to get triggered every day," Ethan said adamantly.

I smiled gratefully at them.

"No, I need to. It keeps the swelling down, and it does feel better after," I reassured them. "I can get through it, just don't distract me."

The guys gave in, none of them liking it.

Zeke was back with the towel and ice packs, and I was about to lay down when Miles stopped me.

"Lexie, what if we put the ice on the floor, and you laid your back onto them?" he suggested quietly. "Changing the way you're facing might stop you from having a flashback."

I shrugged, it was worth a shot. Zeke tossed me the ice packs, veggie bags, and towel. I put everything in line and slowly lowered myself. It hurt a little at first, but then the cold seeped through the towel. I waited, expecting the memories to push forward again. When they didn't, my body went weak with relief. I lifted my head and looked at Miles down the line of my body.

"Miles, you're a genius," I told him earnestly. He grinned at me.

I looked back up at the ceiling and gestured toward the boxes they were going through. "What are we doing?" I asked like there was nothing weird about this.

"Zeke was trying to explain what this stuff is and what we're supposed to do with it," Asher answered.

"Only, I can't remember half of what she said." Zeke bit out the words, obviously grumpy.

I tilted my head back and to the side so I could see Zeke and Asher. They were upside down, but I could see them.

"Pull something out and show me," I said thoughtlessly.

Isaac started snickering, Ethan joined in. Asher was holding back a laugh, his cheeks turning pink.

I thought about what I said and started laughing. There are just some things you can't say in a room full of guys. "That's not what I meant." I groaned.

Even Zeke was covering his mouth, his eyes sparkling.

When everyone got control of themselves, Zeke reached into the box and pulled out a purple cloth bag. He opened it and pulled out medium sized bead, then handed it down to me. It was heavier than it looked which meant it was stone.

"That's the bag of onyx beads she gave me. They keep the dead from touching you. I'm planning to make bracelets with them."

I handed the bead back to Zeke. He dropped it into the bag, closed it, then set it aside. He pulled out a big silver ring with a black stone inside.

I pointed at it. "That's an onyx ring, I thought Ethan might like it since it's more his style."

Zeke tossed the ring over to Ethan.

"Oh, nice," Ethan said. "Does this mean we're engaged?"

I snorted and ignored him.

Zeke was holding out a black leather necklace with a vial of water attached to it.

"That's mine." I held out my hand to Zeke. He handed it over before digging into the box again.

"What is that?" Asher asked.

"It's a vial of salted holy water," I explained, slipping the necklace over my neck. "Serena told me to load up on everything for a while, then slowly take one level of protection off over a few days until I get exactly the level I need." I held up the little vial. "If I'm getting jumped, just open the vial and pour it into my mouth. It'll force the ghost to leave."

"So, it's a ghost epi-pen?" Asher asked, an eyebrow raised.

I thought about it and nodded. That was rather accurate.

"How much protection are us muggles going to need?" Isaac asked, pulling books out of one of the boxes and handing them down to Miles.

"She said two items should do it for you guys," I said, looking at a silver coin-like medallion Zeke was holding up. It had a hole so you could hang it from something. "That's for Asher; I was going to string it on leather for a necklace."

"Okay, it sounds like we're going to have to make jewelry," Isaac said.

"Oh yeah," I said, watching Asher upside down as he got to his feet and moved out of view. "She asked me to pick up a few jewelry-making kits."

Zeke held a malachite pendant above me for identification.

"That's for Miles, again protection from the dead. And it'll match his eyes."

I heard someone chuckle at that. Zeke tossed the pendant over towards Miles.

"Thank you, Lexie," Miles said.

Asher came back in. Upside down, I watched him sit back down with big thin plastic boxes in his hands. He started to hand out boxes when I got tired of lying there. I looked up at Zeke.

"Did you send a picture yet?"

Zeke nodded.

"About 2 minutes after you laid down," he said.

I groaned as I sat up. I picked up the bags behind me and started to get up.

"I got 'em," Zeke said, taking the packs from me.

"Ooh, an ice bitch," I said, teasing him., I was trying to let him know I wasn't mad about earlier. It wasn't really his fault, he had no idea how bad I would react.

He grumbled. "I deserved that," he said as he took the ice packs and walked into the kitchen.

I scooted around towards the coffee table. Asher handed me a jewelry making kit. I took it, opened it and reached for the bag of onyx beads. Asher held up a brown leather braided bracelet with a beautiful flat triangular blue stone woven in.

"That's for Isaac," I said.

Asher tossed it over to Isaac who smiled.

"Thanks, Red."

Zeke came back in and sat down as Asher pulled out another necklace. Hung from black cord was a black obsidian stone that looked raw and was roughly in the shape of a shark's tooth.

"That's Zeke's." I got on my knees and pulled out the other bags of beads as Asher handed the necklace to Zeke who put it on immediately.

"Okay guys, here's what's going on. There was only so much jewelry at the store, but she had lots of stone beads." I put the onyx in front of me and set the other bags on the table. Some were hematite, some were agate, there were others, but they were all for general protection. "In every kit, there is some needle nose pliers, a wire cutter along with leather cord and wire for beading. There's even stretchy plastic if you want a flexible bracelet."

I looked up to see I had most of their attention; Isaac was opening another kit.

"What you have now is specifically for the dead," I continued, putting my hand over the bags of stone beads they were going to use. "These are for protection in general. Serena said it's better to have different kinds on."

Everyone got to work. It wasn't long before someone was talking.

"I hate to ask this but how much did all this cost?" Isaac asked.

I was trying to figure out how much stretchy cord I needed around my wrist when I answered.

"Enough that all of you owe Rory 10 days of yard work each," I said, smiling while I worked.

"Seems fair," Asher said, cutting some leather cord. The others made sounds of agreement.

The room was so quiet that I looked up. All the boys were frowning as they concentrated on making their jewelry, it was cute. I hid my smile and went back to work, wishing I could get a picture of this. Everyone started talking about movies; which new ones looked good.

Ethan's phone started vibrating on the table; everyone ignored it as he picked it up.

"So Red, what's the plan for tonight?" Isaac asked absently as he focused on putting a string through the hole of a bead.

"Well, Serena told me no dead for three to six days. And I'm sure that Zeke is going to make me follow that," I said, not really paying attention.

"Now she's getting it," Zeke mumbled.

I rolled my eyes.

"So, the plan is to get some uninterrupted sleep tonight. Hopefully. Rest tomorrow and avoid Bitch Ghost while I go over those books Serena gave me." I didn't like it, but I needed more information on how to deal with a ghost this amped up with energy. It wasn't fun, but it's what I needed to do.

"I'm sorry, Miles, but you might be stuck with us for a few days."

"As long as you need," Miles answered, his voice calm as always.

"Well, Asher's got a football game on Friday, so let's go to that," Ethan said. "I mean, we usually do anyway."

"We need to keep Lexie safe, guys," Zeke reminded them.

I rolled my eyes. Again.

"Safe doesn't mean I can't go out and have fun." I didn't bother looking up from my beading as I answered.

"There's usually a party somewhere afterward, too," Asher added, sounding distracted.

"Oh, come on," Zeke groaned.

I looked up to see he had stopped working on his beading to glare around the group.

"She has a pissed off ghost that has almost killed her already, and you want to take her to a kegger?" he asked.

"If this stuff works, then she'll be fine," Isaac pointed out. "Red almost died, she deserves to have a little fun this weekend."

Heads nodded around the group. Zeke took a deep breath and let it out while shaking his head with his jaw clenched.

"Fine, but I want to test the damn charms before we go to the game." His tone told us not to argue.

"Yes, Grandpa," I said sweetly. Everyone but Zeke laughed, though the corner of his mouth did twitch as he got back to work.

Everyone was quiet while we worked. It was a while later that I realized something.

"We didn't do our homework," I said with a groan, looking up from my bracelets.

"Screw it," several voices said at once.

"Damn, I should get jumped more often. No homework," I said, thinking myself funny.

"NO!" they all shouted vehemently.

I jumped. Their shouts actually echoed through the house, they were so loud. I looked around at them with wide eyes. Everyone looked up from their work to explain.

"That's not even funny, Ally, you scared the crap out of us," Asher said, his fingers holding a bracelet he was making.

"You just sort of crumbled to the ground," Isaac added, wincing.

"Then your nose started pouring," Ethan continued, shaking his head as if to get the image out.

"Who freaked out the most?" I asked, genuinely curious but also wanting to lighten the conversation.

Everyone pointed at Zeke. He frowned at all them his eyes narrowing, his shoulders growing tense.

"Me? Really?" Zeke scoffed. The guys burst out laughing while Zeke scowled at them.

"We're not telling, Lexie. There's a guy rule that when a freak out occurs, you don't talk about it," Miles said, being the first to get control of himself.

I looked at him suspiciously. His ears were turning pink, and he was looking anywhere but at me.

"And when was this rule created?" I asked.

"The second you dropped like a rock." Ethan grinned at me unrepentant.

I looked around the group again. They were all very eager to get off this topic. All of them were shifting in their seats, avoiding looking at me or focusing way too hard on their work. Warmth filled my chest again; that feeling of being cared about came back. It was a little less weird this time.

"So basically, you all freaked out," I stated knowingly. I couldn't stop smiling: they were all acting so evasive and well, cute.

"We'll never tell," Zeke said before smirking at me.

Oh yeah, it had to be all of them.

"Aw, you all do care," I said, only half-teasing. I guess it was really starting to sink in that they really did care.

Isaac threw a bead at me.

"Knock it off Red. You're messing with the guy rule." He chided me. The conversation changed to what everyone had scheduled this week as we worked on our jewelry.

THE GUYS WERE DONE before I was. They stoked the fire and made smores while talking about the game on Friday. When I finally finished, I had eight onyx bracelets lined up, covering a couple inches of wrist and forearm like a big cuff, and a small hematite beaded necklace that dropped down between my breasts with my other necklace.

Miles checked his watch.

"It's getting late; I guess we should start moving furniture," Miles announced.

"Hey, Red didn't get any smores," Isaac pointed out as he got to his feet.

I shrugged; my mind was more on what was coming tonight than smores. I was packing up the jewelry kits when Asher pulled me away from the coffee table with his hands on my shoulders.

"What?" I asked as he turned me and gave me a small shove towards the fireplace.

"Go sit on the fireplace and make smores while we move the furniture."

Asher's voice told me not to argue.

So, I sat on the stone in front of the fireplace and ate smores while the guys talked about where to put the furniture. They decided to move everything against the walls as far as possible. I watched as they moved everything, enjoying the view as the guys used their muscles. They were my friends but damn, they were ripped, and I was only human. By the time they were done, my cheeks were a bit warm.

Miles gestured to me.

I hopped off the hearth and took charge.

"We'll have to sleep in a circle, heads toward the middle, feet toward the salt line. Let's set up the sleeping bags, and then we'll see how much room we have to work with."

In the end, we all ended up within arms-reach of each other.

Everyone disappeared into the house to get ready for bed. I brushed my teeth and washed my face in the bathroom downstairs. When I came out, I looked around the great room again, looking for any dangers that I didn't notice before.

I was contemplating the moose head above the fireplace when Miles came downstairs in blue flannel pajama bottoms; he was still pulling his shirt on when I caught a look at his upper body. My heart slammed in my chest. While not bulked up like Zeke or Asher, Miles' muscles were hard and defined. My eyes ran over the lines of his muscled abs when he pulled his shirt down over his chest. I looked away, taking a breath and hoping he didn't notice my ogling.

"So, what do we do now?" Miles asked.

I gestured to the floor, still a little flustered by my sight of his chest and abs. I so really needed to work out.

"Um, we make the salt circle," I told him lamely, trying to get my thoughts together again.

There wasn't much else to do.

Miles nodded. "I'll go get the salt," he said, padding off toward the kitchen.

It wasn't long before the others were coming down the stairs in their pajamas. Asher came down in blue and white striped, drawstring bottoms and a white, ribbed tank top that showed off the muscles in his arms and his wide chest that tapered down to narrow hips.

I took a deep breath; this being friends with hot guys was going to be harder than I thought.

Isaac was right behind him, pulling on a black shirt and wearing a pair of blue mesh shorts that reached his shins. and his shoulders weren't as broad as Asher's, though he had more muscle than Miles with even more definition. Ethan came down the stairs with Zeke. Ethan was only wearing gray sweats. Not surprisingly, he had the same build as his brother, only he had less definition, but still, very nice lines. Zeke was also wearing black sweats but also a fitted, black, crew neck, sleeveless shirt that showed off his barrel chest, his wide shoulders, and his thick arms. He had bulk but softer definition, like he worked out but not for the way it made him look.

Seeing one of them like this I could handle, but seeing all of them together... I had to remind myself to breathe. Thankfully, no one seemed to notice my ogling. Rule one of being friends with guys: don't get caught drooling. I had to remember that.

Miles came back in carrying four tubs of salt. Time to get to work.

"Okay guys," I said. "Can you lay in your bags? I need to see where your feet are going to be so I can make sure you're not going to hit the line in your sleep."

Everyone got into their bags; Isaac scooted down a good foot from where he began. It was actually kind of cute how he snuggled down into his sleeping bag.

I took the tubs and started pouring. We ended up in the center of the living room, with the salt line four feet from the guy's feet. I made sure to make the line thick, using all four tubs. When I was done, I shut off the light and carefully stepped over the line using the firelight to see. My sleeping bag was between Ethan and Isaac. I slid into my bag and zipped up.

"Should we put out the fire?" Miles asked from across the circle.

I sat up to judge the distance.

"It'll die out soon enough," Asher answered.

"Night guys," I whispered.

There was a chorus of good nights. Everything was quiet for a while. I shifted, trying not to lie on my back--the hardwood floor hurt. After a while, I rolled onto my stomach, but I instantly hated that. Soon enough, I was shifting again onto my side. My hipbone bit into the floor. I shifted again.

"Beautiful, what are you doing?" Ethan asked from my left.

"She can't get comfortable," Asher mumbled from across the circle. "Can't lie on her back."

"She doesn't like her stomach," Zeke chimed in.

"And girls got those pointy hips," Isaac added his voice muffled.

"I'll figure it out," I said, grumbling and trying a half side-half stomach position with my knee up and out.

A sleeping bag unzipped.

I looked up in time to see Miles passing me and heading up the stairs. It wasn't long before I heard him coming back. I watched him carefully step over the salt line with his arms full of a white blanket.

"Get up for a second, Lexie."

I got up and picked up my sleeping bag.

Miles unfolded then refolded a thick, fluffy blanket and put it in my spot. "This is a king sized down feather comforter. Folded to your size, it should give you some cushion from the floor," he explained as he took my sleeping bag and put it on the blanket. When he got to his feet, I hugged him. It was so sweet and considerate that I couldn't help it.

"Thank you," I said.

He tensed, but after a heartbeat, relaxed and then squeezed me back.

"No problem."

We let go at the same time. He went back to his sleeping bag, and I climbed into mine. It was a thousand times better; I could actually sleep on my back.

"Miles, you're my hero for tomorrow," I announced across the circle. I heard him chuckle.

"Hey, why don't the rest of us get a comforter too?" Isaac asked.

"When you're as pretty as she is, I'll get you one," Miles shot back. "Otherwise get it yourself."

Small chuckles went around the circle.

"Can't argue with that," Isaac mumbled. "It's too far anyway."

Ethan, on the other hand, got up and went upstairs. It wasn't long before he was coming back downstairs, his arms full of his own blanket. Soon he was back in his sleeping bag.

I smiled to myself as I snuggled down into my comfy spot and fell asleep.

I WOKE to that familiar chill down my neck. This time it felt like a knife running down a nerve. That woke me up fast. I slowly unzipped my sleeping bag and slid out. I sat back on one knee, the other foot planted on the floor. My hands braced on the floor. The room was dark; the fire had burned down to coals. Moonlight poured through the giant windows, lighting the room almost as well as sunlight. Only beyond the doorway to the long hall was it completely dark.

Bitch Ghost stepped into the living room, frowning. She practically vibrated with energy. The room started to go cold as she sucked in even more energy from the air. She eyed the salt line as she walked towards us.

I got up slowly, quietly, not wanting the guys to wake up. I met her at the line from this side. She had changed; one side of her face looked like it was melting away, a large glistening hole had opened up in her cheek showing the white of her jaw bone and bottom teeth. It looked like she was decomposing, though that didn't make sense. Ghost don't do that.

The smell of patchouli was thick on my tongue.

"You aren't so stupid after all," Bitch Ghost said, taunting me. "I almost thought that tonight wouldn't be a challenge."

I was amazed; for the first time in my life, I was standing near a ghost and not drowning in their memories. Thank you, Serena! I really needed to send her a gift basket or something. I pushed the thought away and focused on the now.

"Where are you getting so much energy?" I whispered.

Ghost Bitch smiled. It was disturbing with half her face like goop. She looked over my shoulder at the guys still sleeping.

"Sweet boys you have there." Her eyes came back to me, I ignored her.

"Why are you doing this?"

I tried again to find some trace of the girl she'd been. Sharing her memories, I understood why she was pissed. Being murdered by your boyfriend sucks, but it didn't give her the right to hurt people. I needed to reach this chick.

"I know your life wasn't great, and I know being killed by your boyfriend was awful-."

Her gaze snapped back to me, scowling.

"You know nothing," she snarled.

I met her eyes and tried again.

"Your name is Mary Summers. You were born here in Spring Mountain in the fifties," I began, using the memories she had poured into me when she tried to possess me. "When you were 8 years old, you broke your arm falling out of a tree. Six weeks later, the day after the cast was taken off, you broke it again climbing that same tree. You loved music, and you sang beautifully."

Her eyes welled up as I continued. I needed to get her to remember the good that was in her life.

"You were going to go to the Peace Corps. You wanted nothing more than to make the world a better place." my heart ached for her as I sorted through her memories. "You were beautiful, caring, and tenacious." I swallowed hard as I remembered her death. "That fucker took your life. Don't let him destroy everything that you are, too."

She eyed me silently, and for a moment, I thought I had gotten through to her. Then her face twisted into a snarl.

"I should have had more time, so I'm going to take it." Her voice was clear in the quiet of the house. "I'm going to take you. Then I'm going to hurt and twist your boys. I'm going to take everything from you."

I let go of any hope I had of helping her. I had tried to help her remember who she was, but you can't help the ones who don't want to be helped. She wanted my body; she wanted to hurt my friends. She could fuck off.

Bitch Ghost reached a hand out and tried to reach across the circle. I stepped back smiling. Her hand began to burn. The more she tried, the more she burned.

She grunted as she pulled her hand back. "You're going to have to come out of there sometime," she said.

I snorted.

"Not till morning, sweetheart," I told her, my voice matter-of-fact. "You'll run out of energy before then."

"Red?"

I turned to look behind me. Isaac had woken up and was rubbing his eyes. When he looked up, he grew white.

"Holy fucking shit!" He jerked back, his mouth open. His eyes were on the ghost, not me. He started slapping the floor hard. "Wake the fuck up, guys, there's a ghost in the fucking living room."

Everyone woke up, some slow like Zeke, and some fast like Isaac. Miles put his glasses on and looked over towards me.

"That's her? That's the dead girl?" Miles asked, his voice still full of sleep.

My mouth dropped. I turned my back on the ghost since she couldn't do anything anyway.

"Wait, you guys can see her?" I asked.

Zeke finally turned towards us, his face drowsy as he looked around. When he saw the ghost his eyebrow raised, his eyes still groggy.

"Yeah, we can see her," he mumbled, still half asleep. He laid back down as if to go back to sleep. "Can she cross the salt line?"

"Nope." I gestured towards the boys then towards the ghost. "Everyone, meet Bitch Ghost. Bitch Ghost. meet everyone," I announced in my sweetest voices.

Bless the guys, they all waved to her, even Zeke from his sleeping bag. A couple actually said hi.

She sputtered with indignation.

Yeah, I had been polite before when there was a chance of helping her move on. Mary Summers was dead set on taking my life from me, and she hurt Miles. I wasn't going to be polite now.

"Why's her face half rotted?" Asher asked, yawning.

I turned back to the ghost who was getting pissed off now.

"I think it's a reaction from having so much juice." I hazarded a guess. "I don't think the spirit is meant to hold that much." I leaned in a little, making sure not to cross the salt line. "Or at least hers isn't."

I turned my back on her and walked over to where the boys were sitting at the heads of their sleeping bags. I turned, sat down at the head of my sleeping bag and watched the ghost get even more furious.

"If she's using this much energy for you guys to see her," I said, "then she'll be out soon, and we can go back to sleep."

The temperature in the room was still dropping, I was starting to shiver. Someone shifted behind me.

"Ally, come over here, it's freezing."

I took a quick look at Asher. He was sitting in the very middle of the circle now, his legs crossed under him, his arms open. I looked back at the ghost who was pacing along the line, thinking of her next move. I kept my eyes on her as I scooted on my butt towards him. When I was close, enough he wrapped an arm around my waist and slid me to him then lifted me in his lap. With my back to his chest, his body heat made me realize how cold I really was. His hands moved to my arms and started rubbing.

Isaac snagged the comforter under my sleeping bag and dragged it over. I opened it up more so the others could use it too. Everyone slid closer. Well, except Zeke, he was still in his sleeping bag. Asher's arms were around my waist, Miles' shoulder was against mine, and Ethan's side was against my left thigh, his hand wrapped around my left ankle. His thumb making circles on my anklebone. Isaac was against my right thigh, his left hand wrapped around my calf. Touching me seemed to keep the twins calm.

"Asher, you are right next to my head, man. I swear if you fart, I'll beat you," Zeke growled out from behind us.

We burst into giggles.

Bitch Ghost met my eyes and smiled in a really creepy way.

"Where did she go?" Ethan's hand on my ankle tightened a bit.

"Oh, she's still here," I answered, watching her as she walked toward the bookcases. "She's going to try to scare one of you into breaking the circle or out of the circle." I kept my voice matter-of-fact for the guys; I wanted to make this easier on them.

Bitch Ghost reached up for the books.

"Cue scary book movement," I told them.

She shoved an entire row of books to the floor. The boys jumped. Bitch Ghost was glaring at me as she walked around us to an end table with an ashtray. She reached for it.

"Duck!" Everyone ducked and covered their heads as the ashtray flew over us and shattered against the fireplace.

"I thought we hid all the breakable stuff," Ethan grumbled, looking behind us at the shattered glass.

Bitch Ghost scowled at us.

"No, just the expensive stuff," Miles admitted.

I watched as she walked over to the photos on the wall and began reaching for them.

"Cue frame smashing," I warned them sarcastically. When the photos dropped to the floor, no one jumped.

"She's not going to stop, is she?" Zeke groaned.

"Not until she's out of energy." I reached around Asher to stroke Zeke's hair in apology. "We could piss her off more, that should drain her faster," I offered in a whisper.

"Oh. That sounds fun," Isaac said with his usual mischievous glee." Hey, ghost chick! What's it like being dead? I mean, was there a white light?"

"A tunnel?" Ethan chimed in.

"All evidence says that those things are caused by the body shutting down," Miles explained patiently.

Asher added, "We have an actual ghost here, Miles, doesn't that prove that people have souls? And that maybe the whole tunnel with a light at the end of it might not be just the body shutting down?" Asher gestured around me towards where he thought the ghost was.

The ghost went over to the painting on the wall

"Painting," I warned. When it fell, the boys didn't notice and continued their debate on whether or not an actual ghost proved there was a heaven or hell. Even Zeke joined in from his sleeping bag from time to time. I continued to narrate what the ghost was doing. They continued to throw questions at her even though they knew she wouldn't answer. We snuggled under the blanket while she tried to scare us.

When nothing she was doing was working, she screamed at me.

"I will tear this house apart!" she said, though her color was already getting paler. She was getting weaker.

I relayed what she said to the others. Miles flicked his hand dismissively.

"Feel free, I hate this house."

The others chuckled.

She walked to the open French doors to the foyer, the French glass doors.

"Doors!" I warned.

One of the French doors slammed closed, the glass shattering. The next one followed. The room was so big that the glass never even reached the salt line. Bitch Ghost screamed in frustration. Then her eyes met mine, something sparkled there. She came to the line and began walking around it, around us.

"It was ridiculously easy to get a hold of your friend there," Bitch

234

Ghost began. "He was dead asleep; I had knocked over a few things in his room. But he's a sound sleeper."

I went still, keeping my eyes ahead of me. I knew what she was doing; she was trying to piss me off.

"You should have seen his face when I dug my fingers into his throat." She came back around the circle and stopped directly in front of me.

That spark in me started to grow, every word she said was feeding it. I took deep breaths and clenched my jaw as she kept describing how she strangled Miles in detail. I kept focused on breathing as I got angrier. Eventually, the boys realized something was wrong. Hands were on my shoulders, the hands on my legs started rubbing.

"You know what the funny part is?" she asked, tilting her head. "I could have kept going. I still had enough power to strangle him to death." She looked at Miles and licked her bottom lip. "I chose to let him live." Her dead eyes met mine. "Next time I won't."

I slowly, calmly removed their hands, got out of Asher's lap and walked to the line. She was right; it was easy to get to Miles, and we needed to know if the charms worked. She was weak enough now that I doubt she could do more than give me a nosebleed.

Bitch Ghost stood up expecting me to break the line.

I stepped over the line. The guys cursed.

The ghost grinned as if it was Christmas morning and she got exactly what she asked for. She reached out to touch me. Her hand stopped an inch away from me. Her eyes grew wider.

"Things have changed, bitch, and you're almost out of juice." I leaned forward, getting into her face this time. She stepped back, eyes wide. I put everything in me behind my next words.

"Now get out."

She let out a piercing shriek. Glass shattered as every light bulb in the living room broke. Then, as if a wind ran through the house, Bitch Ghost was shoved right out through the front window.

I felt my lips curl into a satisfied half grin. "She's gone."

"Why the fuck did you leave the circle?" Isaac shot at me.

"She was bothering me, besides, we needed to see if the charms worked before tomorrow," I answered. "And they do." I walked back into the circle and picked up the comforter.

"Stupid fucking risk," Zeke growled from where he was sitting up.

I shrugged. "Maybe, but if she kept talking about strangling Miles, I was going to blow a gasket." I folded the big comfort back up and put it back in my sleeping spot.

"Lexie, you can't take-" Zeke began, clearly getting ready to lecture.

"What's done is done." I stopped him before he could gather steam. "Now, do you want to lecture me or do you want to sleep?"

Zeke grumbled and lay back down. Isaac and Ethan shared a grin before climbing into their bags.

I was half-asleep when I remembered all the damage in the living room.

"Sorry about the mess, Miles."

"I'm rich, I have a maid," he called back, half-asleep.

I smiled sleepily, and then I was out.

CHAPTER 13

I woke up to an alarm going off, comfortable, warm and snuggled. I vaguely noticed that Isaac had slid over and snuggled into me sometime in the night. My back was pressed against the front of his body. His arm was around my waist holding me against him. His face buried against the back of my neck. In my half-awake state, I barely noticed it.

"Someone turn that thing off," Asher groaned.

There was a rustle, and the alarm stopped.

"We still have to get up." Miles' voice was rough this morning. Through the fog of half-sleep, I wondered if that happened every morning.

"No," Isaac grumbled into my hair and shifted into me some more.

My eyes were still closed when I felt something hard press along my butt and up towards my hip. I vaguely realized what it was.

"Isaac," I called.

"Hmm?"

"Think about baseball for me," I mumbled into my pillow.

Isaac shifted, his lower body pulled away. "Sorry, it's morning." His voice was muffled against my skin.

The zippers of sleeping bags opened as the others started to move.

"I know." I didn't care; I'd been around enough guys to know they often got morning wood. He couldn't control it.

"When the hell did that happen?"

Asher's question had me opening my eyes and lifting my head to look at him half asleep.

"Huh?" I blinked at him.

"What?" Zeke's voice was more gravelly than usual. He coughed. I saw him start to sit up.

Asher gestured towards Isaac and me.

Oh. I put my head back down and closed my eyes again wanting to go back to sleep.

"She was making weird noises in her sleep, like whimpering and shit," Isaac explained, his face still muffled against my skin. "I touched her shoulder, she stopped. I pulled away, she started again. So, I snuggled."

I didn't remember any of that; I must have been out cold. I smiled into my pillow as my twisted side came out to play.

"That's his story, but I don't buy it," I told the boys, sounding doubtful. "I think he just wanted to lay on my blanket. Get him, Zeke."

I hid my smile into my pillow as I heard footsteps over the wood floor. Isaac's arm was pulled off me.

"That's cold Red, real cold," Isaac told me as Zeke pulled him away from me, dragging him along the floor.

I giggled as I rolled over onto my back and rubbed the sleep from my eyes. "So what's the bathroom situation here?" I asked, dropping my arms and looking at the ceiling. I forced myself to sit up and look around. The living room still looked like it did last night. Destroyed.

I forced myself to start rolling up my sleeping bag.

"There are 5 full bathrooms upstairs, a master bath down here, and plenty of hot water," Miles answered "Lexie, you should probably use the master bathroom. It's the only one that has girl stuff in it, I think."

I tied off the sleeping bag and got to my feet.

"Sounds good to me." I took my sleeping bag, pillow, and blanket over to drop on the couch. I'd get it later. "Where am I going?" I asked, pushing my hair out of my face.

Miles tossed his sleeping bag on the couch. The others were already tiptoeing around the glass to head upstairs.

"Follow me," he said.

I grabbed my overnight bag and followed Miles down the long hall. The Master bedroom was directly across from the bathroom at the end of the house. He opened the door and gestured inside.

"Bathrooms to the right."

"Thanks."

Miles nodded sleepily and walked down the hall.

I stepped into the master bedroom and froze. The room was beautiful, the cream walls were classic. Several landscape paintings hung from the walls. The bed was a huge king-sized bed, the comforter looked soft and rich in a tan and white damask pattern. There were several pillows against the dark wooden headboard.

I walked across the wood floor and into the bathroom. It was beautiful and serene. The walls were a soft teal with white tile halfway up the walls. The floor was covered in gray tile. I passed a big Jacuzzi tub and promised myself a soak before this was over.

I quickly showered and got ready. I wore a pair of black boot-cut jeans and my favorite long-sleeved, scoop-neck indigo shirt. It was my favorite because it was comfy and still looked good when it covered half my hips.

My hair was still wet in its ponytail as I brought my bag back into the living room. I dropped it by the stairs and looked around. Everyone was still upstairs. Did guys usually need longer than 20 minutes? Huh. I walked into the kitchen and found several cereal boxes. I put those on the counter and pulled the milk out. I noticed the coffee maker had automatically made coffee. Searching the cabinets, I found the dishes and grabbed a mug and a bowl. I got coffee first--it was more important to me.

I was almost done eating when Miles and Ethan came into the kitchen. Ethan wore black, and Miles was wearing a Zelda t-shirt, jeans, and his green hoodie. They both grabbed bowls and mugs of coffee.

"Is it really only Wednesday?" Ethan asked, rubbing his hands over his face.

"Yes, it's Wednesday," Miles answered, sounding as tired as Ethan did.

"Sleeping on that floor all week is going to be a bitch," Ethan said with a groan, rubbing his lower back.

"Well, since we know the charms work, we don't have to sleep in a salt circle tonight," I said.

"Red! Don't tell them that." Isaac groaned as he came into the kitchen. "How am I supposed to sneak in cuddles if you're in a different room?"

I chuckled as he sulked.

"Sorry, Cookie Monster. I can't make the guys sleep on the floor just for snuggles," I told him before taking another drink of coffee.

Isaac pointed at me.

"If Bitch Ghost shows up tonight, I'm sleeping with you," he warned, his eyes sparkling with mischief.

"Fine, if Bitch Ghost shows up, you can sleep in my room," I said, smiling at him. I didn't mind a good cuddle from a friend. Truthfully, I hadn't had a boyfriend in a long time. I missed the cuddling. Besides, Isaac would behave himself. Unless there was a pen around. I made a mental note to hide my book bag tonight.

"So, we're sleeping in Lexie's room tonight?" Zeke asked as he came into the kitchen wearing his usual all black. Asher closely following behind wearing jeans, a white shirt, and a blue unbuttoned plaid.

"I told these guys that since the charms work, we don't have to sleep in a salt circle tonight," I explained. "Isaac warned me that if Bitch Ghost shows up tonight, he's sleeping with me." I shrugged.

"Well, you are the only one who can see her," Ethan said thoughtfully. He gestured at me with his coffee mug. "If shit starts flying around, I'm running to your room too."

I burst out laughing at how serious he sounded.

"Huh, that's a good point," Asher admitted.

I looked up at him, seeing where this was going.

"If I smell even a hint of patchouli, I'm hiding behind you," he explained.

Oh my God, this was getting ridiculous. Luckily, I wasn't the only one who saw it.

"We can't all sleep in Lexie's bed," Zeke reminded them.

Isaac looked him up and down.

"Yeah, you can't. You'd wake up smacking her," Isaac said.

Zeke thought about it for a second and nodded in agreement.

"There's always the floor," Asher offered, grinning.

I rolled my eyes. "I'm going to end up sleeping on the floor if you guys keep claiming my bed," I pointed out. There was only so much room, and they were big guys.

Asher seemed to think about this.

"We can stash the sleeping bags in Lexie's room, just in case," Asher suggested to the group.

Everyone nodded.

I really hoped they were joking.

"Why do you guys keep saying my room? What room? Where am I sleeping tonight?" I asked, looking over at Miles.

He shrugged.

"You can stay in the master bedroom."

I cringed a bit. Sleeping in his mom's bed didn't really sit well with me.

"I'll just sleep on the couch; I don't like the idea of using your mom's bed. It's a little creepy." I admitted. I didn't know his mom, and so, yeah, no.

"My mother has never slept in that bed, Lexie. Everything in there is brand new," Miles said before drinking his coffee.

That seemed a little weird to me.

"What?" I asked.

Miles' eyes met mine as he explained. "My mother had that furniture moved in, finished decorating, packed a bag, and left for that spa yesterday." He shrugged before getting up to put his bowl in the sink.

That seemed a little weird to me. You finish decorating your own bedroom, and you don't sleep in it?

"So, no couch surfing for you," Isaac declared, meeting my eyes. He gave me a slight shake of the head, telling me not to ask. I didn't

"Damn it, I'm just going to have to sleep in that big comfy bed then," I said in my 'doesn't it suck' voice. I got some chuckles out of them. But I was still wondering why Miles' mother would leave him here alone like that.

Soon it was time to go. We all made sure everyone had their charms on. I even used the rosemary oil again. I grabbed a book I wanted from the pile, and we were heading out the door.

I was buckling in when the passenger door opened. Isaac climbed in and over the seat to climb to the bench seat behind me. Ethan climbed in and closed the door.

"We're all coming back here anyway," Ethan explained.

I didn't mind, the twins were fun. I queued up my morning 'get moving' play list before I drove off. They were arguing about something ridiculous when I pulled up near the school.

"Why don't you ever park in the student lot?" Isaac asked, ignoring his brother.

"They're assigned," I answered, looking over at Ethan.

He shook his head.

I instantly wanted to smack Tara.

"Who told you that?" Isaac called from the back seat.

"Tara," I said my jaw clenched. I had been walking across campus every day for no damn reason. I looked over to Ethan. "Do you know what spot Tara usually takes?"

Ethan nodded, smiling.

"Show me."

We were somewhat early to school, so when we pulled into the student lot, there weren't that many cars. Ethan directed me toward a nice spot in the front. I shut off the engine and got out, feeling much better about the day.

The morning moved on as usual. In World Civ, the girls to my left actually talked to me. It wasn't long, just small talk about the upcoming essay before class. But it was a first for me. I was sitting in

English waiting for class to start when the brown-haired boy that usually sits behind me sat to my left instead.

"Your Alexis, right?" he asked, turning towards me. I tried to hide my surprise that he was talking to me. He usually sat behind me and texted before class. His brown hair was short, but shaggy on the sides, but longer on top, enough that I could tell he used something to keep it up and back that way. He had a nice open face, a pointed chin and angled jaw. His amber colored eyes were killer, though.

"Yeah, and you're Eric, right?" I asked, hoping my memory was right. He smiled at me; a dimple peeked out of his cheek. The guy had dimples...uhg, dimples killed me.

"That's me." He opened his bag and started pulling out his copy of Romeo and Juliet. "So, what did you do your first weekend in town?"

Oh, nothing big, only helped a couple ghosts move on, found a dead body; you know, the usual girl stuff.

"Slept in," I said immediately.

He chuckled.

"No, I went hiking with some friends and saw one of their bands play over in Dulcet," I told him.

He suddenly looked really interested.

"You were there Saturday?" he asked.

I nodded in response

"What happened that night?" he asked. "I keep hearing different stories. Did Zeke Blackthorn really jump someone for no reason?"

I barely stopped myself from groaning.

"Oh no, he had plenty of reason. The guy shoved a girl, and she hit the floor," I said. Maybe if more people knew the truth, then they'd stop thinking Zeke was to blame. People already seemed to avoid him like the plague.

Eric's eyebrows went up. His eyes were unfocused for a moment as if he was thinking.

"Huh. Guess he did have a reason." Those pretty eyes were on me again. "So, did you like the music? Who was playing anyway?"

"Under Fire was playing that night. Ethan Turner's band." I noticed

Mrs. Hayes starting up the aisle. "I honestly can't wait till they start performing their own songs. I want to hear what they can do."

"So, you really like music huh?" he asked, a grin on his face.

"I like music. I really like music that says things you can't normally say," I told him absently.

His grin spread to a smile as Mrs. Hayes called for everyone's attention.

English went on, as usual, reading and talking about Romeo and Juliet. Dear God, please let us be done with this book soon. It felt like we were moving at a snail's pace. When class was over, I was pulling on my jacket when Eric looked at me.

"I'll see you around, Alexis."

He was gone before I could say anything. Okay, he was a cutie, with dimples. I grabbed my bag and headed out towards my next class.

Zeke and Asher, as usual, spotted me in the hall. I headed towards them, moving to meet them in the middle, when someone stepped close to me.

"Hey sexy."

A guy I never met leaned into me. I felt the sting from a hard smack on my butt. I had a heartbeat of shock, and then I was pissed. Oh, hell no. When he began to move past me, I grabbed his shoulder and forced him to turn towards me. He was still smiling when I drove my right fist into his solar plexus. His eyes grew wide as all the air left his lungs in a rush. He grabbed his stomach and stumbled back into the lockers, his face turning red.

I stepped closer and got in his face as he still struggled to breathe.

"Don't ever smack my ass again," I growled at him. "Or next time I'll kick you in the balls."

The guy finally took a gasping breath and nodded. I stepped back and picked my bag up from where I dropped it. Several girls were clapping, others whooping. Maybe this guy had done this before?

Asher and Zeke finally reached me. Zeke's eyes went from me to the guy I'd hit and back. Asher was frowning.

"What did he do?" Zeke asked, his tone making it sound like this was something I did every day.

"He smacked my ass," I replied, watching with satisfaction as the guy tried to straighten up.

"I don't think he'll be doing that again," Asher said with a grin on his face.

The guy started shaking his head as he moved off into the crowd. I turned and looked up at the guys.

"So how are your mornings going?"

It wasn't until the end of Chemistry that I had a chance to open one of the books Serena had given me. A journal really, from a man in the 1920s. It was full of information about different kinds of ghosts. How they manifest and how to tell them apart. I was hoping to find a solution to our Bitch Ghost problem. I really didn't want to get Miles' house trashed again, we still hadn't cleaned up the mess from last night.

I was finally getting to an interesting part when it was time for lunch. I grabbed my bag and started walking. I was ignoring the guys and barely paying attention to where I was going. A hand grabbed my jacket and jerked me to the right. I stumbled and actually looked up. Ethan had jerked me away from the pole I was about to walk into.

"Red, put the book down and walk," Isaac said disapprovingly. "You can read when we get to the table."

I kept my finger on my page and closed the book. "This book actually has some answers on how to deal with our bitch problem," I said, making sure to be vague in case someone was within earshot.

"It won't do any good if you give yourself a concussion," Miles pointed out as Ethan let go of my jacket.

"Okay, okay." I waved the book around showing it was closed.

When we walked into the area in front of the cafeteria, I noticed Jessica was sitting on Jason's lap not too far away. I made a point to sit with my back towards her. Isaac and Ethan were arguing again something about training this week as I started reading again. I didn't notice the others had arrived until Asher sat down next to me.

I scooted over, my nose still in my book. A hand waved in front of my face. I looked up, blinking.

"What?"

Everyone laughed at me.

"We were talking about going to get lunch in the cafeteria," Asher informed me.

Oh yeah, no one made a lunch this morning. It had completely slipped my mind.

"We can't all go. Someone needs to watch our bags," Miles reminded everyone. I immediately volunteered, pulling my wallet out of my back pocket.

"I'll watch them." I pulled out a five and handed it to Asher. "Get me something cheesy and fattening please."

"You'll get something healthy and like it," Zeke growled at me. I stuck my tongue out at him as they got to their feet and went back to my book.

"How much do you want to bet our bags are gone when we get back? And she has no clue?" Ethan asked as they were walking away.

"I can hear you," I commented. The boys laughed as they walked away. I started reading again but made sure to look up and check the bags every once in a while. I don't know how much time passed I had just found the answer to our ghost problem when the boys got back. Asher handed me a plastic container of salad and grilled chicken.

I glared at Zeke, he smirked back. I thanked Asher.

"I think I found a way to get rid of Bitch Ghost," I announced.

Five pairs of eyes looked up at me.

"Well two actually, but one is kind of illegal."

"So?" Zeke asked bluntly.

I leaned in towards them. "So, it's salting and burning the body of the ghost," I whispered. "I'd rather not get arrested for that. Especially considering my uncle."

"He'd cover for you," Asher reassured me.

"Let's call that plan b for now," Miles suggested. I agreed with him completely. "What's the second way?"

I sighed.

"It talks about linking to the Veil and using it to force her out of this plain and into the next. Pretty much forcing her to move on." I shrugged. "It doesn't say how to link to the Veil; it's going to take time to find more."

Miles held out his hand towards me.

"Can I use your phone, since mine is still in the pool?" he asked me, playing the guilt card.

Joke's on him; I didn't feel guilty at all. Though I did give him my phone.

"What's the Veil?" Ethan chimed in.

"It's the place between this world and the next, at least that's what I'm reading. Souls are supposed to go there to pass on," I explained, looking through the pages to check that I got it right.

"I still like the first way better, it's fast, efficient," Zeke commented before taking another bite of food.

"We'd possibly get caught," I pointed out.

"The bitch tried to strangle Miles. Normally, I'm the last to suggest doing something risky," he argued. "But this I'm okay with." His voice was becoming hard.

"Well, I'm not," I said.

Isaac leaned over to Ethan.

"I've got ten on Red." he staged whispered to his brother.

Ethan snickered.

We ignored them.

"Why?" Zeke all but barked.

"Because it doesn't say where she'd go," I shot back at him.

He blinked at me, not understanding.

"One way," I started to explain, "says it will force her to move on, the other doesn't say what would happen to her." I took a deep breath. "She was 16 when her boyfriend killed her. Yeah, she stayed and didn't want to be dead. I can't blame her for that. Maybe in time she can come to deal with that on her own." I met Zeke's eyes from across the table. "But I can't do something when I don't know where I'd be sending her. Not if she can't touch us anymore."

I took a deep breath before adding. "If she becomes a bigger threat then, yeah, we'll go the other route."

Zeke's eyes softened a bit, and he opened his mouth to speak.

Miles cleared his throat, grabbing everyone's attention.

"As the one who got strangled," Miles began, adjusting his glasses. "I agree with Lexie, she's not really a big threat right now as long as the charms continue to work." He turned to me. "However, knowing where she's buried would allow us to move fast if she does become that threat." He held up the phone. "In the meantime, I've found something on linking to the Veil."

He handed the phone over to me. I started reading.

Apparently linking to the Veil required a lot of meditation and exercises. It took time to develop the ability. Shit. I read the instructions over and over, committing them to memory.

"To do it my way, it's going to take time," I informed them. "It requires a lot of practice. I don't know when we'll be able to move her on."

I dropped the phone and started rubbing my temples. "Are you guys willing to wait to deal with her?" I asked, my eyes closed.

"I am," Isaac assured me.

I opened my eyes to see him wink at me. I gave him a grateful smile.

"Me too," Asher announced.

"I like staying at Miles' house, he's got a hot tub. I say wait," Ethan said.

Zeke sighed.

"Majority rules," Zeke said, his voice neutral.

The conversation quickly moved to a lighter subject. After a few minutes I met Zeke's eyes, he gave me a wink. He wasn't mad at me. My heart felt lighter.

Ethan's phone vibrated on the table, and he picked it up. He was in the middle of a sentence talking about a girl when he stopped. He looked up at me and smiled that mischievous grin of his.

"Lexie, when were you going to tell us about punching Derrick Geeter in the stomach this morning?" Ethan asked sweetly. Asher and

Zeke grinned but kept their mouths shut. Isaac and Miles were looking at me, their questions on their faces.

"Who?" I asked innocently.

"The guy you hit this morning in the hall," Asher reminded me helpfully, his eyes still full of laughter.

"Oh, I never got his name," I admitted, finding that a bit funny myself.

I looked over to Ethan. "If you tell me that it's on Youtube I might have a fit," I told him honestly.

"No, one of the girls I know texted me," Ethan reassured me. "She knows we're friends and is asking why you slugged him."

"Oh, he smacked my ass."

Isaac and Ethan chuckled; Miles gave me a small smile.

"I have a rule. If I don't know you, hands off," I said. The boys grinned at me as if they found it cute or something.

Ethan sent my answer to the girl who asked.

Miles eyes narrowed on me.

"You didn't slug Isaac or Ethan on your first day here," Miles pointed out.

I smiled at that. "They weren't slapping my ass or being jerks." I shrugged. It might be a weird rule, but it was mine. It could be weird. Miles expression told me it made complete sense to him. Our conversation went back to normal.

Soon the bell rang, and I hurried to Gym.

I had just pulled my gym shirt on when Jessica stepped over next to my locker. Oh, great. I'm pantless, and she wants a chat. I pulled my gym shorts out of my locker.

"Can I help you? Or are you just checking me out?" I asked, getting irritated with her watching me. I pulled on my mesh gym shorts and waited.

"You've been hanging out with my brother a lot," Jessica announced to me like this was news. I waited for her to continue. When she kept glaring at me, I realized she was waiting for me to say something.

"And?" I asked before sitting down on the bench and pulling on my sneakers.

"I don't want him hanging out with a skank," she said, practically hissing.

I shook my head and started tying one of my shoes. I ignored her. There was nothing to gain in the conversation, so I didn't even try. She had made up her mind about me. I admit it. I was probably just as big a bitch as I thought she was from her point of view. But I wasn't going to waste my time with this bullshit. I had enough to deal with right now. So, I ignored her.

I was tying my other shoe when I realized some of the other girls were watching us and trying to be stealthy about it. I finished tying my shoe and stood up. I turned around and shut my locker, making sure it latched.

I was pulling my hair up into a messy bun when I met Jessica's eyes. I smiled sweetly.

"Fuck off," I said simply before I turned and walked away.

She wasn't done yet.

"You'll regret this," she shot back.

I stopped and turned around.

"Why am I going to regret this?" I asked, my temper starting to spark. "You're going to destroy my reputation? Spread lies about me?" I asked sarcastically. "I don't really care what people think about me. I know what I am and I know what I'm not." I shrugged casually. "Knock yourself out." I turned to walk out of the now silent locker room.

"I'm going to make you care!" Jessica shouted after me.

I waved my hand goodbye without turning around.

"Doubt it," I shot back over my shoulder. I was out the door before she could say anything more.

The rest of gym was normal; we played basketball and sat around. Jessica didn't approach me again in the locker room. I met Asher on our way to art class as usual.

"You're sure those charms will work, Ally?" Asher asked, his voice uncertain.

"Yep, I couldn't even feel her emotions last night. Not even when I stepped out of the circle." I smiled up at him, trying to be reassuring.

His face relaxed a bit.

"Well, let's not stress test it today," Asher suggested. "No stopping on the path."

"Oh, I'm with you on that." I nodded emphatically.

He finally smiled, his face relaxing a bit. We were getting close to the path when my cell vibrated. I pulled it out and checked it. It was Isaac calling.

"Hey, Cookie Monster."

My phone vibrated telling me there was another call coming in. I ignored it.

"Actually, it's me," said Miles' voice, surprising me. "Isaac let me borrow his phone, since his last classes are with Ethan."

"That was sweet of him."

"Have you walked past her yet?" Miles asked, sounding oddly like Zeke at the moment.

I smiled to myself as Asher's cell phone rang.

"Not yet, we were just getting close."

I watched Asher answer his phone then immediately pulled his phone from his ear wincing. I had a hunch that was Zeke on his phone.

"Are you sure this is going to work?" Miles asked, his voice tense.

I smiled to myself; they were really worried about this.

"I told you guys last night, the charms work. I couldn't feel anything from her at all." I repeated what I had just told Asher. Asher was telling someone to stop yelling.

"You're positive? No doubt in your mind?"

His doubt made me start to think about it. The charms were to keep her from touching me. If she couldn't touch me, she couldn't hurt me.

"Yeah, like ninety-nine-point nine percent sure," I admitted.

"So, you're not a hundred percent sure," he said, his voice getting worried.

I rolled my eyes.

"No one can ever be one hundred percent positive that something isn't going to happen," I told him, wishing he'd just trust me on this.

Asher frowned as he took his phone from his ear held it out to me.

"Zeke wants to talk to you," he said, then gestured that we trade phones. I nodded.

"Miles, honey, I'm going to give you to Asher, Zeke's apparently demanding my attention," I told him before handing the phone over to Asher and taking his. Asher's phone vibrated; someone else was trying to call.

"Greetings, tall and oh so grumpy one," I said to Zeke in the phone, thinking myself funny.

"Why didn't you answer your phone?" Zeke growled into my ear.

I rolled my eyes. "Miles got to me first," I said, snapping back at him.

"Have you walked past her yet?"

Now, I know Asher had told him we hadn't.

"People keep calling and making it harder for us to walk," I pointed out, obviously talking about him.

"Well get walking, I want to listen to what's going on," Zeke demanded.

I thought about what the repercussions would be if I just hung up on him. Knowing Zeke, he'd run across campus to get over here, and it would be over before he got here. But, I did almost die this week, so he wasn't being completely crazy. I sighed as I realized I was going to give in.

"Fine, oh so grumpy and demanding one." I couldn't help mocking him. I mean, really, I tested this last night, we were fine.

I looked up at Asher. "We've been told to walk."

Asher nodded as we headed out to the path.

I turned my attention back to the phone in my hand

"So, how's your day going, Zeke" I asked in a cutesy voice.

He huffed back at me.

I spotted Bitch Ghost; she was waiting in the middle of the path.

"Because mine's going okay." I continued talking to distract him from worrying. And maybe myself a little too.

We started down the path, walking at our normal speed. I kept talking.

"A cute guy talked to me this morning, he asked me about Ethan's band," I began, going over my day. We were almost to Bitch Ghost, and I still felt nothing. It was going to be fine. "Then someone slapped my ass."

She tried to reach out and touch me, but her fingers stopped inches away from me. Her energy was like a blanket in front of me. I felt it only because she was using a lot. The beads on my wrist grew warmer.

"I hit him, but you saw that anyway," I continued in my cutesy voice as we past Bitch Ghost and kept going.

"Yeah, I saw that," Zeke said into the phone. Something about his voice made me think he had that half grin on his face again. At least I was amusing him.

We were almost to class when I decided to have some fun with Zeke.

"Then I hung out with…" I trailed off on purpose and continued in a deadpan voice. "Oh god, the pain. There's a tunnel, a light." I changed to my childlike voice. "Auntie Em? Uncle Henry? Toto? What are you doing here?"

Asher burst out laughing next to me while there was silence on the phone. I couldn't stop myself. I started laughing too.

"That's not fucking funny, Lexie!" Zeke shouted at me.

"Oh, it is from my end." I was still laughing as he cursed at me again. "We're fine, Zeke, we're at the classroom."

Asher's face was red as he doubled over, still laughing. I heard feet running up from behind us and turned. Ethan and Isaac skidded to a stop in front of us.

"And the others just showed up, freaked out because you made me stay on the phone. Baaad Zeke."

The twins looked at me like I was nuts. Asher started laughing harder. Part of it might have been from relief that nothing happened, but I'd like to think it was my smart mouth that had him busting a gut.

"Lexie," Zeke growled into the phone.

"Zeke," I exaggerated a growl back at him. I think I heard him laughing; he was trying to keep it quiet.

"We're fine, don't worry so much. I'll see you in an hour," I told him before hanging up.

Asher was standing, now wiping tears from his face. Isaac had an eyebrow raised as he looked at me, tilted his head in Asher's direction.

"Is he possessed?" Isaac asked seriously.

"No, I was giving Zeke a hard time."

Asher finally pulled himself together enough to put his hand on Isaac's shoulder. "It was awesome."

I MET the twins back at my Blazer after school and headed back to Miles' house. They demanded that I tell them what I said to Zeke that had Asher laughing so much. When I finished, I was pulling up to the gate. The twins were laughing their asses off; it took them two tries to give me the combo for the gate. By the time I reached the circular driveway, the boys had control of themselves.

"Oh, he's going to be pissed," Isaac predicted as I shut off the truck.

"Nah, he was laughing by the end of the call. Besides, I'm too cute to be pissed at for long," I told them sliding out of the Blazer. Zeke's Jeep was coming up the drive. I wondered what happened to the motorcycle from this morning. I reached over my seat and dragged my bag out of the truck.

By the time I was shutting the door, Zeke was walking towards the house.

"Where's the motorcycle?" I asked, heading toward the front door.

Zeke stopped to wait for me.

"It's going to start raining here soon, so I had to put her away until spring," he told me when I reached him. He narrowed his eyes at me. "That wasn't funny by the way." His voice lacked his usual conviction, so I smiled up at him.

"Ooooh yeah, it was," I said over my shoulder as I started walking through the open front door. I looked to see him shaking his head and smiling. My heart lightened. I knew it! He thought it was funny in the end. I win! I felt like shouting wahoo or something, but I kept a lid on it.

My boots crunched over the broken glass all over the floor. Oh yeah, we still had this to clean up. I dropped my bag onto the couch and headed into the kitchen. The twins were raiding the fridge, pulling out sandwich fixings.

"We need to get the living room cleaned up guys," I reminded them as I started looking for a broom and dustpan. The twins groaned.

"Miles said he'd get a maid to come in," Isaac reminded me.

I found the broom and dustpan. The twins were still making sandwiches and Zeke had joined them. I huffed at them as I pulled out a garbage bag and left the kitchen. I quickly put my hair up in a messy bun at the back of my head. I started with the glass on the floor from the French doors. I made sure to get the area around the salt pile; I didn't want to miss any pieces that I'd find later on my foot. When that was cleaned up, I picked up broken frames and pulled the photos out. I piled them onto an end table. I pulled all the broken glass from the frames and leaned them against the wall. They were nice frames; I didn't want to throw them away.

I had cut my fingers a couple times, but I just wiped the blood off on my jeans and kept going. I put the books back on the shelves and swept again. When I had all the glass off the floor I could see, I moved to the French doors. I was on my knees, sitting on my heels, pulling the broken shards of glass from the door frame when the front door opened. I turned to see Miles walking in with a plastic bag and his book bag.

He looked at me his brows drawn together.

"What are you doing?" he asked, closing the door behind him.

I let go of the shard of glass I was trying to pull from the door.

"I've got the living room cleaned up, but I want to vacuum the floor before anyone goes in there barefoot," I said, reaching out and working on that piece of glass again. "I took those photos out of the frames and put them on the end table." I yanked that piece of glass out of the wood, wincing as I sliced a finger again. "I took the glass out of the frames and leaned them against the wall. The glass can probably be replaced." I put the shard into the garbage bag and started working on another one. "The books are back in the case, and now, I'm just trying to get the rest of this broken glass." This piece was being a bitch. "So, you can get the doors fixed before your mom comes back."

I let go of the shard, leaving a bit of blood on the glass from one of my cuts. I was considering breaking the shard into smaller pieces when Miles interrupted my thinking.

"Why? I told you I'd get the maid to do it," he said as he put his book bag down.

"Because the maid didn't make the mess," I offered as I decided to try yanking on the shard one more time, this time from the side. I kept talking, not really paying attention to what I was saying. "Because your maid probably has her hands full keeping the rest of this house clean, and I didn't want to make more work for her." I gave the shard a tug from the right side, and it slid out. Yay! I put that shard in the trash, already looking at the next one.

Miles was quiet while I started tugging on the next shard. My fingers slipped as blood coated the glass.

"Lexie, you're bleeding."

"Yep." I wiped the blood off on my pants. I was reaching for the same shard when Miles stopped me by grabbing my wrist. I looked up at him puzzled.

"What?"

He squatted down beside me; his emerald eyes running over me, his mouth pressed into a hard line.

"Didn't you get the guys to help you?" he asked as he was gently pulling my hand to him and turning it over.

"I told them we needed to, but they wanted to let the maid do it," I admitted.

His fingers were careful as he looked at the cuts on my fingers.

"Don't worry about the cuts," I said. "They're small; they only need a good cleaning out." I gave my hand a little tug, wanting to get back to work.

Miles didn't let go. Instead, he looked at me, his eyes running over my face. That same odd look from last night was back on his face. His eyes were soft as they ran over my face, a small half grin on his lips.

"Go clean out your cuts, Lexie," he said, turning to the door. "I'll finish this up." He let go of my hand and knelt down, pulling the garbage bag out of my reach.

"Are you sure?" I asked uncertainly. I didn't want to stick him with the rest of the clean-up.

Miles pulled a shard out and tossed it into the bag.

"Yes, I'm sure." He was already reaching for another shard. "There's a first aid kit in the downstairs bathroom." He yanked out the shard and tossed it into the bag. "Be sure to use the blue antibacterial cleanser that's in the kit before washing with soap."

"Aye, aye, captain." I gave a small salute before getting to my feet.

Miles smiled as he reached for another shard.

I headed toward the long hallway. He said he was okay cleaning up; I had to take him at his word. I looked back over my shoulder to see him pulling the glass out of the door frame. Miles really was very sweet.

I smiled to myself as I walked down to the bathroom. I found the first aid kit, opened it and pulled out the blue bottle of cleanser. I made sure I was using the right stuff, then started squirting it over my fingers on my right hand. Oh, holy shit!

"Ow, mother fucker, that fucking hurts," I cursed as the cleanser did its job, making the cuts on my fingers burn. I poured some more on until I was sure the cuts were clean. "Shit, shit, shit." I kept cursing over and over.

I heard a vacuum running in the house. I smiled to myself. Miles must have finished with the doors and remembered that I wanted to vacuum to be sure I got the rest of the glass. I focused back on what I was doing. I took a deep breath and squirted the cleanser over the cuts on my left hand. "Shit, shit, shit." I kept cursing as I forced myself to clean the cuts until I was sure it was done. My hands were shaking as I washed with soap and water. I dried my hands and took a good look at the cuts on my fingers. A few were deeper than I thought. I pulled a couple bandages out of the kit to cover my deeper cuts. Ooh, they were a pretty blue color. I liked them better than the beige ones.

I ended up with three on my right hand and two on my left. I put everything back in the kit and put it away. I made sure to throw the trash away before leaving the bathroom. I was almost to the kitchen when I heard the guys' voices coming through the doorway.

"Why didn't you guys help Lexie?" Miles' voice drifted from the kitchen.

Curious, I stopped walking to listen in.

"What are you talking about?" Zeke asked with his gravelly voice.

"Where is she anyway?" Ethan's smoky voice chimed in.

"With what?" Isaac asked.

"She's been cleaning up the mess from last night," Miles announced.

I bit my lip wondering where he was going with this. Was he mad at me for cleaning?

"When I got home she was kneeling in the foyer, pulling out the broken glass from the living room doors. She said it was so I could get them repaired before my mother got back." There was tense silence from the kitchen. I bit the corner of my lower lip. "Where were you guys?"

A few heartbeats of silence went by.

"I didn't hear her say anything about cleaning the mess up," Zeke said honestly. He was right; he hadn't been in the room when I mentioned it.

"She mentioned that we needed to clean it up when we got here," Ethan admitted.

"I told her to let the maid handle it," Isaac explained, sounding uncertain. "She didn't mention it again."

"Because she was out there taking care of it," Miles said, his voice still calm. "While she was pulling glass out of the door frame, she told me she was going to vacuum the living room next to make sure she got all the glass up."

I smiled to myself, Miles was lecturing the guys. It sounded like he was giving them a guilt trip for not helping me clean up. But it didn't sound like he was trying to do that. More like he was letting them know what had happened, and the guilt trip wasn't intentional, it was just a side effect. I liked Miles.

"I'll go do that," Isaac offered. Wood scraped across the tile.

"I already did it," Miles said his voice still calm and neutral. "After I sent her to wash up, I finished the doors and vacuumed the living room."

"Why'd she have to wash up?" Zeke's voice sounded like he had already guessed the reason and was just looking for confirmation.

"She cut her hands up cleaning all the glass off the floor," Miles informed them. The other guys cursed. "So, next time she mentions all of us cleaning something up, you guys might want to check to make sure she's not just doing it herself."

The guys agreed, sounding apologetic.

I tiptoed back down the hallway and closed the bathroom door a little harder than I needed to. Not a slam, just a hard close. Then I walked back up the hall and into the kitchen as if I hadn't heard a thing. Everyone looked at me. I smiled, went to the fridge, and pulled out a cold bottle of water. I came over to the breakfast bar and stood next to Miles across from the guys. I was opening my bottle when Miles broke the silence.

"So, you did have some deep ones," he said, gesturing at my fingers.

"Not that deep, just bad enough to need a band-aid for a couple days." I held up my bandaged fingers and wiggled them. "Look. I got blue," I said, trying to show the guys I wasn't mad at them.

Miles smiled down at me.

"Sorry, Lexie, I didn't realize you were cleaning up the living room." Zeke's voice was sincere. I shrugged.

"Sorry, Red, next time just smack us if we aren't listening," Isaac said, wincing.

"Sorry Beautiful, I just thought you were taking some girl time away from us guys." Ethan shrugged, his face apologetic.

"It's okay; you guys can do dishes tonight." I waited a beat before adding, "And tomorrow." I waited another beat. "And the day after that." I leaned over to Miles and stage whispered. "Think I could get any more out of them than that?"

Miles looked like he was actually considering it. Zeke was shaking his head, the corner of his mouth twitching, and the twins looked like they were expecting bad news.

"You'd be pushing your luck," Miles stage-whispered back. "But if you pout, I think you can get a couple more days."

Zeke's face went hard as he got to his feet.

"No, no, no." Zeke pointed at me as he headed out of the room. "I'm not dealing with that fucking pout again." He strode from the room fuming. I burst out laughing, the other guys looked confused. Isaac ran to the doorway.

"Is it really that bad?!" Isaac shouted down the hall.

"Find out for yourself!" Zeke shouted back.

Everyone started laughing.

When I managed to get control of myself, I opened my water bottle and looked up at Miles.

"What took you so long to get home?"

Miles smirked at me and pulled a new cell phone out of his pocket.

"Had to pick up a new phone, my other one is still in the pool." Miles turned it on and swiped at the screen. I pulled out my phone and handed it to him.

"Share contacts, it'll be faster," I said.

Miles grinned and took my phone.

I leaned over the breakfast counter to grab a chip out of the bag. I had just popped it into my mouth when Zeke walked back in, his book bag over his shoulder.

"I saw that," he said from the doorway.

I narrowed my eyes at him, grabbed another chip, and popped it in my mouth while he watched. I chewed then swallowed it.

"You saw that too," I said, stating the obvious before turning to the others. "Let's get our homework out of the way." The twins shared a grin and got up. Miles agreed. Zeke came over and put the chips up high where I couldn't reach them.

I like a challenge.

CHAPTER 14

*A*sher came in from practice an hour later. He called from the front door that he needed a shower, and he'd be down in a bit. I finished my rough draft for my World Civ. essay on my laptop and decided I wanted a snack. I got up and headed into the kitchen.

As I passed the living room, I noticed that Miles had rearranged the furniture. One leather couch faced the fireplace with the coffee table in front of it, and the other was just to the left of the coffee table. It looked nice.

I had just pulled down the chips from Zeke's hiding spot when Asher came in. His hair was still wet from the shower. He was wearing dark-gray sweatpants and a blue t-shirt. He looked up and went still. Then he smiled.

"Ally girl, why are you standing on the counter?" he asked, smiling.

I sat down on the counter and grinned wickedly. "Because Zeke hid the chips too high for me to reach. Or so he thought."

Asher laughed as I opened the bag and ate a chip. I raised an eyebrow at him. "Are you in your jammies?" I asked before eating another chip.

Asher smiled as he dug in the pantry.

"Yes, I am. No point in getting dressed again when I'm just going to bed soon anyway," he said, turning around with his hands full of ingredients.

I scooted over to the breakfast bar to give him more work room as I watched him collect some chicken and fresh veggies from the fridge. I sat cross-legged on the tiled counter and watched him working in the kitchen.

"What ya doing?" I asked in my cutesy voice. He smiled as he pulled out a cutting board with the word meat burned into it.

"I am cooking dinner for everyone.," He went to the sink and washed his hands. "Do you want to help?"

"Sure." I hopped down from the counter then gave him an appraising eye. "Do I need to be in my jammies?"

Asher chuckled. "Yes, this is a wearing jammies cooking night," Asher declared before tilting his head toward the doorway. "Hurry and change."

I hurried out the door then jogged down the hall. I went into the master bedroom and changed into my black flannel bottoms. A faded black Red Hot Chili Peppers shirt. I redid my messy bun and hurried back to the kitchen. Asher was cutting up the chicken, so I went to the kitchen and washed my hands.

"Okay, what do you want me to do?" I asked, drying my hands. Asher stopped cutting chicken and gestured me over near him. He pointed at a drawer.

"Open the drawer and take out the cutting board that says veggies on it," he instructed, keeping his hands away from anything. I pulled out the cutting board. He seemed to think for a second, then went to wash his hands. "We're making stir fry chicken, with a yellow curry sauce." He quickly washed his hand and then was back beside me. He pulled out a smaller knife than he'd been using on the chicken. Then he grabbed the head of broccoli and put it on my cutting board.

"Normally I make the sauce myself, but I still have homework to do so we're going with the jar kind tonight." He grumbled as he set the knife on the cutting board. "Stir fry is all about the prep," he began to explain.

I noticed that small light was back in his eyes.

"Stir-fry cooking is fast and at high heat. The pain is cutting every-thing up, especially for this many people."

I nodded.

"Do you know how to cut up raw broccoli?" he asked.

I shook my head.

He smiled down at me before putting the broccoli back and grab-bing a bunch of carrots. "Okay, let's start with knife cuts on the carrots." That light in his eyes was getting bigger as he became more animated. "What you're going to do is julienne cuts. This is how you do it." He took an already washed carrot and cut it into large chunks about an inch long. He cut the sides off till it was a block of carrot. Then he made slices out of that block. He then stacked the slices and cut down the sides, creating little pieces of carrot. He did it so quickly it was obvious he'd done this a lot. "You got that, Ally?"

"Yeah, let me at those carrots."

He chuckled as he handed me the knife, with him holding the blade. I took it carefully, not wanting to cut him. He stepped away and continued cutting the chicken.

I worked in silence while I got used to what I was doing, then I was able to talk and not cut myself. "So, you usually make yellow curry from scratch?"

"Yeah, it's just so much better when you make it yourself. The flavor isn't watered down, and you can add different things to change it as you go."

I smiled to myself as Asher began talking about cooking. The recipes he loved and the ones that crashed and burned. Apparently, Asher was having trouble with a banana foster; he said he just sucked at desserts. I asked him questions about why you do this or that when cooking and he actually knew the answers. Over the next hour, he was animated, excited, and happy as he talked about food and cook-ing. It made my heart melt a little. He needed to be a chef, it's what he loved. When we finished with the prep, I sat on the breakfast bar again and watched him cook. He impressed me. He put everything in a huge serving bowl and told me to grab mine before the guys came in as he headed out to tell the guys dinner was ready.

I had just finished dishing up my bowl when the others came in. I quickly got out of their way and headed back to the dining room.

I sat back down in my spot and took a bite. Oh, my god... that is soo good. Okay, Asher was a cooking God, and I needed to make him see that. I put it on my to-do list in the back of my head. Make Asher go to culinary school. There is no way I'd forget that.

Everyone else came in and sat down. Asher pulled his books out before he ate dinner.

"Asher, will you marry me?" I asked down the table, covering my mouth since I was talking with my mouth full. Everyone chuckled.

Those blue eyes flashed down the table at me.

"You just want me for my cooking," he accused me, smiling. I swallowed my food and scoffed in mock outrage.

"No, you're my wonderful friend Asher," I told him honestly. Then I mumbled. "Who could also cook like a god."

Asher burst out laughing, his cheeks turning pink.

"I don't think so, Ally girl." He said shaking my head.

"Can't blame a girl for trying," I grumbled before taking another bite. The boys laughed at me. I didn't care; I was stuffing myself on Asher's cooking.

EVERYONE WAS STILL in the dining room an hour later. Asher had just finished his homework and was putting his books away when Zeke got to his feet.

"I've got to go to work," Zeke grumbled as he headed out the door to the hallway. Everyone said bye. He waved without turning around then he was gone.

I couldn't stall anymore. I had to go do those meditation exercises.

"Miles, is there anywhere in the house that is, well, peaceful?" I asked. Miles looked down the table at me. "I need to start those meditation exercises."

He seemed to think about it, and he smiled.

"There is one place. Come on, I'll show you." He got to his feet, and I followed as he led me down the left side of the long hallway. I looked around as I followed; I'd never been past the dining room on this side of the house. He took me all the way to the end to a glass wall and door. Through the glass, I saw a lot of green plants. He opened the door, switched on the light and gestured for me to go first. I walked into a giant glass room filled with plants and the sound of flowing water.

"You have a conservatory?" I couldn't believe it. Climbing plants covered some of the glass walls. Flowering vines covered every column. There was green everywhere, with flowers of every color imaginable tucked here and there.

"My mother is a botanist, or was before she stopped working. She still loves plants," Miles explained as I walked further into the room.

I followed the path through the forest of plants. When I reached the center of the room, I found a round cement fountain in the center of the clearing with water streaming out of the mouths of three frogs into the blue-tiled basin. It was amazing. I was also pretty sure my mouth had dropped opened, so I made a point to close it.

"Wow," I muttered; it was all I could manage. I looked up to see a curved glass ceiling, twenty feet above. I bet if you shut off the lights you'd be able to see the stars in here.

"I take it you like it?" he asked, his voice quiet again.

I nodded.

"I would rather have an observatory," Miles admitted.

I pulled my eyes off the flowers to look at him.

"That would be pretty cool too," I admitted before I went back to getting a closer look at the flowers on one of the columns. "But you're talking to a girl who lived in a trailer for four years. Not to mention I kill every plant I ever get." I decided not to touch any of the flowers just in case my luck was transferable.

"Good point," Miles said. "Do you think this would work for trying to meditate?"

I nodded, my eyes still running over all the colors.

"If I can't do it here, I'll never be able too," I admitted. I heard him blow air through his nose.

"Then I'll leave you to it," he said, walking back up the path.

"Thank you, Miles," I called out before he got out of earshot.

"You're welcome, Lexie."

The door closed, and I was alone in the big beautiful room. I looked around and found a cushioned patio couch. I sat down and pulled out my cell phone. I looked up the directions on how to begin meditating to link to the Veil. I closed my eyes and focused on my breathing. I tried to clear my mind, but things kept popping up. Memories of my mother, memories of getting jumped, the boys showing up after I woke up. Everything over the last week kept popping up into my head, distracting me. I tried to do what the instructions said and let the thought go to keep my mind clear. I was having a hard time with it. I sat there cross-legged on the couch and tried to clear my head.

THIS WASN'T WORKING. I opened my eyes and sighed. I had been at it for almost two hours and I still couldn't even get past step one. I got up and walked back into the house. I was trying to figure out what I was doing wrong when raised voices caught my attention.

"What the hell happened?" Asher shouted.

I raised an eyebrow.

"It's nothing, I'm fine." Zeke's growl rolled from the kitchen.

"Let me take a look," Miles ordered Zeke. "I'm calling in Dr. Tayes."

"I'll take care of it!" Zeke growled.

Something was wrong; I walked faster.

"Then you'll have no problem showing us your hand." Asher pointed out, his voice rising.

I was jogging by the time I reached the kitchen. Zeke was on the kitchen side of the breakfast counter, a first aid kit open in front of him. His left hand was wrapped in bloody gauze; he was wrapping more gauze on top of the old.

"What happened?" I asked, my voice hard as I strode into the kitchen. Zeke was the only one who glanced at me, then he was back dealing with his hand again.

"I had an accident at work." Zeke snapped as he pulled the gauze tight.

I stood across from Zeke at the breakfast bar and watched as blood continued to soak through the bandages. That wasn't good.

"Miles, call the doctor. Tell him Zeke will probably need stitches," I told him in a calm voice. I reached into the first aid kit and pulled out a pair of gloves. Miles pulled out his phone and dialed.

"I don't need stitches," Zeke was shouting now, his body becoming rigid.

I pulled on the gloves.

"Zeke you're bleeding through a lot of gauze. That's not fine," I snapped back at him as I grabbed more gauze and grabbed his hand. The mound of gauze was on the top of his hand, I put his hand on flat on the counter, covering the top with my palm and pressed down with everything I had. Zeke grunted and clenched his teeth.

"That fucking hurts!" he snarled at me, hitting his other fist into the tile counter.

"Too fucking bad!" I snapped back. His scalding eyes rose to meet mine from across the counter. "We need to stop the bleeding, so suck it up!"

He bent over. His head faced down, looking at the floor in front him, his arms braced on the counter. He was taking deep breaths and letting them out slowly, his body shaking.

"Now what the fuck happened?!" I shouted at him, demanding an answer. The other guys backing up a step away from us.

"A fucking hood slammed down on my hand." He growled at me, his head still down. "I managed to catch it just before it hit."

A weight settled in my chest. How would a hood slam down on his hand? Zeke worked on cars a lot; it didn't sound like a mistake he would make.

"What are you leaving out, Zeke?" I growled, hoping my instinct was wrong.

Zeke hit the counter again.

"Zeke!" I barked at him again.

He looked up at me; his jaw clenched his eyes blazing.

"I fucking smelled patchouli right before it slammed down," he snarled.

The guys cursed.

I felt myself go quiet inside, my head was clear and my body was still. I had only felt this one other time in my life, and I ended up beating the shit out of someone with a short crowbar.

"Okay, did you see any broken bones?" I asked, my voice calm now.

Zeke dropped his head again, his body still shaking. He hit the counter again.

"No broken bones. I can move everything," he said, practically growling. "It just won't stop bleeding."

I kept the pressure on his hand. Zeke slammed his other fist into the counter again and again.

"Yeah, break your other hand, that'll help," Isaac snapped from somewhere behind me.

There was a buzzing sound in the kitchen. Miles went to the monitor on the wall and pressed the button to open the front gate.

"Doctor's here."

It turned out Zeke needed a dozen stitches. I watched silently as the doctor Miles had called worked to close the big gash across the top of his hand. When I thought no one would notice, I slipped out of the dining room and headed down the hall. I went into the kitchen and grabbed a tub of salt. I ignored the pounding in my ears as I headed outside and tossed that into the back of the Blazer. I walked around the outside of the house and found where the gardeners kept their tools. I picked up a shovel and a full gas can. I walked back to the blazer. I put those down and pulled down the tailgate.

The doctor's car was gone. He must have been finished with Zeke's hand. My pulse was racing when I realized I didn't have a lighter. I remembered seeing matches in a kitchen drawer. Still, in that numb calm, I walked inside and went to the kitchen. I opened the drawer.

"You okay, Beautiful?" Ethan asked.

I didn't even see him in the room. That didn't really bother me right now; I had something I needed to do. I nodded and pulled the matches out.

"What are you doing with the matches, Red?"

I hadn't seen Isaac either, that's okay. I was going to make sure they were out of this from now on. I closed the drawer and headed out of the kitchen.

"Lexie!" Isaac shouted after me. "What are you doing?"

I didn't answer; I was trying to remember what else I needed. I was driving to the cemetery. Keys. I need the keys. Without keys, the truck wouldn't start.

"Guys! Lexie has matches and has gotten real fucking quiet!" Ethan shouted down the hall as I walked into the living room.

I picked up my jacket and checked the pockets. Vaguely, I heard feet running down the hall. I found my keys.

"What's going on?" Miles' voice was quiet behind me. I ignored them; I was almost out the door anyway.

"She came in, she got matches and hasn't said..."

Isaac's voice went out of earshot as I stepped outside. I reached the truck and picked up the shovel. I needed to get going. I had a lot of digging to do before dawn.

"Lexie, what do you think you're doing?" Zeke's voice came from behind me. I didn't even hear him come out.

"Taking care of a problem," I said as I put the shovel inside the back of the truck with shaking hands. Why was I shaking? Huh, I'll figure it out later. I have to get going.

"You said you didn't want to go that route, remember?" Miles' voice was gentle.

When did he get here? I focused on picking up the gas can and putting that in the back too.

"Things change." I slammed the gate shut. The pounding in my ears was getting louder. I headed around the truck. Asher was standing in front of the driver side door. Where did he come from?

"Please move, Asher." That numbness was starting to fade, and I wanted to get this done before that. I needed to get this done before that happened.

"Can't do that, Ally."

I needed to get in the Blazer, and Asher was blocking me. My skin was hot, edgy, the cool fall air was feeling really good right now. The other side. I can use the other door. I went to walk around Asher, but he stepped in front of me.

"We can't let you do something when you're angry that you'll regret later."

I shook my head. I didn't understand what he was saying. I wasn't angry. I just needed to get this done now.

"I'm not angry, things are just very clear right now," I said, my voice calm and flat. There was a curse, but Asher's mouth didn't move.

"Lexie, you're severely pissed off and aren't thinking straight." Ethan's voice was calm next to me.

I turned my head to see him standing there. I was confused; when did he get here? The numbness was starting to pull back. My skin was feeling tight. No. I couldn't just stand around, I needed to keep going, keep moving. Before I began to feel again.

"Doesn't matter," I said as my shoulders grew tense. "She hurt my friends. I hurt her. It's very simple." I reached for the driver door. There was another curse, maybe Ethan? Was Ethan still out here?

Asher moved back to block me.

"You said you didn't want to go this route because you didn't know what would happen to her. Do you remember that?" Isaac's voice surprised me; I didn't know he was here too.

I turned my head to see him stepping around Ethan. Ethan was still out here after all. When I couldn't move forward, that numbness began pulling back. Fire licked in my gut as I pictured the marks on Mile's neck, the blood on Zeke's hand. It needed to stop. I needed to make that bitch stop. I felt my body really starting to shake. I needed to move.

"Screw her," I managed to say through clenched teeth.

I still needed in the truck. I turned to walk around the back of the truck, only to find myself blocked. The others had spread out behind me, boxing me in. Didn't they get it? Didn't they understand that until I did this, this shit would just keep happening? That numbness pulled back further, my body became rigid as the fire in my gut built to a blaze. Feeling was coming back hard and fast. The numbness disappeared completely. The blaze rushed over me, showing me Zeke's hand, Miles' neck. Over and over.

"You are not in the right place to make this decision tonight," Zeke said, his voice calm. How the fuck was he so calm? He should be helping me take care of that bitch, not blocking me.

My blood was boiling. My hands were twitching to get moving, get digging. I took deep breaths through my nose. I wanted to hurt someone. I wanted to hit, beat and tear into someone until the rage was gone. I kept a tight hold on my body. I didn't want to hit them; I didn't want to hurt them. But they wouldn't fucking move. I couldn't get to that bitch.

I locked my body down, not daring to move an inch. Ethan saw the change in me; I saw it in his eyes.

"Maybe we should do this like Zeke and just hold her till she calms down?" Isaac suggested,

I looked from Ethan and glared at Isaac. Not if you want to live asshole. I held back a fresh wave a heat that tinged my vision red. I closed my eyes. Something was wrong. That wasn't right. That was Isaac; I'd never want to hurt Isaac. What was wrong with me? I focused on breathing and keeping myself still. Something was very wrong.

"That would be a very bad idea," Ethan advised. "She's one wrong move from swinging at us."

I really was, I was holding on by a thread. I could barely think, but I was trying to. I opened my eyes and looked at the gravel of the driveway. Still taking deep breaths.

"She needs an outlet, and we're cutting her off from the only one she's knows right now." A hand was held out to me, palm up. "Lexie, you need to let all that out. Come with me, and I'll show you what works for me."

I stared at Ethan's hand for a couple minutes, oddly noticing the calluses on his fingers from guitar strings. I kept taking deep breaths, trying to swim up through the rage. It had taken a while before I had enough control to trust myself to move. I lifted my eyes from the gravel to Ethan's.

His amber eyes met mine and waited. He waited patiently for me to be ready to move. I reached out and put my shaking hand in his. His hand closed around mine.

"Brother, get my iPod from my room." Ethan kept eye contact with me as he started walking backward, pulling me out from between the others. After a few steps, he must have realized I wasn't going to fight him. He turned and led me back into the house, at a slow walk.

My blood was still boiling, my stomach a hard knot. I felt my jaw still clenched. I focused on moving, on not hitting anyone. On keeping myself under control. I had all this rage inside me, and I didn't know how to get rid of it. He led me through the foyer and into the living room. He walked me carefully around the couch and had me sit looking towards the fireplace. I sat down, crossing my legs under me in the middle of the couch. I tucked my hands under my butt, hoping for a little more control. The pounding in my ears was still there. So, when Isaac was suddenly there; handing Ethan his iPod and head-phones I didn't really notice.

I was looking at the fireplace when Ethan sat down on the coffee table directly in front of me. His warm eyes met mine.

"I noticed something about you over the last week, Beautiful. You're a bit of an audiophile." He turned on his iPod and connected his headphones. He looked back to me, meeting my eyes again; keeping that connection with me. "You love music and sound, it puts you out of your head and changes how you're feeling." He reached out towards me. I went rigid, keeping my body still as he put his big head-phones around my neck. "Right now, you want to rip someone apart, and we need to get that out of you." He reached out again, my body still as stiff as a board. He put his headphones on my ears. "I want you to close your eyes, listen to the music and let yourself feel what you're feeling. And go where the music goes."

I must have looked at him as if he was crazy because he kept talking.

"We're not letting you leave the couch, but you need to get this out. Got it, Beautiful?"

I nodded slowly. He gave me a small smile and fiddled with the iPod. He went to a specific playlist that was labeled "pissed off". He hit play and handed the iPod out to me. I pulled my right hand out from under me and took it gently. I closed my eyes as Drowning Pool's Bodies began playing in my ears. I turned it up so I couldn't hear anything else. And I did what Ethan told me to. I listened to the music and felt the rage I was holding inside. I didn't fight it; I didn't do anything about it. I just gave myself permission to feel how I was feeling. Then Disturbed's Down With The Sickness came on. Then Korn, Then Metallica. Then Linkin Park.

Then when I felt like I needed to move, to do something else to get this out, I felt a touch on my hand. When did my hands move to my lap? I opened my eyes to find Ethan still sitting on the coffee table, pushing a large sketchpad and soft pastels into my lap. I took them gratefully, rocking with the beat of the music I was listening to. I didn't ask where the art supplies came from, I just took them and started to use them. I drew dark scenes that poured from me in my anger. I drew, blended, and smudged. I wiped my fingers on my pants and kept going, ignoring everything and everyone else. I poured everything out of me onto the pages.

Then the music changed, it was subtle at first. Less driving beats and shouting, to less harsh songs. Seether, Halestorm, Within-temptation, and then more rock music blended with violins and then pianos. The tempo changed again. The songs became slower, vocals, piano, and violin. It ended with Disturbed's The Sound of Silence.

When the music stopped, I blinked hard. I felt weak, my arms heavy. My heart was no longer racing. My breathing was smooth and even. I was drained, empty, and no longer needing to tear someone apart. I looked up to find Ethan still sitting on the coffee table, still watching me. I took off his headphones and looked at him with fresh eyes. I'd never seen Ethan angry except that business with my back, but he knew exactly how I had felt out there. That raging calm that took over. He understood it; he'd felt it himself. So often, that he had a play list specifically for it.

He sat waiting, his body was tense. His fingers were spinning one of his rings constantly. His knee started to bounce. I didn't know how to tell him I understood how hard that was, letting me see that much of him. So, I untucked my feet, scooted to the edge of the sofa, my knees going between his legs. I reached out, pulling him into a hug. After a heartbeat, he wrapped his arms around me and squeezed me back. His body relaxed, his face resting against my hair. His spicy cologne filling my lungs.

"Thank you," I whispered into his shoulder.

One of his hands moved to cup the back of my head.

"Always," he whispered back, his smoky voice low.

"I might need a copy of that play list before this is over," I admitted as I started to shake. I wasn't ready to let go of him yet. He nodded against my hair. He let me hold onto him as long as I needed. He didn't get impatient; he didn't even shift his weight. He just held me as long as I needed. Warmth was flooding through me again. There was no wall there anymore. Not against him, not against any of them. When I finally stopped shaking I let go, he let me pull away. He brushed the hair from my face. His eyes were watching me still.

"Do you know why you decided to go to the cemetery?" he whispered, his face only inches from mine.

I dropped my gaze down to my knees. His black jean-clad legs were on the outside of mine. His hands cupping the sides of my legs, one of his thumbs rubbing back and forth. My throat was tight as I nodded.

"Can you tell me?" His voice was gentle again, soft and soothing.

"Meditating didn't go well tonight," I whispered back my cheeks burning. I scoffed at myself. "I couldn't even get past the first step." It was pathetic, I managed to fail immediately. "Zeke got hurt, he needed stitches." I took a deep calming breath. "She's escalating and getting stronger." I looked at my black and red pastel covered fingers twisting in my lap. "The longer it takes to link with the Veil, the bigger the chance is that you guys will get hurt."

"That's the risk we all agreed to take," he said, his voice rolling through my ears, making it hard not to listen.

I shook my head. "Zeke didn't, majority rules," I reminded him as I looked back up into his dark eyes.

Ethan gave me a gentle smile, his eyes running over my face again.

"He could have appealed, Lexie," he said. "If Zeke felt that strongly about it, he would have appealed. We would have discussed it again." He reached out and wiped his thumb across my cheek. It came back with black pastel on the tip. "He changed his mind when you told him why you didn't want to use the cemetery route."

I looked at him as if he was nuts.

"Zeke? Changed his mind?" I asked slowly just to be sure I heard correctly.

Ethan chuckled softly, his teeth flashing in a smile.

"It does happen on occasion, Beautiful."

I didn't know if I really believed him. I didn't know what else to say, so I looked around the living room. It was empty, it was just us. My gaze went back to my lap.

"I have an idea to help you meditate that we can try tomorrow," he said

"I'll try anything," I admitted, my cheeks still warm. I needed to get this right and soon. I pulled my gaze from my lap to his handsome face. I gestured behind me. "Everyone go to bed?"

He snorted quietly. He gave my legs one last squeeze before letting go and scooting further back on the coffee table.

"The guys forced Zeke to take a couple pain pills, so he's sleeping up in his room," he began. "When the others saw that you were calming down they went to bed. Miles put me in charge of making sure you go to bed."

I felt lighter knowing I wouldn't have to see anyone else tonight.

Ethan gestured at the drawings in my lap. "What do you want to do with these?"

I looked down in my lap. I picked them up, frowning. I couldn't understand what I was seeing until I laid the four pictures out in my lap. I'd created several dark pictures, all interconnecting in a mosaic.

My chest went tight as I realized what I was seeing. I scooped them up quickly, not wanting Ethan to see what I had drawn tonight. He didn't need to know, the guys didn't need to know.

"Burn them," I whispered quietly, my voice small.

One of his eyebrows arched as he met my eyes. Asking me silently if I was serious.

"Please."

His eyes turned into warm chocolate before he nodded and held his hand out for them. I didn't even hesitate before handing them over.

I couldn't get rid of them fast enough. Ethan got to his feet and walked around the coffee table. My body was twitchy, on edge. I needed to do something tonight to protect the guys; I couldn't just wait till tomorrow. The knot in my stomach wouldn't let me. I went into the kitchen and pulled down another tub of salt. When I stepped back into the living room, the drawings were burning in the fireplace. When they were ashes, I felt better, less naked.

Ethan turned, his worried eyes meeting mine. He had looked at them. He knew what I drew; I could see it in his eyes. The naked feeling came back as I looked away from him and at the tub in my hands. I swallowed hard before I could say anything.

"I just want to throw some salt on your guys' bedroom floors." I peeked back up at him knowing my cheeks were a little pink.

His eyes were understanding as he nodded. He took me upstairs and opened each of the guys' bedroom doors. I tiptoed into every room and scattered salt by hand onto every floor. When we reached Zeke's, Ethan grabbed my arm, stopping me from going inside. He took the salt from me and salted Zeke's room himself. When he came back out, he handed it back to me. Ethan even watched me quietly as I did the same in his room. When we were done, those rooms were just as safe as being in a salt circle.

When I was satisfied, he walked me back downstairs. I was going to put the tub back in the kitchen, but he took it from me and went down the hall. I didn't understand until he stepped into my room. By the time I got there, he had most of the room salted. I didn't even think of salting my own room--it didn't even occur to me.

But it had occurred to Ethan, and he did it himself. When he was done, he gave me a stormy look.

"You don't get to make yourself a target." His smooth voice was firm, his lips pressed together as his eyes held mine.

"I didn't..."

He gave me a gentle smile. "Think past protecting us," he said, finishing my sentence for me.

I nodded, massaging my arm with my other hand.

"Get some sleep, Beautiful."

He walked past me and I heard the door close behind me. I had a sudden urge to call him back. I didn't want to be alone. I kept my mouth closed as I went into the bathroom and washed the pastel chalk from my hands. When I was done, I looked in the mirror. My face was pale, my eyes wider than usual. There was black chalk on my face still. I washed my face as I remembered my drawings. I used a towel to dry, wishing I could wash the image of those five headstones out of my mind. And their lone guardian standing barefoot in the dead grass. I didn't sleep well that night.

CHAPTER 15

I stayed up late into the night, my eyes on the ceiling. I thought about ways that Ghost Bitch could hurt the others. It made my chest tight most of the night. At least until I started coming up with ways to prevent it. The more ideas I had about preventing the boys getting hurt, the better I felt.

I was still awake when the sun came up, but I felt like myself again this morning. I got up and got ready for school. When I pulled on my black bra I winced, my girls were hurting. I hissed, just the bra was going to ache today. The joys of being a girl. I wore dark blue jeans, a black cami, and a faded purple, green and white plaid, which I tucked into my jeans and buttoned up until I was comfortable. The cami was in case a button popped open.

I headed into the kitchen as I pulled my hair back into a ponytail. I was the first one up again, which meant there was a full carafe of coffee. I grabbed a cup of coffee. Not feeling real hungry, I just made some buttered toast. I was actually starting to be a bit optimistic about my chances of protecting the guys as long as they paid attention around them it should be all right.

I had just started on my second cup of coffee when the others started coming downstairs. Miles eyed the carafe and eyed me. I wasn't really paying attention. I was staring at the corner of the kitchen, still lost in my head, going over the ideas I had last night again and trying to punch holes in them.

"Lexie, are you alright?"

I jerked my eyes away from the corner and brought myself back to the present. Miles was standing across the breakfast bar from me wearing a dark green hoodie, a Mario Brothers shirt, and jeans.

His eyebrows drew together as his eyes ran over me.

"I didn't get any sleep," I admitted, taking a drink of coffee. His ears were pink as he looked uncomfortable gesturing towards my shirt.

"I can tell, your shirt buttons are all crooked," he said politely.

I looked down at my shirt to see he was right. I snorted at myself and jerked at my shirt, popping the metal snap buttons open. Miles spun around fast, almost spilling his coffee.

"Whoa. Okay, um. Lexie..."

I laughed. He thought I just whipped out the girls.

"I'm wearing a cami underneath. Relax, Miles." I was still laughing as I started buttoning my shirt up properly.

Miles looked at me out of the corner of his eye. When he saw I was telling the truth he turned back around, his face pink. I just shook my head at him smiling. His blushing totally made my morning. He went about getting himself breakfast while ignoring me.

Isaac came into the kitchen and froze, watching me. I had just unbuttoned my jeans to tuck in my shirt.

"Are you getting naked in the kitchen?" His voice didn't sound like he was that much against it if I was.

I laughed at the look of excitement on his face. "I'm tucking my shirt in," I informed him, smiling as I started doing just that. "Miles thought I was, too, for a minute."

Miles' ears turned red as he poured himself cereal.

"Well, I didn't expect you to just rip your shirt open to fix your buttons," Miles pointed out.

"What happened?" Asher walked in, an eyebrow already raised.

I started laughing as Miles turned a little redder.

"Miles thought I was stripping," I told him, teasing Miles.

Miles put the cereal box down a little harder than necessary his eyes narrowing at me.

"I told the girl that her buttons were crooked on her shirt. She just reaches up and rips her shirt open without a word," Miles said, defending himself. "How was I supposed to know she's wearing something underneath?" Miles' voice was asking me to drop it.

My smile faded. He was really uncomfortable with this topic. The guys burst out laughing, making his face turn redder. His eyes were on his cereal, focusing more than anyone ever needed to. He was really embarrassed. Shit. I felt awful. I had only meant to tease him; I had to fix this.

"Being the gentlemen that he is, he turned his back as fast as possible," I admitted. I buttoned my pants and started pulling the shirt out a little until it was comfortable. I walked around the counter with my empty mug. I stopped next to Miles, leaned into him, and nudged his shoulder gently with mine. "Thank you for being such a gentleman, Miles. Most guys would have just watched with their mouths hanging open." I shot a look specifically at Isaac before looking back at Miles profile.

"Just warn me next time," Miles mumbled before drinking out of his mug.

"Promise," I whispered back.

He nodded letting me know that he heard me. I smiled to myself as I went over to refill my mug.

"I wasn't even in here, and I get the stink eye," Isaac said as he went to get breakfast.

I just chuckled at him as I was putting the carafe back.

"Why did Isaac get the stink eye?" Zeke asked as he strode into the kitchen.

I could practically hear Miles turning redder.

"For being a guy. It's that kind of morning," I answered before anyone could embarrass Miles further. I put cream and sugar in my coffee and headed back to sit on the counter by the sink since all the bar stools were taken now.

Zeke poured himself some coffee.

Miles looked at the mug in my hands. "How much coffee have you had this morning?" he asked me, his face now back to his normal color.

"This is my third cup, and I'm finally waking up," I admitted. "I didn't sleep last night. Zeke's accident got me thinking about some things."

The room was filled with tense silence as Ethan walked in, wearing his usual black clothes and silver jewelry. He looked at everyone's serious expressions and stopped cold.

"We only just got up," he said with a moan. "Did something happen already?"

I chuckled at the almost whine in his voice. Poor Ethan.

"No, I think I just made all the guys nervous at the same time," I observed, looking over each of the guys' faces as I took a drink of coffee. "Unclench your butt cheeks, boys; I'm not heading out to the cemetery."

Ethan and Isaac snickered as everyone relaxed. Everyone went about eating and getting breakfast as I started talking again.

"I was thinking of ways that Bitch Ghost could hurt you guys with what's around you." I gestured towards Zeke. "Like with the hood on Zeke's hand. How are you feeling anyway?"

Zeke shrugged his mouth full when he swallowed he answered. "I'll live." That's all he said.

A small knot formed in my stomach again, it made me glad I only had toast for breakfast. Okay, Zeke wasn't going to tell me how he is feeling.

"What stuff do you think she could do to hurt us?" Ethan asked before pouring his coffee.

"If she can slam a car hood down like that, then she could probably mess with your brake lines, knock stuff over on to you. Anything that doesn't actually involve touching you." The room went quiet. Yeah, that's how I felt all night. Luckily, I had already come up with an answer to at least one issue. "If we throw salt over and in the cars. Then at the engine-"

"Wait, you didn't say in the engine, did you?" Zeke interrupted, his brow drawing down.

"No, *at* the engine," I assured him. "Then she couldn't touch the car or anything attached to it." I shrugged and continued. "And we only have to check the brake lines this morning before leaving, and we won't have to worry about it again. Just throw some salt around every day until we deal with her."

Some of the guys were nodding. Zeke got to his feet, picking up his bowl and coffee mug.

"Let's take one car today...we don't have the time for me to check everything for more than one right now," Zeke suggested as he put his bowl and mug in the sink. He turned and leaned against it while looking at the guys.

"Okay, whose car seats six without too much squishing?" Isaac asked.

Zeke raised his hand.

"Mine, we can pull it off if someone short rides in the middle, in front." He looked pointedly at me.

"Do I have to ride bitch?" I asked, really wanting a seat and my own seat belt.

Zeke gave me a half grin. "No, the console lifts up, and there's a seat." He explained, pushing away from the sink.

"No problem." I said.

"I'll get on it." Zeke nodded once before he headed out of the kitchen.

It wasn't until Zeke was outside that I remembered Asher had football practice after school.

"Uh, you have practice, don't you?" I asked uncertainly.

Asher nodded but finished chewing and swallowing his food before answering.

"Zeke can bring you guys back, and he'll just have to come get me later." Asher shrugged. Isaac snickered.

"Zeke the taxi service," Isaac announced.

Everyone chuckled.

It wasn't long before Zeke came back into the kitchen. He came over to the sink and washed the grease off his right hand.

"Brake lines are fine, so are the fuel lines." He reached over and tore off a paper towel to dry his hands. He looked over at me. "Go do your thing, Lexie."

I smirked at him and hopped down off the counter. I went to the pantry and grabbed a salt tub. As I was heading out, I passed my book bag and remembered the rosemary oil.

"Hey, Zeke. Do you care if your Jeep smells like rosemary?" I called towards the kitchen.

"No, go ahead," Zeke answered from the kitchen.

I pulled the oil out of my bag and tucked it into my pocket. I went outside and shivered. Shit, it was cold. I went over to Zeke's Jeep and opened the driver's side door. I opened the tub and poured salt into my hand, then I flicked the salt around the front seat. I even tucked some into the pockets on the door. I went to the back seat and did the same thing. I did the same for the passenger side, both front and back. I walked around to the front of the truck. Zeke had left the hood up for me. I took another handful of salt and threw it around the engine.

When I was done with the salt, I closed the lid and tossed it into the back seat. Might as well keep some with us, just in case. I pulled the oil out and used it on myself first. Then I climbed into the front seat and sat on my knees. I ran the oil along the interior. All along the jeep, near the ceiling. The smell was so strong when I was done that I rolled the windows down to air it out a bit. I hopped out and headed back inside to the kitchen.

"We should be good." I looked to Zeke and gave him a tense smile. "Your Jeep really smells like rosemary, though." I picked up my coffee mug and leaned against the counter. "I rolled the windows down to help clear it out a bit."

"I'm not worried about it, Lexie." He shrugged.

Isaac eyed me from his spot at the counter.

"I went to bed last night, and when I got up, there was salt all over my bedroom floor," Isaac announced eyeing me across the counter.

"Mine too." Zeke's voice was its usual grumpy self.

"Same here." Asher's eyes narrowed on me.

"Lexie? Did you salt everyone's room last night?" Miles asked politely.

"Maybe." I hedged in my sweet girly voice.

Zeke's jaw clenched.

"You came in my room when I was asleep? Lexie, I could have-" Zeke began gathering steam.

"That was me," Ethan interrupted, cutting him off before Zeke could get going. Zeke looked so relieved that I had to poke at him.

"Yeah, you probably sleep naked, and I don't need to see your bare ass," I shot back at him, everyone laughed. Even Zeke chuckled.

"Why'd you salt our rooms? Did something happen?" Miles asked before taking a bite of cereal.

My eyes met Ethan's for a second before looking at the counter.

"I figured if Bitch Ghost can't get into the room, she can't throw stuff at you guys. Or knock stuff over on you," I said, my mind going back to the drawings from last night.

Miles eyes narrowed on me while he chewed.

"Did you salt your room last night?" Miles asked, being entirely too observant.

"I made sure of it," Ethan answered for me.

The conversation went back to normal around me, but I wasn't really paying attention. I still had that image in my head, the five headstones. Their headstones. I really needed to link to the Veil and fast.

SOON ENOUGH IT was time to go. We got our jackets and backpacks. When we got to the door I stopped everyone.

"Charm check!" I announced, feeling my own body to make sure I had everything I needed.

When everyone said they were good, we headed out the door to the Jeep. Everyone put their bags in the back cargo area then began to climb in. Ethan, Asher, and Miles climbed into the back. I climbed in through the driver side, flipped up the console, and sat in the seat there. Isaac hopped in on my right and Zeke on my left. I had to scoot a little more to the right due to Zeke's shoulder size. He ended up having to keep his shoulder in front of mine for us to be comfortable; though his shoulder reached the middle of my chest.

Zeke started the Jeep. I was just thinking about my World Civ. essay that was due tomorrow when Zeke went to shift into drive. He cursed.

"I need to fix this transmission, it's still sticking," he said, grumbling. He jiggled the shifter on the steering column a bit before he used his strength to shift it down into drive. His elbow shot back, hitting my breast hard.

"Fuck!" I cursed, then clenched my teeth, sucking in air. Pain shot through my left breast as I crumbled to the right against Isaac's shoulder. My whole breast throbbed as my right hand cupped the poor girl, and my other hand crossed over my chest just to make sure nothing hit it again.

"Shit!" Zeke cursed, yanking his elbow up and away from me. "Oh fuck, fuck. Lexie, I'm so sorry!"

I just whimpered as I tried to relearn to breathe through the pain. Right on the nipple too. And since my luck was legendary, I was a week away from the end of my cycle. My breasts were hurting already.

"Shit Zeke!" Isaac cursed at him; he lifted his arm to wrap around my shoulders, giving me more room to move over. My eyes started watering.

"Lexie, are you okay?" Zeke asked, his gravelly voice had a strange note to it.

If I weren't in so much pain, I would try to figure it out. As it was, I was trying not to whimper anymore; it sounded pathetic.

"I heard that from back here, what happened?" Ethan asked.

"Zeke just elbowed her in the chest," Isaac called over his shoulder.

"Right on the fucking nipple too," I groaned, pulling away from Isaac. I folded myself in half, my chin over my knees, just waiting for the pain to stop. A big hand went to my back, rubbing up and down my spine gently.

"I'm so fucking sorry, Lexie." Zeke apologized again. "I didn't mean to do that, I swear."

"We are so fucking even for the car hood," I groaned out as I was getting my breath back.

The guys in back laughed.

"Yeah, it's real fucking funny assholes!" Zeke snapped at them.

I used my left hand to wipe the tears from my face since I was still folded in half. I didn't want to sit up just yet.

"Shit! Asher, you have any tissues?" Zeke snapped over his shoulder.

The laughing stopped, there was movement in the back.

"Is she really crying?" Ethan asked.

Zeke handed tissues to me, and I used them on my face.

"No, I'm fucking asking for me!" Zeke barked at the guys in the back.

Zeke was getting more and more upset. He needed to calm down, and that wasn't going to happen with me bent over like this. My breast was still throbbing, but it wasn't taking my breath away anymore. I didn't want to sit up. If I sat up, my boob was going to shift, and it was going to hurt. But Zeke was still rubbing my back, and I could tell he was getting pissed. Not at anyone else, just at himself.

I sat up, still cupping my breast; I really didn't want it to get hit again. I could already tell it was going to be hurting all day. I took a couple deep breaths and wiped my eyes again. I crossed my other arm over my chest, my hand on my shoulder. I wasn't guarding my breast; I was positive Zeke would never do that again. It was just instinctive.

"Just start driving, or we'll be late," I told him, pointing toward the driveway, my voice strained.

"I'm so sorry, Lexie. I swear I didn't mean to get you like that." Zeke's normally deep voice was even deeper than usual.

I looked up at him. His face was hard as he watched me, his eyes burning with anger at himself.

"It's okay." I offered. My breast was finally just throbbing down to an annoying level. Zeke clearly didn't believe me. "If it was any other time in my cycle it wouldn't have been so bad."

He stared at me not understanding. Oh yeah--he was a guy. I was going to have to spell it out for him. "My boobs were hurting already from hormones. You just happened to get me when they're super sensitive."

"I'm so fucking sorry, Lexie," he began earnestly again, reaching for the wheel.

"I know. I'll be fine," I reassured him. "I'll be extra sore the rest of the day, but I'll live."

Zeke started down the driveway.

"Though if someone else hits my girl, you beat them up. I'll be in the fetal position," I said.

Zeke's mouth twitched. "Just tell me who," he agreed with enthusiasm.

"Um, my girl?" Isaac asked, his eyebrow raised.

"Oh, like you don't have names you call your body parts," I shot at him, letting go of my breast now that she wasn't hurting so much. The guys burst out laughing. I leaned my head back and closed my eyes, hating being a girl at the moment.

"You really okay, Ally girl?" Asher asked, his fingers brushing hair from my face. I nodded. We were pulling into a parking space when something occurred to me and my twisted sense of humor.

"You know, Zeke just got to second base, and I didn't even get dinner first. I'm feeling gypped," I announced to guys. Everyone burst out laughing, I lifted my head to see Zeke shaking his head and smirking again. Ha Ha, cheered him up. I smiled to myself.

He shut off the Jeep and got out. Instead of sliding out, I got on my knees and moved the rear-view mirror so I could check my eyeliner. My eyeliner was a little smudged. I licked a corner of my tissue and used it to fix my makeup. When I was done, I scooted over to the driver side door. I slid to the cement to find Zeke still holding open the door. He crooked a finger at me to come closer. I took a few steps closer until I was looking up at him.

"Are you sure you're alright?" he asked, his voice quieter than usual. His broad fingers reached out and tucked a hair behind my ear. I smirked up at him and nodded.

"Zeke, I'm okay."

His frown still there.

"Like I said before, the only reason it hurt so much was unlucky timing," I told him.

He sighed, finally accepting what I was telling him. He nodded, letting me know he believed me this time. I went to the back of the truck to get my book bag followed closely by Zeke. We had just closed the back when the bell rang. We scattered, everyone running to their own class.

WORLD CIV WAS BORING as usual. I was heading to English when my cell phone vibrated. I pulled it out and checked my messages as I headed down the hall.

Ethan: A girl just told me you had it out with Jessica yesterday in the locker room, why didn't I hear about this?

I sighed, Ethan knew too many girls to keep anything a secret.

Alexis: She got all pissy because I was hanging out with Asher. She told me to stop, I told her to fuck off. That's about it.

Ethan: LOL, I love the way you handle that girl.

I smiled to myself and sent him a winking emoticon. I put my phone away as I headed into English class. I was pulling out my book when Eric sat next to me again.

"Hey, Alexis, how's it going?" His voice seemed distracted this morning.

"Looking forward to Friday as usual. How about you?" I asked, watching him pull his book out of his bag.

"The same." He seemed to come to a decision. He leaned into the aisle towards me, his face weirdly serious. "You're not friends with Zeke Blackthorn, are you?"

Okay, that's weird. Not the question, but the way he said it. As if he couldn't believe I could be friends with him. It irked me a bit.

"Yeah, he's one of my friends," I admitted. I ran my eyes over him wondering where he was going with this. "Why do you ask?"

He was staring at me with his eyes unfocused.

"I wanted to ask you about some rumors I heard, but I don't know how," he admitted, his eyes focusing on me again.

I sighed; rumors, great.

"Just ask." I shrugged as if it was no big deal to me.

A small smile crossed his face, showing off that dimple. "Okay." He waited a beat and continued, "Are you dating him?"

I rolled my eyes, I couldn't stop myself.

"No, we're just friends," I told him simply.

"A friend that moves your hair out of your face?" he asked, his eyebrows up.

I burst out laughing. His eyebrows dropped as his eyes ran over me.

"Have you seen my hair? It's everywhere all the time," I pointed out, trying to not laugh at him again. "I need all the help I can get to keep it off my face."

He grinned at that.

"Were you the girl he beat up that guy over?" he asked as his knee started to bounce.

Why does everyone keep thinking Zeke was a bad guy? If someone had one conversation.... no, two.... Okay, I can see how they might think he's an asshole. But I was going to put this rumor down now.

"That guy shoved me into the bar, and I hit the floor. And he did it because I didn't want to fool around with him." I told him making eye contact. "Zeke doesn't like guys hitting girls. Even if that hadn't been me, but some other girl he didn't even know. Zeke still would have beaten the shit out of him." He could believe me or not. If he liked to listen to rumors and not think for himself, that was on him.

He was looking at the wall, clearly thinking it through.

"I get that," Eric admitted; his gaze was on my face again. "Are all your friends guys?" he asked wearily.

I fought the urge to clench my teeth. I was starting to get tired of his questions.

289

"Yep, all guys." I kept my voice light and friendly. I don't know how I managed it, but I did.

"Why?"

I frowned at him, starting to get irritated.

"Why not? They make me laugh, they teach me stuff, they're fun, and they have my back," I explained, my voice showing my irritation. "I've never had a lot of girls as friends. I've seen a lot of backstabbing and drama. Guys will just tell you if they are pissed at you, you talk about it or duke it out on a video game and it's over. No grudges, no drama. It's done." I smiled as I thought about how easy it was with the guys.

"I can understand that," he admitted.

I looked over to see him smirking down at his book. I don't understand some boys.

Mrs. Hayes called for our attention. English dragged on as usual. I hate this play. It felt like forever before I was pulling my jacket back on and picking up my bag. Eric flashed that dimple at me as he said goodbye before he headed off. I headed down the hall thinking about the way Eric seemed to get weirded out by my guy friends. It didn't seem weird to me, it just seemed normal. I decided not to bother thinking about it.

I spotted Asher and Zeke in the hallway, Asher was chatting up a blonde. He was smiling down at her as he was listening. Aw, she was cute. Zeke spotted me and left Asher to the blonde. He met in the middle of the hall.

"Shit, I thought my head was going to explode." Zeke cursed, his fingers pinching the bridge between his eyes.

"What? She looks sweet," I said, taking a peek around Zeke to take another look. She was wearing designer jeans and a pink sweater. Her jacket also looked expensive.

"She's very sweet and polite. Very girl next door." Zeke sighed. "Very much what Asher goes for, but that doesn't mean I have to stand there and listen to her."

I chuckled at him.

"You could have left earlier," I pointed out.

Zeke shrugged. "I didn't realize it was going to be a long conversation," he admitted.

My twisted sense of humor came out to play.

"Aw, poor tortured Zeke," I cooed at him.

His eyes narrowed at me.

"Stop it," he warned.

I smiled wickedly. "Are you scared of the small, sweet girl?" I continued in that 'I'm talking to a little kid' voice. "Did she say hi to you? Did she try to hug you?" He glared down at me, but I saw the corners of his mouth twitch. "You want to hide behind me? I'll protect you from the nice girl."

That did it. He started chuckling.

I smiled up at him feeling lighter, I really liked that I could make him laugh.

"I'll see you at later, Lexie."

"See ya."

We went our separate ways; I waved to Asher when he spotted me. He waved back before he continued his conversation with the cute girl. Though she did send me a strange look when Asher's back was turned. Dating was going to be complicated.

THE REST of my day went on as usual. By the time I was walking to art class with Asher, I was exhausted. It was getting hard to just keep my eyes open. I really needed coffee. When my cell phone vibrated, I pulled the phone out of my jacket and answered it.

"Hello."

"Have you walked down the path yet?" Zeke's voice was demanding and right now, it irked me.

"Zeke, everything is fine, stop worrying," I assured him, hoping he'd back off. I was tired and that always made me irritable. That wasn't his fault.

"Start walking. I want to make sure those charms are still working," Zeke ordered.

I sighed; my shoulders getting tense. This is getting ridiculous.

"They are working, they are fine. Will you please stop worrying?" I snapped at him as we stepped onto the path. Bitch Ghost was standing in the middle of the path again with that creepy smile on her face. "You can't do this every day, Zeke."

"Wanna bet?" he countered.

I growled; I was tired. I wanted a nap and Zeke was being an over-protective shit. So, I did what I wanted to do yesterday. I hung up the phone and kept walking.

"Did you just hang up on Zeke?" Asher asked. I nodded. He winced. "He's not going to take that well."

"I'm sure we'll see him any minute now," I said grumpily as we got closer to Ghost Bitch. Asher chuckled. The bracelets on my left wrist started to heat up.

"Oh, we will," Asher assured me. "I wouldn't want to be you when that happens, though. He's going to be mad."

I wasn't really listening; the heat on my wrist was starting to burn. I gritted my teeth and walked faster down the path.

"Asher, I didn't sleep last night, I'm tired, and when I'm tired, I get cranky," I explained to him as my beads got hotter. "So, if he comes looking for a fight he'll get one."

We passed Bitch Ghost, the pain increasing, I knew my skin was getting burnt, but I couldn't say anything. If I said something, everyone would get worried, and I really didn't want to deal with it right now. I was tired. I was real close to just saying fuck it and sleeping in Zeke's Jeep until school was over. So, I kept my mouth shut as my beads burned into my skin. I walked faster, the farther from Bitch Ghost, the less my wrist burned. We were almost to class, and the beads were still warm on my arm when I heard Zeke

"Lexie!"

I groaned and turned around. Zeke was striding through the avenue of trailer classrooms, and judging by his face, he was severely pissed off. I really didn't want to deal with this.

"What?" I asked as he strode up to me and stopped. He towered over me.

"Why the fuck did you hang up?" he snapped, his eyes running over my face looking for something.

"Because you were being ridiculous," I snapped back.

His brow drew down; his mouth becoming a hard line.

"Walking on that path every day and demanding that you listen is ridiculous, Zeke."

Zeke looked around us; he noted the other people around and stepped closer. He leaned down so only I could hear him.

"You almost died in front of us two days ago," he whispered in my ear, his voice hard. "You kept a secret that almost got you killed." I swallowed as I heard the anger in his voice as he continued, "That is ridiculous."

I jerked my head back ready to defend myself, but I didn't get the chance. His hands went around my arms holding me in place, his grip firm but gentle. Not hurting me, just holding.

He moved his head so that he was whispering in my ear again. "Talking to me on the phone for three fucking minutes so I know you're okay. That isn't much to fucking ask considering the situation we're in." He pulled back from my ear and looked at me. His furious gaze meeting mine.

That's when I saw it. It was small, nothing more than a brief flicker. But it was there. Fear. I had scared him by hanging up the phone, by not letting him hear that I was fine. This whole situation scared him, and he was trying to handle it the only way he could. By worrying and trying to keep me safe, the best way he knew how. That feeling of being cared for washed over me. Was I ever going to get used to feeling this? Would I have hung up the phone on him if I had known this was how he was feeling? Shit. I knew the answer. I would have talked to him as much as he needed if I had known. I was wrong, but I wasn't the only one in the wrong here. I crooked my finger at him. He bent down so I could whisper in his ear.

"If you need me to help you deal with something, tell me," I whispered my voice firm. "If you need to hear me while I walk past Bitch Ghost so you don't freak out, fine. But you need to tell me why, otherwise you come off like an overprotective asshole." I leaned back and met his eyes as he straightened to his full height. "You hear me?" I used his words to make him understand I was serious.

He took a deep breath and let it out slowly.

"I hear you." His gravelly voice filled my ears. He gave my arms a small squeeze before letting me go. "I'll see you after class. Asher, I'll pick you up after practice."

Zeke headed back in the direction he came from. I turned to see Asher looking from me to Zeke's retreating back. His eyebrows went up.

"I expected a much bigger fight than that," he admitted.

"It was apparently a miscommunication." I hedged; Asher didn't need to know that Zeke had freaked out. Asher shrugged, and we headed into class.

During our drawing time, I went to the sink and pulled the beads off my arm. All along my arm, in the shape of my beads, were red burns but luckily no blistering. I turned the water on and ran it over my skin--it felt really good. How good it felt told me it would be a couple days before the burns disappeared. Where the hell is Bitch Ghost getting her energy? How long did I have until she shatters my beads with heat? I didn't have any answers. I needed to get that link to the veil working soon. I didn't know how much time I had left. I put my bracelets back on and went back to the table. I said nothing about it to Asher.

After class, I met everyone at Zeke's Jeep. The boys gave me the front seat. We were headed back to Miles' house when I decided to just close my eyes for a bit.

CHAPTER 16

I woke up in a dark bedroom. It took me a few seconds to recognize the master bedroom at Miles' house. I rubbed the grit out of my eyes and tried to remember how I got here. I remember buckling up, listening to the boys talk about the weekend, and pulling out of the student parking lot. Then nothing. Someone must have carried me into the house and put me in the bedroom. I smiled at that warm feeling in my chest again. It wasn't so odd this time.

I sat up and checked the clock. It was six o'clock, and I still had homework. I groaned as I got out of bed. When I felt the wood floor under my feet, I jerked. Apparently, someone had taken my shoes off, too. I pulled my jacket off and tucked my cell phone into my back pocket. I opened the door and headed down the hall, still wiping the sleep from my face. I heard voices coming from the kitchen, so I went in. Asher was putting fried rice into a big serving bowl, and Isaac was standing at the breakfast bar with Miles next to him.

"There she is," Miles greeted me.

I smiled and ran my hand back through my hair.

"What happened?" I asked, still a bit drowsy.

Miles and Isaac smiled.

"We got one block from school, and you were out like a light," Miles explained, coming around the counter. He headed for the dishes cupboard and opened it.

"Huh." I walked around the counter and sat down at the breakfast bar. "Who carried me into the house?"

"What makes you think you were carried?" Isaac asked, chuckling. "You were out, gone. We could have dragged you into the house, and you still wouldn't have woken up."

Miles brought a stack of plates over the counter and set them down. "Isaac did," Miles answered over his shoulder as he headed for the silverware drawer.

I looked over to Isaac. He was eyeing the big bowl of fried rice.

"Thanks for bringing me in, Cookie Monster."

Isaac glanced back at me and winked before grabbing a plate. "No problem Red, you're light."

"He didn't bang my head on anything on the way in, did he?"

Asher laughed.

Miles looked concerned. "Not that I know of, do you have a headache?" Miles asked, adjusting his glasses.

I smiled and shook my head no.

"Good, cause dinner's ready," Asher announced.

All of us dished up and headed for the dining room. When I walked in, I saw everyone's books out on the table. Shit, I still had that essay due tomorrow.

"Food's ready," I told Zeke and Ethan.

They both popped up and headed down the hall. I saw my book bag and brought it to the table. I was still pulling out my books when the guys came back in with their dinner.

"Don't bother, Red, we did your homework for you," Isaac announced.

My eyebrows went up.

"Seriously?"

They all nodded.

"You guys are awesome. Thank you so much." I was about to get up to get my laptop when I noticed it over by Miles. "Miles did you finish my essay?"

His ears tinged pink. "Yes."

"You're an angel," I told him sweetly. He sent a smile down the table.

"So, all I have left tonight is to try and fail at meditating," I grumbled taking a bite of chicken.

"Actually, I think I've got something that will help," Ethan said. "I'll show you after dinner."

"Anything is worth a shot right now," I mumbled, my mind on the burns on my arm. I was going over possibilities when my phone vibrated in my back pocket. I pulled it out and saw I got a text.

Unknown: Hey, it's Dylan from last Saturday. What have you been up to?

I bit my lip trying not to smile. Almost a week and he finally texts me. I decided to make him wait a little. I looked down the table to see Asher had finished eating.

"Looks like I can't guilt you anymore, Asher," I said. Asher looked across the table at me. "Dylan just texted me."

Asher scowled. "Oh, come on man," Asher muttered. He tilted his chin at my phone. "Have you texted him back yet?"

I shook my head, smiling. "I'm making him sweat for a couple minutes," I admitted.

The other guys groaned. I looked around the table at them with an eyebrow raised.

"I hate that," Isaac complained.

"That's cruel, Beautiful," Ethan chimed in.

"You do know that guy is just sitting there waiting for you to text back, right?" Miles asked, pointing at my phone. I smiled at Miles.

"He got my number Sunday morning, and he waited until Thursday night to text me," I said being very clear.

"Oooh. Yeah, let him sweat a couple minutes," Zeke agreed before going back to his Physics homework.

"When you do text him back, tell him I said 'weak game.'" Asher grinned mischievously.

I sent him one back. After a couple minutes had passed, I picked up my phone.

Alexis: The usual stuff, school, sleep. I'm having dinner with the guys right now. Asher says 'weak game.'

I giggled as I hit send.

"She's giggling, that can't be good," Isaac said.

"No, I'm giggling at the weak game thing," I admitted. I put down my phone to take a bite of food. My phone vibrated on the table.

"Yeah, he better text you back," Asher mumbled.

I snickered as I picked up my phone.

"What, Asher? Not liking the way your friend is texting me?" I taunted him a bit.

Asher gave me a half grin. "When I gave him your number, I told him no stupid dating games." Asher shrugged as he went back to his work.

I snickered again and checked the text.

Dylan: LOL. I deserved that. I would have texted earlier this week but my Dad got sick, and I had to take more shifts at the store.

By the time I read that, he had sent another text.

Dylan: With homework and everything by the time I'd think of texting you, it was always near midnight. Seemed kind of creepy to text someone for the first time that late.

I smiled at my phone. That I could understand.

Alexis: Yeah, that would have been really creepy. I guess I can't give you a hard time over it.

Dylan: Thank you merciful one. So, tell me how's your week been?

Oh, you know, almost died. Found out I was a Necromancer. You know, the usual stuff. I lost my smile. How could I tell him the truth? Simple, I couldn't, so I hedged.

Alexis: A bit hectic, but nothing I can't handle. Sounds like you had the same.

Dylan: Pretty much, but since I worked all week, I get the next three weekends off. Totally worth it.

Alexis: 48-hour rule?

Dylan: .... so not worth it.

I chuckled as I texted back.

Alexis: Lol, sorry couldn't resist that one.

I picked up my fork and took a bite of food.

"You're killing us, Red," Isaac said with a groan.

I looked up and found Isaac and Ethan watching me.

Asher kept taking quick looks once in a while. "What excuse did he have for not texting?"

I shook my head, smiling at Isaac's suffering voice.

"He said his dad got sick, and he had to pick up more shifts at the store. He admitted he didn't want to text me in the middle of the night, he thought it would be creepy."

My phone vibrated again.

"Yeah, that sounds more like Dylan than just not calling," Asher admitted going back to his work as the others started to pick up their dishes.

I went back to texting Dylan.

Dylan: No, that was a good one. You make me laugh.

Alexis: I try; you should hear the bad ones. The guys all groan and roll their eyes.

Dylan: Lol.

Dylan: Asher told me you had all guy friends. You don't see that very often.

I groaned and put my head back on my chair.

"What?" Asher asked.

I looked back to realize that the others were gone.

"He's subtly asking why I only have guy friends. Do you know how often I get that question? This is the second time today," I complained.

Asher grinned. "Tell him that."

"Really?"

Asher nodded. "Yeah, he doesn't want to irritate you." Asher started packing up his bags.

"Where is everyone?" I asked, getting up and picking up my dish.

"Family room, are you coming?" Asher stretched.

I nodded.

"Just got to put away my dish, dinner was delicious by the way," I called over my shoulder as I headed down the long hallway.

"Thank you, Ally."

I went into the kitchen and put my dish in the sink, and texted Dylan back.

Alexis: You are the second guy to ask me that today. I didn't think it was that strange.

I headed down the hallway and walked into the family room. Zeke and Isaac had the couch to the left, Ethan and Miles were with their backs to the door. My phone vibrated as I climbed over the back and plopped between the boys. Asher laid out on his back on the floor, groaning. I was looking down at my cell phone when Ethan nudged my shoulder. I smiled and nudged back. The guys talked about the movie while I read Dylan's text.

Dylan: It's not strange just different. Don't you like hanging out with other girls?

I rolled my eyes and turned the tables on him.

Alexis: Do you like hanging out with a bunch of girls?

"Nice one, Beautiful." Ethan grabbed my attention. I looked up to see him reading over my shoulder.

"Really?" I asked, a bit irked. I elbowed him in the side for spying on me.

My phone vibrated.

"Yeah, you don't want your phone to end up in the pool," Miles warned him.

I smirked as the guys chuckled. I read Dylan's text.

Dylan: Well, no, but I'm a guy.

I snorted.

Alexis: I don't have a lot of great girls-as-friends experiences. Guys are easy; if they're mad, you know.

Dylan: But don't you miss having girls as friends sometimes?

I thought about that for a second before I was texting him back.

Alexis: When I'm not sure if an outfit works or if a color is right for me, otherwise no.

I smirked and added.

Alexis: Besides, guys gossip just as much as girls do. Ethan's sitting here trying to read over my shoulder.

"Thanks for that, Beautiful," Ethan grumbled.

"You deserved it."

"If he wanted to talk to you this long, he should have just called." Ethan pointed out still looking over my shoulder. "Texts are for short talks or flirts."

"He's being a chicken shit," Zeke announced still watching the movie.

"He waited too long to call, so he's feeling her out," Miles chimed in.

The guys agreed. I looked around at them.

"Okay, I know you guys don't sit around talking about who Ethan is texting," I pointed out to them.

They all grinned.

"If we did, we'd be stuck talking all day," Isaac countered.

We burst out laughing. Ethan just grinned. My phone rang.

"That'a boy, have a pair," Asher said proudly.

I was laughing as I answered. "Hello?"

"Thought calling might make it harder for Ethan to snoop." Dylan's husky voice filled my ear. Damn it, I had forgotten about his voice.

"I don't know; he's practically in my lap now, trying to listen." I elbowed Ethan in the gut hard. He grunted. "There we go, nothing an elbow to the gut doesn't fix."

Dylan chuckled.

I looked around, the movie was paused. The boys were all watching me.

I dropped the phone from my mouth but kept it to my ear. "You guys actually paused the movie to listen in?"

Dylan was laughing now.

I put the phone back to my cheek. "I told you, they're just as bad as girls."

The guys laughed at me as I got up and headed around the couch.

"I'm just going to go somewhere with less ears." I walked into the long hall and down to the living room. I took the couch facing the doorway so the guys couldn't sneak up on me. "Okay, it's clear. Hi."

"Hi, do they do that a lot?"

"What, be nosey?" I couldn't seem to stop grinning. His voice just rolled through my ears. It was a damn good voice.

"Yeah, do they do that when all the guys call?"

I snorted. "I've been here just over a week; you're the only guy to call. Well, that wasn't one of them." I admitted.

"Really?"

"Yep."

"When did the guys at that school get so stupid? I met you once and asked for your number." His voice was warm, sending butterflies through my stomach.

"Oh, and you go in for the hard flirt. Interesting choice," I said, teasing him and totally loving it.

DYLAN CHUCKLED IN MY EAR. "Yeah, I kinda have to make up for lost time here," he admitted. "I only got one dance with you before all that went down."

"Yeah, but it was a damn good dance." I flirted back. I felt a little rusty.

"Well, it was a memorable night after all."

I chuckled quietly.

"And then Zeke beat that guy into the ground," Dylan continued.

I shifted, crossing my legs under me. "Yeah, but I can't really blame him." And I kind of didn't want Dylan blaming him either.

"Asher told me the guy had it coming but didn't go into detail. Will you tell me?"

I sighed and explained all at once. I didn't want to keep talking about it. "Basically, a guy groped me and tried to pin my back against the bar, so I pushed him off me. He got pissed and pushed me back. My back hit the bar, I hit the floor. Then Zeke hit him, a lot." I waited, heart pounding, wondering if he was going to get scared off by Zeke.

He was quiet for a couple beats.

"He hurt you?" Dylan's voice changed turning harder. It sent the butterflies fluttering again.

"It only hurt for a few minutes. The air was knocked out of me, and since my spine hit the bar, my hands shook for a while." I gave him a half lie. There was no way I was telling him about my bruises.

"Are you okay?"

"Yeah, I'm fine." I felt like I needed to explain Zeke's reaction. "Zeke just really hates guys who hurt girls."

"Remind me to thank him next time I see you." His voice was back to his normal husky.

I smiled a big girly smile.

"You're going to see me again, huh?"

I heard him let out a breath before answering. "Well, it's going to be hard dating you if I don't get to see you again." His voice was full of confidence that I'm pretty sure was fake.

"You don't know me well enough to want to date me; I could be some crazy girl." I pointed out still smiling.

He chuckled. "Well, I'm trying to get to know you, but I'm running behind here. Especially if I want to see you this weekend."

My stomach did that hard flip. I winced.

"This weekend?" I asked, my voice pained. I rested my head back on the sofa.

"I take it you can't this weekend?" His voice was full of disappointment, he wasn't the only one.

"If I really make some progress on this project, and work at it all day Saturday, then I should be able to swing Saturday night for a few hours." If I can connect to the Veil by then, I could take care of Bitch Ghost on Sunday or later Saturday night--if I could figure it out. Then I got an idea. "Wait, I am going to Asher's football game with everyone tomorrow night. Can you come to that?"

He sighed deeply. "I'm playing out at Northridge tomorrow night."

"Okay, schedules suck," I declared.

He chuckled. "Yeah, they do. Especially with you almost an hour away." He laughed.

"Only from your point of view; to me you're the one an hour away," I told him.

"Wait, what's in the middle?" I heard him moving around. "Come on, wake up computer."

I smiled. "It's only forty-five minutes," I pointed out.

I heard typing.

"Yeah, but if there is something in the middle, that's less time driving and more time I get to see you," he said distractedly.

I couldn't seem to stop smiling.

"Hmm, and less gas used. I like it," I admitted.

He laughed. "A girl who knows the value of gas, be still my heart." His voice was adoring. "Okay, something in between. I've found a park."

I started laughing.

"If I told the guys I was meeting you in a park at night, they would all come and glare at you the whole time," I told him.

He laughed again. "I was thinking more during the day next weekend or something," he said. "There's a really small town. I'll look up what's there later; I'd rather talk to you right now."

"You are really working the hard flirt," I said fighting the urge to giggle. What was wrong with me? I have never giggled because of a guy.

"Yeah, I am. Is it working?" he asked. His voice had an edge of uncertainty. He was so cute.

"Oh, yeah, it's working," I admitted happily. I heard a deep exhale of relief.

"Good."

I snickered.

"Think you can make it out to Vegabond Saturday night?" he asked me.

I bit my lip.

"If I make progress on that project, then it's a definite yes." I hedged; I didn't want to say yes and have to back out.

"But if you don't?"

"I'll be busting my ass every night to make sure that doesn't happen," I admitted. I decided then and there that I was going to reach my center on Saturday, no matter how long it took.

"Alright." His voice got softer in my ear. "So, what did you draw today?"

"I was practicing roses today."

Before I could say more, Ethan walked into the living room carrying his iPod and headphones.

"Hey Beautiful, you've got that thing you're working on," he called from across the room.

"Did he just call you beautiful?"

I winced.

"Yeah, it's his nickname for me. So far, I haven't picked his, but Nosey Brat is starting to sound good."

Dylan and Ethan laughed at me.

"I do have to get working, though," I said "if you want to see me Saturday night and all."

"Get moving, I want another dance," Dylan ordered making me chuckle. "I'll try to call tomorrow, but you'll definitely get texts."

"Uh-huh, now tomorrow or a week from tomorrow?" I teased.

He groaned.

I snickered.

"I'll make it up to you I promise."

"Alright. Night," I said, still smiling.

"Night."

I hung up the phone and glared playfully at Ethan who had a big shit-eating grin on his face.

"Lexie's got a boyfriend," he sang.

"Lexie's got a date Saturday night," I sing-songed right back.

"Oh. Nice, where?"

"Vegabond."

He tilted his head, his eyes unfocused. "Now I need a date." He shook his head and focused back on me. "Come on Beautiful, let's go."

I followed Ethan down the long hallway and into the conservatory. He led me to the center of the glass room and gestured for me to pick a seat. I sat down in one of the chairs. Ethan brought the other chair closer, the metal feet scraping along the stone tile. He sat in front of me like last night.

"So, what is involved in linking with the Veil?" he asked, playing with the cord on his headphones.

"Well, first you have to meditate, get a clear head. Free of emotion and conscious thought. Then you have to find your center," I explained, still trying to understand it myself. "Your center is supposed to be this place inside you, the you that is at the very core of who you are. The good, the bad. It's all there. You have to face that to reach out and link with the Veil."

Ethan licked his lips. "Well, let's start with part one," he offered.

I smiled gratefully. He handed me his iPod and headphones.

"I've downloaded a pretty good guided meditation for you. It should be able to help get you there."

I nodded and put the headphones on.

"Are you staying?" I asked, settling into the chair. He nodded. I hit play on the file marked "Lexie's". I placed my hands on my lap and closed my eyes. The music was soft, a flute, and tranquil. Then the guide started to speak. I winced; his voice was hard on my ears. It was a higher pitched man's voice, and it had a slight accent that I ended up trying to place rather than listening to the actual guide. I brought my attention back to what I was supposed to be doing.

Ten minutes later, I couldn't take it anymore. I pulled the head-phones off.

"Nope, nada, no way," I said in a strained, frustrated voice. Ethan frowned at me.

"What happened?"

"The guy has a slight accent I've been trying to place for a good five minutes and his voice is higher pitched. It's like a knife in my ear," I told him honestly. I hated how picky I was about sound. But this wasn't working. What the hell was I going to do?

Ethan's face became thoughtful. He was silent for a couple minutes before he grinned at me. He reached over and took the headphones from me.

"Alright, I have an idea." He put the headphones on but left one off his ear. He queued up the iPod. Then he met my eyes. "Close your eyes."

I raised an eyebrow at him and sighed. I was willing to try anything right now. I closed my eyes.

"Take deep, slow breaths."

Ethan's voice went low and smoother than usual. It wasn't his toe-curling voice or his normal one, it was somewhere in between. His voice filled my ears slowly, softly till his voice was all I could hear.

"Focus on feeling your body breathing, the air coming in through your nose. Your lungs filling with air. Feel yourself exhale."

I did as he said; I couldn't resist that voice of his. It went on like that for half an hour. Ethan saying the instructions, following and me listening. The world disappeared. There was only the sound of water and Ethan's voice. When my mind was completely blank, free of emotion and thought. I gave him a thumbs up, letting him know I was where I needed to be. Then Ethan began again, this time giving me instructions on how to reach my center. I don't know where he found them and I didn't care. I just listened.

"Feel yourself relaxing, sinking deeper into your mind."

I relaxed my hold on everything, my body, my stress, all the pressure I felt to get this right. I just let it go and sank down inside myself.

"Where does your instinct come from, Beautiful? That place in your mind that is all instinct. The instinct that you used with Zeke today. That instinct you had when you calmed me down the day before my gig."

I knew the vague area in my mind where that came from, it was lower, deeper. So, I sank further.

"That's where your center is. That is what you need to find," Ethan's voice told me.

I was closer, I could feel it. I felt stronger, more me. Images flashed through my mind, not all of them good, not all of them bad. The big moments in my life. Seeing my first ghost, Clair saving me, Claire protecting me. Dad. I saw Dad reading me The Hobbit before bedtime. Then I saw his casket. My heart ached as I fell deeper. I knew what was coming. I saw myself being alone at night. Trying to understand why Mom wanted to go out instead of stay with me. I saw how I tried every day to make things better for my mother, how every day she blew me off. I watched the color of my world leach away until there was barely any color at all. I felt my breathing speed up and let it. I knew what was coming. I watched as Jacob Noon tried to pin me down in the park. His hand going up my skirt as I said no. He'd asked me to go stargazing, and I thought it would be fun. I watched as I fought him off, driving my knee into his groin. Then pushing him off me. I watched the white-hot rage in my eyes as I walked to the Blazer. I watched myself pick up the short crowbar. I didn't hesitate, I didn't think. Then I watched myself smash that crowbar across his face, over and over. When he was unconscious, I watched myself pull my cell phone out and call the police and an ambulance. My chest felt tight. It was horrifying to see myself that way, to see what I was capable of doing. I didn't want to see my dark side, I knew it was there, but I didn't want to see it. I didn't want to see anymore. I didn't want to see myself. I didn't want to know what kind of monster I really was. I began to swim up, and up. Desperate to get away from the knowledge that lay below. I was coming up when a loud bang yanked me out of my head.

I opened my eyes, disoriented, not quite knowing where I was. It took me a couple minutes of blinking and looking around for me to remember I was at Miles house. Asher was walking towards us, grimacing. When he realized we were both watching him, he smiled tensely.

"Sorry, I didn't know the door opened that easily," Asher admitted.

I waved a hand dismissively.

"No, it's fine I was trying to come out of it anyway."

Ethan looked at me curiously.

"Ethan, your mom is on the house phone. She's pissed you're not answering your cell," Asher said, handing Ethan the cordless phone. Ethan winced as he took it.

I got to my feet and walked out of the conservatory with Asher.

"So how did it go?" Asher asked as he closed the conservatory door behind us.

"We managed to get through the first step," I began. As we walked down the long hall, my stomach knotted. "I was almost at the second when I hit a snag."

"What's the second step?"

"Finding my center; it's the root of who you are and everything you will become." My voice got quiet as I remembered seeing myself in the park. "You see everything you are, those big moments in your life that shaped you. You see it in a way that you didn't then." I swallowed hard, my eyes on the carpet runner in the hallway.

"Is that so bad?" he asked gently.

I licked my lips before answering.

"What if who you are, is something far worse than you ever thought you could be?" I bit the corner of my bottom lip looking down the hallway. "What if you are something awful-?"

I never got to finish my sentence. A woman burst through the wall in front of us. I jerked back, falling on my butt, then scooted back a few feet all the while yelling, "Ghost, ghost, fuck a ghost!'

I tried to calm down as she turned and noticed me seeing her. She stepped closer, her color fading in and out. Like a bad signal on an old TV.

"Please, you have to help me! My son!" she begged, her voice frantic. "My son is still in the car!"

I watched, not feeling anything from her. I got to my feet slowly, looking closely at her.

"What do you mean?" I asked, watching her fade in and out again, the color leaching from her, then bouncing back.

Asher grabbed my arm and tried to pull me back down the hall.

"No dead, Ally, not for another couple of days," he reminded me as he tried to pull me away.

I tugged my arm away from him and looked into that woman's eyes. I felt nothing. She kept fading in and out. That wasn't normal. I had a horrible thought. I reached for my bracelets and began pulling them off, one by one.

Asher grabbed my hands, stopping me. "Ally, don't!"

"I just need a peek; something's not right," I mumbled before pulling off another bracelet. "She's fading in and out like a radio signal."

I continued taking off the bracelets and handing them to Asher. When I finally felt her, it was light, a pressure in my side. Panic in her chest. That wasn't right. I'd never felt panic from the dead. I pulled another bracelet off. Pain stabbed through my side, my heart stuttered. No, not my heart. Hers. "Holy shit."

The woman nodded, tears pouring down her face.

My mind went blank, my mouth hanging open like a barn door.

"My car crashed down on the highway, I went off the road. My son is in the car!" she yelled at me, pointing out towards the road.

"Show me." I was running down the hall, the woman's spirit following right on my heels.

"Ally!" Asher was to my right as I turned into the living room; I grabbed my jacket and yanked out my keys and cell phone.

"Car wreck!" I shouted, running for the front door. I heard other feet behind me. "She's not fucking dead yet!" I shouted behind me as I yanked the door open and ran for my Blazer. I jumped into the driver's seat. The woman jumped through the wall of the truck and knelt between the front seats. I had just started the truck when the passenger side opened and Asher jumped in. My heart raced as he slammed the door shut and I gunned it. I tossed my phone to Asher. He held on for dear life as I raced down the driveway. "Call Rory!" The front gate opened, and I was through almost scraping paint as we went by.

"Where did you wreck?" I asked her.

"About a mile east, just past the freeway sign. We're off the road." Her voice was shaking. She was still fading in and out, so I was guessing her body was still alive.

I repeated to Asher the location as I turned left onto the freeway. Tires squealed as I pushed down the accelerator. Come on, come on, don't let me be too late. Please, God. For once in my life, don't let me be too late. It felt like it was taking forever but I later learned it had only taken us five minutes from the front door to the crash site. I saw burned tire marks in the road leading off into the trees.

"Here!"

I hit the brakes. I threw on my hazards and jumped out of the truck. The woman ran in front of me down the side of the road. Heart in my throat, I followed, ignoring the underbrush. The car wasn't far, just far enough to not be seen from the road at night. The blue sedan was bashed around as if it was made out of play dough.

Adrenaline pumping, I ran to the driver's side and yanked the door open. She was sitting there, seat belt strapped across her chest, a head wound, and blood pouring out of her side. A sharp piece of blood-soaked metal lay in her open hand. I heard crying.

"Mommy!" A little boy's voice was crying, big sobbing tears.

Asher reached us.

"You take care of him, I've got her," I told him calmly as I ripped my shirt open, tore it off and started pushing against her side, trying to stop the bleeding.

"Hey, buddy, my name is Asher, and that's Lexie, we're here to help," Asher told the kid in the back seat. I heard him open the door.

"I want Mommy."

I looked across the car at the woman's soul and met her eyes.

"Your Mommy's hurt right now, honey. I'm taking care of her," I told him in my most soothing voice.

I pressed everything I had against the wound. I wasn't going to let her go anywhere.

"Is the ambulance on the way?" I asked grunting with effort, hot blood covering my hands. Asher stopped consoling the little boy long enough to answer me.

"Yeah, a couple minutes out." He went back to talking to the kid. His name was Joshua, but his mom called him Joshy. He liked dinosaurs and the color green. He had a friend named Marty who had a big pool at his house. And he wanted to be a dinosaur finder when he grew up. Asher kept asking him questions, getting him to calm down enough that he wasn't sobbing hysterically. I noticed the woman's spirit's color getting stronger. A weight settled in my chest, my stomach knotting.

"Asher get him out of here." I kept my eyes on her soul.

"I don't know if I should move him."

"Can he move his arms and legs?" I asked, getting desperate--I had to talk to the woman, and I couldn't do it in front of the kid.

"I'm not risking it, Ally." he told me over his shoulder.

Fair enough.

I looked the woman's soul in the eyes.

"Don't you fucking dare," I growled low. "Your son is sitting right behind you. You fucking fight until you have nothing left, fight to get back to him."

The woman's gaze went to the back seat.

"Yeah it sucks, it hurts, and you're tired. But your son will remember this day for the rest of his life." I pushed all my weight against the woman's wound. I felt her blood run down my forearms. "It's up to you whether or not it has a good ending or a bad one." I heard sirens coming down the freeway. I refused to look away from her face. "Make the decision now. Is this the day he's going to hear his mother die in front of him, or is this the day that his mother fought to stay?" I heard tires screeching on the road. Come on woman, make the right fucking choice. Don't leave your kid here.

The woman's soul met my eyes again, hard determination glowing in her eyes. She looked down at her body and slipped back inside. Relief left me shaking; I focused on keeping the pressure on.

"Down here!" Asher was shouting.

I kept talking to the little boy's mother.

"You got this, honey, it's going to suck. But it'll be worth it when you see him grow up and find dinosaur bones."

I heard feet crashing through the brush. I saw lights shooting through the night, running over the car and us. The first paramedic came to me first; he took a quick look and knelt on the ground next to me.

"Keep the pressure on," he said in a calm voice as he opened his kit.

"No shit," I growled, pushing even more of my weight onto the wound. He pulled out a lot of large gauze pads and began covering my shirt with it. I shifted a hand here and there, pushing the pad against the wound as we tried to stop the bleeding. I don't remember how long it was till the second paramedic came to take my spot. I made him repeat three times that he was pushing on the wound before I let go.

I slipped out from under his arms and stepped away; now that I didn't have a job to do, I was shaking. I became sharply aware that I was cold, and barefoot. I shivered and looked around me. Another ambulance had arrived; the other paramedics were bringing down a backboard from the road. I spotted Rory coming down the embankment in gray sweatpants and university shirt. The paramedics were talking into the radios on their shoulders as they put a neck brace on the woman. The bleeding stopped soaking through the bandages, and that's when I knew she was going to be okay. I knew it was okay to let her go now, she wasn't going anywhere.

I moved towards Rory, trying to get out of the way of the other paramedics coming in. I winced as rocks bit into my feet. Rory met me halfway to the road. His eyes ran over me, his face white.

"What happened?"

I looked up at the road and saw five familiar silhouettes. One was holding a kid on his hip. I wasn't too surprised to see them. I was oddly calm, my mind quiet. I gestured toward the road.

"How's the kid?" I asked my voice rough.

"He's okay, some bumps and bruises but he'll be fine," Rory answered stepping to the side and wrapping his hand around my arm.

I looked down and saw blood covering my hands up to the middle of my forearms. Oh, I wouldn't want to touch me either. I started walking toward the road, Rory helping me around the sharper rocks. Rory ended up climbing up to the road and reaching down to grab my upper arm, he gave me a tug as I pushed to climb up the steep embankment. I stood up straight and walked over to the little boy. He couldn't have been more than four years old. He had chubby cheeks and pretty blue eyes. He clung to Asher as if he was his new favorite toy. I looked up at him and gave him a sweet smile.

"Josh, your mom asked me to tell you something," I said gently, keeping my voice soft. He looked down at me, his eyes big and scared. "You're Mommy loves you very much, she's going to be okay."

"Lexie, you can't-" Rory bit out.

"This time I can." I looked over at him. "This time I know. She's not leaving him." I suddenly felt disgusting.

I looked over at the guys. They were all watching me with different levels of curiosity and concern. "Is there any way to get this blood off me?" I asked, my voice rough again.

Rory nodded and brought me to the back of the second ambulance. It was empty; they were bringing the woman up the embankment. It took everyone, even the guys pitched in. Asher kept holding Josh. Rory handed me big antiseptic wipes. I took them and began scrubbing the blood off of me.

"How did you learn about the crash?" Rory asked, his voice quiet. I tossed a now useless wipe into the trash and opened another one.

"Her soul came to me at Miles' house," I told him honestly, just starting to really think about it. "She kept fading in and out like a radio signal. I took off enough protection to get a bit of what she was feeling." I shrugged, a bit bewildered myself. "I felt her heartbeat, and I knew she was alive." I kept wiping my arms, trying to get them clean. "I don't know how the fuck it happened, but she found me. Ran right through the wall in front me." I threw away another wipe and opened another one; I almost had one arm clean. Though I was seriously thinking of wiping down with bleach when we got back to Miles' house.

Rory's brow drew down. "Has this ever happened before?"

I scoffed, fighting back tears. I swallowed hard and looked around at anything but him. I kept cleaning my arms.

"I see the dead, Rory; by the time they get to me, there is nothing left to save," I admitted to him and to myself. I was Death's clean-up crew; I swept up the souls that got left behind or refused to leave. It wasn't fun, it didn't feel good, and it wasn't even something I wanted to do. But it was my reality, my life.

"Not anymore, apparently," Rory pointed out, he had a small smile on his face.

"Yeah, it was nice to help someone before they died for once," I admitted. This one felt good, and I really needed that today.

I kept cleaning my arms. When I finally had all the blood off my arms and out from under my nails. Thank you to the paramedics that stayed behind! Asher gave Josh to Rory. He looked at me then at Rory and back again. Apparently, we looked enough alike that he didn't mind being held by him. Asher drove back to the house. The others following behind us.

I was still thinking about the woman in the car when Asher got my attention.

"Ally, that was pretty amazing," he said, his voice sounding impressed.

I looked out the side window feeling my face grow warm.

"That's never happened before," I admitted, my voice rough. I didn't know why it kept sounding like that. "I've never seen anyone who was alive before, their soul, I mean."

"Not that, Ally." Asher's baritone was earnest as we pulled up to the gate. He leaned out and punched in the combo. The gate started moving. "That woman was slipping away, and you made her stay."

I kept my gaze out the window. "Her son kept her here, not me."

"Ally, I heard you," he told me simply. "She was slipping away, and you reminded her of what she had to live for."

I swallowed hard around the knot in my throat; I didn't understand where he was going with this. It put me on edge.

He pulled the Blazer into the driveway and parked. "Remember what we were talking about before the ghost came in?"

"Yeah, I remember," I mumbled, hoping he'd drop the subject. I didn't really want to think about my issues with centering. I just wanted to go inside and pass out.

"I don't think you have to worry about finding out you're anything bad, Ally." he said, his voice gentle. "You have too big of a heart for that."

That feeling of being cared for washed over me again, bringing tears to my eyes. Oh, I really needed to get used to this. I couldn't keep tearing up every time someone shows that they cared.

My voice was thick when I finally answered him.

"Thanks, Ash."

CHAPTER 17

$\mathcal{T}$he guys let me go to bed without too many questions, though I did take a shower and scrub my arms for a good half hour before I was done. The next morning, I woke up earlier than usual. I took a shower and did my usual morning routine. Today I wore my usual boot-cut dark blue jeans and a black boyfriend shirt. I made sure to put all my cleaned bracelets back on. I pulled my hair back into a ponytail and headed into the kitchen. I woke up early enough that we could have a real breakfast today, so I pulled out eggs and a big slab of bacon. By the time the guys started coming downstairs, I had a huge plate of eggs and a huge plate of bacon waiting.

I was sitting on a stool at the breakfast bar, finishing my last piece of bacon, when Miles came into the kitchen. He wore dark blue jeans, black converse, and a white shirt with a large picture that looked like it was taken from the Hubble telescope. That I now kind of wanted to steal; I liked the colors.

He looked around then over at me.

"You are my favorite person today," he declared as he headed to get himself a cup of coffee.

"Did I make enough?" I asked, worrying. The guys ate so much I didn't know how much to make.

Miles looked over the counter. "Yes. That should fill up everyone, even Isaac and Zeke."

I got up and washed my plate then sat back down. It wasn't long before the others walked in. Asher looked around and grabbed a plate. Today he was wearing a pair of dark jeans and a green and gold football jersey with the number six on his chest. It didn't do much for his eyes.

"Who cooked?" He dumped a big spoonful of eggs on his plate. Mile pointed at me while he took a drink from his mug. Asher's eyebrow rose. "When did you get up?"

"I've been up for an hour." I shrugged then gestured at his shirt. "What's with the jersey?" It looked odd on him, not his usual style.

He came and sat down on the other side of me.

"All the football players wear their jersey on games days, well, when we have home games," he explained before he began eating.

Huh. I'd never heard of that. Then again, I'd never paid much attention to what was going on around the other schools I attended.

Zeke came in next, his hair wet but combed. He had actually shaved this morning. It made him look more "the scary guy next door" rather than his usual "menace to society" look. For the first time since I met him, he wore dark blue jeans and a scoop-neck, long-sleeved black t-shirt. The neckline showed the dip between his collarbones at the base of his throat. I wondered if it was laundry day and he was out of black jeans.

He raised an eyebrow at the food. "Did Asher cook?" He was looking wearily at Miles.

"Ally did," Asher answered before biting into a piece of bacon.

Zeke raised an eyebrow at me and then eyed the food wearily.

"It's not as good as Asher's cooking, but it's food," I told him honestly.

Zeke grabbed a plate and dished up his breakfast.

Ethan came in next; his midnight black hair was wet and tucked behind his ears, the ends resting on his jaw line. The silver earrings against the black of his hair, as always, they caught my eye. Today he wore a faded black Metallica shirt and his usual black jeans. When his chocolate eyes saw the eggs, they lit up.

"Food!" He hurried over, avoiding Zeke who ate with his back leaning against the sink.

He was dishing himself up some eggs when he paused. "Did Miles cook?" Ethan's voice was filled with dread.

"Lexie did." Zeke supplied.

Ethan looked at me and blew me a kiss.

"Thanks, Beautiful." He dished himself breakfast then stood at the end of the breakfast bar, his plate on the counter.

I heard stomping down the stairs.

"Very fucking funny guys!" Isaac shouted. He turned from the stairs and stormed into the kitchen, still wet from the shower, wearing only a towel around his waist.

The guys burst out laughing while I took the time to ogle him a little. The muscles in his broad shoulders caught my eye, which then ran down to his defined chest. He didn't have Zeke's mass, but he did have more muscle than most guys did. Then there were his abs, he had the definition everyone wished they had. His Adonis belt was defined, making the v that disappeared into the white towel. The guy had definition all over. I forced my eyes back up at his face, which was scowling at the other guys.

"Where are my clothes?" The guys burst out laughing again. Isaac just shook his head and waited it out.

"Upstairs, linen closet," Ethan and Asher told him still laughing. Isaac turned and headed off to get dressed.

"Why did you guys do that?" I asked, making a mental note to lock the door next time I take a shower.

"Isaac pranks us so much, that when an opportunity to mess with him comes up, we take it," Asher explained as he took his plate to the sink. It wasn't long before Isaac came back downstairs fully clothed, wearing his usual jeans and sneakers. Today he wore a green long-sleeve shirt and his blue hoodie.

"Who made food?" he asked, already grabbing a plate and dishing himself up some food.

"Lexie." Miles and Zeke answered at the same time.

Isaac looked over at me then gave me puppy eyes. "Marry me?"

I rolled my eyes as the other guys threw wadded up napkins at him. Isaac smiled at me before biting into a piece of bacon. I ignored the proposal and finished off my coffee.

"So, is everyone coming back here after school?" Zeke asked, putting his plate into the sink and leaning against the counter near it.

"I won't, I have to stay after to get ready for the game," Asher announced, taking his coffee mug to the sink.

"Wait, are we still only taking one car?" I asked looking around the group.

The guys shook their heads.

"Last night I checked everyone's car out, and then Ethan salted everything. So we should be good." Zeke said, rolling his neck; I heard it crack from here.

"I'll probably stop by my house to pick up a change of clothes; I'm meeting Kristina at the game," Ethan announced. "Then hopefully to the party."

"Have you asked?" Isaac asked.

"Not yet, but I'm sure she'll say yes." Ethan boasted.

I rolled my eyes. Ethan did have charm; I couldn't deny that.

"I should pick up some clothes then, too," Isaac said, thinking out loud. "We can get ready for the party here."

It made me think about the party tonight. What did I have in my closet that would look good?

I got to my feet and headed toward the sink with my empty mug. "Well hell, if everyone else is getting pretty," I muttered as I stepped past Zeke and put my mug in the sink. "I might as well too."

"You don't have to," Zeke pointed out, shrugging. "I'm not changing."

"Guys don't have to look pretty, Zeke, but girls? It's kind of our thing. So I'm going to do the girly thing tonight." I kept my voice matter of fact before turning and leaning against the sink.

"Are we going to see Red in a skirt?" Isaac exclaimed, his face lighting up as if it was Christmas.

I laughed sarcastically.

"No," I told him flatly.

His face fell.

I looked over to Miles. "Miles, do you mind if I use that big tub in the master bath tonight? Cause it's kind of calling my name," I asked sweetly.

He smiled at me. "Of course."

I SMILED CUTELY AT HIM. "Thank you."

"You might want to add a layer today, Ally, it's going to be cold," Asher advised, taking his mug to the sink.

I looked around at the guys.

"Okay, who has an extra hoodie I can steal?" I asked them. I could probably get away without one, but I really didn't want to be cold. Cold was really cold up here in the mountains.

The guys looked at each other expectantly.

"I don't have one," Zeke announced. "Even if I did, it would be huge on her."

"I've got a red one, but it smells from band practice," Ethan admitted apologetically.

"Same here, from football," Asher added.

"I'll get her one," Miles announced, narrowing his eyes at the guys. "The girl needs a hoodie, not an appendage."

I raised my eyebrows at that as he left the kitchen to go upstairs. The guys laughed when he was out of earshot.

"What did you guys do?" I asked suspiciously.

"We just annoyed Miles," Isaac explained. "He's a big believer in chivalry. You know, treating girls like ladies and all that."

I smiled. That did sound like Miles.

"Besides," Isaac continued, "he's the one closest in size, and his hoodie will still be big on you."

Made sense to me.

Miles came back downstairs and handed me his gray hoodie. I leaned over and kissed him on the cheek.

"Thank you, Miles."

His ears turned pink as I pulled away.

"Wait, he lends you a hoodie, and he gets a kiss on the cheek?" Isaac scoffed, his voice full of disbelief.

I saw the mischievous gleam in his eye; he was messing with Miles or me.

"Damn straight."

Isaac chuckled. "So classy, Red," he said, teasing me.

I stuck my tongue out at him, and everyone laughed. I put on the hoodie--it reached mid-thigh. I held my arms out and laughed.

"If I had leggings, I could wear it as a short dress." I giggled at myself. The boys chuckled at how small I was.

When it was time to go, we all made sure everyone had their charms on. I made sure to use my rosemary oil again. We decided to split into two cars; I was planning on riding with Miles, Isaac, and Ethan. I pulled on my leather jacket over Miles' hoodie and stepped outside. Then immediately wanted to step back inside. There was actual frost on the windshields, and my nose felt frozen already.

"Holy, freaking, mother... it's cold," I complained pulling the sleeves of Miles hoodie over my hands. The guys laughed at me as I hopped into the back of Miles' car.

"You still need a scarf and gloves, Beautiful," Ethan informed me as he got in the front seat.

"I haven't exactly had time to go shopping," I reminded him.

"Excuses, excuses," he muttered.

I narrowed my eyes at him then scooted up behind his seat. I took my freezing hands and shoved them down his back under his shirt and jacket. He shouted, wiggled, and cursed.

"Oh look, I found a heater!" I taunted as he continued to complain.

Miles and Isaac laughed so hard that we were almost late to school.

THE MORNING WENT on as usual. In World Civ. the girls to my left talked to me again this time about the coming weekend. It was nice to talk to other girls for once.

I was on my way to English when I got a text from Rory. Looks like the woman, Emily Hanns, was going to live and make a full recovery. It made my morning.

I was sitting in English waiting for class to start, when Eric sat to my left again.

"Hey Alexis, what are your plans for the weekend?" he asked, flashing me that dimple.

Oh, the usual, use my freaky abilities to beat a Bitch Ghost into staying away from my friends. I was even a smart ass in my head. Instead, I shook my head.

"I have a project I need to finish, and probably a lot of sleeping in." I shrugged "What is there to do in town?" I asked curiously.

He gave me a friendly half-grin.

"Not much in the fall, really. Mostly the movies, hiking trails, or parties." He snapped his fingers and pointed at me. "There's a party after the game tonight. Out at the Dotson's, their parents are out of town. If you want to go."

Was he asking me out? Or was he just letting me know?

"Yeah, I heard about that one. My friends were going to take me tonight," I said, hoping to sound vague.

The teacher walked to the front of the classroom, class started, and I was miserable. I hated the story of Romeo and Juliet, how other girls fawned over the tragic love story. I couldn't see the appeal. A little communication and honesty on their part and the whole death thing could have been avoided. But judging by the way that the girls were gushing as they answered questions, I was in the minority.

When class was over Eric walked out with me.

"Which way are you headed?" Eric stopped and turned around. I pointed toward the east hall. He smiled.

"I'll walk you," he offered, already walking along side me.

Okay, this was a first. The only people who ever walked the halls with me were the guys.

"This town doesn't really have a lot to do in the fall, but after the first good snow, there's a lot more going on," he said.

He told me about parts of the lake freezing over, the pickup hockey games that happened every Saturday. I couldn't tell if he was trying to be nice, or if he was working his way up to asking me out.

He was talking about going to the game with a group of his friends when Zeke and Asher found us in the hallway. They were walking along when Asher spotted me, saw Eric, grinned and said something to Zeke. Zeke smirked. Oh no. They made a beeline towards us.

"So, if you want to go to the game..." Eric trailed off and stopped walking when Zeke and Asher reached us.

"Hey, Ally," Asher greeted me before his eyes went to Eric. "Who's this?"

Zeke stopped in front of Eric. He eyed Eric up and down, being obvious about it. His frown was very much in place.

Great.

"Eric, this is Asher and Zeke, a couple of my friends." I gestured from the boys to Eric. "Eric's in my English class."

Asher smiled, his face open and friendly. Zeke was his usual frowning self.

"We were just talking about the football game tonight," I told them both.

"It should be a good game," Eric offered, his gaze still on Zeke who had crossed his arms over his chest.

That shit!

Eric looked uneasy as he looked back at me. "I'll see you later, Alexis." Then he disappeared into the crowd.

I looked up to see Zeke's smirk back in place.

"What was that about?" I asked, trying not to laugh.

"We wanted to meet the guy who was asking you out on a date," Asher explained.

"He didn't ask me out," I argued.

"He was trying too." Zeke chuckled.

I shook my head at them. I didn't know if I should be mad, annoyed or just laugh.

"And you stopped him," I pointed out. "Is this going to become a thing?"

"Isn't it better if you know right off if he has a problem with your five guy friends?" Asher asked.

I rolled my eyes. He had a point; that didn't mean I liked it, but he was right.

"Good point." I shrugged dismissively. "Besides, I got a date with Dylan tomorrow night."

Asher's eyebrows went up, his eyes widened. He wrapped his arm around me and pulled me to his side smiling.

"And when did this happen?"

I snickered as I wrapped my arm around his waist. "On the phone last night."

"Where is he taking you?" Zeke asked, adjusting his bag and looking a bit tense.

"I'm meeting him at Vegabond." I looked up at Zeke. "By the way, he wants to thank you for kicking that guy's ass last Saturday."

Zeke made a puzzled face. "It had nothing to do with him," he said, looking uncomfortable.

"That's what he told me." I offered.

I gave Asher a squeeze and looked up at him. "Hey, I got a text from Rory. That woman, Emily Hann, is going to live."

He gave me a big smile. "That totally makes my morning."

I nodded and let go of Asher before heading down the hall.

"See you guys at lunch."

WHEN WE GOT to our table at lunch, Zeke and Asher were already there. Zeke offered to watch our bags, as long as someone grabbed him something. I volunteered immediately. He handed me his money, and we headed to the cafeteria. As we went through the line, I picked the most healthy, tasteless food I could find. Revenge is sweet. I was headed back when my conscious twinged at me. I stopped and picked him up a candy bar I'd seen him eat earlier this week. That, I stuck in my pocket.

The look on his face when I handed him his steamed rice, chicken, and veggies was priceless.

"Lexie, what the fuck?" he asked, stunned at what I picked up.

The other guys burst out laughing.

"Revenge is sweet, Zeke." I smiled at him across the table.

His eyes met mine as he glared.

"I made a point to pick you up healthy food that tasted good," he pointed out.

I did feel a little guilty. I was still smiling when I pulled out the teriyaki sauce packets and put them in front of him. He was still glaring at me as he picked them up. I started laughing again as he looked at his food with a pained look. Okay, yeah, I was starting to feel bad. A little. I pulled out the candy bar and tossed it to him.

"You think I would do that to you?" I asked in my sweet voice.

Zeke smirked at me and started eating his lunch.

"So, have you asked Kristina to the game yet?" I asked Ethan as I started eating my tuna salad sandwich.

He nodded, his mouth fill. When he finished chewing, he answered. "Yep, I'll be meeting her there tonight. Don't really want it to be too date-like; girls get weird after that."

"Speaking of dating, some guy was hitting on Ally in the hallway today," Asher announced, his eyes sparkling.

I rolled my eyes and continued eating.

"Oh, who?" Isaac asked excitedly.

"What's his name?" Ethan chimed in, resting his chin on his hand, giving me his full attention.

"How did you meet?" Isaac continued in a girly voice.

"Was he cute?" Ethan said in the exact same tone.

The other guys burst out laughing.

"Oh my god, stop please," I said as they continued to make doe eyes at me. "His name's Eric, and he's in my English class."

"Oh, never date someone you have a class with it, gets weird when you break up," Ethan cautioned as he went back to eating.

"Yeah, there's that, 'We've done stuff with each other, but now we don't talk awkwardness when you're near each other.'" Isaac added.

"Don't worry about that. Zeke scared him off," I told them dismissively.

Heads turned to Zeke who shrugged unrepentant.

"What did you do Zeke?" Miles asked, his voice growing colder.

He smirked. "Mild glaring," he admitted to them before turning to me. "If that scared him away, you're better off. Because any guy that comes around, we're going to be asking him questions."

"What are your intentions?" Asher offered.

"Where are you going?" Ethan added.

"When will you be back?" Isaac supplied.

I looked around the table at them to see if they were serious. They were all nodding, including Miles.

"And does this rule apply to Dylan?" I asked, hoping to hear a no.

They all smirked.

"We all just happen to be going to Vegabond Saturday night, so we might as well carpool," Asher said nonchalantly.

I sighed and rested my forehead on my hand.

"I'm never going to date again." I groaned.

The guys thought it was hilarious.

I looked up and pointed at them. "I am warning all of you. If you scare off every guy that wants to ask me out, one of you are going to have to go to homecoming with me, and winter formal. And prom. And anything else I want to go to."

They didn't stop laughing until after the bell for 6th period rang.

THE REST of the day went on as usual. Gym was dull. But when I was on the phone talking to Zeke as we walked the path, I couldn't see Bitch Ghost. It sent a chill down my spine. She could be somewhere else on campus. Then I put it out of my mind.

During art class, Asher drew stick figures jumping to their deaths. This time out of an airplane--at least there was a variation.

After class, I headed out to the parking lot, only to see Miles' car gone. I went and waited next to Zeke's Jeep. Isaac soon joined me.

"Where did Miles and Ethan take off to?" Isaac asked.

I shrugged, I hadn't texted them to find out. Isaac pulled his phone out and started texting. He had a small smile on his face when they answered.

"They say they're running errands," Isaac told me.

As we waited for Zeke, we talked about the party. Isaac told me about the girl he had his eye on for a while now. I asked him all the questions they had asked me earlier. He promised never to do that again.

Revenge is sweet.

AFTER A GREAT DEAL OF BITCHING, Zeke drove us by Isaac's house and mine to pick up clothes. Soon after, we pulled into the circular drive in front of the house. We walked into the living room to hear shouting from deeper into the house. I dropped my bags on one of the couches and followed Zeke and Isaac into the family room.

Ethan and Miles were on the big couch, their backs towards me. I watched as one character on the screen continued to beat the other into submission. Zeke sat next to Miles, and Isaac took the other couch to the left. I took off my shoes and walked over behind Isaac's couch. I climbed over the back and plopped down next to him. He bumped his shoulder into me. I bumped mine back.

"Who's winning?" I asked, crossing my legs under me.

"Miles." Isaac and Zeke said at the same time.

I looked over at the other boys. Ethan was cursing under his breath as he hit buttons. He didn't look happy. I watched the screen as his character was knocked out. Ethan cursed and tossed the controller to Zeke.

"I give up. He wins every time," Ethan grumbled. Miles smiled before leaning forward and tossing me the controller. I caught it.

"Before we start, what are we doing for dinner since Asher isn't here?" I asked, eyeing the boys. They all looked at each other, seeing if anyone had an idea. I rolled my eyes. "Is there food in the kitchen? Like, ingredients?"

"Usually," Miles replied.

"I'll go see what I can make." I got to my feet and headed for the door. "Since none of you are getting off your asses."

"Oh, wait, we'll help," Isaac called in a very uninterested voice. I left the family room, walked into the kitchen, and opened the fridge. I pulled out 2lbs of hamburger and put it on the counter. If we had breadcrumbs, we were having meatloaf. I checked the pantry and found breadcrumbs. Yay, I can make something I know how to cook. I preheated the oven and began looking for the rest of what I needed. I was trying to reach a big metal mixing bowl when a hand with silver rings reached up and snagged it. I jumped and turned my head, Ethan was bringing down the bowl from the cabinet. He held it out to me.

"Thought you might like help." His smoky voice was back. I had to remind myself not to curl my toes. That voice should really be illegal.

"I'll take it; can you get the eggs out of the fridge?" I asked as I started looking for the spices.

"So, what are we making?" he asked, closing the fridge door.

I was pulling down the spices I wanted when I answered.

"Meatloaf. It'll take an hour to cook." I washed my hands, opened the meat, and dumped it in the bowl. "Take off your rings, hon; you're getting your hands messy."

He groaned as he went to the sink and washed his hands.

"How did you learn to cook?" he asked with his back to me.

I chewed on the corner of my lip as I picked up the breadcrumbs. "My mom taught me before Dad died." I shrugged, pushing away memories. "After that, if I wanted something not cooked in a microwave, I had to make it myself."

"That sucks, Lexie." Ethan came back over to stand in front of the bowl his hands clear of his rings. "You can always come over to our house; Mom makes bad-ass enchiladas." He pointed to the mixing bowl. "I take it I've got to mix?"

I nodded and reached for the pepper. The idea of a home cooked meal made by a real mom sounded much better than it probably should have. I pushed that thought away before adding pepper to the mix.

"I might just take you up on that. I like enchiladas," I said, reaching for the salt.

We talked about the party tonight while we finished making the meat loaf. I put it in the pan and waited for the oven to heat up. He slipped his rings back on. I hopped up on the counter and watched as Ethan did the same on the other side.

"So, tell me about Kristina," I asked, genuinely curious.

"She's a nice, sweet girl. That doesn't even curse. She's also kind of shy." He kicked his foot against the cabinet. "She's the opposite of what I usually go for," he admitted.

I raised an eyebrow at him.

"What are you talking about?" I asked trying to understand. "I don't know the history here, catch me up."

"I've dated all kinds of girls," he began, fiddling with one of his rings. "Goth, Punk, Emo, geek, band geek, now I'm up to the prim and proper. And I always have the same problem."

"Which is?"

He started to shake his head.

"Nu-uh." I said. "No, you don't get to squirm out of this topic; you guys know almost all my shit, now spill."

He chuckled softly. "Fair enough." He looked toward the door as if to see if the guys were around, then he looked back at me. "Physically we click, it's great, and it's hot. But eventually, she realizes I'm not who she thought I was, and she's not who I thought she was. So we split." His eyes darted to the doorway and back to me. "So, I'm trying to date girls that I normally wouldn't go for, like Kristina."

"Sounds like a good idea," I said, trying to figure out how to say the next part. "You really do need something more in common with someone besides you both thinking the other one is hot," I offered, trying not to overstep.

Ethan snorted. "Yeah, Miles said that too."

I kicked my foot against the counter under me.

"Miles usually gives pretty good advice, Ethan said.

"Yeah, why is that?" I asked, dying to know the answer. "He knew I was freaking out Tuesday. And I thought I hid it pretty well."

Ethan looked at me his eyebrows raised.

"You were freaking out?" he asked, eyebrows raised, his eyes wide.

Apparently, I hid it good enough to fool the others.

"He didn't tell you?" Oops.

Ethan shook his head. "Guy code, Beautiful," he reminded me.

Shit. I just ratted myself out. I was going to have to get the hang of this.

"That's not the point," I said, really not wanting to talk about it. "The point was, he noticed it."

Ethan took the hint.

"Well, it has to do with Zeke, really," Ethan explained. "A lot of messed up shit went down with his family, and his Aunt Sylvia wanted him to deal with it in a healthy way. So, Zeke went to a lot of therapy. Miles wanted to help him deal, so he learned everything he could about psychology."

I looked up to see Ethan watching me, his face serious.

"I'm not telling you about Zeke's shit, Lexie, that's not my story to tell."

"I can respect that."

"Just know that even when Zeke is barking at you and bossing you around, he genuinely wants the best for you," Ethan said, eyeing the doorway again.

"That's why you guys put up with it?" I asked, getting up to put the meatloaf in the oven.

"Yeah, it's how he deals." Ethan shrugged.

A tense silence filled the kitchen.

I eyed him suspiciously. "Your cell phone isn't on, right?"

Ethan burst out laughing.

DINNER WAS READY AN HOUR LATER. I microwaved some bags of green beans and put them into a serving bowl. It wasn't Asher's cooking, but it was food. The guys were coming down the hall as I was pulling the meatloaf from the oven. Everyone dished themselves up some and thanked me for cooking. After we had eaten, Isaac and

Ethan agreed to clean up. The rest of us went back to the family room.

I was in the middle of trying to kick Zeke's butt at the fighting game when they came back.

"It's a party, I need to blow off some steam," Isaac snapped at his brother as they walked in.

"Blowing off some steam is fine, but you have training tomorrow--"

"And I'll deal with it." Isaac interrupted, his tone making it clear the subject was closed.

I have never heard Isaac serious about something. It was weird. It distracted me enough that Zeke got the upper hand and knocked out my character. I checked the clock and saw the time; it was 5:45 pm.

"Well, I'm going to go soak in the tub, then get ready." I got to my feet and handed the controller to Miles. "Miles avenge my honor."

Zeke cursed.

"As my lady wills it," Miles said in a gallant puffed up voice.

I walked into the bedroom and dropped my bags on the bed. I pulled out everything I'd need for my soak including my mp3 player. I left my clothes and makeup to grab later, though I did take my cell phone with me. I went into the bathroom and started the tub. Soon I was soaking away all my worries with the jets on. I dunked my head once to get my hair wet, then I put my earbuds in and started my music. Everything drifted away. All the stress of the last week disappeared. It always amazes me the way a good tub soak could make you feel like new.

I was playing Angry Birds when I remembered that Dylan had a game today, so I sent him a message.

Alexis: Good luck at your game tonight.

I was just about to go back to the game when my phone vibrated. Wow, that was quick.

Dylan: Thanks, it should be a good game. How was your day?

I smiled as I texted back, feeling girly.

Alexis: Not bad. Miles had to lend me a hoodie to go under my jacket today. Why is it so freaking cold here?

Dylan: Lol, we're in the mountains, sweetie. It even snows here.

I tried to ignore the warm feeling in my stomach I had when he called me sweetie.

Alexis: I'm going to freeze. How was your day?

Dylan: Lol, the usual. Just killing time until we need to get in our gear.

Alexis: What position do you play? You never told me.

Dylan: I'm a running back.

I smiled, that meant he was quick, light on his feet and ran the ball a lot.

Alexis: What're your yards per carry?

There were a couple heartbeats of silence before he answered.

Dylan: You know what stats are?

Alexis: Yeah, watched football with my dad a lot. He always answered any question I had. And I wanted to understand what was going on.

Dylan. Let me get somewhere quieter, and I'll call you. I need to hear you talking about stats.

Panic clutched my chest tight.

Alexis: NO!

I winced as I sent that then quickly tried to explain.

Alexis: I can't talk on the phone right now. I just remembered you had a game today and I figured you'd be too busy to talk to me.

I felt my face turn pink as I hit send.

Dylan: Where are you that you can't talk?

I groaned, he probably thought I was on the toilet or something. That was worse than the truth. Sighing, I texted him back.

Alexis: I'm kind of soaking in the tub. I just wanted to wish you luck tonight, didn't think you could talk.

It was a couple minutes before he replied.

Dylan: Damn, Lexie.

I snickered to myself.

Alexis: I tried not telling you.

Dylan: I'm calling.

Alexis: I won't answer.

Dylan: I'm so going to talk to you when you're naked.

Alexis: Not today, you're not.

Dylan: Tell me there are bubbles.

I started laughing so hard I almost dropped my phone into the water.

Alexis: LMAO.

Dylan: Fine, don't tell me if there are bubbles. Or if your hair is down or up.

Alexis: Okay, I'm hanging up now.

Dylan: Okay, I'll behave. What are you doing tonight after the game?

Alexis: The guys are taking me to a party somewhere.

Dylan: Zeke going?

I looked at my phone suspiciously. Why did he want to know about Zeke?

Alexis: Yeah, why?

Dylan: Just suddenly very grateful you have guy friends.

My heart melted as I texted him back. But I was also a little irked he thought I needed protecting, it was a weird feeling.

Alexis: You're sweet, but I can handle a party.

Dylan: I bet you can, but you're small, honey. There's only so much you can do against a guy bigger than you.

I hated to admit it, but he was right. Hell, Zeke had proved that on Tuesday. I sighed, resigned.

Alexis: You want me to stick near the guys, don't you?

Dylan: It would help me not worry about you.

I groaned. I could just tell him that I was going to stick near the guys, hell I probably was anyway. They were the only ones at school I really knew. But he didn't need to know that.

Alexis: Alright, I'll stick with the guys.

Dylan: Thank you.

Alexis: What are you doing after the game?

Dylan: Heading home, we'll get back around 11:30 tonight. Then I was going to take a shower and text you to see if you were awake to talk.

Alexis: Sounds good to me.

Dylan: It's a date. Now seriously...bubbles?

I burst out laughing and shaking my head.

Alexis: Lol, I'll talk to you later tonight. Good luck at the game.

Dylan: ttyl

I put my phone down and laid my head back smiling. I started getting into the music and began to sing along. After I was done, I turned off the jets and unplugged the tub. I was still singing along to Halestorm's Amen when I tied a towel around me and was dabbing my wet hair with another.

When I opened the door, still singing, I froze. All four boys were sitting there looking at me, red-faced and laughing. Miles was the only one looking apologetic standing by the bed his hands in his pockets. Oh god, they heard me singing. My face went red instantly as I yanked the buds out. Their laughter filled my ears. I grabbed both ends of the towel in my hands, flipping it into a rat-tail.

"You assholes!" I shouted at them and started whipping one end of the towel at the boys on the bed. They kept laughing as they scattered out of range. I chased them out of the bedroom, nailing a few on their butts.

"Worth it!" Isaac shouted on his way out the door.

In the hall, Ethan turned around out of range of the towel.

"Your voice is actually pretty good-"

I threw the towel at his face and slammed the door, this time locking it. I'll never forget to lock the bedroom door again.

I finished getting ready. I did my normal hair stuff; combing, anti-frizz. But this time I added leave in conditioner and dried my hair with a hair dryer while I waited for my face to turn back to normal. Then I did my usual sunscreen moisturizer--I know it's nighttime but damn it, I'm very white. I did my usual makeup, only tonight I made the shadow a few shades darker and the black liner thicker, bringing my eyes out more. I looked at my face and thought about using a deep red lipstick. Nah, I'm wearing red already. I put on a rosy pink lipstick that was a couple shades darker than my natural lips.

I stepped back and looked in the mirror. The makeup wasn't as subtle as normally, but it still looked good. I put on my black bra and underwear. I pulled on black skinny jeans, a dark red Henley long sleeve shirt. I made sure to unbutton a only a couple buttons to show a little cleavage; I didn't want to fall out of my shirt tonight. I pulled on my tall, black boots with black leather straps on the outside, making sure to tuck my pants into the boots.

I left the bathroom and looked in the full-length mirror in the bedroom. My hair was in sleek curls for once, no frizz or fly-aways. The skinny jeans showed the shape of my hips and thighs even more than my usual boot cut jeans. And with the still somewhat-modest shirt, I didn't look real sexy until you were standing near; that's what I liked, subtle but sexy. I used a quick layer of nice smelling hairspray to keep my hair from frizzing. I made sure to put my two necklaces on, tucking them into my shirt, then my onyx beads which I pulled my shirt sleeve over. I even made a point to put on the rosemary oil again. I was going to have fun tonight. No ghost drama, just normal teenage fun. Whatever the hell that means.

I grabbed my keys, cell, and wallet before leaving the bedroom. I found the guys waiting in the living room. When they spotted me, eyebrows went up and talking stopped. I took a look at them. Zeke and Miles were still in their clothes from this morning. Ethan was wearing black jeans, a black collared shirt unbuttoned, showing a black t-shirt underneath, along with his usual rings on his fingers and in his ear. But he was freshly shaved. Isaac was still wearing his dark blue jeans, only his orange t-shirt had a vintage look. He also wore an olive green short-sleeved, collared shirt unbuttoned. Isaac's hair was actually combed.

"You guys clean up pretty good," I told them. "Well?" I held my hands out and did a turn.

I heard Zeke curse.

When I was facing them again, I looked at them questioningly.

Isaac had a confused look on his face.

"What?" I looked down, thinking I got makeup on my clothes or something. When I saw nothing, I looked back at him with an eyebrow raised.

"How do you do that?" Isaac asked.

"Do what?" I looked down at my outfit again, not understanding what he was asking.

"You are completely dressed, showing almost no skin and still..." Isaac trailed off.

"We're going to spend all night making sure she's not in trouble," Zeke growled out, looking at the others.

Miles' ears had turned a soft pink, Isaac's eyebrows were up, and Ethan was grinning ear to ear. I took it all as a compliment.

"Relax, Zeke. I'm not planning on drinking."

His shoulders relaxed.

"Good." His eyes ran over me again, the worry back on his face.

I wrinkled my nose at him.

"Oh, I almost forgot," Ethan said, going over to the couch and grabbing a shopping bag. He handed it to me. "Miles and I went shopping for you."

I raised an eyebrow and opened the bag. There was a beautiful soft, black scarf with white skulls of different sizes all over it. I loved it instantly.

"This is awesome, where did you get it? I think I need this in every color," I said, having a big girly moment. The guys laughed as I pulled out soft, black, knit gloves and a black beanie with a skull and crossbones design on the front. I loved them. I dropped the bag and hugged Ethan tight. "Thank you, guys. I love them!" I let go of Ethan and hugged Miles who went tense but then relaxed after a couple heartbeats.

"No problem, Lexie," Miles told me, patting my back.

"Yeah, I was only thinking about my poor neck," Ethan teased. I threw my scarf on and tucked the gloves and beanie into my jean pockets.

"Come on, I'll drive," I told them as I picked up my jacket. Everyone grabbed their coats, checked their charms, and we headed out.

TRYING TO LIVE WITH THE DEAD

WHEN WE PULLED up to the student lot, it was packed. I hadn't realized how popular a football game was in this town. I finally found a spot and parked. We paid and went through the gate. Ethan stayed behind, wanting to wait for Kristina. The crowd was thick enough that we had to go single file. I grabbed Miles' and Isaac's hands to stop us from getting separated. Zeke was in front, making a path. When we made it to a less crowded area, I let go of the boys and looked around. We were on the far-right side of the bleachers. We followed Zeke down the cement steps till we were around the middle.

"This good?" Zeke asked, pointing to the benches.

We all said yes.

I ended up on the left with Isaac and Miles to the right. Zeke sat behind me. The guys started talking about the game and injuries some of the players had. I asked about Asher's stats and got a couple surprised looks. Then Miles was telling me Asher's numbers.

The bleachers were really filling up when Ethan found us, Kristina in tow. She had a cute face, with a button nose. Long, straight, brown hair and pretty, brown eyes. She was wearing an oversized lavender sweater, white jeans, and a khaki jacket. She was cute; there was no other way to describe her.

"Everyone, this is Kristina," Ethan announced before he pointed at each of us. "That's Zeke, Miles, Isaac, and Lexie,"

Isaac said hi. Miles smiled and turned around quickly, his fingers tapping that staccato rhythm again. Kristina looked really tense, her fingers knotting in on themselves over and over again. I got an idea.

"Thank God! Another girl!" I all but shouted dramatically, I stood up and hurried across the bench in front of us to get past the boys. I was soon sitting next to Kristina, her face lit up, her eyes wide. I gave her my pleading face. "Please talk to me about girl stuff. I'm begging you."

The guys burst out laughing, even Kristina chuckled.

"No one wants to hear that stuff, Red," Isaac shot out over his shoulder, a mischievous half-grin on his face. He knew what I was doing. I leaned over and popped him lightly on the shoulder.

"Shut up, we already talked about football stats. It's my turn," I said back before turning back to Ethan's date. I kept asking her questions to get her to start talking. She was in the school band, played the flute and piano. She was hoping to go on to college with a great music program. The more I got her to talk, the more she relaxed and talked to the others. She asked me what it was like to have so many guy friends. I told her it was a hoot, in a deadpan voice. I told her about this afternoon and the whole boys listening to me sing incident. I left out that I was in a towel part. The guys snickered; I shot each of them a glare. Kristina giggled. Kristina also showed me several ways to fold and use my new scarf. I didn't know there was more than one way to use a scarf. Huh, learn something new every day.

When the game started, I got up to go back to my spot. Ethan caught my eye and mouthed a thank you. I gave him a wink and went back to my spot. As the game went on, we cheered and booed the bad calls.

It wasn't until it was well into the second quarter that I realized the temperature had dropped. I could see my breath. It was cold. I had mostly lived in southern California, Arizona, and New Mexico. It did not get this cold there. The metal bench under my butt seemed to steal any warmth I had. I pulled on my gloves and my beanie; I was a bit warmer but still freezing.

"Shit, it's cold," I finally muttered.

"What's wrong Lexie? Didn't it get cold in California?" Isaac taunted.

I blew into my gloved hands.

"Not this freaking cold." I was starting to seriously consider sitting in one of the guy's laps. I was even trying to decide whose lap I was jumping into when Zeke caught my attention.

"There's hot chocolate at the snack bar if you want something warm."

I was up and down the aisle in a blink. I only stopped long enough to ask if someone else wanted something. They all said no, laughing as I ran up the steps. I didn't care; I was not used to this weather. I was on my way back from the snack bar with my large hot chocolate

TRYING TO LIVE WITH THE DEAD

warming my hands when I heard my name. I stopped and looked around. Eric waved to me as he hurried over through the crowd.

"So, you made it," Eric observed. "Where are you sitting?"

I gestured over my shoulder towards the other end of the bleachers. "With the guys on the end over there. It's less crowded." I took a sip of my cocoa.

"Do you think your friends will mind if I join you?" he asked, his voice uncertain.

Surprised, I really didn't know how to answer. I had a date with Dylan tomorrow and a phone date tonight. Did that make it weird if Eric came to sit with us during the game? I was really rusty at this.

"I-I don't think so." I stammered, still not knowing how to answer.

Eric seemed to relax and started walking with me.

I had just finished telling him that Zeke wasn't as protective as he seemed today when we reached the guys.

"Hey guys, this is Eric," I announced, narrowing my eyes at Zeke, warning him not to start glaring. He gave me a smirk and went back to watching the game.

I pointed out everyone as I introduced them. "This is Kristina, Ethan, you know Zeke, Isaac, and Miles." Everyone said hi, except Zeke. I decided to sit down next to Miles; keeping Zeke away from Eric seemed a good idea. I might not want to date the guy, but I didn't want to have him shit himself if Zeke sneezed. The game went on, and the conversation flowed. Half time came, and my phone vibrated. I checked it.

Ethan: Who's this guy?

I made sure Eric couldn't see my phone and then answered.

Alexis: Guy from English Zeke scared off. He wanted to sit with me, and I didn't know how to answer. I'm actually not dating anyone, but at the same time, I have a phone date with Dylan tonight and a regular one tomorrow.

It wasn't long before he wrote back.

Ethan: A double pull...nice, Beautiful.

I snickered and put my phone away. No judgment from Ethan; I liked that about him. I went back to watching the halftime show.

We were in the third quarter when it happened. Hoots and whistles went up through the crowd. I didn't understand until Miles touched my shoulder gently.

"Lexie," Miles said his voice serious. "The big screen."

I looked up and my heart dropped. There was a photo of me in my underwear. It was obvious I was changing in the locker room and that I had no idea the photo was being taken. Words flashed across the bottom of the screen: "Call for a good time", followed by a phone number. My mouth dropped. More cheers and laughter rang out through the crowd.

"Oh my goodness." Kristina's voice was shocked.

"What the fuck?" Ethan cursed, his voice low with controlled anger.

"Who the hell did that?" Isaac growled.

"Why is it still up there?" Even Miles' voice was cold.

I didn't hear anything from Zeke, and I knew that wasn't good.

"Is that your phone number?" Eric asked, stunned.

I read the number again.

"No," I said as I took a really good look at the picture. At first, it looked bad--I admit; I was in my underwear on a big screen. My underwear wasn't skimpy; in fact, it covered more than some swimsuits. Once I thought of that, I felt better, and it didn't bother me so much. It looked like I was wearing a two-piece swimsuit. The only reason anyone knew it was underwear was because of the locker next to me and the jeans in my hand. I decided to look on the bright side and laugh this off. "At least I don't look half bad."

I heard Kristina make a surprised laugh behind me. The twins immediately agreed with me, if only to make me feel better. That's when I heard Zeke get to his feet and step into the spot where I was sitting earlier.

Then everything happened fast.

"Zeke!" Isaac called out a warning.

Zeke stepped down onto the next bench and started walking up that bench toward the center aisle.

"Oh-no," Miles muttered.

"Lexie, stop him!" Ethan shouted. I got to my feet as he began to pass me and jumped onto his back like a spider monkey.

"Zeke! Stop! Calm down!" I told him, my voice hard as I was clinging to his back with my knees around his ribs and my arms around his neck. I had managed to get high enough on his back that my face was near his ear.

Zeke barely noticed my weight. He kept going and stepped out into the center aisle.

"It was a girl," I told him. "I was in the locker room. You can't kill a girl. And you can't do it with me on your back, you'll make me an accessory to murder!" I pointed out, hoping that would stop him. He stopped walking.

"Get off me, baby," he growled; his whole body was tense under me. His hands went to my arms as if to pry me off. I grabbed his wrists and squeezed tighter with my legs.

"It was probably Jessica; we have gym the same period. You can't beat up a girl," I explained desperately. He was so pissed he was actually shaking to hit someone under my weight. He twisted his wrists from my grasp and started back up the steps. Oh, shit.

Miles, Isaac, and Ethan had run up the steps and were trying to stop him.

"But the guy running the damn screen isn't. And he hasn't taken the fucking thing down," Zeke snarled, still climbing.

"Miles will get him to take it down," I assured him as I looked up desperately at Miles. "Miles go get them to take it down!"

Miles instantly turned and ran up the steps two at a time. Isaac took Miles' spot, blocking Zeke, but it wasn't working. They were just slowing him down. So, I kept talking.

"Yeah, I'm in my underwear, but that covers more than most swimsuits do. It's not even my real phone number." I kept going as he kept climbing. "I'm not that embarrassed, I don't look too bad. Sure, I need some muscle tone, so I'll probably start working out with you guys. But otherwise-"

"It's down," Ethan announced, not relaxing from his defensive position. Zeke stopped a step down from them. I felt his back rising and falling as he took deep breaths. I kept talking.

"Zeke, I don't care about it. It's okay," I whispered to him.

He shook his head.

"It's not okay, Lexie. Some assholes putting up a picture of you like that is not okay," he said, snapping over his shoulder at me. He kept taking deep breaths as he was fighting to keep control.

Miles came back down the stairs his face pink, his eyes running over us.

"Are we good?" he asked, watching Zeke like you would a wolf.

I shook my head. We weren't good, we were out of "emergency", but we weren't good. An idea sparked in my mind.

"Zeke, if you calm down we can call Rory," I offered calmly. At my words, Zeke looked at me over his shoulder. I continued, "I just turned 17 in August, and someone just put a photo of me in my underwear on display."

"Technically, that is child pornography. It's a felony," Miles chimed in, seeing where I was going with this.

"And I am the niece of a very overprotective cop," I reminded him. Personally, it only irritated me, but if I had to call Rory to get Zeke to calm down, I'd call Rory. I felt Zeke's body relax a little under me. "Rory will scare the shit out of her and whoever helped her," I said in a singsong voice.

He ran a hand through his hair and gave a big hard sigh.

"Fine, call Rory." Zeke's voice was still not back to normal.

I gave him a nudge in the ribs with my right knee.

"Take me back to my seat first. Mush," I said, teasing him and hoping to get a mouth twitch.

I got a snort, even better.

Zeke turned around and walked down the steps carefully. We were almost back to our seats when Eric met us.

His eyes went from Zeke to me on Zeke's back "Not that protective, huh?" he asked. Zeke didn't stop so I could talk to Eric, he kept moving

"Can ya blame him?" I asked sarcastically. If he didn't understand why one of my friends would be pissed over this, then he could fuck off.

"See you in English, Alexis," he said before heading back up the stairs.

Zeke's hands came back and wrapped around my knees, giving me more support as he continued down the stairs. He gave me a gentle squeeze, probably apologizing.

"You know it's like I'm riding a dinosaur up here," I told him so he knew I wasn't upset, the other boys laughing behind me. I sat up a bit and started looking around. "So, this is what you see if you're tall." I felt him chuckle. I smiled, pleased with myself.

When we reached where Kristina was sitting, Zeke went down another step before he let go of my legs and squatted down enough for me to touch the ground. I let go and waited for him to get back to his feet.

He looked at me expectantly.

"Call Rory," he demanded.

I pulled out my phone and dialed as everyone else sat back down. I started back to my seat only to see that I had knocked my hot chocolate to the ground. I picked up the now empty cup and set it aside to throw away. Rory answered as I was scooting in to sit next to Miles, Zeke sat next to me. I explained to him the situation and how I wanted to scare the shit out of the ones responsible. Rory agreed completely; he was going to send a couple guys on duty over to the game and take care of it.

"I don't want to charge them," I repeated for the fifth time to Rory. My uncle sounded so pissed that I felt I had to keep reminding him.

"I got it, Lexie. Trust me. We'll have them in cuffs by the end of the game, and it'll be very public." Rory reassured me before hanging up.

I tucked my cell phone away. Then I looked up at Zeke.

"He says they'll have them in cuffs before the end of the game, and it'll be public," I announced.

"Good," Zeke said in a satisfied voice.

Everyone agreed.

Then I remembered Asher. If Jessica were responsible, it would be his sister that was put in cuffs. I cursed.

"Asher's going to be mad, isn't he?" I asked no one in particular, biting the corner of my lip.

"Nah," Isaac reassured me. "He probably saw the photo, too."

Zeke shook his head, the worry back on his face. "You know what's going to happen now, right?" he asked, getting all our attention. "Guys are going to start catcalling you, harassing you, the creeps are going to start coming around...." Zeke trailed off. He was clearly dreading the fallout of the photo.

"Then I'll deal, and if anyone gets handsy, I'll punch them." I bumped my shoulder into his, getting his attention. "It'll be okay, Zeke. I'm a big girl. I can sock a guy in the jaw just as easily as you can."

That made the corner of his mouth twitch. He looked away from me his eyes finding my empty paper cup.

"I owe you a hot chocolate." He heaved himself to his feet and headed toward the center aisle.

"No killing, Zeke," I called after him.

"No killing," he grumbled back.

"Or maiming!"

He turned to me with that smirk finally on his face. "No maiming," he assured me before heading up the stairs.

It was only a few moments later when Ethan started laughing. Then Isaac started up, then Miles. Then even I was laughing, the relief actually leaving me light headed. But for the others, it was something else.

"When I said to stop him, I didn't mean for you to jump on him, Lexie." Ethan managed through his laughing.

"It just kind of happened," I explained. "Besides, Zeke wouldn't go into a fight with me on his back. And I was clinging like a monkey."

That brought another round of laughing.

"Oh, I wish I had that on camera," Isaac admitted.

Soon we all settled down and watched the game. It wasn't long till Zeke was back and I had my hot chocolate warming my hands again.

It was near the end of the fourth quarter when Zeke looked to our left. I turned, and sure enough, two uniformed police officers were going down the stairs toward the front of the bleachers. I couldn't help but smile as they approached the cheerleaders.

"Oh, here it comes! Here it comes!" Isaac said excitedly. He even had his phone out, recording as Jessica was handcuffed and taken back up the stairs in front of everyone. When they were out of sight, Isaac stopped recording.

I leaned over to him.

"Send me that video," I whispered to him.

"Are you kidding? I'm putting it on Youtube."

I watched as he did just that. I looked to my right at Zeke.

"Feel better now?"

He nodded his head, grinning. "Yeah, I do," Zeke admitted.

I nodded myself. "I kind of do, too."

THE GAME WAS OVER SOON after that, and we all headed out to wait by Asher's car. Kristina had left after the game, saying she had a curfew. We all turned our backs and walked away a bit to try to give them some privacy. We made small talk loudly so we couldn't hear them till they walked off into the parking lot. Ethan came back after walking her to her car, frowning.

"Didn't go well?" I asked, wincing.

Ethan shook his head. "It's all right; we managed to stop Zeke from killing someone, so it wasn't so bad," Ethan said as he leaned against the car next to me.

I leaned over and rested my head against his shoulder.

"Sorry."

Ethan's arm moved to wrap around my shoulders, giving me a squeeze. I put my head back on his shoulder.

"Not your fault," he said.

"We are going to a party," I reminded him, hoping to cheer him up. "Lots of girls to use that smoky toe-curling voice on."

Ethan smiled down at me. His chocolate eyes warm.

"Yeah, you're right." he nodded.

"Besides, it looks like one of you guys is going to have to take me to homecoming and winter formal," I informed them, sulking a little.

"Yeah, what was up with that Eric guy?" Isaac asked, moving to stand across from us. "Your photo gets put on the big screen, and one of your friends goes berserk." Isaac spread his arms palms up. "You help calm him down, and he bails?"

"I think it was because that friend was a guy," I suggested and then added, "That Zeke is protective of me just tipped the scale."

"That's ridiculous." Miles chimed in. "Zeke's protective of all of us."

"I can hear you, you know," Zeke called over to us from a few steps away.

We giggled.

"It doesn't matter, anyone I date has to hold their own around you guys otherwise they can go," I told them honestly. Ethan pulled me close and kissed the top of my head. It made me feel warm. That cared-for feeling washed over me again; I think I was starting to get used to it.

"You mean like Dylan?" Ethan teased.

I snorted. "We'll find out tomorrow night."

"I'm just speculating, here but Eric could have not liked what he saw on the big screen," Miles suggested.

My mouth dropped as I looked at him. The other boys groaned. I heard Zeke curse.

"Miles, I know I need some muscle tone, but did I look that bad?" I asked, using the question to point out what he had said wrong.

His eyes went wide when he realized his mistake.

"No, no, no, no." He waved his hand in front of himself as if he could erase what he said and start over. "I mean the attention; he might be a more low-key person."

I looked over to Isaac. "Can I start working out with you guys? I want that muscle tone."

"We start tomorrow at 7 am," Isaac said, grinning at me.

"Sadists."

"Who's a sadist?" Asher asked coming up to the group. His blonde hair was wet but combed. He was back in blue jeans, a white long-sleeve shirt, and dark blue hoodie. His eyes went to my face assessing. "And what the hell happened on the big screen?"

"Your sister snapped a picture of me in the locker room," I explained. "She got some guy to put it up on the screen with a fake cell phone number."

"Zeke was dead-set to go on a rampage, but Beautiful here jumped onto his back. She latched onto him like a monkey," Ethan said.

"Red managed to stall him long enough for Miles to run up and get the picture off the screen before Zeke killed the guy." Isaac continued for Ethan.

"And once the screen was off, Lexie calmed Zeke down by offering to call Rory. Since she is only 17 and that was her... not dressed," Miles continued for Isaac.

"This made it child porn, which is a felony. The guy controlling the big screen and your sister were cuffed and taken to the police station." Zeke finished for all of us.

Asher's face was stunned.

"I'm not pressing charges, my uncle's cop buddies are just scaring the shit out of them," I assured him before he started worrying. It took him a minute to process everything before he responded.

"Okay, she deserved it. Let's hit the party."

CHAPTER 18

$\mathcal{W}$e ended up taking two cars, Zeke and Miles went with Asher. The twins came with me. I followed Asher to a house outside of town. The house looked like it had been a barn at one time, but had been renovated and had new additions. The party was in full swing when we arrived. I parked far enough back from the house that even if more people showed up, the Blazer wouldn't be buried. Isaac was out the door as soon as I stopped. I shut off the truck, climbed out and met Ethan on the other side. We both watched as Isaac ran through the cars and into the house.

Ethan sighed sadly.

"That's not a good sign," Ethan announced.

We started walking toward the house.

"Why's that? Isaac's always excited."

Ethan shook his head. "My brother is different when he drinks," he explained. "We all end up keeping an eye on him to make sure he doesn't do anything stupid."

"Like what?" I asked as Zeke, Asher and Miles spotted us and began making their way over. We stopped to wait.

"One time he got on the roof of the house and wanted to jump into the pool. That was over 10 feet from the house."

I winced thinking about how much that would hurt, hitting cement like that.

"Asher had to tackle him. We got real lucky neither of them went off the roof," he said.

"Wow."

The others joined us. Asher raised an eyebrow at me.

"I'm just telling Beautiful about Isaac when he drinks," Ethan explained.

Asher nodded.

"Did you tell her about the time he was punching a tree for almost an hour before we found him?" Asher asked Ethan.

"Seriously?" It was hard to imagine sweet, funny, energetic Isaac like that.

"Yeah, then there was that girlfriend he had," Zeke answered shaking his head as we all headed for the house.

"Yeah, she treated him like shit, and he just took it." Ethan stepped behind me as we slipped through the cars. "I mean bad, she called him names, put him down all the time. It was insane."

"He'd probably still be dating her if her family hadn't moved away," Asher added.

"You remember him climbing without gear on our hike?" Ethan asked me, I nodded. "That sort of shit."

"He also likes to pick fights with groups of guys at these things," Miles added.

"Does he ever say why he does this stuff?" I was genuinely worried about him. I was half-tempted to go in that house, yank him out, and take him back to Miles' house.

They all shook their heads.

"When he gets like that he doesn't talk to us. Not until after he's sober. And never about what happened," Ethan admitted.

We were getting close to the house now; I could hear the music thumping.

"So what do you do when he starts a fight?" I asked just in case.

The guys shrugged.

"Get a grip on him and get him outside," Miles said simply.

Well shit.

"Alright, guys, one of us in the room with Isaac at all times," Zeke said as if this was routine. "Lexie and Miles are the sober drivers. If you see Brandon Zimmer, watch him carefully."

I raised an eyebrow at that. Zeke didn't notice.

"If he tries to drop something in a girl's drink," Zeke continued, "kick his ass out and don't be gentle about it." Zeke gaze zeroed in on me. "And you. Don't accept a drink from anyone that isn't one of us. Don't put your drink down and drink from it. Get a new one. And if Brandon Zimmer comes to talk to you, kick him in the balls for me."

I smiled sweetly at that, I had no problem with that.

"Try to stay in the same room as one of us," Zeke added.

I frowned at him.

"Please," he added quickly. "If you get into trouble you can't handle just shout for Asher and your location. Guy's got the hearing of a blind man."

Asher smiled. "It's true; if you give even a half shout in there, I'll be able to hear you from the second floor," Asher admitted nonchalantly.

"Even over the music?"

They all nodded.

Damn that was impressive. "Remind me never to use the bathroom with you in the next room."

We were on the porch of the house when Asher waved his hand dismissively.

"Just turn on the faucet, that's what my sister does," Asher called over his shoulder.

We walked into the house. It was huge. The old barn's main room went all the way to the roof. Railings showed it was open on the second floor. We made our way into the house and almost immediately got separated. A hand grabbed mine; I turned to see Miles tugging me through the dance floor. A hand went around my waist as someone started to grind on my hip. My elbow shot out, knocking the air from the guy's lungs. He let go, gasping as I followed Miles. We came out of the dense crowd. Zeke took a beer bottle from Asher as he was searching the room. I imagine he was looking for Isaac. Miles pulled me to the drink table and grabbed a red plastic cup.

"Have you ever had orange juice with 7-up?" he asked, pouring the drink.

"Nope."

Miles grinned as he handed me the cup. "Try it." He went about making himself one.

I took a sip and liked it. It was sweet, light, and made my tongue tingle from the carbonation

"Okay, that's good," I told him.

Miles smiled, putting down the 7up.

"And no one will hassle you about not drinking."

He lifted his cup up, I hit his with mine. We both drank. I liked Miles' way of thinking.

Ethan came out of the crowd, a red cup in his hand.

"Isaac's found the ping pong table," he announced.

"Beer pong?" I asked.

He shook his head. "Shot pong."

I groaned. That was awful.

The guys cursed.

I tapped Miles' shoulder and pointed to the table.

"Get me a can of soda please?" I asked.

Miles turned and did as I asked as the others were debating who was going to watch Isaac first. Miles handed me the can.

I nudged Ethan's arm. "Show me where Isaac is, I'll take the first watch and try to slow him down. Maybe I'll be able to get him to do something else for a while."

The guys all thought about that for a moment.

"That might just work," Asher announced.

"Hell, if she can get Zeke to calm down she might be able to keep Isaac from doing something stupid," Ethan agreed.

"We'll rotate out every 30 minutes. Sound good?" Zeke asked, looking at everyone. Everyone agreed. We split up.

Ethan took my elbow and led me to the far side of the house. It looked like a recreation room. There was an air hockey table, darts, and video games in addition to the ping pong table. Ethan stopped before Isaac could see him; he pointed me in the right direction. I nodded when I saw Isaac's blue hair. Ethan melted back into the crowd near the door. I moved around the group that was watching other people play video games.

"Hey, you're the girl from the big screen," I heard someone say as I kept walking.

The voice followed. "Hey, I'm looking for a good time, honey."

"Find it somewhere else," I shot over my shoulder.

His friends laughed. It sounded like he took it well since he backed off. I just hoped anyone else who tries does, too.

I stepped into Isaac's line of sight. The boys had taken the net down and had 6 cups in front of each of them. Isaac had just landed a ball into the other guy's cup, making him drink, when I sidled up next to him, touching his arm with my hip. "Hey, Cookie Monster," I greeted him smiling.

Isaac looked up and smiled.

"Red, there you are. Where is everyone?" he greeted me.

"They ditched me for some girls." I sighed with fake disappointment. I held out the soda to him. "And I heard you might need a chaser."

Isaac took the soda from me.

"Yeah, I did. Thanks, Red." He gestured to one of the other chairs. "Have a seat, stay a while."

I sat down and watched as the other guy missed on Isaac's end. They went back and forth for a while, both missing. The other guy made it into Isaac's cup. I watched as he drank the shot. And refilled it with tequila and put it back in line. I started thinking about how I could get Isaac away from the pong table.

I had come up with an idea when a guy approached me.

"You're the new girl, right?" he asked, already slurring his words.

"I'm Alexis," I offered, trying to be polite.

"That is a cool name," he said before tapping his chest. "I'm Anthony, everyone calls me Tony."

I noticed out of the corner of my eye that Isaac had sunk another ball.

"It's nice to meet you, Tony." I turned back to watch the game.

"Hey, what was with the big screen at the game? Who would do that to you?" he asked, leaning closer.

I shrugged. "I pissed someone off, and they tried to get back at me," I explained, watching Isaac drink another shot. Okay, two shots down that I've seen; I needed to get Isaac away from the table. I was about to get up when Tony put his hand on my knee.

"That's a shame, you're a pretty girl. They shouldn't have put your photo up like that."

I turned my head and looked him in the eye.

"Move your hand, or I will break it," I said in a dead calm voice.

He lifted his hand away and backed up. "Can't blame a guy for trying," he said before disappearing into the crowd.

I turned to see Isaac down another shot. Shit. I got up and went over to him.

"Cookie Monster?" I asked in a sweet voice. He looked up at me, smiling. He wasn't drunk yet.

"Yeah, Red?"

I used my best pout on him. "Will you come dance with me?" I asked, almost pleading. His eyebrows rose in surprise. "You're one of the few guys around here I trust not to get handsy."

His eyebrows dropped as he understood; no one wanted a repeat of the bar.

"You got it, Red," he told me. He looked down the table at the other guy. "Sorry man, but a lady calls."

Isaac took my hand and led me through the house, back into the front room. I spotted Zeke leaning against the wall, talking to a girl with purple hair. When he spotted us, I winked at him as Isaac pulled me onto the dance floor. We danced. I moved to the music next to Isaac, ignoring everyone else in the room. When a guy crowded close, I'd throw an elbow just before Isaac pulled me closer, his arm going around my waist as he glared over my shoulder. The music changed to a loud thumping rhythm. We put our arms in the air, jumping along with everyone else.

When the music changed to a slow song, he pulled me in close with one arm around my waist. I leaned in and proceeded to tell him the worst jokes I had ever heard. He shot some back. Soon we were going back and forth. We kept getting weird looks on the dance floor. I don't know how long we danced, I'm sure it was over my 30 minutes. But it kept Isaac away from the shot pong table.

Eventually, I needed a break; I waved a hand at my face and pointed off the dance floor. He nodded and took my hand, leading me off the dance floor and towards the drink station. Shit. He handed me a bottle of water before pouring himself a rum and coke.

I had tried. I checked the seal on the bottle making sure it hadn't been opened then opened it myself. I took a long drink. I was sweating a lot. I reached back and pulled the mass of hair off my neck. I wish I hadn't worn a long sleeve shirt. I wished I knew where to put my jacket without it getting stolen. Isaac leaned into me so I could hear him over the music.

"I'm going to go check out some games," he told me.

My eyes darted around the room. I spotted Ethan sitting on a couch and talking with a group of people. I nodded to Isaac.

"I'll see you later, thanks for the dance, Red." He disappeared back toward the game room.

I made my way over to Ethan and tapped him on the shoulder. He looked up at me, smiling, his cheeks a little pink, though his eyes were clear as glass.

I leaned down and whispered into his ear, "Your turn."

His head jerked back from me. I stood up, not wanting him to get that good of a look at the girls. He got to his feet, checked his watch, and looked at me, puzzled.

He leaned in, talking into my ear. "You've had him all this time?"

I pressed my cheek against his so we could talk. "Yeah, he had three shots when I found him. We've been dancing since then, but he just made himself a drink."

Ethan suddenly seemed to tackle me. His body slammed into mine, his arms wrapping around me, squeezing tight. We stumbled, but he managed to keep us upright.

"Beautiful, you are amazing. It's been an hour and a half! Normally we'd be pulling him out of a fight by now."

"Don't thank me yet, he just went to check out the games." I said, hugging him back. The twins really were affectionate, I was getting used to it. Hell, I was really starting to like it.

Ethan nodded against my head.

"I'm going to buy you some jewelry, woman!" Ethan declared before surprising me by kissing my forehead before heading in the direction Isaac had taken.

I took a drink and looked around; it was really hot in here. I headed for the front door; I wanted some air. The outside air was cold, and the sweat on my skin chilled me instantly, but I didn't want to go back in yet. I leaned out over the railing of the porch looking at a cat that seemed to be sleeping through the party.

"Lexie!"

I knew that bark. I looked up to see Zeke across the lawn, standing with a group of guys around a black muscle car. Zeke waved me over before taking a drink from his beer.

I went down the stairs, passing a couple making out, and crossed the lawn. I stepped up to the group of guys. Zeke wrapped his arm around my shoulders, bringing my side against his. I took a peek up at him, he seemed completely sober.

"Guys, this is Lexie." Zeke gestured at me with the hand that held his beer bottle.

I waved to the guys. They all seemed big and scary. A lot like Zeke, actually.

"If you see someone messing with her, you kick their ass."

I elbowed him in the side and glared up at him.

He grunted then looked down at me. Then back to the group. "Okay, fine, if you see someone messing with her, watch for a minute to see if she kicks his ass. If she's trying and can't, then you kick their ass."

Everyone burst out laughing.

Zeke looked down at me, his brow drawn together. "Where have you been all night?"

"I had Isaac," I explained gesturing toward the house. "I kept him dancing as long as I could, but it's freaking hot in there." I wrapped my hair in my hands and lifted the mass off my neck.

"Wait. You had Isaac this whole time?" Zeke asked, eyes wide.

"Yep, he was mostly sober when I last saw him." I waved a hand at my neck.

"Isn't that your friend that always gets in fights at these parties?" the guy with a shaved head asked.

Zeke nodded.

The guy looked surprised. "I thought he just wasn't here tonight."

"I was keeping him busy." I switched my hair to my other hand. "Seriously, does anyone have a rubber band or something?"

One of the guys dug into their pockets.

"My girl always forgets her hair ties." He pulled out a tie and reached across the group to hand it to me. "I'm always carrying extras for her." He shrugged. The other guys laughed at him. His cheeks turned pink.

"You, sir, are the world's best boyfriend," I exclaimed, putting my hair into a ponytail. I looked at the other guys. "That man." I pointed to the guy with the pink face. "Knows how to keep a woman happy," I declared, finishing with my hair. "And probably in more ways than one."

They all burst out laughing.

I tilted my chin toward the car engine. "What are you guys doing?"

"I'm just ogling my dream car," Zeke admitted.

"A '67 Chevy Impala?" I asked, feeling everyone's eyes on me.

Zeke raised an eyebrow at me.

"If you're not dating her, can I?" one of the guys asked.

Everyone burst out laughing, including me. Zeke didn't find it funny, he glared at the guy.

"Don't even think about it, Ian." Zeke shot at his friend. "I know you too well, man."

The guy, Ian, chuckled, admitting that Zeke was right.

I rolled my eyes at them.

Zeke gave me a squeeze to get my attention. "I didn't know you liked cars," Zeke said.

I shrugged. "I don't know a lot, but I know I like the sound of the old muscle cars." I leaned into him as I stage whispered. "I only knew the car because it's the same one on that show Supernatural."

Zeke burst out laughing, the other guys groaned.

"You gave us hope, Lexie," one of them accused me.

"Sorry." I smiled at them, but they didn't seem to care.

"So, you managed to keep Isaac sober?" Zeke asked.

I nodded.

"I really appreciate that, Lexie; we haven't been able to enjoy a party for a couple years now."

I snorted at him, it really wasn't that hard.

"Ethan said he's buying me jewelry," I informed him.

Zeke smirked. "I'll buy you shoes," he offered.

I looked at him as if he was insane.

"How about you find out why my Blazer shakes when I go over 70?" I countered.

Zeke gave me a big smile, with teeth and everything. I'd never seen his teeth before.

"Deal."

"Wait, you rather have your car fixed then shoes?" The guy, Ian, asked, not quite believing it.

I nodded.

He looked at Zeke as if he was in pain. "What the fuck man? Where have you been hiding her all my life?"

"As far from you as possible," Zeke shot back, completely serious.

Everyone laughed. I just rolled my eyes again.

Zeke's friends started asking questions about the Blazer; when did it shake, what kind of shaking it did. I described it as best I could. They debated the problem, then started talking about other cars. I was starting to get cold, so I poked Zeke in the side to get his attention. He bent down bringing his ear to me.

"I'm getting cold, so I'm going back inside. Do you know where any of the others are?" I asked, tucking my hands in my pockets.

"Last I saw, Miles was on the second floor in a sitting area with a bunch of his gaming friends."

I nodded that I heard him. I said bye to Zeke's friends and headed back into the house.

The party was still in full swing. I managed to get past the dance floor without anyone trying to grope me. Yay! I found the stairs and slipped past a flirting couple. I found Miles in the second story sitting room with a group of people. I stepped into the room and paused; they all seemed to be in the middle of a card game. Miles looked up and saw me standing in the doorway.

"Come on in, Lexie." He gave me a big smile.

I walked in and took the only empty chair.

"Everyone, this is Lexie."

I waved at everyone and watched Miles as the group continued playing.

"I'm kicking down the door," he announced, picking up a card that read "door". He tossed down a card with a funny looking monster on it. He pointed out several of his cards to the others. "I have enough, I defeat the monster. Earning another point, this brings me to ten. I win."

The others groaned and began picking up their cards.

"What are you guys playing?" I asked, watching as they began setting up another game.

"It's called Munchkin," Miles explained. "Basically, you're in a dungeon full of doors and monsters. You collect armor and weapons as you go." He held out a character card for me. His character happened to be a girl. "You can either knock down a door and take on a monster. Or loot the room you're in and get an item." He held up a monster card and pointed at the number in the corner. "This is the number of attack points you need to kill the monster. You get those from items you've gotten. Or you can team up with other people."

"Or they can sabotage you," offered the only other girl in the group." You're trying to get 10 victory points. The first person to 10, wins."

"Okay, that sounds fun. Can I play?"

Everyone nodded. They finished setting up the game. Then it was all out war. I kept picking at Miles, throwing curses and poisons at him. I wasn't even trying to win, I just went after Miles.

"Lexie, you're killing me here." Miles groaned as I stripped him of his armor for the third time.

Whenever I got a good card, I made a little giggle. Miles started to hate that sound. It went on for an hour. Till finally, I formed an alliance with the only other girl and took down a monster. She won. Miles threw his cards down and glared at me, but the effect was ruined by his smile.

"That is just cruel, Lexie."

I snickered at him.

Everyone began to clean up for another game.

"Where have you been anyway?" Miles asked.

"I managed to keep Isaac mostly sober for a while, and I handed him off to Ethan. Went outside to cool off and ran into Zeke." I shrugged. "Zeke told me you were up here, so here I am." I put my cards back in the right pile and looked up. Miles was looking at me strangely.

"You managed to keep Isaac sober?"

I nodded.

"Mostly, for about 90 minutes, yeah."

He blinked at me. "You're a miracle worker; you have no idea how much that means to us," he told me plainly.

I rolled my eyes.

"Ethan said he's buying me jewelry, Zeke is fixing my truck. I think I'm getting the idea."

Miles smiled at me.

"I'll be your IT guy any time," he told me simply.

I smiled big at him. "Sounds good to me," I told him honestly, I had a new computer I really didn't want to fuck up.

I got to my feet wanting to move. "Do you know where any of the others are?"

Miles shook his head apologetically.

I pulled out my phone and texted Asher.

Alexis: Where are you?

Asher: Isaac duty in the kitchen. I'm bored out of my mind.

Alexis: Want some company?

Asher: Of course.

I smiled to myself and said goodbye to everyone still at the coffee table. I headed downstairs.

I was making my way across the crowded room when an arm snagged me around the waist.

"Hold on sugar, where you runnin' off too?"

Some guy I'd never met stepped around me, pulling me close. I leaned back away from his tequila breath.

"Let go of me," I told him clearly, in case he was drunk.

"Don't be like that. My name is Brandon, what's yours?"

I looked around and saw Ethan heading my way through the crowd, his face dark. I looked back to the guy touching me.

"Brandon Zimmer?" I asked wanting to be sure.

The guy smiled at him, showing all his teeth.

"That's right, you want a drink?"

I smiled sweetly up at him, my hands going to his shoulders. I slammed my knee right up into his balls. He sucked in air and dropped like a stone. People spread out, most of them laughing at the guy on the floor.

Ethan reached me, laughing so hard he doubled over. He pulled out his cell phone and took a photo of the now fetal Brandon Zimmer. The guy was starting to cry.

Ethan's eyes watered as he did something with his phone.

"Oh, Zeke is going to love this."

It wasn't a minute later that I felt the floor shaking as Zeke came running inside. Several of his friends following.

The crowd parted for them like water, and suddenly he was standing next to me, his hand on the back of my neck. I felt his eyes running over me, but I just watched, smiling, as Brandon was moaning on the floor.

"What he do?" Zeke asked.

Ethan was wiping tears away as he tried to get control of himself.

I smiled sweetly up at Zeke. "He grabbed my waist, wouldn't let go, and offered me a drink," I explained simply. "You said Brandon Zimmer, right?"

Zeke smiled down at me, big with teeth again.

"I said Brandon Zimmer," he confirmed before squatting down near the guy's head. He slapped the guy on the cheek getting, his attention.

"Hey Brandon, didn't we tell you to stop coming to these parties?" Zeke growled at him. He began patting the guy down and pulled out a small bottle of pills. Zeke looked like he was going to kill someone. He straightened again before gently nudging me over to make room. "Get him out of here guys, I'll go flush these."

The guys I had met earlier with Zeke reached down, lifted the still whimpering guy up, and headed out the door. A couple guys stayed behind.

"Let's do a quick look around, make sure there aren't any unconscious girls," Zeke said. The guys agreed and headed out in different directions.

Zeke looked back down to me. "You good?"

"I'm good; I was headed over to see Asher," I explained looking over at Ethan whose face was dark red from laughing; he was finally getting control of himself. Zeke gave my neck a squeeze before heading off down a hallway towards what I assumed was the bathroom.

"I'm sending that photo to Asher; he's going to love this," Ethan told me, his voice cracking.

I shook my head as he disappeared back into the crowd. Moving through the crowd was much easier now; no one tried to grope or stop me. I found Asher leaning against the counter, his cell phone in his hand.

I hopped up on the counter next to him and nudged his arm.

His face was a little flushed, his smile a little too big. Asher was buzzed at the very least. I found Isaac at the kitchen table playing quarters. His face was bright red, his eyes glossy. I could tell he was wasted from here. That was before he yelled and threw his arms in the air as if he'd just won the lotto. Yeah, he had to have been buzzed on the dance floor. That settled, I decided to forget about it.

"Ally girl, did you do this?" Asher asked, holding up the photo of Brandon Zimmer curled in the fetal position.

"He grabbed me and wouldn't let go," I explained. "And it was Brandon Zimmer."

Asher hopped up on the counter beside me and bumped his shoulder against mine.

"Ally girl, you always surprise me." He smiled down at me. He was handsome with that smile.

"Are you drunk, Asher?"

He smiled as he did something with his phone. "Not really, just a buzz and I'm tired," he explained, kicking his foot against the bottom cabinet. "We never usually stay this long; we usually have to take Isaac out by now."

"Maybe this time he won't start a fight?" I offered hopefully.

Asher shook his head. "He will. It's getting close." He gestured toward Isaac who was resting his temple against his hand with his elbow on the table. "When he gets quiet is usually the first sign."

"Why come to the parties at all?" I asked. If it was really that bad, then they needed to keep Isaac away from these situations.

"He'd come on his own even if we weren't here," Asher explained to me. "He needs to slow down, though, or he's going to be too sick tomorrow for training."

Isaac was just playing now, not really talking. I hopped down, went and grabbed another unopened water bottle, and came back into the kitchen. I walked around the table into Isaac's line of sight.

He gave me a lopsided grin.

"Hey, Red, how are ya doin?" he asked, his words slurring.

I smiled and handed him the bottle of water.

I leaned in and whispered sweetly, "Cookie Monster, can you drink some water for me?"

He leaned back and eyed me suspiciously.

"You don't have to stop drinking; I just want you to drink this too," I kept my voice sweet.

He pursed his lips together and opened the bottle.

"Thank you, sweetie." I pushed some of his hair back from his face before I walked around the table. I hopped back on the counter next to Asher.

"How do you do that?" Asher asked.

"Do what?" I asked keeping my eyes on Isaac.

"How do you get him to listen to you?" He was genuinely curious.

"Boobs," I told him plainly. I took my eyes off Isaac and looked at Asher. "And big eyes, soft voice, and a good pout if he resists."

Asher chuckled. "So basically, being a girl?"

I nodded, smiling. "Yep."

We were quiet for a while as we watched Isaac. Asher nudged my shoulder again. I looked up to see he'd moved closer.

"I'm sorry about what my sister did you," he whispered, his eyes running over my face.

I shrugged. "It's not your fault,"

"You're not angry?" He looked at me, surprised.

I smiled. "I didn't look too bad, right?" I asked, only half joking.

He snorted.

"No Ally, you didn't look bad at all," he reassured me as he shook his head.

I smirked up at him.

"Now, if I did look bad then I'd be pissed."

He burst out laughing. "It was still messed up."

I looked up at him and dove in. "What is her deal?"

Asher sighed looking back at Isaac.

"I don't really know." He tilted his head thinking. "I can tell you what I think."

"Spill, any insight would help," I admitted. I wanted to understand why his sister came at me, and then maybe I could get her to stop.

"Well, our dad didn't pay her much attention. He was always just about me and my shit." Asher shrugged. "I never understood that, but that's the way he's always been." Asher licked his lips and looked down at my knee next to his. "Our mom always split her attention between us. Then Mom got sick, she died, and Dad is gone all the time."

"So, you think she's angry?" I asked, needing more information.

Asher shrugged, looking me in the eye. "I know she's angry. Hell, I am too, but she's taking everything out on other people and that I don't get." He sighed. "She's my twin, and I don't even recognize her anymore."

"Wait, your twins?" I asked, surprised. How many twins were in this town?

Asher smiled down at me. "Fraternal, yeah."

He went back to watching Isaac. I leaned my head against his shoulder.

"I'm sorry about your mom," I said.

He sighed wearily. "Sorry about your dad."

"What was she like?" I was genuinely curious. I barely had any good memories left of my mother. At least any I could remember right now.

He was quiet for a while; I shifted my head so I could look at his face. He swallowed hard and clenched his jaw before answering me.

"Ask me again when I haven't been drinking, Ally girl." He looked down at me smiling sadly. "I'll tell you then."

I nodded and wrapped my arms around his and gave a squeeze. "Sorry."

"Don't be." His ocean blue eyes were full of shadows that my question had brought on. I needed to fix that.

I smiled up at him wickedly.

"Do you want to mess with Isaac when he passes out tonight?" I asked hopefully. "I'm thinking something involving a stun gun and an alarm clock for the morning, and a hand in warm water tonight. At the very least."

Asher burst out laughing, the shadows leaving his eyes.

"You and that damn smile of yours, it's going to get me into trouble," he mumbled under his breath.

"Maybe, but it'll be fun trouble," I offered, still smiling. He chuckled again, Asher had a nice laugh.

He looked over at Isaac and frowned. "I need to go to the bathroom; can you watch him for a minute?"

"Yep."

Asher hopped down off the counter and smirked at me.

"By the way, I sent that photo to Dylan."

My mouth dropped. "The big screen one?"

His eyes went wide.

"No. The Brandon Zimmer one," he said, reassuring me.

"You didn't."

Asher snickered. "With the tag 'what happens when someone touches Lexie without permission.'" He smiled big as I groaned.

"We're not even dating, Ash!" I pointed out as he headed out of the kitchen.

I took a drink from my water and put the lid back on it. I watched the game and bounced the heel of my boot against the cabinet. My phone vibrated. I winced before answering.

"Hello."

"What happened?" Dylan's husky voice was hard in my ear. He didn't sound too happy.

"I don't know what you're talking about," I said. I tried for innocence, but it came out more smart ass.

"The photo Asher sent me, this guy grabbed you?"

I sighed. Mental note: Write on Ash's face after he passes out tonight.

"Oh, he put his arm around my waist and wouldn't let go. So, I kneed him in the balls," I said casually. It really wasn't that big of a deal.

"Good." His voice was back to his usual husky. "Who was he anyway?"

"Brandon Zimmer."

Dylan burst out laughing.

I smiled as I waited till he was done. It was about a full minute.

"Yeah, Zeke filled me in on his party habits."

"Oh, Lexie, that is awesome," he said, his voice still a little breathless from laughing.

"So I've been told." I smiled to myself. I took a look at Isaac and noticed he had started talking to a girl. Maybe we'd get a reprieve. "How was the game?"

"It sucked, we lost. A couple of our guys decided to wing it during some important plays." He grumbled.

"I'm sorry."

"Eh, it's over. How'd Asher do?"

"He did pretty well, from what I saw. Only a couple sacks in the whole game, any fumbles weren't due to a bad throw. No interceptions." I debated telling him about the billboard stunt for a second and decided against it. He didn't need to know about it. "We did win, though."

"That win puts them in the playoffs this year." He grunted. I raised an eyebrow. "I might get to see a game with you after all."

"Why are you grunting?" I asked suspiciously. Please tell me you were lifting something.

"I was stretching, honey," he said, his voice growing warm. "I had a couple bad hits tonight. So I'm not moving so great right now."

"Take some aspirin and suck it up."

He burst out laughing.

"Ya know most girls would be all 'aw poor baby.' But not you, Lexie." It sounded like he was smiling.

"Yeah, well, I'm not like most girls."

Isaac took a shot. I decided to keep my eyes on him.

"No, no you aren't." His voice sounded like it wasn't a bad thing.

I smiled. But I wanted to know. I didn't like not knowing where I stood.

"Is that good or bad?" I bit my lip waiting.

"Oh, it's good."

I smiled and tried not to get too excited about it. Isaac drank another shot.

"You never did tell me about your yards per carry."

He chuckled in my ear. "Seven."

Wow, that was a damn good number.

"And you guys lost? Does the rest of the team suck?" I asked, still watching Isaac.

He laughed. "No, everyone just had a bad night." He took a deep breath. "It just means football will be over soon, and I'll have more time to see you."

I smiled. Isaac was quiet again. Where the hell was Asher?

"We haven't even gone on a date yet," I pointed out as butterflies fluttered in my stomach.

I was watching as the guy to the left of Isaac saw me, leaned over, and said something to Isaac. Isaac went still. Oh, come on.

"What did you say?" Isaac asked clearly, his face growing dark.

Oh, shit.

"You don't fucking say that shit about her," he growled at the other guy.

"I have liked everything I've heard so far," Dylan said in my ear.

Shit.

"Hang on, I need to go stop a fight before it happens-"

Isaac bolted out of his chair, leaped over the table, and slammed down on the guy. The table knocked over. The chair broke under their combined weight.

"Shit!" I dropped my phone on the counter and jumped to the floor as Isaac sat on the guy, his fist coming down fast over and over, as he pummeled the guy.

Okay, I'll admit the guy probably deserved the first couple punches, but then Isaac was scaring the shit out of me. Girls were screaming, people were yelling. I didn't know where the guys were so I did the first thing I could think of. I strode over to Isaac, grabbed his ear and twisted hard. He stopped hitting the guy as he bent towards me.

"Ow, ow, ow. Fuck, Red!"

I kept a tight hold on his ear.

"Get up." I told him calmly, my voice hard, though inside I was kind of shaking. Watching Isaac pummel that guy into the floor really hit home that he was a trained fighter.

Isaac got to his feet, leaning his head down so as not to yank on his ear more.

"We are going outside for you to cool off."

I began pulling Isaac towards the back door. I saw Asher pushing through the crowd, his eyes wide.

"Asher! Grab my phone, check the other guy, and then get your ass out here! And bring Zeke!" I ordered as I opened the door.

I made Isaac follow me outside. He shut the door behind us. I pulled him off the porch and halfway across the large backyard before letting him go.

"What the fuck, Lexie?!" he yelled at me, his hand going to his now red ear.

"That's what I was going to ask you!" I said, my voice hard. I crossed my arms over my chest watching as he kept pacing. "What the fuck, Isaac?!"

"That guy was talking shit about you!" he shouted, gesturing towards the house.

I nodded. "And that's why I let you get a few swings in!" I shouted back.

He blinked hard at me.

So, I kept on speaking in a normal voice. "But this wasn't about me; this was about you looking for a fight."

Isaac waved his hand dismissively at me as he started pacing. That wasn't going to fly with me.

I stepped forward, holding onto my temper. I needed to get him to talk. "What's going on Isaac?"

I heard the screen door open and close.

Isaac turned around and glared at me.

"If I don't want to tell you something, respect that. I'll tell you when I'm ready." He shot my own words back at me.

Shit. That just bit me in the ass.

He didn't want to talk. I remembered what Ethan said about finding another outlet.

Asher stepped up next to me, holding my phone to his ear. Zeke stepped up on my other side. I didn't look away from Isaac and his pacing.

"Which one of you is up for sparring?" I asked the guys next to me. Isaac didn't hear us, he kept pacing back and forth his hands running through his hair, his fingers digging into his scalp.

"I'm sober," Zeke volunteered.

I nodded and pointed at Isaac.

"You want a fight? You're sparring with Zeke," I shouted at Isaac to get his attention.

He stopped pacing and looked at me, trying to figure out if I was serious.

Zeke smirked and stepped forward, stretching his arms and loosening his muscles.

"You're looking for a fight, Isaac; this is the only one you're getting tonight," I told him simply, my voice hard.

Isaac started eyeing Zeke who now stood across from us on our left, Isaac on the right.

"Let's see who can drop the other guy to the grass the most," I said.

Isaac scoffed at me in disbelief.

"He's almost twice my size!" he complained.

I smirked. "Then you'll just have to work harder now, won't you?" I shot back sarcastically. I heard Asher smother a laugh next to me. "No full-strength hits," I declared, looking at both of them. "Go."

I backed up a couple more steps, and Asher did the same.

Zeke and Isaac went at it. Holy shit. Isaac went in hard and fast trying to distract Zeke enough to drop him. Zeke wasn't having it. He moved much faster than I thought he could. He was a big guy, and big guys usually couldn't move that fast.

"She's fine, not a scratch, not a bruise. She split it up fast and got Isaac out of there." Asher was talking on my phone. I wasn't really paying attention; I was still stunned by the way the guys were trying to take each other down.

"Remind me not to piss off Zeke," I mumbled to Asher.

Asher snickered.

"You piss off Zeke on a daily basis," he reminded me. "And we all love watching it." He held out the phone to me, smiling. "Your future boyfriend is still on the phone."

I snorted and took the phone. "He's met me once and talked to me a few times. He might not like me after tomorrow." I reminded him and myself.

Asher gave me a shit-eating grin.

"I don't know, when I picked up the phone he said, 'where's my girl?'"

My stomach fluttered again, and I fought off a smile.

"I told him you were stopping a fight and had your hands full; he got pissed at me for not taking care of it. I told him you got there first and had it taken care of by the time I got there."

I playfully narrowed my eyes at him. "Watch the sparring and stop talking about my love life," I said, smiling. Asher burst out laughing as I put the phone to my ear before stepping away. "I'm back."

"What just happened?" Dylan's husky voice was calm, but it was a forced calm.

"Isaac started beating the crap out of someone, I jumped in, yanked him away and out the door. Zeke and Isaac are now sparring in the backyard to give Isaac a better outlet for his anger or whatever this is."

There was silence for a few heartbeats.

"How did you yank Isaac out?"

I snickered.

"I yanked and twisted his ear until he came with me," I told him in my sweet voice.

He was quiet for a while.

My heart sank. "Still think me not being like other girls is a good thing?" I asked, pretty sure he was going to bail on tomorrow.

"Lexie, I love that you can kick a guy in the balls, yank a guy out of a fight by the ear, and still sound cute on the phone."

I smiled a big smile as my heart melted. Okay, I might be in trouble here.

"Really? What's wrong with you?" I said half joking, not know what else to say. "You should be running in the other direction."

He laughed. "I like a challenge." His voice had gone soft, making me bite my lip.

"Zeke one," Asher announced.

I turned around and watched Isaac pick himself back up.

"I should probably keep an eye the guys sparring. Isaac's drunk, and we don't want any accidents." I said, concerned at the gleam in Isaac's eye.

"You probably should, you might need to do some more ear pulling," Dylan admitted. "I'll see you tomorrow at seven?"

"Sounds like a plan." Then I remembered something. "You might want to expect the guys, too. They're going to try and give you a hard time."

He chuckled. "Bring it."

I laughed, feeling myself blushing.

"Night."

"Night."

I hung up. When I was sure my blush was gone, I turned back around. I was just in time to watch Isaac drop Zeke. Holy shit. Zeke went down hard.

"Isaac one, Zeke one," Asher announced turning to me as I came back. "How's the future, boyfriend?"

"A little crazy considering he's still interested," I admitted, smirking. Asher chuckled. My phone vibrated. I checked it.

Ethan: What happened? Where is everyone?

Alexis: Outback, we're wearing Isaac out, get out here.

It wasn't long before the screen door opened behind us. I turned and watched Ethan and Miles heading across the lawn. Ethan was frowning as we watched Isaac get dropped again.

"Zeke two, Isaac one," Asher announced.

"Whose idea was this?" Miles asked, stepping up on the other side of Ethan.

"Mine." I looked down the line to see Miles smiling.

"Good idea, Lexie."

"You know what the funny part is?" I asked, smiling mischievously. Isaac got dropped again hard. Ouch.

"Zeke three, Isaac one," Asher called.

"What's the funny part, Beautiful?"

"Isaac still has to go to training in the morning," I said.

The guys burst out laughing as we watched Zeke drop. This time it took him a second to get his air back.

"Zeke three, Isaac two." This time Miles called it.

"How long are they going?" Ethan asked.

"Till Isaac is done working out his shit tonight?" I offered, not really sure if that was a good idea or not.

Miles nodded. "That's sounds good to me."

Zeke dropped Isaac again; he landed on his back hard. Everyone said ouch. Zeke was starting to breathe heavy.

"Zeke four, Isaac two," Ethan called.

"Anyone want to tag in?" I asked, worried that Zeke might hurt his hand more.

"We're trying to wear him out?" Miles asked.

"Yep."

The guys next to me chuckled. Miles took off his jacket, handed it to me and headed toward the guys. Zeke and Isaac stepped back from each other.

"Um, what's so funny?" I looked down the line to see them all grinning.

"If you think Isaac is fast, wait till you see Miles. Guy's like a fucking eel," Ethan told me. "You just can't get your hands on him."

Zeke headed towards us. Isaac was frowning at Miles before getting into position. Zeke came back to stand by Asher. I looked over at him, his face was red, and he was sweating, but he seemed fine.

"Zeke, you are fast," I said, watching as Isaac and Miles circle each other. He chuckled.

"For my size, yeah," Zeke admitted. "Wait till you see this."

I watched as they continued circling. Isaac had his hands up like a boxer; Miles just had his hands ready at his waist. Isaac moved to strike Miles. Miles just simply wasn't there anymore, he'd dodged Isaac's fist and quickly used Isaac's own momentum to throw him to the ground.

"Shit," I said, causing the boys to laugh. "Miles one, Isaac zero."

Then they really went at it. No matter where Isaac went to grab Miles, he simply slipped through and moved on to a better position. Sometimes dropping Isaac, and sometimes just making him run after him.

I smiled. He was wearing him down fast. "See, that right there is what I need to learn."

"Come to training and you will," Zeke said simply. "We'll work you up a program for defense and jiu-jitsu."

"Throw some krav maga and kick-boxing in there then she'll be good to go," Ethan added as we watched Miles drop Isaac again.

"Miles two, Isaac zero," I called out before answering the guys. "Sounds good to me, I'm sure Rory won't mind." Isaac was starting to breathe harder, his arms coming down.

"Here comes the take-down," Asher warned; I didn't look, but it sounded like he was smiling. Isaac went at Miles. Miles grabbed Isaac, twisted, and slipped his leg around the inside of Isaac's. Miles threw Isaac over his hip, using his leg to flip Isaac completely off the ground. Isaac landed hard on his back, Miles lying across his chest pinning him to the grass.

"Holy shit." I was pretty sure my mouth had dropped open. The guys snickered. I just watched as Miles got up and headed back towards us. Isaac didn't move; he just kept taking deep breaths. He was done.

"Give me a minute. I'll see if he's ready to talk." I headed towards the others. When I passed Miles, I smiled at him and handed him his jacket. His face was red, and he was sweating, but he seemed fine. He grinned at me as he headed back to the guys. When I reached Isaac, I sat down next to his side and looked at his face. He was just starting to get his breath back, his eyes were closed, his arms out to his sides. "Hey, sweetie."

"I hate it when Miles makes that move, it makes the world spin." He groaned sitting up next to me, his knees spread. I fought off a laugh because it looked pretty cool from my point of view.

"Ready to talk?" I asked, watching his face.

His eyes were hard as they met mine.

"No, Red," he said flatly.

I nodded. That was okay, he didn't have to.

"Isaac, you're a trained fighter. Do you understand what that means for the rest of your life outside of the ring?"

He raised an eyebrow and looked at me. I finally had his attention.

"If you get into a fight, you could kill someone. And because of that, judges and juries will hold you to a higher standard. If you accidentally kill someone in a fight, you will be prosecuted for it. And you will be found guilty." Then I repeated to him what my kick-boxing instructor had told me in LA; you get a lot of training. you get a target on your back if you fuck up.

"Cookie Monster, if you're going to keep coming to these parties then you need some rules." He just looked at me. "Asher knew you were getting close to a fight before he went to the bathroom. You got quiet, stopped talking to people."

Isaac looked down at the grass between his legs again and nodded.

"If one of us sees you doing that, we're going to suggest that you take a walk. Will you do that for me?" I asked him.

Isaac was looking down at the grass in front of him, and he nodded."And if I don't want too?" he asked, his dark eyes meeting mine.

"Then it won't be a suggestion." I gestured around the yard. "I'll grab that ear and we'll be right back here. You'll be sparring with the guys again until you get whatever it is out of your system."

When he didn't look at me, I continued. "We're not going to let you destroy your life, so we'll manage whatever this is until you are ready to talk about it. Sound good?"

Isaac was quiet for a few minutes, that was fine. I wasn't going anywhere. Finally, he looked at me again.

"You're right," he admitted, resigned. "I could really hurt someone or kill them."

"So, if one of us says take a walk?"

"I'll take a walk," he agreed.

"Thank you, Cookie Monster."

He got to his feet and reached down to me. I took his hands, and he pulled me up to my feet. After I was standing, he pulled me into a hug. I wrapped my arms around him and squeezed back.

"You're a pain in the ass, Red," he whispered into my hair.

I snickered. "Especially when I'm right."

He huffed before pulling away.

We headed back to the others. I was tired and done for the night. I wanted my bed at Miles' house and sleep.

"We have a new rule in place," I said getting their attention.

"If I do that quiet thing at another party, tell me to take a walk," Isaac said to the guys, his voice tired.

"And if you don't?" Zeke asked, frowning at him.

Isaac snorted. "Get Red. She'll get me outside," he admitted. "There might be more sparring involved then."

Ethan snorted. "Good, because you are rusty as fuck," Ethan said emphatically. "Mom's never going to let you back into the ring like that."

Isaac snorted in response.

"Everyone ready to leave?" Zeke asked, looking down the line.

Everyone nodded. We headed inside. It was quieter, the party was winding down. When we reached the big room, I paused.

"I'm going to use the bathroom real quick. I'll meet you guys outside," I said. They all nodded and headed for the door.

I went down the hall next to the kitchen and found the bathroom. When I was done, I opened the door and froze. Jason was standing there, his hands on the door frame, blocking off the hallway.

"I've been looking for you," Jason said. He blinked hard. His voice changed. "Now we're going to have fun." It wasn't Jason's voice anymore. It was Bitch Ghost.

My heart slammed in my chest. He or she tackled me. I hit the floor hard, my head hitting the tile. My back in agony. Adrenaline slammed through me, and suddenly I didn't hurt anymore, I wasn't tired. I was pissed. When Jason's body sat up, with his legs straddling my waist. I made a fist with both hands and brought it down towards Jason's groin. Bitch Ghost grabbed my arms before I connected. She forced my arms back over my head. I head butted Jason's face, his nose burst, blood poured. It probably hurt like hell, but it didn't stop Bitch Ghost. She dropped all of Jason's weight onto me, pinning me by the elbows. I struggled against the weight; it was getting harder to breathe. She let go of my right arm and pulled back the sleeve of my left. I brought a fist down on Jason's face, again and again. It did nothing but split Jason's lip and give him a black eye. She reached for my beads. My chest burned as terror ran through me. I screamed.

"Asher! Downstairs bathroom!"

Bitch Ghost ripped my bracelets apart. Beads flew everywhere, I vaguely heard them bouncing off the tile. Suddenly my head was in a vice, my pulse in my ears as I felt Bitch Ghost pressing against my mind. It wasn't as bad as last time, but that's like saying this stab wound was less likely to kill me than the others.

Jason's hands wrapped around my face as she brought his body in closer. I bucked, trying to throw his weight off of me as my barriers held against her. Suddenly, Jason's weight was pulled off me. I looked up to see Asher and Zeke slamming Jason against the opposite door.

"That's not Jason!" I croaked, getting to my feet.

I darted into the hallway where they were struggling to hold him. Jason's body bucked, bringing his body off the door. They slammed him back, this time through the door. Ethan, Isaac, and Miles were running down the hall towards us. I followed Asher and Zeke into the room where they grappled with Bitch Ghost; her energy making Jason's body stronger than he should be.

"Get him on his back on the floor!" I shouted.

Zeke and Asher glanced at me, then at each other. They got a better grip on Jason's body; Asher on one side, Zeke on the other. They both kicked the back of Jason's knees. They dropped like a rock. Zeke and Asher's body weight dragged Jason down, landing on top of Zeke and Asher. Bitch Ghost was trying to break free of their grip.

Heart racing, I jumped on top of Jason, pinning his chest with my body weight. The others ran in and were struggling to pin his arms.

"Someone get his mouth open!" I yelled.

Ethan's hands went to Jason's face and pried his mouth open. I reached down, jerked the vial from my necklace. I popped it open with my thumb then poured the salted holy water down Jason's throat. Bitch Ghost gave out a scream that was cut off when Jason's body went limp. The salted holy water had forced Bitch Ghost out of Jason's body.

Trying to catch my breath, I looked down at Zeke and Asher over Jason's shoulders. They were out of breath, too.

Zeke met my eyes.

"Can we do plan b now?" he asked seriously.

I nodded and tried to get off Jason's chest. Hands steadied me as I wobbled; I looked up to see Miles holding me. Ethan and Isaac pulled Jason's body off of the others. Zeke and Asher groaned as they got to their feet.

My mind ran through Bitch Ghosts memories, looking for her grave site. St Michael's. Fourth row in, north corner lot. I shook my head pushing them away again.

When everyone got their breath back, they all looked at me.

"We're ending this now," I announced, my voice hard.

Everyone nodded.

"We'll need shovels, salt, gas and a lighter," I said.

I turned around, strode out the door and through the house, the boys right on my heels. We were walking across the now empty lawn before anyone spoke again.

"Miles, Isaac, go get the salt from the house and pick up a lighter," Zeke said, taking charge. "We'll get some shovels and the fuel."

"Wait, where is the grave?" Miles asked.

Everyone cursed.

"I know where it is," I told them, opening the door to the blazer. They looked at me quizzically. I wave a hand. "It's part of Bitch Ghost's memory download."

They accepted that. Everyone agreed to meet at the graveyard.

"Be careful, she has enough juice to jump another person," I warned them before we split up.

Asher, Zeke, and Ethan climbed into my blazer. My heart still racing, I took off like a bat out of hell.

"Easy there. Beautiful. We need to get there in one piece," Ethan said, his hand on my shoulder.

"Where are we going to find shovels at this time of night?" Asher asked, his voice tense.

"We don't have to," I said. "There's a groundskeeper shed at the cemetery. That's where they'll keep the shovels." I pulled onto the highway. "They'll probably have a gas can with the lawnmower." I wanted to push the pedal down, but the gauge said I was already doing ten over the speed limit. Was the gauge even right? Are we really doing sixty-five? I don't think that's right, it feels too slow. Tension hung in the air as I drove to the cemetery.

"How are you going to feel about this, Lexie? You don't know where she's going," Asher said from the back seat.

I didn't want to think about that, I couldn't. Bitch Ghost was pushing things too far. It was time to push back.

"I think she forfeited that consideration tonight," I said under my breath as I finally pulled into the cemetery.

I pulled to a stop near the groundskeeper shed. I didn't even bother shutting off the Blazer. I was out and running to the door in a blink. The door to the shed was locked. I immediately slammed my shoulder into it. It didn't budge. I was stepping back to do it again when hands caught me.

"Let's have someone with a lot more mass do the breaking, huh sweetie?" Asher said, pulling me away from the door, his hands giving me a squeeze.

Zeke stepped towards the door.

Why the hell didn't I think of that? I really needed to calm down; I focused on taking deep calming breaths as Zeke broke through the door with his shoulder. I darted into the shed behind Zeke. They grabbed the shovels while I looked for the lawn mower and the gas can. I found the can, but it was empty. I cursed.

"What's wrong?" Ethan asked, stepping up to me.

"No gas."

"We can siphon the gas from the truck, we just need a tube." he said.

I looked around the shed, my eyes finding a garden hose.

"There's a box cutter in the toolbox in the back, we can cut the garden hose," I told him, already running out the door and to the back of the blazer.

The back gate was already open, so I jumped in and crawled to where I kept my dad's toolbox. I opened it and found the box cutter. I ran back past Zeke and Asher who were loading the shovels into the truck. Ethan took the box cutter from me.

"Let me do it, you're shaking so much that you'll just cut yourself," Ethan said as he measured out the length he wanted. "We still need to dig, Beautiful. "It's still going to be awhile, calm down, or you'll wear yourself out before we're even done," he told me, cutting the hose.

I nodded. He was right. I focused on taking deep, calming breaths as we all got into the truck again. I kept breathing like that as I drove to the ghost's grave site.

Zeke looked at me confused.

"What's wrong? Why are you breathing like that?" he snapped.

"She's having a big adrenaline rush, I told her to calm down," Ethan said.

Zeke just went back to looking out the window. I stopped the truck. We got out, the boys grabbing the shovels as I lead them to the grave. It was exactly where Bitch Ghost's memories told me. It had a modest headstone. Asher used the flashlight on his keys to look at the name on the headstone.

"That's her," I confirmed, looking away from the name. I couldn't think of her as having a name right now.

"Move, Ally," Asher said.

I got off the grave as Asher and Zeke started digging. Ethan pulled me away from the grave and back to the blazer. He opened the gas cap and started explaining what he was doing. He put the hose into the gas tank, the gas can on the ground. Then he sucked on the end of the hose. It only took a few seconds, then he was spitting out a little gas and put the end of the hose into the gas can.

"Oh, that's disgusting," Ethan told me, making a face. "You owe me cookies for this."

I gave him a small smile, my stomach in knots. My hands were starting to shake again. I didn't have my beads, and she was still out there. She's going to realize what we're doing.

When Ethan thought we had enough fuel, he took the hose out of the tank and put the cap back on. Now that we had the gas, we both grabbed shovels and started digging. We had to get down eight feet, burn a body, and then put all that dirt back before morning.

I lost myself in the rhythm of digging; I didn't want to think about what I was doing. I hated what I was doing. The dead should be allowed to rest, but this bitch wasn't giving me a choice.

I wasn't aware that the others arrived until Isaac was taking my shovel from me. I blinked up at him confused.

His eyes ran over me, his face worried.

"Go sit down, Red, I'll take over."

I bit the corner of my lip and looked at the others. Asher and Zeke were in the grave too, no one else would fit. They worked fast; we were already down three feet. I nodded and let go of my shovel. Isaac gave me a boost so I could climb out of the grave.

When I had nothing to do, my mind ran around in circles. Miles and Ethan stayed close by, keeping an eye out for anyone coming. This was wrong, wasn't it? I didn't know where I was sending this girl. But she wasn't giving me much of a choice. Well, she was--be possessed the rest of my life or burn her body. Not much of a choice.

Without something to do, my hands started shaking again. I knew I had to do this to keep people safe from her, but it didn't stop my stomach from knotting tightly.

I knew exactly when the ghost became aware of what we were doing. We had three feet left, and it was as if a bell was hit. Only you couldn't hear it. I felt the vibration along my skin, I instantly knew she had another body and was heading here.

"She's coming," I told the guys. Miles came over to me.

"How do you know?" he asked, his voice gentle.

"I can feel her, and she's getting close," I said, my voice shaking. I started going over the plan I've been making since I was jumped. How I was going to keep her out? I went over it, again and again.

Miles took my hand and squeezed it reassuringly.

"We're here, Lexie; you're not alone in this," Miles told me calmly.

It helped me calm down a bit more, knowing they were there. If she jumped me again, the guys knew what to do. I wasn't at risk of dying in an emergency room.

"Lexie, you're freezing."

Was I? I didn't really notice. I was watching the roads, trying to figure out where she was coming from. Still going over my plan again and again. It helped keep the fear from crashing down on me.

Miles put my hand between both of his trying to warm it. His hands stopped rubbing. "Lexie, where are your bracelets?"

Everyone looked at me. I'd never seen fear on one of their faces before. Now I saw it on all of them.

"She broke them back at the house," I told them, my hands shaking again.

Curses went around as the guys went back to work, digging faster. Ethan walked over to us.

"What about your necklaces?" Ethan asked.

I swallowed hard. "I used the holy water on Jason, and the other is just general protection," I explained, squeezing Miles' hand.

"That means she can jump you, right?" Ethan asked, his jaw clenching.

I felt her enter the cemetery.

"Yeah." I pulled my hands from Miles looking out at the road.

"Then what the hell is the plan if she gets here before we're done?" Ethan asked me, his voice getting low.

"I try to keep her from jumping me while you guys salt and burn her bones," I said.

Headlights glowed on the road, the driver going too fast on the gravel.

I looked at Ethan, his face was dark. "Why do you think I've been so jittery this whole time?" I looked back to the road as the car made its way towards us. I recognized that car.

Ethan shouted for the guys to dig faster.

The red Ford Focus came to a sliding stop. Tara got out of the car, a snarl on her face. Oh, hell no. That bitch was not fucking with my cousin. I suddenly felt solid again, my temper boiling. It felt good right now. If the bitch wanted a fight, she was going to get one.

Tara walked around her car her eyes fixed on me.

"Salt, then burning," I reminded them before I stepped away. "You have about twenty minutes if she gets through me."

I met Tara's body halfway to the road. I heard Ethan shouting at the guys, Miles' voice joining in. I didn't hear what they said; my total concentration was in front of me.

"Get the fuck out of my cousin bitch," I growled.

She smirked using Tara's face.

"Gladly." She reached out to grab me; I caught her hand with mine.

The world disappeared as we went to war. Adrenaline surged as Bitch Ghost slammed her energy against me. My barriers shook. Pain burst behind my eyes as she tried brute force. I didn't attack her. I had been thinking about this in the back of my mind since she jumped me. I shored up my barriers; I used my memories like stone blocks reinforcing the weak parts, closing them off before she could use them. I kept breathing as I ignored the pain running through my head. I pushed every emotion I had out of my head, every thought except one. Don't let her in.

She sent wave after wave of energy at me, knocking chunks of my barrier away. I kept reinforcing it. When she backed off for a heartbeat, I wrapped myself into a ball, with a hard barrier around me. She slammed through my barriers using everything she had. I felt them like a physical snap as they broke. She poured in. She tried to pour over my soul, drowning me. I sank down in the blackness in my little ball. She thrashed above me as I sank, she couldn't find me. She felt me, but couldn't find me. That's when I reached for that place inside me where my anger lived; always there, always waiting. It had been growing ever since she went after Miles; it grew when she went after Zeke. And I let it out. Hot boiling waves boiled up through her blackness, lighting her up like a torch. She couldn't flee, she could only try to cool my rage. But you can't use rage to stop rage. She changed tactics. She threw her happy, blissful memories around her like a geode hiding in molten rock.

I thought of the boys, how they were hurrying to save my ass. I thought of how they had adopted me and made me feel cared for again. It was a powerful memory, hard as diamond. I used that memory like a chisel, and I went a-knockin. I tore down her walls, grabbed her around the metaphysical neck, and threw her out.

I opened my eyes, gasping, my head exploding in pain. Disoriented. The world spinning. Hot wetness on my face. I couldn't focus. I saw Bitch Ghost's complete shock on Tara's face, my vision watery. Then she snarled and tackled me. My back hit a flat tombstone, stunning me with pain. It gave her the opening she needed. She wrapped her hands around my throat and started to squeeze. I heard shouting around me as I tried to pry her hands off me. I felt feet running through the ground. It was disorienting... like the grass in the cemetery was my skin and I could feel everyone and everything in it. It was only a flash, and then it was gone.

I blinked up at Tara's face.

"You fucking bitch!" she screamed at me. "You don't deserve to live!"

A loud whoosh filled my ears. Tara's body froze above me, a look of pure horror on her face. Her mouth was open in a silent scream as the flames ripped through Bitch Ghost's soul. I heard her screaming, and I was screaming inside with her. With my barriers down, I felt it all; the agony, as the fire tore into us.

We were going to die, going to be wiped away. There was nothing! Black despair poured through us, shaking our bodies. Our lungs burned as we continued to be torn apart. Tears fell down our face as we felt the end coming. We saw that stone ledge in the dark above the abyss of black. We saw it coming as we burned, singed, and ripped. We tried to crawl away from it, fingers digging into the dirt. Only here the dirt was sand, and it wanted to go with you. Our hearts clenched, our limbs shook, our very souls cried out shivering and shaking as we slipped closer along the stone. Our chest clutched, our heart was slowing, our soul fading. Our feet were off the edge, dangling over that dark pit. Our hands clinging to the ledge that was sand covered rock. No, she was off the edge; she was desperately clinging to the ledge. I was laying across from her, my eyes on hers. I saw the terror in her eyes. I saw the tears, I saw her. As she was in life, as she had been. Singing in choir like an angel, helping everyone around her. I saw her at that moment. Completely, utterly beautiful and unique. There was no other like Mary Summers.

No. no, no! I felt my heart shatter as I realized what I had done. I reached for her and grabbed her hands hard. I couldn't let her go into that nothingness. I couldn't. She was a soul. She didn't deserve that black void. This was WRONG! I tried to pull her back. I pulled and pulled, but she was being sucked down into the void. Tears falling, I could barely hold on to her anymore, the pull on her was too strong. Panicking, I met her cerulean blue eyes. They were terrified. I kept trying to pull her back to this world, to keep her here. But she was fading in front of me. Her face was fading, her body, her hands in mine. I tried to keep hold of her. I kept looking her in the eye as she faded into nothing. Because no one should die alone, no one should go this way. So I held her gaze, tears falling down my face as I watched her soul die in front of me on that sandy ledge.

Then she was gone.

Not even dust remained on the hot wind blowing across the stone. Lightning cracked above me in the silence. I looked up to see the green smoke moving through the clouds. They boiled. That wasn't right. I don't know how I knew, but I knew that wasn't right. I looked around the ledge of the pit; trees were dead and burnt to a crisp. That wasn't right either. I looked up again and understood what I was seeing. Souls that cross over go up through those clouds, but nothing was crossing over.

I looked around me at the burnt and dead Veil. I saw how the dead came, like a movie playing in my head. The Veil was thin; it was supposed to allow you to come here. It was the natural order. I don't know how I knew this, I just did. But now the Veil was thick and fogged over. I found one last clear spot just before it was poured over by fog. The Veil was shut. Souls couldn't get inside to cross over naturally. Someone had shut them out. It's going to take someone to let them in.

At that moment, I have never felt more hatred than I did for the one who did this. This was the reason the area was wrong, this was the reason souls had more energy. I saw it all, understood it all in a heartbeat. Then I was jerked backward, hard.

I opened my eyes not understanding what I was seeing. Stars above, something hard underneath me, my heart being shredded. A heavy weight was across me, pushing me down. I took great, big, gulping breaths, trying to ease the burn in my lungs. My throat tight. I was still seeing her eyes as she disappeared, as if she had been nothing. Like she had never loved, never laughed, never even existed.

I vaguely registered the guys pulling Tara off me. Miles pulling my upper body from the ground, his arms wrapping around me. His mouth was moving, but I couldn't hear him.

Mary Summers had been a person, a soul. And I had wiped her from existence as if she were nothing.

CHAPTER 19

*S*omeone must have called Rory because he was standing in front of me, talking to me, but I couldn't hear him; I was still trying to grasp what I had done. I couldn't talk until then, not until I was ready to tell them what I did.

My chest was one raw, clenching ache, my lungs kept burning like I couldn't get enough air. My cheeks were wet, I was crying quietly. I didn't care. Someone should cry for her. There was a blanket around me, it was warm and rough against my skin. Someone was next to me. Rory walked away and towards the open grave. My chest threatened to explode. I didn't want him to know what I did, how I fucked up so badly. I had done something that never was meant to be done. Souls weren't meant to be destroyed. We were supposed to keep going. And I had just... My stomach lurched.

I turned to the side and threw up. Over and over again until I was empty. Hot hands were on my head, holding my hair, I think. I didn't care. I deserved so much worse. It was my area of talent, my responsibility.

When I was done being sick, I wiped my mouth with the back of my shaking hand. I blinked. Rory was back, his mouth moving again. He looked at Miles, his mouth still moving. He was moving too fast for me right now; he was reaching out and touching my face. I felt it; I just didn't want to move. I couldn't with this burning pit in my chest. I was still trying to breathe, my lungs still starving.

Someone lifted me, an arm around my back and another under my knees. It hurt, it hurt a lot, but I didn't want to move. I looked up to see that Isaac had me, his face worried, his skin pale. I didn't like his face like that. I blinked, and we were at the back of the Blazer, the back gate down. Ethan was sitting in the back on the floor his arms reaching out. Isaac passed me to him. Ethan tucked me into his lap. He was looking at me his face drawn too, his chocolate eyes were scared. I didn't like that either. Ethan's mouth was moving, his fingers wiping at my face. I heard him; it was just too fast right now.

We were moving. I blinked, and Ethan was handing me off to Asher. Asher's ocean eyes looked down at me, fear written in the lines of his face. I didn't like that at all. Asher walked through a familiar door. I recognized the high ceiling. We were at Miles' house. Asher put me down on something soft. I recognized the living room. Isaac was at the fireplace doing something. Ethan was kneeling in front of me, wiping my face with something wet. I felt the edge of one of his rings. Miles came in with his arms full of blanket. He put it around me; it was soft. Asher came in carrying my book bag; he poured it out and found the journal I had been reading all week. He shoved it into Miles' hands, his mouth moving. I heard a noise; I knew they were talking. Everything was just happening so fast. Isaac stepped away from the fireplace and started pulling out books from the boxes that were still on the coffee table. Everyone grabbed one, except Ethan. Ethan was still in front of me, wiping my face gently. He was telling me something; the only word I could make out was 'back.'

Zeke strode into the room, four weird bags in his hands. He took Ethan's spot in front of me, his sky-blue eyes running over me. His face hard, a flame of fear in his eyes. I really didn't like that. His hand was hot on my face. Zeke scowled and took off his jacket. He was talking, saying something about heat; it was the only word I could make out. He was talking too fast. Zeke pushed the blanket off my shoulders. He lifted me against his chest, an arm under my knees, and an arm around my back. Pain exploded across my back. I jerked. I turned in his arms and pressed against his chest, knowing I was making pain filled noises. I blinked. I was sitting wrapped against Zeke's chest, my forehead resting against his throat. Hot bags in my lap against my stomach, a blanket wrapped around both of us. I vaguely heard crackling nearby. I could see the others around the coffee table. They were going through the books. They kept stealing glances at me, then going back to what they were doing.

Soon, I felt warm. Zeke's body heat, the blanket, and the weird hot bags were making me warm. Hot packs, they were hot packs. How long had I been sitting here? Sunlight was pouring through the windows. Isaac got to his feet. He threw the book at the wall. I heard the thump. His face was red, tears running down his cheeks as he pressed his hands against his scalp, rubbing hard. He began pacing across the room and back. He was freaking out. I looked at the others and saw the same signs. Miles' hands were fists as he tapped against his thigh. Ethan was taking deep controlled breaths, his fingers constantly spinning one of his rings. Asher was rocking himself slightly, his neck red from where he'd been rubbing. And Zeke. I could feel Zeke holding me tight, a hand rubbing up and down my arm, trying to warm me. His hands were shaking.

They were all freaking out. I wanted to tell them I was fine, but I didn't move my mouth. That wasn't fine. Shit. Okay, time to climb out of this, Lexie. You can't leave them hanging like this.

As soon as I made the decision, I felt myself start to rise. Like a bubble from the bottom of a pond, I was moving upwards. The further up I went, the more I seemed to catch up to the world. Then the pain hit. I felt like I got hit by a truck. My gut was knotted with embers, my throat still tight. It felt like a hand was clutching my heart in its fist and squeezing. How could I have done that? What had I been thinking? I was such a fucking idiot. I was standing in that graveyard, and I KNEW it was wrong!

I sank a little more into Zeke. He noticed the shift; his hand moved to the back of my neck.

"Guys, she shifted a bit."

I understood Zeke's words this time. They were loud, but I understood them.

The others looked up at me, everyone's face was white.

I was still rising. I wanted to scream, I was furious with myself. WHY?! Why did I fucking do that? You fucking idiot! Then the world snapped into terrifyingly sharp techno color. My entire body started shaking, I was gasping. What the fuck were you thinking, Lexie?! You knew on a gut level!! You KNEW it was bad!

I scrambled off Zeke's lap--no one should touch me. They didn't know what I did. My knees came to my chest, my forehead rested on my knees. I wrapped my arms over my head, my hands and nails digging into my scalp. I rocked myself back and forth, trying to get through the next second and the next. Hands touched my back, pulled my hair out of my face. I knew they were talking to me, but everything I had was focused on just breathing through the next moment. My chest felt like it was an aching void that would forever burn. It was what I deserved. I was so fucking stupid! I didn't even understand what was happening here. All I had seen was the surface. If I had just waited longer, just tried harder, Mary Summers would still exist somewhere. It's my fault, my responsibility, my fault.

I kept rocking, kept breathing and trying to not lose my mind.

Time passed; I don't know how long. I stayed curled up and kept rocking. But I became aware of sound again. "My fault, my fault, my fault." That was me. I was whimpering...my voice so small and cracked.

"Lexie, tell us." Ethan's voice rolled through my ears grabbing my attention.

I blinked and lifted my head. Ethan was on my left, sitting on the hearth beside me. Zeke was to my right, his arm still around me. Asher and Miles sat on the coffee table, waiting. Isaac was pacing. I was stopped rocking. They needed to know.

"I erased her," I whispered, the words catching in my throat. "I erased her from existence." My chest ached so much it felt like it was on fire.

The guys seemed to understand me now. They all had looks of horror on their faces.

"I saw it all, felt it all. I fucking deserved it." Tears started falling down my face.

"Why do you say that, Lexie?" Zeke asked, his voice rougher than usual.

I wiped my cheeks with shaking hands. Every breath I took burned.

"Because the problem wasn't her." I swallowed hard before I told them. "It was the energy, it fucked her up." I started rocking again. "The Veil is shut now. There is nowhere for them to go."

Hands were on my face; I blinked hard and saw Miles. His emerald eyes examining mine.

"Tell us what happened," he said softly.

I blinked hard and focused. Miles sat back on the coffee table.

"When her bones were salted and burned, she went into the Veil," I said. I knew my face was blank, but I was just concentrating on getting it out. "You guys salted and burned her bones, but I was the Necromancer there. It's my responsibility." I needed to focus. I pressed my nails into the palms of my hands and squeezed. The pain brought me back a bit more. I needed something, I was so fucking tired. "Coffee please."

Isaac immediately ran into the kitchen. I kept pressing my nails into my palms so I could keep talking.

"There are two ways out of the Veil. One's moving on, the other is the pit." I was starting to shake again, I was bone-deep cold. I looked for the blanket and saw it on the floor. I began to move, to reach for it when Zeke seemed to read my mind. He picked up the blanket and wrapped it around me. I moved my legs down, crossing them underneath me and held the blanket to me. I looked at the floor not really seeing it anymore.

"In the Veil," I continued, "the sky is how you move on to the next part, the pit is below. The sky was wrong, it was filled with boiling clouds, green smoke, and lightning. The trees around the pit were burnt down to charcoal. It was all wrong."

Isaac came back in and carefully handed me a mug. I took a sip. It warmed my insides, and I really needed that right now. I took another drink feeling stronger. I can break down later; they needed to know what was going on.

"The Veil walls have been shut. The dead can't get there now," I told them, still feeling cold. I took another drink before looking at each of them. "The dead can't move on, not until it's open again. And the energy is just going to keep building."

Asher's brow drew down.

"Ally, what are you saying?"

I sniffed, feeling almost manic to make them understand. They needed to understand, they needed to know.

"The world is like a water balloon filling with water. This one is usually a tube, but someone has put a knot in one end. But the water, the energy, is still filling it up. And this balloon will never break. It just gets bigger." I looked around the circle at them, my hands shaking still. "And someone is planning to use it."

Curses went around the circle.

"Ally, if the energy made Mary Summers go nuts, does that mean-"

I scoffed, interrupting him, tears filling my eyes at the mention of Mary.

"We ain't seen anything yet," I warned him.

"You said there were two ways out of the Veil. The sky and the pit." Miles said. "What is the pit?"

I took a deep shaking breath.

"Hell?" Asher asked.

I shook my head. "Worse. It's nothing. It's where things go to be unmade." Tears filled my eyes as I remembered Mary's face. "That's where I sent her. I tried to pull her back, I held her hands, and I pulled, but the pit kept pulling her harder. I couldn't let her go like that. I couldn't let her go feeling alone."

Tears were pouring down my face as I continued. "I felt everything she did. She was terrified. The least I could fucking do was make sure she didn't feel alone." I wiped my face and my breathing shaky. "There is nothing left of Mary Summers." I broke down. I stopped talking and cried.

When the crying turned to sobbing, the guys still held me. Miles brought me tissues and Ethan grabbed a trash can. I don't remember how long I cried, but I do remember that they took turns holding me, rocking me, telling me all the things you say when someone you care about is breaking down. I do remember, that during that time, not one of them left my side; they were there with me through all of it.

THE BOYS: MILES

I adjusted my glasses as I watched Zeke looking out the kitchen door. He was spying again. I understood the urge, but Lexie had said she wanted to do this alone. I didn't like it myself, but it was her choice.

"Zeke, stop watching," I said, still managing to keep my voice calm.

Everyone was on edge, waiting for Lexie to finish talking to Rory. Lexie breaking down had bothered everyone. She had such a big personality that you never really noticed how small she was. Not until she starts crying. Then you remember that she's breakable.

I looked down at the counter and focused on tapping out a staccato rhythm. It helped, barely. I needed to be the calm one.

Zeke was still watching.

"Zeke," I bit out, not asking this time.

Zeke ran a hand through his hair and stepped away from the door.

"She's fucking crying again," Zeke growled as he walked further into the kitchen and leaned against the cabinets, his face troubled.

"She's going to cry for a while. We killed a soul, and she felt that soul die," I said, my own voice growing colder. I needed to be the calm one, the rational one. "That's going to take time to heal, for all of us." I took a deep calming breath and let it out. "She's going to need time.

The guilt might not go away, but eventually, it will become bearable. For all of us."

I looked over at Asher. He was leaning against the cabinets on the wall closest to the hallway. His eyes were unfocused. I sighed. I couldn't really stop him from listening in. He couldn't help it.

"She keeps saying 'I,'" Asher announced. Asher's eyes focused before he looked around the room.

"She's saying 'I killed her', 'I destroyed her.'" He shook his head, his face blank.

"She thinks that since it's her area of talent, it's her responsibility," I tried to explain. "That she somehow should have known what to do. She's taking all the guilt onto her."

"She's not the one who lit the fucking match," Ethan said, his voice was hard as he leaned in front of the sink.

Heart heavy, I tried to get through to them again.

"She's going to try and take all the blame, and we can't let her."

Everyone looked at me. Good, now they were listening.

I continued.

"We have to make her realize she wasn't alone in this mistake, that we did this, too." The guys all nodded at this, all of their faces were haunted. "We also have to convince her that with the knowledge we had at the time, we didn't see another choice. It was a mistake. We didn't go out there to kill Mary Summers' soul. We went out there to protect Lexie." The guys nodded again. "We tell her it was an honest, horrible mistake that we all made."

Everyone agreed.

Asher's eyes were on the floor again.

"She's telling him about the Veil now," Asher told us. He closed his eyes and pinched the bridge of his nose.

"What the hell are we supposed to do about the Veil?" Ethan grumbled.

Everyone was silent for a while.

"We help her any way we can," I told them honestly. "We're there for her when she needs us." I nodded at my own words, already making a list. "I'll hire someone to start digging into Necromancy and anything to do with the Veil. Anything about controlling the dead." I didn't know if it would work, but I had resources, and I'd use everything I had so I never have to watch Lexie break down like that again. "Heck, I'll hire a team if I have too."

Isaac was nodding. "I'll design her a training program like we talked about last night. It'll keep her mind off things. Plus, self-defense for someone her size is never a bad thing to have." He lifted his head and looked around the group. "You guys willing to help her train?"

Everyone nodded.

"She's already scheduled three climbing lessons a week for the next three months," Asher said to the room. "She really liked climbing."

Ethan looked around at us, with a strange look on his face.

He said, "What she needs to do is a link to the Veil. We need to find out how she's supposed to do that before anything else."

"More meditation exercises," I offered. Then I realized how much was really there. "We're going to need to help her make a schedule. Schedule some recreation time around all this, too."

"She also needs to eat right," Zeke said, drawing everyone's attention. "Serena said taking care of herself was not an option. She needs to eat right and sleep eight hours at night."

Everyone else cursed. I sighed.

"She never sleeps eight hours," Isaac snapped. "Hell, last night she was screaming after two."

"Then again after another three," Ethan said, his face dark. "Isaac said she stopped whimpering when he touched her." He looked up and around the room. "Maybe that's the answer."

The others were silent at his words.

I started thinking about a different solution, but there was another issue we needed to talk about before Lexie finished talking to Rory.

"I know everyone cares about Lexie, but right now, we need to know how much." I said, a bit distracted.

Everyone glared at me, Zeke looked downright hostile.

What did I say?

"We aren't bailing on her," Zeke growled at me.

Oh. That's what it sounded like?

"I'm not trying to say we should." I looked around at each of them and tried again. "I mean, how do you guys feel about her? How does she fit in our group? She's a girl, and that's going to change the dynamics a bit."

The room was quiet.

"I don't want to watch romantic girly movies," Isaac said with a groan.

Ethan laughed. "You won't. Have you seen the movies she likes? Deadpool is a favorite. Monty Python and The Holy Grail is another. Oh, and Tremors 1, 2, and 3. Not to mention Star Wars."

Everyone chuckled.

"She fits," Zeke admitted. "I noticed it the first night studying at Rory's."

"Me too." Isaac nodded. "It's like she's been with us for years."

"Like puzzle pieces and we didn't know we were missing one," Ethan added.

"She already feels like family," Asher agreed. "Like she's always been here."

"Then we should have a no dating Lexie rule," I told them seriously.

They all looked surprised.

"Do we really need one?" Ethan asked; his face puzzled. "Anyone want to date her?"

No one answered.

I sighed; no one was going to fess up now if they did.

"We're all going to be spending lots of time together," I told them. "She's new, different, she's funny and well, she's..."

"Cute. The word you're looking for is cute," Isaac said then frowned at me. "Because if you call her hot I'm going to smack you."

I sighed and tried to explain again.

"I just want to cut off trouble before it starts." I swallowed and tried again. "Imagine if she dated one of us and it didn't work out. How would she still be able to hang out with us? Be friends with the rest of us? Or worse, what if one of us starts dating her and someone else liked her, too?"

Everyone started thinking about it. The room was quiet for a time.

"I see where you're going," Zeke said.

"That makes sense," Isaac mumbled.

"I can get on board with that." Ethan chimed in.

"You do realize you guys are assuming she'd *want* to date one of us?" Asher asked.

That made everyone stop and think.

"She canceled on Dylan last night, but he's still very much on the radar," Asher continued.

"What did she end up telling him?" Ethan asked, rubbing an eyebrow.

"She told him a relative died, and she won't be able to see him for a couple weeks," Asher replied. "I backed her story up to him. I don't think it'll be a problem."

"So, this whole thing might not even be necessary," Zeke pointed out.

"I still think it is," I told them honestly. "I make a motion to have a no dating Lexie policy, within the group."

Ethan sighed. "Seconded."

Ethan's voice told me he clearly didn't see the point of this.

"Third," Asher agreed distractedly as he pulled out his cell phone.

"Motion passed," I said. "No dating Lexie."

Asher tilted his head to the side. "They're done talking."

EPILOGUE

*R*ory let me stay at Miles' over the weekend and into the week. He understood that I couldn't see Tara just yet. I spent a lot of my time at Miles' house, sleeping and talking to the guys. It took a lot of conversations, but I realized I wasn't the only one who felt guilty over Mary Summers; that the guys thought themselves responsible, too. I didn't want them to be right, so I talked to Serena about what happened. It was an awful conversation. She said everything comes with a price--I paid that price. But we were all responsible. I'm still working on believing that. But the guys all keep saying the same thing. We should feel guilty, but it was an honest, horrible mistake. All we could do is make sure it never happened again.

My time sleeping at Miles' wasn't so great at first. If I were alone, I'd wake up screaming, with Mary Summers' face as she died fresh in my mind again. The guys were never far away. Though on the second night after I had woken everyone up again, Ethan said 'Fuck it' and climbed into bed with me. When I slept through the night, that became our norm. One of the twins would sleep next to me and the other, the next night. It made going back to Rory's harder. I still wake up at night, though I'm able to stop myself before I start screaming now.

JESSICA'S PHOTO of me in the locker room had unexpected consequences for her. It was the Tuesday after the game, and pictures of Jessica changing in the locker room were sent from person to person. She broke the rules of the locker room and faced the consequences. I thought it was rather funny. Asher didn't like it, but he also thought it was poetic justice.

DYLAN and I are having trouble getting our schedules to sync up for a date. Someone quit at their hardware store, and Dylan is having to pick up the slack. We're still talking or texting every day. And we have a break coming up from school, so we'll meet up sometime. No, he isn't my boyfriend.

ZEKE WAS RIGHT about the repercussions from the big screen photo. I get catcalled and harassed any time I'm in the hallway now. I'm thinking of getting a middle finger sign and putting it on the back of my jacket just to save me some time. Miles isn't handling it well, but I've managed to keep him from hitting anyone.

I'M STILL LOOKING for anything on the Veil and how to control this 'gift' of mine. Not to mention how to open the Veil for spirits again. But I keep coming up with nothing. I sent Claire out of town; I didn't want the extra energy messing her up the way it did Mary Summers. She had a few leads she wanted to try, anyway. It's going to take her awhile. Ghosts don't really travel fast.

THE DEAD STILL COME TO me every now and then. But the lulls

between are getting smaller. They are finding me, somehow. I tell them why they can't move on. I listen to their lives and talk to them if they need it. I still draw their portraits in my sketchbook, along with their stories. I put Mary Summer in there, too. Someone should remember.

FOR THE LATEST NEWS ON THE VEIL DIARIES

Check out :

blbrunnemer.com

Or follow on face book

https://www.facebook.com/BLBrunnemer-1575614369409677/?fref=ts

or Twitter

https://twitter.com/blbrunnemer

FROM THE AUTHOR

I love to hear from my readers, so if you have question, or spot a
grammar error.
Please contact me at

Blb@blbrunnemer.com

CPSIA information can be obtained
at www.ICGtesting.com
Printed in the USA
FSHW04n0755220318
46038FS